Also by Sarah Rees Brennan

The Demon's Lexicon
The Demon's Covenant

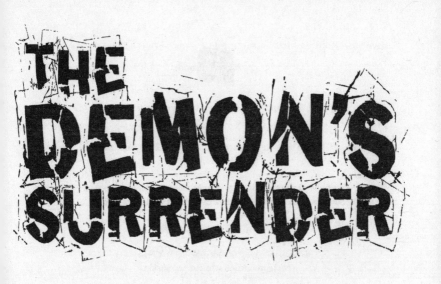

THE DEMON'S SURRENDER

SARAH REES BRENNAN

SIMON AND SCHUSTER

A **simon pulse** book

Simon Pulse and its colophon are registered trademarks of
Simon and Schuster UK Ltd.

First published in Great Britain in 2011 by Simon and Schuster UK Ltd,
A CBS COMPANY

First published in the USA in 2011 by Margaret K McElderry Books,
an imprint of Simon & Schuster Children's Publishing Division.

Simon & Schuster UK Ltd
1st Floor, 222 Gray's Inn Road
London WC1X 8HB

This book is a work of fiction. Names, characters, places and incidents are either the
product of the author's imagination or are used fictitiously. Any resemblance to actual
people living or dead, events or locales is entirely coincidental.

A CIP catalogue record for this book is available from the British Library.

ISBN: 978-1-84738-291-7

1 3 5 7 9 10 8 6 4 2

Printed in the UK by CPI Cox & Wyman, Reading, Berkshire RG1 8EX

www.simonandschuster.co.uk
www.simonpulse.co.uk

This trilogy is all about family, and especially about siblings. So it seems fitting to dedicate the last book in the series to the sibling who reads my books.

This one is for Gen, my favourite sister.

Okay, my only sister. But if I had another one . . . my hypothetical other sister would be seriously out of luck.

Summer Past

MAGIC WAS LIKE A SPECIAL GUEST IN SIN'S LIFE. IT APPEARED all too rarely, stayed for a brief interval and she spent the rest of her time preparing for it to come again.

She had taken the day off school so she and her dancers could set up the lights. She and Chiara had spent an hour singing into Phyllis's new music boxes, which echoed back their voices transformed into strange, sweet melodies. Then she'd had to rush away and help Carl set up his display of knives with luck stones in the hilts.

The magic had been worth waiting for. The Market at Dover Beach was one of the most beautiful Markets she'd seen this year.

The musicians were high on the white cliffs, streaked with shadows by the twilight, and the Market itself was being held on a platform a few steps up from the shingled beach. The sea lay sparkling and still in the curve of the bay, like water held in the hollow of a pale hand, and fainter than the light of the stars, Sin could see the night-time lights of the French coast.

There were other Goblin Markets held in other countries. She wanted to dance at them all one day.

For now she was glad to be at this one.

Sin was watching Toby while Mama put the finishing touches on the fortune-telling stall. The lanterns swinging over their heads cast rainbow gleams over the surface of the crystal balls, in the depths of the jewels on Mama's hands. Sin rocked Toby and Mama sang a Goblin Market song to them both as she laid out the cards.

> *"Hush little baby, don't say a word.*
> *If you have two marks never get a third.*
> *Hush little baby, don't you cry.*
> *Mama never falls and demons never lie.*
> *Hush little baby, don't say a thing.*
> *Mama's going to buy you a magic ring.*
> *And if your ring won't give you a wish,*
> *We'll be all right, baby, just like this."*

Sin smiled. "Who are you planning to dance with tonight?"

"The best-looking man who asks me," Mama replied, and they both laughed.

Mama was in a good mood for the first time in a long time. She had been sick too long after Toby was born and Victor had left with no word since to Mama, the woman he'd said he loved, or to Toby and Lydie, his children.

He wasn't Sin's father, and they were better off without him, but money had been tight since he went. What tourists really paid for were answers from demons, and to get those you had to dance. Mama had been too sick to dance, and she never accepted help from anyone. She'd never even let Dad help after

2

he left. They had barely been able to scrape by on what Sin made dancing.

But now Mama was finally ready to dance again, they would be all right. Just like this.

"How about you?" Mama asked.

Sin just smiled, which meant she was holding out for Nick Ryves. He hadn't been to the Market in a couple of months, so he was due back.

Nick and Sin weren't exactly friends. It was hard to be friends with Nick.

He was the best dancer she'd ever seen, though, and that made her like him. Sin respected talent, and it was hard to dislike anyone when you loved to watch them move. Besides, you learned a lot about people dancing with them. That was why Sin made sure to dance with every new dancer once.

"Don't tell me it's Nick Ryves." Mama wrinkled her nose. "That boy's creepy. I'm saying this as someone personally acquainted with fifteen necromancers."

Sin shrugged. "He's better than his brother."

"I don't see what you have against Alan," Mama said predictably. "He's very gifted."

Alan Ryves was the kind of boy all the parents and grandparents and busybodies of the Market thought everyone should be like: perfect, studious, ever so polite and ever so politely disdainful of the dancers. He got up Sin's nose more than anyone she had ever met.

"I know. Being so boring and yet so irritating at once, that's a gift."

Mama did not respond. Sin glanced up to see that her mother's eyes had gone wide, pools of brightness reflected from the lanterns, and Sin immediately twisted round to see the threat.

3

There was no threat. There was just Alan Ryves and his annoying face, and at his shoulder where Nick always stood there was . . . well, there was Nick.

It wasn't that Sin did not recognise him. It was unmistakably Nick, all dead-white skin, dead-black hair and drop-dead stare, but those sullen, too-sharp, and too-strong features of Nick's had clicked into place: he was almost as tall as his brother now. Muscles that had made him look squat before, like a surly, full-grown goblin rather than a kid, fitted on his new frame in easy rippling lines as he walked.

He still moved like a dancer, smooth and sure.

This was Nick made new under the burning lanterns, light racing golden along the angular line of his cheekbones, fire kindling in the depths of his black eyes.

Mama whistled.

Sin smiled absently. It wasn't that she was not interested by Nick's sudden ridiculous good looks. She was just distracted by something even more unexpected.

She found herself feeling a little sorry for Nick.

Sin had always been a cute kid. She'd known that ever since she could remember: there was no way not to know, when she and Mama had to use it. She'd been using curls and ribbons and a sweet smile to get people to come to Mama's stall and have their fortunes told since she was five years old.

She'd been dancing almost as long. First just to amuse the tourists, providing entertainment that was more about her smiles and her pretty costumes than the fact that she could dance, and then for the demons, when it was only talent that really counted. But making it look good never hurt.

She was used to attention and admiration. But it did change

4

when you grew up, new and sometimes unexpectedly painful, like aching muscles.

Last year she had been at the stall of a potion-maker she'd known for years, and he'd given her a present because she looked so pretty that night. He'd spelled out her name in dandelion seeds, shining like stars in the moonlight.

He'd spelled it Sin. She'd always spelled it Cyn before. But now people looked at her and saw something different.

Mama had put her arm round Sin's shoulders as they left the potion-maker's stall.

"So make the name yours," she'd said.

A stage name was the truest name a dancer could have. She'd learned to use what people saw when they looked at her. She'd always been a performer.

Heads were turning as the brothers moved through the crowd, and Nick did not look even slightly fazed. Sin saw him meet a few gazes for an instant and then let his eyes slide deliberately away, his mouth curling. Nick, who never wanted to talk or play or be friends, looked as comfortable as he did in the dancing circle with the demons. As if he had always known he was going to be beautiful.

Nick had never been one for performance. But it looked like he knew how to use this new power he had as a weapon.

She could understand that.

Sin rose from her place by Toby's crib, and took a moment to let the lights of the Market and the wind from the beach wash over her.

Her mother caught her eye and winked. "Go and get your partner."

"Oh, I will, but Nick can wait," Sin said. "First I want an audience."

5

It was the night of the Goblin Market, a night for seeing someone in a new light.

She thought Nick was human at the time.

Sin spotted her mark right away. He was a guy in a suit who had the air of someone who'd been to the Market a few times before and was trying to give the impression it had been more than a few. He was also handing over a lot more money than the German book of witchcraft he was paying for was worth.

"Welcome to the Market," Sin said.

When he spun round, she was already positioned so that the fairy lights caught the red glints in her hair and left her face wearing shadows and a slow, scarlet smile.

It was a lot like placing her mother's crystal balls on the stall so they were shown off to their best advantage. Sin wasn't for sale, but it did no harm to let tourists believe she might be.

The man visibly hesitated, then swallowed. "It's not my first time."

"Oh," said Sin. "I could tell."

"I guess," the guy said, his eyes travelling over Sin's bright clothes and gleaming skin, "that you're one of the attractions?"

"I'm the star attraction," Sin murmured. "Follow the music when it starts, and you'll see me dance."

The man took a step towards her and she felt a flash of triumph. She had him, like a fish on a line.

"What are you doing right now?" he asked.

"She's busy being underage," said the most irritating voice in the world.

They both looked round to the book stall, which Alan Ryves was leaning his bad leg against, a book in one hand and his usual expression of righteousness on his face.

"So perhaps what you should do right now is leave," he continued in his gentle voice, the one he used as he limped around the Market charming every old biddy in the place. Such a nice boy, they all said.

Nice boys were such a pain.

"Er, so I'll just be going," said the tourist, and then stepped backwards and away, into the crowd.

Alan gave her a little smile, as if he expected her to thank him for scaring away her audience. As if he'd done something nice for her, and he was expecting her to be pleased. There were fairy lights over his head, too, making his glasses catch the light and his red hair seem to catch fire. He looked even more ridiculous than usual.

He was wearing a T-shirt that said I GET MY FUN BETWEEN THE COVERS. It had a picture of a book on it.

"Hi, Cynthia," he said.

"What is wrong with you?" Sin demanded. "Besides the obvious."

Alan's smile twisted in on itself, and Sin bit her lip as she realised what he thought she'd meant. She hadn't been thinking about – well, she had been, it was hard not to notice – but she hadn't intended for him to assume she was talking about his leg.

She didn't feel like losing any ground before the ever-so-saintly Ryves brother, though, so she just sneered, turning her face pointedly away to look at the rest of the Market. There were a lot of sights that deserved her attention far more than Alan.

7

One of them was her little sister Lydie, being carried past in Trish's arms. Trish made fever wine during the day before the Market, but at night she often volunteered to babysit.

"Lydie," said Sin, and brushed a kiss at the golden curls at her sister's temple. Lydie looked past her and reached her arms out for Alan.

"Hi, sweetheart," said Alan, his voice turning slow and sweet as honey. Lydie's arms stretched forward, questing and imperious, and Alan leaned his weight against the stall and reached out to hold her.

Sin had to look away as he lurched.

"You're so irresistible to women, Alan," she remarked. "Pity your charm only works on those over fifty or under five."

"Poor me," Alan said. "I just missed my chance of dazzling you. You're what, seven by now?"

He gave her the smug look of a boy a bare three years older than she was. Sin rolled her eyes.

"Same age as your brother," she remarked. "And he's looking pretty grown-up these days."

Alan's stance shifted suddenly, and Sin realised that there was one of the Ryves brothers at least who was not entirely comfortable with Nick's transformation. Alan's T-shirt might as well have read MY BROTHER IS JAILBAIT. IT'S MAKING ME ANXIOUS.

Sin smiled with glorious and terrible joy.

"You've seen Nick," Alan said, his voice suddenly wary. "Did you talk to him?"

She raised her eyebrows. "I'm sorry. I wasn't aware that he needed a signed permission slip to play with the other children. I have seen him. I had a lot of fun looking."

"Yes, all right, Cynthia," said Alan, who apparently felt he needed to use her full name at all times in order to achieve the maximum possible level of condescension. "Look, I'm just – I'm just saying, maybe be a little careful."

"Careful?" Sin repeated. "You're telling me to be careful of your own brother."

Alan coloured a deep, unhappy red. Sin did not give a damn.

Market opinion was divided on what Nick thought of Alan, their guesses ranging from "total indifference" to "sullen adoration". But Alan had always seemed to love Nick, sticking close to him, taking care of him as Nick scowled about it. It was the only thing about Alan that Sin actually approved of.

She reached out and pulled her sister out of his arms, rocking Lydie when she made a noise of extreme dissatisfaction. She pressed Lydie's cheek to her talisman, the enchanted web of net and crystal against her heart.

"I can't count the ways you make me sick," she said conversationally to Alan. "Besides the obvious."

She wielded the words with vicious, deliberate emphasis like one of her long knives, and saw them cut deep. The colour drained out of Alan's face.

"Stay out of my way," Sin ordered. "And don't you dare interfere with any of my audiences ever again."

"He was a creep," Alan mumbled. "It's wrong to objectify women."

He turned away towards the piles of books, as if retreating to a refuge, and sounded a little awkward when he said that, like he really believed it but knew it sounded stupid. Alan was supposed to be so smart; Sin could not understand why he didn't see that he was insulting her by implying she hadn't known exactly what she was doing, and exactly what that guy was.

She gave Lydie to Trish and stepped in close to Alan, whose

eyes widened slightly. Sin ignored her own surprise that Alan was so tall and leaned in closer still, almost resting her chin against his shoulder, so close she could feel his body heat. She concentrated her gaze until he followed it, and saw who she was watching.

She gave him a slow, sweet smile.

"Guess what," she said. "I'm objectifying your brother right now."

She left without another look at him, sliding through the Market. She smiled, seeing first-time tourists arrive looking wary about the mysterious invitations they'd received from strangers, and then seeing their faces wiped clean of everything but wonder. The stalls were full of glittering marvels like treasure chests newly discovered and just opened for the first time, and even the stars shone bright as new coins under lamplight against the black velvet drape of a stall. Sin remembered being very small, walking through the Market holding her father's hand, dazzled by everything.

Sin was part of the marvels now.

As she listened to the pipers, the music from above changed, became something intense, with a beat that rang out to the sky. Sin tipped her head back to see white cliffs painted violet and black by the falling night, the pipers at the edge with their instruments gleaming in the moonlight, and above them walls and a castle keep.

Then she lowered her gaze and saw that everyone was looking at her.

She had already positioned herself under a lantern that beamed white light in a pattern like lace: a lantern enchanted to make everything it touched radiant. Sin knew it was making her silvery dress glow like moonlight on steel, that it made the fever blossoms woven through the pale material and her dark hair kindle with crimson fire.

She sent her body rippling to the music, bringing attention to the shifting, whisper-soft material over her skin, to the sway of her hips. Her movement called the other dancers to her, spilling in from every corner of the Market to join her dance.

She swayed a few more times, slow and sinuous. The whispers and gasps of the audience stroked over her like caresses.

When she pulled a fever blossom slowly out of her hair, dark locks unravelling from the flower like ribbons, the noise from the audience rose to an excited pitch.

Clearly, this crowd had been informed that whoever was thrown a fever blossom had the dancer's favour.

Sin laughed, and threw.

The single point of red drew every eye and painted a fiery streak against the sky, like a tiny falling star.

Nick was standing alone and looking bored, his eyes hooded. He caught the fever blossom in one hand.

Sin left the dance and walked towards him. His lids lifted as she came close. There was a gleam in his eyes.

"You ready to dance?" Sin asked.

"With you?"

"Don't tell me you were considering someone else."

Nick smirked. "Why, will it break your heart?"

"No," said Sin. "I just won't believe you."

She saw the glint of appreciation touch his cold face, curving his mouth at the very edges. Nick never showed much emotion, but even the smallest hint of a reaction was like a victory. And he'd always appreciated directness.

"Well, I don't lie," he said, tucking away the fever blossom and offering her his hand. "And I don't want to dance with anyone but you."

The summoning circles were cut, the drums were beating and Nick was in the circle overlapping hers before she spoke to him again. Even then, he didn't speak back.

He couldn't. They always used a speaking charm so Alan could talk to the demons for him.

"Good luck," Sin murmured, and they both smiled because the idea he might need luck was a joke.

The music had started as a trickle and became a flood now, cascading over the sand and into the ocean, echoing off the pale cliffs, coursing like sweet electric shocks through Sin's bones. Sin could see the tourists' heads turning even more than usual, as she looked at them with eyes that lured them into drawing closer and Nick stared at them with eyes that said to draw closer if they dared.

The music from the new drums was better, the tiny rattle of skulls adding an edge to the melody. Lines and circles leaped into fire under Sin's feet.

She turned to fire with them, muscles burning as she twisted and turned and pushed them to their limit, blood burning in her veins as she spun. She was never so aware of her body as she was when she danced, of her body as a weapon honed to a perfect edge and a decoration polished until it was perfectly irresistible. Every pair of eyes resting on her, every breath she took away, was a triumph.

Sin never doubted the demon would come.

And Anzu did, golden wings meeting over his head like a crown, empty, glass-coloured eyes fixed on Nick's. Nick stared back without flinching: a real dancer, who would never in a thousand years stumble or fall.

Alan's voice came out of the darkness beyond their burning circle, sure and calm. Sin had to admit, he always knew just what to say.

She'd hardly been aware of her partner as she danced, aside from the fact that she could trust Nick never to make a wrong move. But she was always most grateful for Nick when the demons came. Nothing ever frightened him.

Sin looked at him and saw the same satisfaction she felt, the same rush and thrill of daring death and doing it just right, and was absolutely certain that later tonight there would be making out.

Then a magician sent a fireball through a stall.

Merris Cromwell sent the alarm bells ringing for an attack, Matthias and his pipers started playing music to work everyone into a battle frenzy and Carl from the weapons stall threw an axe at the head of the first magician in the sweeping rush.

Sin and Nick had to stay perfectly still. If they moved, they might break through one of the lines, they might cross the circle, and that meant the demon could tear off their talismans. That meant possession: that meant worse than death.

They were left totally exposed.

"Scared, my beautiful dancer?" Anzu the demon whispered in her ear. "Sure you don't want to run?"

"I dismiss you," Alan said coolly, as if nothing was happening. The demon's fury curled round Sin's heart like a fist as his balefire started to dim.

Sin lifted her chin and ignored him. Part of dancing was knowing when to stay still.

The demon was leaving, the fire dying. Soon the circle could be broken.

She could see only three magicians, but the three were cutting through the Market people like a spearhead, their demons clearing them a path, their hands streaming lightning and darkness. They rushed down the pier, and Sin realised in a moment of cold horror that they were coming straight at Nick.

The circle would not be broken in time.

Then there was the sharp crack of a gun firing, and the head of the man in front exploded. Blood splashed hot into Sin's face. There was another shot and the glint of a knife in the night. Sin did not let herself even tremble.

Then there was nothing but three dead men between Alan Ryves and his brother.

Alan stepped over them without a glance, a gun in one hand and a bloody knife in the other.

"Are you all right, Nick?" he demanded, and pulled the speaking charm off Nick's neck, chain breaking in the hand that held his knife, so Nick could answer.

Nick nodded silently. He had not moved a muscle, and he did not look even slightly surprised.

Once reassured, Alan lowered his knife and looked over his shoulder at the trail of dead bodies he'd left behind. Apparently now he could register that he had killed three people in less than a minute and look a little startled and a little sorry.

That was why Sin didn't like guns. Apart from the fact that they sometimes didn't work on magicians, it was too easy to use them. There was no physical, visceral awareness of what you had done when you used one.

She did like knives. And as the last of the balefire died, she stepped out of her circle and drew hers, though there was no threat left to face.

It was excellent that there hadn't been many magicians, that they had been neutralised quickly, that the Market night could go on. But it left her with the blood racing in her veins, her heart battering her chest as if it wanted to take wing.

She had meant to stay and see Mama do her first dance.

Instead, when Nick caught her eye and turned away, she followed him.

It was dark and cool down on the shore, white seashells and sand crackling beneath her feet. Sin moved towards the shoreline, where the surf was kissing the sand in a rush of exuberant foam, looked around and saw no sign of Nick.

Sin walked along the water's edge, the lights of the Market behind her, sea and sand stretching to either side, and waited until the moon-iced surface of the ocean broke.

Nick pushed back black hair, drenched and sleek as seal fur, and smiled at her. He might as well have beckoned. The angles of his face looked more sharply cut than ever, his shoulders white and wet, all the planes of his body given gleaming definition by moonlight.

She walked into the surf and he walked out of it towards her: the water of the English Channel was cold even in August, rushing up to meet Sin mid-thigh almost at once and hitting her at waist-height as she waded in deeper, washing the sweat off her skin and all the tiredness out of her muscles, leaving her with nothing but a sweet ache along her body.

She reached out and trailed her fingertips down the ridges of Nick's stomach, curious, until her hand met the cool shock of water and the leather of his belt.

"I'm a little disappointed," Sin said.

Nick smirked. "I'm a little shy."

Sin caught hold of the wet rope securing his talisman,

knotted it round her hand and pulled his head down to hers. He caught her small, delighted laugh with his mouth.

His skin was cool and his mouth hot against hers, and she stood on her tiptoes to get more. It wasn't like Sin was short: these Ryves boys were both too tall.

Nick rescued her from the passing and disturbing moment when Alan Ryves crossed her mind by solving her problem and picking her up, hands sure on the small of her back, and bending her backwards so she was lying on the water like a mermaid in her bed, her hair spreading out with the waves. Then he pulled her back up to him, and she slid her arms round his neck and kissed him again.

"Come on," Nick murmured against her mouth. "I don't like the sea. Why don't we get out?"

Sin smiled. "Why don't we?"

He carried her out of the ocean and laid her down on the shoreline, the place where the pebbles lay washed by the surf until they looked like jewels. Her soaked hair fanned out in the sand like seaweed, and Sin arched up so he could slide his hands under her back and save her from the chill. He stroked up and down her back obligingly, and slid down her body a little, nudging her talisman sharply to one side as if it irritated him, so the wet rope bit hard against her neck as his mouth opened on her throat, warm and lingering.

Sin pulled his wet hair a little as a punishment for the sting of the rope, and arched up against him again.

Then an alarm shattered the silence from cliffs to sea. Sin went rigid with fear; she levered herself up and met Nick's gleaming black eyes.

"Alan," he growled.

"Mama," Sin said, and now that they'd both named what

they had back at the Market, what could be in danger, the spell of the moment was broken. Sin was up and running, not caring if Nick was running, too, or where he was, only caring that she got back.

She launched herself up on to the cement platform and landed hard, skinning her knees bloody and not caring about that, either, rolling to her feet and running.

There were magicians all around them. The first three magicians had been a decoy, something to make them feel as if they were safe from attack. This was real.

Sin saw the tourist Alan had warned away from her, magic glowing in his hand. His eyes went wide as he recognised her.

She was faster on the draw than he was. Her knife was buried in his throat before the magic ever left his hand, and she was running on.

Everywhere across the Market her people were fighting, and they beat the magicians back. Sin was shivering with triumph and exhaustion by the time she finally reached the dancers, ready to find Mama and rest, with Mama singing that they would be all right.

It was very quiet where the dancers were. It was so still.

Mama was lying face down in her circle. The balefire had all gone out.

Sin stepped into the dead summoning circle, knelt down on the earth and turned her mother over, so gently. For a moment she was absolutely, blessedly relieved: Mama's breath was coming steadily, stirring the fall of her golden-brown hair over her face, and Sin thought she was just hurt, that everything was going to be fine.

Mama opened her eyes.

All the light and joy of the Market, all the light and joy Sin knew in this world, drained away in the terrible demon darkness of those eyes.

"No," Sin said, her voice a lonely whisper, drowned out by the sound of the sea, by the terrible sucking silence emanating from the thing that had moments ago been her mother.

"Mama!" came Lydie's voice, and Sin looked up to see her little sister come dashing towards them, and thought, No, no, no with the force of a scream she could not let loose, with the force of a prayer.

Alan scooped Lydie up fast as she went by, turning her face towards his with his free hand, talking to her in rapid, soothing tones, comforting her, not allowing her to see.

There was nobody to comfort Sin, and she had to see.

The demon seemed to be registering its success, its body coming to terrible life in Sin's arms, Mama's mouth curving into a gradual, awful smile.

Mama was nothing but a shell with a demon inside her; Mama herself was caged in the back of her own mind. That was what happened whenever an ordinary person had dreams of demons and opened a window to let them in. Or whenever a dancer fell in a summoning circle.

In the distance Sin could hear Merris giving the orders to those in the know for taking a possessed person, for dragging the demon-infested body to Mezentius House, where it would be held prisoner until the body rotted away from the inside out, until the body died. The necromancers were coming and the men with chains, those who had spells to throw.

Her mother was still inside there, helpless, with the demon in command.

"Mama," said Sin, finding her voice in extremity, the words

tumbling desperately out. "Mama. I'll come with you. Don't be too scared. I'll come, I'll stay. Mama, I love you."

Her voice rose then, in a high, childish wail, but she couldn't afford to be childish now. As the Market people came to deal with her mother, Sin surged to her feet and went to deal with Merris Cromwell.

"You certainly cannot come to Mezentius House," Merris informed her. "You're far too valuable to risk."

Sin had always been awed and scared by Merris before. She'd always seen her at a remove, knowing that her mother would probably inherit the Market someday, since she was a Davies and the best dancer they had. She'd left her mother to deal with Merris.

Her mother was as good as dead. Which meant Sin was the best dancer in the Market, and she was the next in line to be leader.

"My mother's in there," Sin said. "I'm going to stay with her. And if you don't let me, I'll leave the Market."

It was an insane thing to say. What would she do if she left the Market, especially now Mama was gone, now Toby and Lydie had only her? She couldn't do anything but dance. She would have to become one of the dancers not attached to the Market, who danced for demons alone, who usually died in less than a year.

It was an insane thing to say, but she meant it.

"You can let me go to Mezentius House, or you can find a new heir. I will not let my mother die alone!"

Merris let her go. Sin promised Trish and Carl all her tips for the next season, anything, if they would care for Lydie and Toby until she came back. Toby was asleep, but Lydie cried, and Sin was terribly grateful that Alan was still holding Lydie, his eyes wide and so sorry for them both. Sin wasn't going to let herself cry in front of Alan Ryves.

She cried at the House of Mezentius. She stayed with her possessed mother for three nightmarish weeks, cried and bled and screamed and stayed, until her mother died. And she went back to the Market, still able to dance.

That was one mercy. There was nobody else to inherit the Market, and nobody else to take care of Lydie and Toby.

Sin did not need anyone else. She could do it, just like dancing; it didn't matter how hard it was. What mattered was never, ever to falter.

She didn't falter, and she did not fall once over the year and more that passed, not when they found out that Nick Ryves was a demon that had been put in a child and raised among them all this time. Not when they discovered that Alan was the greatest traitor imaginable, someone who had chosen a demon above his own kind. Not when the threat of the magicians became so great and Merris got so sick that they had to make a bargain with the demon and the traitor.

Not even when Alan Ryves, the boy Sin had never liked, gave her a gift she could never have imagined and could never repay when he put himself in the power of magicians to save her brother.

So Sin was not going to hesitate for a moment now, though a demon had strolled into her ordinary London classroom with its greying blackboards and harsh fluorescent lights. Sin's magic world and her normal world were meant to be kept apart, but here was Nick Ryves at her school.

He looked much the same as he had more than a year ago, when he'd stood looking down at her with wet hair fringed by moonlight.

"Sin?" asked Nick, who she had thought was human once. He seemed, as far as you could tell with Nick, startled and perhaps even pleased to see her.

Sin crossed her legs under her rough uniform skirt.

"I'm sorry," she said smoothly. "My name's Cynthia Davies. I don't believe we've ever met."

2

The Final Test

"S IN," NICK SAID, SOUNDING VAGUELY ANNOYED, "WHAT ARE you—"

He tugged on his school tie as if it was a choke chain and scowled, then fortunately the bell rang and everyone sprang up. The next class was French and their teacher was pretty strict: nobody was going to hang around and get in trouble, no matter how good-looking the new boy was.

Nobody was paying attention, and in the bustle of the other kids leaving, Sin could seize her chance to act and not be noticed.

She made a point of never being noticed at school.

"Listen closely," she said, speaking very quietly and exercising great self-restraint by not grabbing Nick by his rumpled tie to make him listen. "We don't know each other, have you got that? I'm not at all the kind of girl who knows boys like you."

"What?" Nick said flatly.

"I study really hard: I have to because I'm not that smart.

I'm good at gym, and I have some friends on the lacrosse team. In school I never wear make-up, and I don't talk much to boys. Not that many people notice me and that is the way I like it."

It was all true, as well. She needed to study, and she didn't want the attention of any normal boys. This was just the way she wanted to be, as well as keeping her profile low in case the authorities took a second look at her unorthodox lifestyle living in a wagon with two little kids. It wasn't any more or less of an act than how she was at Market nights.

Nick was frowning at her. "I don't expect you to understand," Sin snapped. "But I expect you not to screw this up for me."

"Fine," Nick grated out. "We don't know each other."

"Good."

She was just about to take a deep breath and calm down when something else occurred to her: here was Nick, inserted into their class in the middle of a school day. There was only one person Sin knew who could talk people round like that.

"Your brother," Sin got out, feeling strange and hesitant about saying the words. "Is he here?"

"Yeah," Nick said offhandedly. "He's probably still wrapping stuff up with the headmistress."

"Okay," Sin said, and made up her mind. She picked up her own French book and slammed it into Nick's chest, possibly too hard. "You take this," she told him. "You need to get to French. I need to – go somewhere else. Um. Right now."

Nick gave her a blank look, but most of Nick's looks were pretty unreadable anyway, and Sin did not have time to explain herself. She bolted out of the door, ran down one flight of stairs, stood in the stairwell with another flight to go and saw Alan limping down the hallway to the main doors.

Then she yelled, "Stop!"

Alan spun round, one hand going to the end of his shirt where she presumed his gun was concealed. Then he stood, squinting up at her through his glasses, looking a little uncertain.

Sin was always conscious of the light she was standing in, and she knew she must be little more than a girl's shape against the big casement window behind her. A girl's shape with curly hair escaping from a braid, wearing a bulky grey uniform. Alan had never seen her look anything like this before.

So when he said, "Cynthia?" with a measure of confidence, she understood he'd known she went to school here all along.

She descended the stairs. She was surprised by how much she didn't want to: she was used to having the advantage over Alan, being in a place that set her off like a stage. Now here they were in a school in Ealing, surrounded by white walls that had gone grey and grey tiles worn to white. She was without costume or backdrop or audience.

Sin lifted her chin as she came down. She didn't need props.

"You wanted Nick to be in class with me."

"Well, yeah," Alan said mildly. "We're all up in London for the same reason, aren't we? I thought it would be nice for Nick to have someone he knew at school."

They were all up in London for the same reason. The Aventurine Circle was there: a Circle with magicians in it who would not forgive the Goblin Market's recent attack, a Circle with one magician in particular who had his mark on Alan and could do whatever he wanted to him at any moment.

Sin nodded. "That's totally reasonable. Is there any particular reason you didn't tell me you were going to do it? Is there any reason Nick had no idea until he walked into my class? Do you ever tell anyone anything?"

There was a beat, and Sin realised that it must look like she'd run through the school purely in order to abuse Alan.

His mouth twisted, colour rising high on his cheekbones, as if she'd hit a sore spot. "Not often."

Sin bit her lip. "I didn't come down here to yell at you."

Alan looked slightly alarmed. "Did you come down here to throw things?"

"Everything was so crazy before. We had to bury the dead, and organise a move, and I never got a chance to talk to you."

"Did you want to?" Alan asked, sounding incredulous.

"Yes," Sin snapped. "I wanted to say thank you."

Alan looked startled. "For—"

"For my brother," Sin said.

She heard her voice come out rough again. She knew she was doing this all wrong; she didn't know how to thank someone for something like this. Sin was a Market girl born and bred. She understood bargains, she understood trading. She had always paid off her debts and tried to be fair exacting her prices.

Now all she could do was say thank you. It felt like revealing exactly how pathetic she was, that she had nothing else to offer.

She could not put a price on Toby's life. There was nothing she had to give that could ever come close to paying back what she owed. If Alan Ryves ever asked her for anything, she would have to give it to him.

She wished he would ask for something, instead of standing there looking politely surprised.

"Cynthia," he said, in a gentle voice she hated. That was the way he talked to children. "I would have done it for anybody."

"I would have thanked anybody!" Sin said, and then there

25

was a sound against the stairwell window like a storm of hailstones.

Sin's head turned to a window that showed a clear blue sky. Then she looked back, meeting Alan's serious gaze, and they both flattened themselves against the walls on either side of the stairs and waited.

The sound was less like hailstones now and more like dozens of fists slamming into the window harder and harder until Sin heard a creak like ice underfoot and then the ringing, tinkling sound of glass hitting the floor.

She slid her knife out of the sheath under her shirt and eased carefully along the wall until she could peep up the stairs.

There was a nightmare creature there, tapping its way through the shards of broken glass like a fastidious old lady. It was made of mismatched bones. It had a fox skull for an elbow, and a human skull perched on top of the whole gleaming construction.

The bones were held together by bits of ribbon. Sin could see the tiny twists of fabric jerk just before the thing moved its bone limbs. They made it look like a huge, horrible puppet.

The long bones it had in the approximate place of forearms looked like they'd been taken from horses' legs, sharpened to a point.

They didn't have much time. Somebody was going to come investigating the noise.

Sin waited to hear the click of bones on the stairs once, twice, three times.

Then Alan stepped out from his place against the other wall, took aim and fired. The human skull on top of the creature exploded into dust and fragments.

Somebody was definitely going to come investigating *that* noise. And the thing was still advancing.

Sin darted up the stairs, pressing her side to the wall. Once she was a few steps up she launched herself off the wall and into the tower of bone.

Her knife found the ribbon tying the fox skull to the horse leg. When she slashed it, the creature's arm fell off.

She grabbed at the thing and climbed it, using the pieces of bone as handholds, and scythed ribbons to cut it off at the point that was more or less its knees.

It was still able to lash out at her, now little more than a rattling whirl of bone, like a mobile over a cradle come to life and turned savage and hungry. Shards of bone stung her face. She thrust her knife through the tangle.

The creature collapsed into a heap of knots and bone, not an instant before Sin heard someone clattering down the stairs.

Sin leaped up and away, ducking her head to hide the cuts on her face. When she glanced up apprehensively, she was in equal parts annoyed and relieved that it was only Nick.

He stood with a short sword in hand, the broken window behind him, body braced for a fight. His eyes lit on his brother. "Don't tell me I missed all the fun."

"Maybe next time we'll save you some," Alan said, grinning.

And then they heard a door open down the hall, and Sin restored her knife to its sheath. When she looked up, Ms Popplewell was advancing, and Alan and Nick had both hidden their own weapons. Alan was wearing a very convincing air of shock and helplessness.

Nick looked vaguely homicidal, but that was sort of his default expression.

"What on earth is going on here?" demanded Ms Popplewell.

"That's exactly what I would like to know," Alan said. "Does this happen often? Somebody chucked this disgusting heap through the window – any one of us could've been really hurt!"

The rising note of indignation in Alan's voice was good, Sin had to admit. Damn good.

Just in case Ms Popplewell's eyes strayed either to the cuts on Sin's cheeks or Mr Tall, Dark and Homicidal, Sin decided to attract attention by covering her face and saying in a fraught whisper, "It was just so loud—"

"There, there," Alan murmured soothingly, patting her on the back.

"I didn't know what was going on!" Sin exclaimed. She let her shoulders go up and down once, but decided that sobbing might be a step too far.

"Has this happened before?" asked Alan, sounding scandalised.

"No!" Ms Popplewell exclaimed, her voice harried and not suspicious at all. "Cynthia, perhaps you should go to the nurse's office. Don't worry about missing French."

"Thank you," Sin offered piteously.

Nick spoke for the first time.

"Can I go to the nurse's office, too?"

Ms Popplewell looked at him. It obviously took her only one look to decide. "No."

"I'm traumatised, too," Nick claimed, his voice completely flat.

"He's a delicate flower," Alan said under his breath.

Sin started to wend her way obediently towards the nurse's office just in case those two brought the whole house of cards down on their heads. She made sure to keep her shoulders a little sad and hunched, lest Ms Popplewell look after her as she went. The key to a performance was in the details.

She did cast one fleeting glance back, caught Alan's eye and sent him a small smile. In a flicker almost too brief to notice, the corner of his mouth turned up in response.

That evening Sin slammed into the wagon that Merris used as her office whenever she was travelling with the Market. Merris looked up from a tablet on her desk, her eyes filled with blackness. The chair on the other side of Merris's desk was occupied by someone who had got there before Sin.

Neither of these things did much to improve Sin's mood.

"I was attacked today," Sin announced without greeting either of them.

"Well," Merris murmured. Her voice always had a different inflection now that she was carrying a demon: almost like a foreign accent, a flavour of some faraway and terrible land. "We are at war."

"Which I'd understand, if I'd been attacked by magicians!"

Merris's office was set up to impress, with heavier furniture than a wagon should have, a charm set up on the desk that changed colours depending on whether the people in front of her lied or told the truth and wall hangings depicting scenes from old books. One was all black strokes on red paper, and it showed a crowd of beggars trying to fight a genie, uncurling from its prison and looking murderous. Sin did not think that would go well for them.

Sin was not in the mood to be impressed. She strode across the floor and threw a small, grubby knot of ribbon down on the desk before Merris's clasped hands.

"I know what a magician attack looks like. And I know what the necromancers can conjure up. You sent a necromancer's sharp-edged little plaything into my school! Someone could have been hurt."

"I take it nobody was," Merris said. "Well done."

Sin took a deep breath and said what she'd been burning to say for weeks.

"These tests are crazy, they are a waste of time and they have to stop now."

There was a silence. Sin stood at the desk because there was no chair for her and waited for the consequences. She knew what this looked like: it looked like she was weak.

She'd thought it was a joke when Merris first suggested that Mae Crawford might inherit the Market instead of Sin. It wasn't a good joke: it was insane, offensive and hurtful, but Sin hadn't been able to think of it as something that could actually happen.

The Davies family had travelled in the Market for four generations. Sin was the best dancer in the Market. Mae was a tourist girl who was really good at dancing for a beginner, and that was all. She didn't know enough, she didn't belong and she'd been brought to the Market, by the Ryves brothers of all people, barely five months ago.

Sin hadn't been worried.

Now she was.

Merris had set them problems about the economy of the Market that Sin hadn't really understood. Mae had not only understood them but had come back with suggestions for improvements. A few weeks ago Merris had asked them to choose a spot in London to move the Market to, and while Sin was still asking around, Mae had got on the Internet and then on the phone. She'd chosen the location on Horsenden Hill where they were settled now, which had enough open space to house all their wagons under concealing charms. It was surrounded on two sides by a canal, and was on the site of an ancient hill fort. It was the ideal choice.

Sin knew that understanding property and finances wasn't really important, was nothing more than glorified homework. She knew that it was the heart and the soul of the Market that mattered, something Mae could never touch. She just didn't know if Merris would see it her way.

"They have to stop now?" Merris repeated, her voice crackling in weird and terrible ways. "I was under the impression I gave the orders here."

Merris would have died if she had not let the demon Liannan into her body on the basis that she would have control during the day and the demon would take the nights. Sin knew that.

It did not make it any easier to look into her dark-brimming eyes, to hear that voice. It did not make it easy to trust Merris, especially when she no longer seemed to trust Sin.

"I agree with Sin," said Mae from the depths of her chair.

Merris's attention turned to Mae, both eyebrows rising. Mae did not flinch at the cold look.

Mae looked small curled up in the chair, the back rising half a foot above her pink hair. She was wearing it in pigtails today.

It was ridiculous that a tourist girl was causing Sin so many problems. This was Sin's place.

"It's not good strategy to keep us at each other's throats," Mae went on. "You said it yourself, Merris. We're at war. Stunts like the creatures today—"

"What?" Sin snapped, and grabbed at the desk. "You sent something after Mae? She can't fight, she's a tourist. She could have been killed!"

"If she is going to be the leader of the Market," Merris said, and Sin felt a chill wash all through her body in case Merris was indicating she had made a decision, "then she has to know what it is like to face danger. She handled it all right."

"I sprayed it with a fire extinguisher," Mae told Sin, her mouth tilting into a rueful, dimpled smile. "When it slowed down, I hit it with the fire extinguisher. Then I hit it again. It was a triumph of mind and fire extinguisher over matter."

Sin had to resist the urge to smile back. Then Merris spoke, and Sin no longer felt any temptation to smile whatsoever.

"Of course," she said, her voice sleek with satisfaction, like a great animal curling up after a good hunt and a feast of flesh, "you did both have help."

Sin flashed Mae a look of inquiry and was irritated to see Mae directing the same glance her way. She didn't have to answer to tourists.

She did have to answer to Merris.

"Alan Ryves happened to be there and shot at it. I didn't ask for his help, and I didn't need it."

"Nick worked out what was going on and came to help me," Mae said, and Sin remembered Nick's sudden request to go to the nurse's office. "I didn't need it, either. And it doesn't matter. The point stands. We have to devote all our energy to stopping the magicians. Can't we put off this contest?"

"This contest will give you both an edge," Merris told her. "I want you to push each other to be the best you can. I want you to be motivated."

"The magicians killed my mother!" Mae snarled. "I am motivated. I don't need to be distracted."

Merris glanced at Sin, as if questioning whether she was

going to continue with this challenge to Merris's authority. Sin had a terrible moment of wondering whether this might be the final test, if she should prove her loyalty by agreeing to submit to Merris's will. She'd always tried to do what Merris wanted; she'd always struggled to please her.

Look how much good that had done her.

She didn't speak.

Merris looked into the space between Sin and Mae. For an instant Sin thought she was regretting the distance between them, but then she realised that Merris was looking through the open door of her wagon.

Those tar-black eyes reflected nothing, but Sin knew as surely as if she'd seen the setting sun in them that night was coming, and Liannan with it.

"I believe you have both seen Celeste Drake," Merris said, her voice unhurried, as if the sun and her own body were not slipping away from her.

Celeste Drake was the leader of the Aventurine Circle, the big London Circle that had joined with the Obsidian Circle, which the Goblin Market had just fought. Sin did not think she could ever forget Celeste, and how she had appeared in the midst of the battle when Sin had just started to truly believe they could win. Celeste was small and very fair, wrapped in white, and she had swallowed their victory so casually, as if it was a plum she happened to fancy.

"Yeah," Mae said warily. Sin just nodded.

"Did you happen to notice the black pearl she wears?"

"Yes," said Mae, as of course she would. Sin didn't want to lie to Merris, so she said nothing. Maybe Celeste had worn a necklace, dark against the pallor of her clothes and skin; Sin hadn't taken much notice.

"It's supposed to be enchanted to wholly protect its wearer from demons," Merris said. "No demon charisma can touch you, none of their words sway you: they have no power over you at all. No matter what."

Sin touched the talisman at her own throat; it warned you of magic coming, protected you from possession unless a demon managed to get it off, shielded you from some spells. The pearl sounded a lot more efficient.

"No matter what," Mae repeated, and Sin looked sharply over at her. There was a new note in her voice that Sin couldn't quite understand. Her hands were clasping the arms of her chair too tightly, her whole body straining forward a little.

"Call this the final test," Merris said. "Whichever of you takes Celeste Drake's pearl wins."

"She's the leader of the Circle trying to kill us!" Sin exploded. "It's impossible."

"It's not meant to be easy," said Merris. "Nor is taking over the Goblin Market."

Sin was sure taking over the Goblin Market was not actually impossible, not like infiltrating a stronghold of magicians, any of whom would kill her on sight, and taking a priceless treasure off the most powerful of them all. This was just throwing away their lives.

"Of course," Merris said, eyes on Sin's, "there is an alternative. Give up."

"What?" Sin demanded.

"Either one of you could surrender your claim," Merris continued as calmly as if Sin hadn't spoken. "Either one of you is free to give up, and swear to follow the other as their leader."

Sin glanced at Mae, whose face was set in determined lines.

Mae wasn't the type to give up on anything. Sin had liked that about her once, the way Mae could go around with that candy pink hair, being as short as she was, and shove her way into being taken seriously anyhow.

She would still like it, if Mae hadn't been trying to shove her way into Sin's place in the world.

"No," Sin said. "I don't think either of us will be doing that."

Merris nodded as if they were all in agreement, and Mae uncurled herself from the chair, murmuring something about helping Ivy and Iris with their back catalogue. The silent sisters, who had traded their tongues for the ability to read any language ever written, had taken a real shine to Mae.

Sin had once accidentally landed on top of a lot of papyri when another dancer had thrown her too hard during a rehearsal. The sisters still acted as if she'd landed on a baby.

Sin did not take the chair Mae had vacated, even once she had left the room. She remained standing by the desk, and Merris pushed her chair back and stood as well. They were exactly the same height. That still startled Sin sometimes.

Merris went over to the window of the wagon. There was a crescent moon carved in one of the shutters she opened, and the setting sun filled her hair with red.

It wasn't just the sun. It was the demon closing its claws round her, her black and silver hair starting to twist in the air like reaching hands, changing as it moved until it was the colour of blood.

Sin could not see her face clearly any longer. She was glad.

"I did not understand the bargain I was making, you know," Merris said quietly.

It was so unexpected that Sin had no idea what to say.

35

Merris had refused to discuss the demon's bargain she'd made with anyone. Sin had begun to think she'd been a fool when she'd believed Merris felt anything like affection for her at all.

Merris had agreed to be possessed, but it was meant to be different with her. Other people were made into shells animated by demons, but she had her body half the time.

It had been clear from the first that it was not that simple.

"Demons always take more than you can afford to pay," Merris continued, the alien note in her voice growing stronger. "I knew that. But I thought, if what I received in return was my life . . . I thought it would be worth it. Only it's not my life now. It's hers."

"Liannan," Sin breathed, as if she was a magician, as if she could name the demon and control its power.

Merris nodded, hair tangling in on itself like a nest of snakes.

"She's in here with me, always," Merris said. "Colouring everything. Wrapped up in everything. Whispering to me, as if she was my own heart. Soon I will only want what she wants. Do you know, when I was a girl, I never wanted anything but to dance? I wouldn't have wanted to be a leader, at your age. I didn't even want to be part of a Market. But when I couldn't dance any more, I made this Market my whole life, and she wants to leave. Every morning I wake up in a place further from it, further from you all, and every morning I think to myself that I could stay gone."

Sin swallowed. She had been able to accept Merris's bargain because she had thought it was the only way to keep her, because the Market needed her so badly.

That was a demon's bargain, though. They took more than you could afford, and they gave you back nothing.

Merris had not been saved for the Market, not really.

"But if I had that pearl," Merris whispered, "I think I could silence her. I think I could stay here, and be myself again."

Hope was harder to swallow than horror. Sin felt like she was choking, at how the stakes had been raised, how the impossible had now become something that absolutely must be done.

Merris continued talking.

"You know, in all the tests I devised for you Mae has achieved much better results, has shown herself able to be a stronger leader than you could be. You're too close to the Market, I think sometimes. You have to be able to step back and see it as a business. And something to die for: that, too. Maybe you have to be a stranger. I was a stranger here once myself."

"No," Sin said.

"I wish it wasn't true," Merris told her. "You walked into Mezentius House and back out again unbowed. You know how I feel about you."

Sin had thought she'd known.

"What good would it be, giving you the Market?" Merris murmured, and Sin drew closer, came to stand at the window by her, and Merris reached up and touched her hair as she'd used to. "If I gave it to you and the Market was destroyed, or you were destroyed by it, what use would this demon's bargain be? I have to choose right, and I have to choose fast. I wish I could choose you. But I don't know if you're the right one: I don't know if you can bear more responsibility than you already have, if you can turn life and death into a business. If you bring me this pearl, we would have time. I would have time to teach you. I want to believe you can be the leader this Market needs."

Sin bowed her head under Merris's lightly stroking hand.

She wanted to cry, but she knew Merris wouldn't appreciate that.

"I am the leader this Market needs," she insisted past the knot in her throat that wanted to become tears. "This is my place."

When she looked up, deadly pallor was rushing over her leader's face, terrible beauty claiming it the same way shadows were claiming the city below as the sun retreated.

From lips twisting into a shape not their own, Merris whispered, "Prove it."

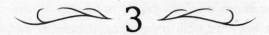

3

Throwing the Fever Blossom

THERE HAD BEEN A GREAT FOREST BY HORSENDEN HILL ONCE.
The houses of Wembley lay spread at the foot of the hill
like a glittering carpet now, but the trees enclosing their
Marketplace were tall and strong, the survivors of the ancient
forest. Every arching branch bore a lantern swaying in the wind,
throwing bright beams of magic against the long grass.

Merris might be lost to a demon, Mae might be impressing
the silent sisters, but the night of the Goblin Market had always
belonged to Sin.

Tonight was her chance to remind everyone that this was
her rightful place.

"Welcome to the Market," Sin murmured to the first rush
of tourists, who were milling about the stalls, watching her.

There was a full moon, a bright circle like a pale, open
flower against the dark sky, and Sin had dressed for it. She was
wearing black with silver lines shot all through it like
spiderwebs, silver that caught the moonlight and turned her
from shadow to gleaming ghost and then back again, mocking,

elusive, the only point of colour about her a crown of crimson flowers.

Mae might be smart and she might be cute enough, but she did not know about performing. She didn't know that if you made a performance good enough, you made it true: that by playing a queen Sin could transform herself.

"It takes you a while to learn the ropes here," said a tourist walking with his girl, who judging by her wide eyes was here for the first time. "Helps if you've got magic blood in you, of course. My mum's Scottish, so that helps. Very mystical people, the Scots."

"Good to see you again," Sin murmured to him as she went past, and he stood and stared after her in pleased bewilderment, thinking she remembered him.

That was part of the performance, making other people feel special, until dozens of people were thinking of you as special. Sin was good-looking, but it took belief to make you the most desirable woman in a crowd. It took an audience to be beautiful.

"Welcome to the – oh, it's you," said Sin, almost colliding with a broad chest and tipping her head back to see Nick.

"We thought we should make an appearance," Nick drawled. "Since we're meant to be allies."

It was a jolt to look into his black eyes, after Merris's. But there was no human struggling in there, Sin reminded herself. There was just this boy she'd known for years; there was just this demon, eternal and cold, and nothing else.

She didn't know what that meant.

She did know that he was dressed all in black, for dancing, and whether he was boy or demon, he was the best partner she'd ever had.

Sin smiled at him. "Welcome to the Market."

He looked down at her, a dark lock of hair falling into his eyes, mouth curving. He looked like the perfect partner for tonight.

"Did you save me the first dance?"

Beyond Nick's shoulder Sin saw Alan lingering at Carl's stall, bright head bent over an array of bows and arrows. She waited for a second, but he didn't seem aware of the weight of her attention, didn't look up to catch her eye.

Alan presented a problem, but for the first time Sin had an idea how to solve it. Before the attack at school, it would not have occurred to her that Alan might appreciate a performance.

"Better than that," she told Nick. "I saved you the last one."

Sin took a break from dances and accepted a plastic cup of water from Chiara. Then she noticed the slice of fever fruit floating in it.

"You're just basically a bad person," Sin told her, and sipped.

Chiara gave her a serene smile, which changed into a slightly more wicked smile at a hovering tourist. Sin took a gulp of water, laced with a taste that raced down her throat burning sweet and strong.

She swallowed and said, "What does everyone think about Alan Ryves?"

"I never think about Alan Ryves," said Chiara.

Matthias the piper, thin as his own instrument, came by and stole the cup right out of Sin's hand. "Personally, I like him."

The dancers en masse gave Matthias a very startled look.

Matthias gestured to his throat and said appreciatively, "Beautiful voice."

41

"Do you care about anything but people's voices?" Chiara asked.

"Yes," said Matthias, considering. "But I can't think of anything I care about half as much."

Tonight's theme for the dances, the ones intended to attract tourists who might then stay to pay for answers from demons, was fire. September had come in cold, and the tourists could huddle round the lines of flame and see dancers catapult through them, dance along them, juggle lit torches enchanted to draw scenes on the air. More Market people had come to watch than usual because of the beckoning warmth of the flames.

Nick was taking his own break from the dancing and sitting with Alan on a log by one of the banked-up fires. Alan was talking to Nick and laughing, his hands making shapes of shadows against the firelight.

"Tell you what I'd do," Chiara concluded after a thoughtful pause. "I'd take them both. That might be fun."

"They're brothers," said another dancer, Jonas. "That's sick."

"No, it's okay because they're not actually related," Chiara argued.

"That's a demon," Matthias observed mildly. "Nothing about it is okay."

Everyone fell silent at that reminder. Nobody wanted to think about demons these days, to admit that if demons were unspeakably corrupt, then they should not let Merris lead them. To think about what lay behind Nick's eyes was admitting that they were all treading on black ice.

Everything had been so much simpler when Sin could just hate both brothers.

Except she had not been able to hate Nick for long, only from the time when she'd learned what he was until she'd met him again.

She'd always found it easy to hate Alan. But she couldn't do that, either. Not any more.

"We made a bargain with them," Sin said. "The Market always keeps its bargains."

She remembered Merris's face, and how demons kept their bargains. That did not stop her from swinging to her feet, taking another drink of fever-touched water and going over to the spot by the fire where Nick and Alan were sitting. Nick was stretched out like a portrait in charcoal, all black and white in lovely lines, and Alan animated and firelit in red and gold.

They looked up as she came towards them, identically wary.

"Time for our dance?" Nick asked.

"Yes," said Sin. "And I wondered if Alan might like to sing for us."

Alan stared. Sin widened her eyes at him, schooling her face into a picture of innocent inquiry.

"Are the dancers going to play nice?"

"If you are," Sin said. "Maybe."

She didn't know what she expected, but it wasn't for things to be easy, after years of being at daggers drawn, as if all she'd needed to do was reach out once.

She reached out and Alan took her hand. She was startled by how that felt: Alan's hand strong and gun-calloused, but holding hers rather carefully, as if he was worried he might hurt her.

It was ridiculous to be startled. She knew Alan was usually gentle. She'd been watching him play with children for years. And she'd seen Alan kill whoever got in his way, whenever he had to.

She'd just never really thought about the contrast of how he presented himself and who he actually was. Not until he'd stepped between two armies and taken her brother and a magician's mark.

Sin looked away as he levered himself up from the log – surely he didn't want her to see him struggling – but she didn't let go of his hand when he was up. She led Alan to where the dancers were talking, Nick stalking in their footsteps like a jungle cat on bodyguard detail.

"Alan's going to sing," she announced.

"Cool," said Chiara, who knew a cue when she heard one.

"I can't tell you how pleased I am," Matthias told Alan.

Alan slid his fingers easily out from between Sin's, watch glinting in the firelight under the frayed edge of his shirt cuff. He hesitated briefly and then curled his fingers round one of the belt loops on his jeans, as if he felt he should do something with his hand.

"Didn't you try to throw me to the magicians last time we met?" he asked Matthias.

"Sure," Matthias replied, flashing his skull-like grin. "But I didn't mean anything personal by it."

"That's all right, then," Alan said, sounding truly amused. He smiled by degrees, like a stage curtain being opened by someone who knew how to do it, making you wait just long enough.

Most of the dancers thawed enough to smile back, and Sin was startled to realise that she had been wrong all this time when she'd assumed Alan was winning over all the old guard of the Market just by being an enormous nerd. He had charm.

He'd just never bothered to use it on Sin.

"We have the exact right guitar for you," Matthias said,

trying to usher Alan away to the other pied pipers. "Don't ask me how I know. I always know. I've been watching your hands."

"I feel very reassured," said Alan. "Also a little violated. There is that."

More than a few dancers laughed as he limped past on his way to the pipers, and Sin was still lost in amazement that it was all so simple: that Alan could make them laugh like he was any guy.

She'd never had a problem charming other guys. There had to be a way to reach this one, too. She had to be able to thank him somehow.

Sin was still thinking this over when the drums started a new rhythm and the tourists all took notice. Sin exchanged a glance with Nick, then reached out and took his hand. It felt different, Nick's fingers strong enough to break her hand and nothing about his still face to make her think he wouldn't.

The fires were crackling round them both, racing in thin glittering lines on all sides. Sin could see her dancers tumbling through fire, striking poses, getting into position. The audience was waiting. Nothing was moving but the flames, the hissing of the fires like a fraught whisper in the hush.

The drumming and piping rolled together into a soft, thrilling start. The guitar riff rippled out, startling and sweet.

Alan leaned forward, serious and intent. The firelight turned his eyelashes into gold and shadows behind his glasses.

He began to sing.

He had the kind of voice you had to dance to, something that moved honey-sweet and slow through Sin's blood until his voice rose and flowed like a river, and she found she was already in motion, carried along with the sound. Nick's hands grasped her waist and lifted her high into the sky, and Sin planted a foot against his chest and launched herself tumbling and hurtling through the air.

Nick caught her as she came back down. Usually the dances for the tourists were so much less thrilling than those for demons, pale shadows of the real dances, the ones that demanded skill.

She wasn't bored now. Alan was singing a Goblin Market song turned into something new and strange by guitar strings and that voice.

"Sweet to mouth and low to sigh. Come buy, come buy."

Sin was a bit above average height and all muscle. It was a luxury to have a partner strong enough that she didn't have to worry about him doing lifts: a partner strong enough for anything. Nick picked her up and spun with her, and she curled her fingers round the tense swell of his arms. She knew the kind of tableau they made. She slanted a glance over at Alan to see if he was paying attention, but his head was bent over his guitar.

New lines of fire were lit and raced between them, bright lines of flame splitting the earth. Their shadows were cast dark and dramatic against the ground. Sin turned away from flames and partner, swaying into the shadows, Alan's voice following her as she went.

"I have wandered through dark woods, I have been worse than lost."

Sin was warm from dancing, but she shivered at the sound. She danced a few more steps to the strumming of guitar strings, then dived backwards on to her hands, twisting through the air and making it look easy. She was scattering fever blossoms as she went, shreds of scarlet sliding through her hair and down her arms, crushed petals marking the places her bare feet touched.

Through fire and darkness the demon came and caught her.

Sin slipped away from Nick once, twice, their shadows tangling though they did not touch. She fought in a stylised mock battle, neither of them using weapons, the audience making small noises as she dived low and Nick pinned her to the grass, muscles weighing her down effortlessly. Sin shimmied out of his grasp on her wrists, thrown up over her head, and leaped to her feet to flee.

Nick grabbed her before she did and threw her, though it must have looked to the audience as if she'd flown. Sin stretched out her arms, her dress billowing round her like shadows, her legs curled under her, tumbling through the air as if it was water. She landed on the stone pillar in the centre of the hill, poised as if to take flight.

"I have tasted fever fruit. It was worth the cost."

Sin stood outlined against the lights of London, feeling the rapt eyes of the audience on her, the eyes of all but one. She drew her hands up along her body to her head, and heard the ripple rising from the crowd as she began to undo the fever blossoms and ivy binding her hair.

Her dancers were moving slowly and gracefully round the pillar where she stood, arms curving over their heads and swaying. Nick just stood, watching her.

Sin cupped the red flower in her hand and then threw it. It arced through the air like a bright bird flying home, like a compass swinging to true north.

Alan caught it almost automatically, and then paused. For a moment he simply sat with one arm round his guitar, his face wiped clean with shock.

Then he ducked his head and looked up again. With sudden colour staining his cheekbones vivid red, he met Sin's eyes and smiled.

If the last smile had been a curtain drawn back, this one was a sunrise.

"This is a trig point," Alan said.

Sin blinked. This was not the kind of conversation guys typically directed at her after she had thrown them a fever blossom. In fact, this was not the kind of conversation guys typically directed at her at all.

"I don't know what you're talking about," she told him eventually.

"The pillar you ended up on there, when you were dancing," Alan said. "It's a trig point. Those pillars were set up all over England in the 1930s, as the points in a measurement system that covered the whole country. You can work out where roads and bridges are in relation to the trig points."

"Oh, you can?" Sin said helplessly.

"Not really any more," Alan told her. "They're a bit obsolete now we have helicopters and aerial maps and so on. A lot of them are gone. But not this one." He'd fixed the pillar with an intent gaze, but now he turned back to Sin and smiled. "I'm sorry," he said. "I just thought it was interesting."

"It's not that it isn't interesting," Sin said. "I just wasn't expecting geography right now."

They were walking alone together through the Market. The other dancers had peeled away after she'd thrown the fever blossom. They all knew the fever blossom meant Sin had decided to spend time with someone this Market night; whether she was just going to flirt with them a bit or draw them away and kiss them depended on how the spending time went. Occasionally a guy would presume that by tossing him a flower she'd promised something more.

She knew how to deal with those guys. Harshly.

She wasn't sure how to deal with a guy who had seemed pleased by being thrown the flower and then seemed to have no expectations at all, or any hopes.

It was possible Alan was just glad to be getting along with a section of the Goblin Market he'd always had friction with before. It was possible that Alan earnestly talking about geography was his way of turning Sin down, in which case she wanted to tell him that it didn't matter how good his voice was, she hadn't decided anything about him yet.

It was possible Alan just thought it was interesting. Sin really had no idea. She was a little warmed by that thought, though: that he wasn't talking down to her as if she couldn't possibly understand what he was saying. A lot of guys did that, and she'd always known Alan was really smart. She'd always uneasily suspected he thought she was stupid.

She decided to smile at him. "I'm a bit puzzled by you, that's all."

She was expecting Alan to look a little flattered, and to start trying to find out if by puzzled she meant intrigued. She was not expecting him to laugh.

"Well, I'm very mysterious. And inscrutable."

"You really kind of are," Sin said, and took his arm.

Any good performer knew how to lie with his whole body as well as his mouth, and Alan could do it: fading into the background as expertly as Sin stood out. But she'd noticed the way he had seemed uncertain about his hand after she'd taken it.

He did react when she took his arm. He hesitated and almost flinched, and she thought she had made a misstep until he put his hand over hers, in an almost courtly gesture that reminded her of the oddly gentle way he had held her hand before, and they walked on.

It was a little disturbing walking like that. Sin was keenly aware of the fact that Alan could not keep in step with her, always favouring his right leg, his walk a little jerky. It made her think of falling, and she felt a little panicked, her heart beating fast.

She didn't want to pull away.

"So are you going to play for us at the next Goblin Market?" Sin asked.

"I think I could be persuaded," said Alan. "Cynthia. I was wondering if you could do me a favour."

He did not say her name with his usual dismissive intonation. Sin found she didn't mind it like this.

"Yes," she said slowly, and became aware that her heart was not beating faster purely because of panic. It was so strange – this was *Alan Ryves* – but there it was. "I think I could be persuaded."

"My brother keeps pointing out to me that guns don't always work," Alan said, and Sin was amazed both at the fact that Alan could think this was a good time to bring up his brother and also at the tone he used, fond and a little exasperated, so normal, when talking about the demon. "Long-range weapons work better for me, for obvious reasons. I saw you with a bow and arrow, in the square at Huntingdon."

In the square where they had all fought and lost. Sin remembered the weight of the bow and arrow in her hands that night, and remembered, too, the weight of Toby in her arms when Alan had handed him to her, when she'd thought she would never hold him again.

"I wondered, if I bought a bow, would you teach me how to use it?"

It was a strange thing to ask, but Sin found she didn't mind. It was something she knew how to do well, and it was nice to get an acknowledgement of that – like a compliment to her dancing that she could be certain had no ulterior motive, nothing but a simple recognition of skill.

"Of course," Sin said. "We're meant to be allies now. That means your strength is my strength. I'll teach you the bow. But this does mean I can call on you at any time for obscure facts about geography."

Alan laughed, and this time Sin felt it as an accomplishment and not a shock. She noticed that he still had the fever blossom in his free hand, and he was playing with it, turning it thoughtfully over and over round his fingers.

"Fair enough. I also know many obscure historical facts I'm willing to trade."

"Like what?"

"The Scottish invented suspenders," Alan said. "And Isaac Newton, the guy who discovered gravity? He invented the cat flap."

"I can see you're going to be an invaluable asset to our side," Sin told him gravely.

She stopped at Elka's food stall, where Elka sold truth leaves that sometimes got the tourists into a lot of trouble, and where Elka's son was stirring a vat of mulled fever wine.

On top of the stall there was a bowl filled with the crystallised petals of fever blossoms. Sin took one and let it dissolve on her tongue, leaving behind a faint trace of sugar and a wilder sweetness.

"They're wonderful," she said truthfully, and pushed the bowl towards Alan.

Elka smiled at her and Alan both. "Nice to see you taking

a break from the demon dances," she told Sin. "You know you're supposed to do them every other month."

This was the first time in a year Sin hadn't done them. She knew it was important to take a break, and important to be seen walking through the Market talking to people, but she still hated that Mae was dancing and she wasn't.

Elka might have read that on her face, since she leaned forward over the stall and said in a low voice, "You're doing a good job. We're behind you."

Then she pushed the bowl of petals encouragingly towards them and went to serve another customer. Sin had another petal.

"You don't want one?"

"No," said Alan. "I've never had any fever fruit. I don't like being out of control."

Sin tilted a smile towards him. "Who knows what you might be capable of?"

Alan didn't smile back, something that surprised her even though they had only started smiling at each other tonight. He just looked at her, eyes wide open and very dark blue, and he really was not very much older than her at all.

"I know what I'm capable of," said the boy who had set a demon free.

Sin felt a little scared, and that knocked her even further off balance; somehow she still had a hard time thinking of Alan as dangerous.

She was dangerous, too, though.

"I know what you're capable of, too," Sin said. "You can't even shoot a bow yet. It's kind of sad."

Alan did smile then.

The smile acted on Sin like another fever blossom petal,

almost pure sweetness with an edge to it, and she made up her mind and tugged Alan through one of the curtains they had set up from the branches, hiding the brightest Goblin Market lights from the world.

Behind the curtain was a dim little space between the wood at night and the Goblin Market a veil away. Everything was grey and faintly glittering. The autumn air was a little cool, so Sin stepped in close to Alan and his warmth.

"Hi," she whispered.

"Hi," he murmured, sounding slightly puzzled but glad to be there, sounding happy and a little amused. She thought that was promising.

"So," Sin said, moving in closer. "I really am very grateful."

She closed her eyes and tipped her head back. Her lean in was stopped by a light pressure on her face. She blinked, looking up at Alan through her eyelashes, and then realised what was touching her face. It was the fever blossom.

She let her eyelids drift closed again, the petals of the flower stroking lightly over her cheek, shiver-soft, trailing along her skin and catching at the corner of her mouth. She felt Alan lean down, his breath warm against her ear.

"You don't have to do this," Alan said.

Sin blinked. "I know."

He ran musician's fingers down her arm, her skin prickling at the light touch, until he touched her hand. For an instant she thought everything was still as she'd planned.

Then Alan whispered, "And I would never want you to."

He stepped back through the curtain and limped away without a glance.

Sin stood alone outside the Goblin Market. She was shivering a little.

The fever blossom lay, returned unwanted, in the hollow of her hand.

She was going to be the leader of the Goblin Market, and that meant she went out and smiled, welcomed tourists and complimented Market folk, and ignored the fact that she had been utterly and humiliatingly rejected.

It did not mean that she was pleased to be reminded of this fact by running into Nick, who scowled at her. Sin let the fixed smile slide from her face and glared ferociously back, and would have moved on if she hadn't seen that Nick looked sweaty and tired as well as more homicidal than usual.

"Did something happen to my dancers?" she demanded.

"Everyone's alive," Nick snapped. "No thanks to you. What were you off doing while Mae decided to risk her stupid neck dancing with that idiot Jonas?"

"Jonas is a good dancer."

"Not good enough."

"Not as good as you," Sin conceded. "Did you offer to dance with her?"

"Why else would I come here ready to dance?" Nick demanded. "This is only her fourth time, and she could screw up at any moment."

"Told her that, did you?" Sin asked. "And here you are with not a stab mark to show for it. Mae has such a nice nature."

Sin might be having issues with Mae about the Goblin Market, but she was ready to be on Mae's side when Mae was being patronised. She looked around for Mae, and found her pink hair.

She was standing with Alan. Sin felt sheer embarrassment seize her, an almost irresistible compulsion to look down or turn away before he saw her.

Alan did not see her. He was talking to Mae, head bent attentively down to hers, so much taller than her it looked almost silly and very sweet. They were near the silent sisters' stall. Alan was pointing to a yellowed scroll, his smile like a fire in a hearth, warm and welcoming.

But not for her.

She looked back at Nick. He crossed his arms over his chest and looked down at her with cold eyes. He made her think again of Merris, running through the woods with wild red hair and black eyes, but Sin crushed down the thought and tried to think of him as just Nick Ryves in a strop. She could deal with him then.

"Mae is an idiot."

"Are you jealous of Jonas?" Sin asked. After a moment Nick laughed, the sound sharp and unpleasant.

"No. She's practically my brother's girlfriend."

"Is that so?"

"Alan's mad about her," Nick said. "She deserves that. They deserve each other. They're going to be together."

Mae had said she wasn't going out with Alan once before, Sin recalled. She'd added that he was pretty attractive.

At the time, Sin had thought she was crazy.

It should have made her feel better, Sin thought. Alan might not have turned her down because he thought she was an idiot or she made his skin crawl, or anything like that. He just wanted someone else. It was simple enough. Sin had made a mistake.

"So it's that you don't like being turned down," Sin said, and smiled deliberately up at Nick.

"Well," Nick said, "it's just that it doesn't happen to me often. It's like a whole new world. I'd ask for advice, but I imagine it doesn't happen to you that often, either."

He didn't smile back, but the compliment was enough to keep Sin smiling, side by side in the shadow of a tree.

"It never happens to me," Sin told him, her eyes sliding back to Mae and Alan.

Unlike a demon, she could lie.

She'd only glanced over, in time to see Alan reach up to fetch down a scroll for Mae from a high shelf, but when she looked back, Nick was gone, silently, as if direct light had hit a shadow.

She did a swift scan of the crowd, used to picking out one face in an audience, and of course saw Nick beside Alan and Mae. Mae scowled up at him, and Nick leaned against the stall and in towards Mae, whispering something in her ear.

Mae's face turned thoughtful as he spoke. After a moment she nodded briefly and slipped out from between the stall and Nick's body, setting off purposefully through the Market. Alan stayed behind, a book open in his hand.

He did not look after Mae and Nick, but everybody else did.

Everybody saw Nick at Mae's back like a shadow that could not be dispersed, a dark sentinel, like the bodyguard to a queen.

Everybody saw Mae moving through the Market. With every step she took the lights nearest her flared into brilliance, the difference as great as if stars were blooming into suns above her head. The light round her hair spread and shone, as if every moment a new golden crown was being placed on her head, a succession of hundreds and hundreds of crowns.

Sin had taken the night off from dancing to make herself seem like the leader of the Market.

The demon had thrown his support behind her rival,

undone all her efforts, let Mae shine and let everyone know his power was at her command.

Sin had no idea how to match this.

The Market was winding down, Sin on the ground directing the people unwinding the wires that held up their lanterns and curtains from round the trees.

"Careful with that," she called up to one of her dancers. "Break a beacon lamp and we'll never hear the end of it. Coil up the wire: we've got to stow all this away."

She slid her hands to the base of her spine and arched, feeling her back pop and crack a little in a way that said she would be feeling all this tomorrow. She was going to get only a couple of hours' sleep, and then it would be time to wake the kids and bring them to school.

"Hi," Mae's voice said behind her, and Sin straightened her shoulders despite her back hurting. "Haven't seen you around a lot tonight."

"Hope your fourth Market was a good one," Sin said, keeping her voice warm and the fact that Sin herself had been part of more than a hundred Markets implicit.

Mae's eyebrows rose, obviously taking Sin's meaning. She always stood a little combatively, short but filling as much space as she could. Currently her arms were crossed and her elbows sticking out.

"It was, thanks," she said, her voice slightly stiff. Then she uncrossed her arms and reached out, putting one hand on Sin's arm. Sin looked down at Mae's hand, very pale on Sin's skin, her nails painted bright turquoise. "Look, Sin. I don't want Merris to succeed in setting us at each other's throats."

Sin remembered that Mae's mother was gone, and as far as

she could see, Mae's father and brother were out of the picture as well. She was staying with her Aunt Edith in London to be near all of them.

"I don't want that, either," Sin answered slowly, the words sticking in her throat. "I would have welcomed you to the Goblin Market. You know that. But I can't – I won't welcome you into my place."

"I can't stop trying for it," Mae said. "This thing, with Celeste's pearl. I want it." She swallowed and continued. "But if you get it before me, I swear I'll do everything I can to help you. You'll be my leader, too."

Sin couldn't say Mae would be her leader. She couldn't even contemplate that happening. But Mae's hand was gripping her arm tight, and she'd liked Mae from almost the first moment.

"Thanks," she said awkwardly. "I appreciate that."

She usually felt energised by the Market, glowing with all the small victories of the night and filled with new purpose. Not tonight. She summoned up a wicked smile for Mae anyway.

"I like the pigtails you're working tonight," she told her, and thought of Mae laughing at the book stall with Alan. "Anyone interesting around?"

Mae shrugged. "My pigtails are not the irresistible mantraps you might think." She let her hand drop from Sin's arm, but grinned up at her. "It must be kind of awesome. Being – well, you know."

"No, tell me," Sin coaxed, amused.

"Well, being completely gorgeous," Mae said, and went a bit pink. "You could have anyone you wanted. You wouldn't even have to try."

Sin thought about the boys at school and the guys on the street who bothered her because they thought black girls were exotic and easy and not to be taken seriously. It wasn't something she could turn off, not entirely, so it was something she'd learned to use.

She thought about getting up at six in the morning to stand outside in the raw air, mist lying clammy on the grass, and shave her legs using a basin and some cold water. She'd fixed her hair, hung the lanterns, planned the dancers' performances and costumes, and now the Market was being packed up and all her success was fading away with the morning. She had tried everything she knew, and she had not even been able to charm Alan Ryves.

Not that she cared about that.

"It's awesome," she said. "But it's not easy."

Mae rubbed at her face, the only sign she'd given to show she might be just as tired as Sin was. "What is?"

"You've got a point," Sin told her, and felt relaxed enough with Mae to give her a sideways hug before she made for her wagon, already thinking of the luxury of crawling in between soft sheets, the kids breathing slow and steady on either side of her.

She found Matthias the piper sitting on her front step, turning his pipe over and over between his hands.

"Sin," he said, rising gracefully to meet her. "You did well tonight."

"Thanks."

"Not your fault you were outdone."

Sin refused to lose ground in front of a pied piper, so she made herself smile. "You say the sweetest things."

"She's a clever girl, that Mae," Matthias said. "Maybe a bit too clever. You know she's been murmuring about a possible spy at the Goblin Market."

Sin made a face. It was just another of Mae's hundreds of ideas, like that of making profit and loss sheets, or the crazy suggestion she kept floating about inviting necromancers and pied pipers to travel with the Market.

"Maybe she's looking for an excuse if the magicians seem like they know too much, and someone wonders where they got the information," Matthias said. "I heard from a little bird that she's been seen talking to people from the Aventurine Circle."

The sleepiness cleared from Sin's mind suddenly. She was very aware of Matthias's watchful dark eyes, waiting for her reaction, of the cold grass round her ankles, and of the familiar weight of her knives against her back.

"Do you have any proof?"

"If I had any proof, I'd have brought it," Matthias said. "You Market people may not think much of the pipers, and we may think you're a little set in your ways, but neither of us wants a leader beholden to magicians, do we?"

Sin's mouth shaped the word *No*, though she did not say it, simply watching Matthias. She'd trusted Mae. She didn't know if she could trust the piper. They were all mercurial and strange, valuing singing more than speaking, music more than the faces of those they loved.

But if there was any possibility this was true, she could not afford to ignore it.

"Imagine the advantage she has, if the magicians are helping her," Matthias said. "She could beat you. Imagine what would happen to the Market then."

Sin licked her lips. "Any ideas on what I should do?"

"We saw the magicians down by the river near Southwark Cathedral," Matthias said. "Maybe you should go and check the place out for yourself."

Sin nodded slowly. "Thank you."

"One more thing?"

Matthias walked lightly as all the pipers did, noiseless and barely stirring the grass with his passage. He brushed by her on his way down the hill, and his voice hit her ear like the music of the Market, beautiful and sinister.

"Watch your back."

4

Anchor Point

NICK WAS CLEARLY MISERABLE.

At first Sin found it kind of amusing. He'd done what she would have predicted he would if she'd thought about it, and approached the guys who generally hung around the handyman's shed and smoked while sitting on old buckets of paint.

That had not gone so well. Nobody was sure what had happened in the handyman's shed at break time, but everyone was talking about it anyway. By lunchtime Sin had heard quite a few compelling theories, and she saw people leaning away from Nick as he prowled sullenly through the playground and made a couple of phone calls to someone who did not pick up.

Sin found herself chewing vengefully on a peanut butter sandwich and thinking perhaps this would teach certain people that demons did not actually belong in school, which was about the time it occurred to her that she was wishing punishment on Nick not only because he'd decided to support Mae, but because she was angry with his brother.

That made her angry enough with herself to get up, murmuring excuses to the girls from the lacrosse team, and go over to him.

"So I heard you tried to kill a guy with a paintbrush."

"Don't try to stifle my artistic self-expression," Nick said.

Sin laughed. She saw a few heads on the playground turn, and realised with a sinking sensation that they would remember this, when her goal was always to avoid too much attention, any questions about the Market, any focus on her or the kids.

She remembered Alan's maddening voice in a sunlit summer kitchen, asking her to stick around and hang out with Nick. He'd offered her a translation worth a month of groceries to do it. She'd taken it, and she'd played nice with Nick.

She didn't regret it. Those groceries had come in extremely handy.

But she did feel like she owed Nick more than a dismissal now.

"Hey," she said. "I'm sorry about the way I acted before. I was just surprised to see you here. At school."

Nick shrugged.

"It wouldn't have killed your brother to have given us a heads-up," Sin added.

Nick stared at her with even more murderous coldness than usual.

There was a sudden chill wind in the air, striking Sin's face and sending cold fingers crawling tip by freezing tip down her back. She looked into Nick's blank face and thought: *possessed*, and did not know why she hadn't seen it years ago, why everyone didn't see it when they looked at him. There was no human being behind that face, only a creature who owned but could not animate it.

Alan had lived with this for most of his life, knowing exactly what it was. The wave of sympathy that washed over Sin at the thought shocked her with its intensity.

She couldn't work out what kind of man he was, good or evil, terrifying or terrifyingly misguided. She couldn't imagine what it would take to bring up a demon.

All she knew was that she'd had him all wrong.

"Shut up about my brother," Nick said at last. "I know you've always hated him, but I don't need to hear about it." His lip curled. "He doesn't think much of you, either."

If Nick had decided to support Mae's bid to be leader, who was likely to be behind that decision?

Sin picked up her peanut butter sandwich again and bit in. "I got that," she said. "Thanks."

She was in a hurry when she left school, and she didn't need to be distracted by the surprise appearance of Alan Ryves, at the wheel of an ancient blue car and with his head bent over a book.

It was therefore a complete mystery to her why she took a detour through the side gate, went over and tapped on the car window.

Alan used one hand to subtly go for his gun and the other to keep his page, then actually looked at her and sent the window whirring down.

"What are you doing here?" Sin demanded, and was horrified by the words coming out of her mouth.

"Picking my baby brother up from school," Alan told her, sounding faintly puzzled that she would ask something so obvious.

"Well, he's in detention," Sin said in what she hoped was a

more reasonable voice. "Word is he tried to kill someone with a paintbrush."

"Little scamp," Alan said. "Well, boys will be boys. Can I give you a lift anywhere?"

Offended dignity said not in a million years, but Sin had a lot more practicality than pride.

"If you could drive me to my sister's school, that'd be great," she said, going round the car and climbing into the passenger seat.

"Happy to," said Alan, and started the car engine.

She gave him directions, and he turned a corner through the estate by her school and towards Acton Town without comment, obviously already familiar enough with the geography of this part of London. Market people always had to know where they were going, and be able to get there fast when they had to.

Sin was not planning on reaching out and being turned down again, so she turned her face away from Alan and watched the buildings go by, grey towers changing to tan-coloured Victorian buildings and back again.

"I wanted to talk to you about last night," said Alan.

Horror and embarrassment sent a burning-hot flash flood through Sin's veins. But it would be absolutely unacceptable for Alan to know he had inspired those feelings, and since she was a performer, goddamn it, Sin laughed and said lightly, "Really? You have to know it wasn't a big deal."

"Yes, I know that," Alan said, his voice very mild. "But we're going to be working together for some time. I'd like for us to get on better than we have done in the past. God knows that wouldn't be hard."

He doesn't think much of you.

"Sounds good!" Sin responded, forcing herself to sound a

bit incredulous about all the fuss Alan was making instead of desperate for the conversation to be over.

"I had fun at the Market last night," Alan continued. "A lot more fun than I usually have."

Until Sin had thrown herself at him. Yes, she understood perfectly. What she didn't understand was why Alan had to *talk* so much.

"I just wanted to let you know that I understand," Alan told her. "And I don't want you to be embarrassed, or to think I took anything in a different way than it was meant."

"I wasn't embarrassed," Sin said. "I don't care enough about your opinion of me to be embarrassed."

"All right."

There was silence for a moment, during which Sin tried to work out if Alan's response had sounded faintly incredulous or simply indifferent. It was too hot in the car, the air-conditioning obviously not working right, autumnal sunlight flooding through the windows and filling the car with trapped heat. Sin sent a swift glance towards Alan, not under her eyelashes, because guys noticed that and she always meant them to, but sidelong and carefully casual.

He was wearing two shirts, which was ridiculous considering the sun but which he always did, and looking at the road ahead, lashes bright fringes over his dark blue eyes. She looked away almost immediately.

"Just so we're clear," Alan said. "You don't owe me anything."

"Okay, Alan, *I get it*," Sin snapped.

"As long as you're still planning to teach me how to shoot a bow and arrow," he continued calmly. "I mean, I do feel you kind of owe me that."

"What?" Sin asked, and was so startled she found herself laughing.

"Well, I sang at the Market and everything," Alan reminded her. "I'm a diffident guy. I had terrible stage fright."

"I'm not familiar with the concept of 'stage fright'."

"It's pretty awful," Alan said solemnly. "You end up having to picture the entire audience in their underwear. Phyllis was in that audience, you know."

"Why, Alan, I had no idea your tastes ran that way."

"Phyllis is a very nice lady," he said. "And I do not consider her so much aged as matured, like a fine wine. But I still think you owe me an archery lesson."

These brothers were her allies, were the Market's allies, and Alan was right: it would be better for them all to get along. She'd had more fun with Alan than she would've expected last night, before being turned down flat.

She wasn't about to ruin any chance of them reaching an understanding because of being rejected. Lots of people weren't attracted to her. Merris, obviously. Phyllis, with any luck. If she ever went insane and assaulted Matthias in a frenzy of lust, he would probably run away, shrieking, *Your singing voice is nasal! Unclean, unclean!*

Alan had saved her brother. She'd judged him wrongly on more occasions than she cared to count at this point, but she felt pretty confident she was right about this judgement: he was worth knowing.

And he was right. It wasn't like getting along better than they had before would be much of a challenge.

"Drive me and Lydie back to the hill," Sin said at last. "And you can have your lesson." She looked at him under her eyelashes and he noticed, as he was meant to; then she grinned.

"Plus Phyllis will be there. I'm sure she'll be thrilled to see you."

Lydie's new school was in a nice part of Acton, far enough away from the Market and Sin's school to make Sin's life difficult, but there were trees lining the street where it stood and when Sin peeped through the classroom door before going in, she saw Lydie's fair head tipped to another girl's, engaged in close and happy conversation.

She had not asked or particularly wanted Alan to accompany her into the school, but he had done so anyway. Sin was making an effort not to be annoyed at him for being interfering. She was sure he meant well.

"I'm Cynthia Davies, Lydia's sister," she told the teacher, shaking her hand firmly so there would be no comments about thinking Sin was older on the phone.

There was the usual look that meant the teacher had thought Sin was white on the phone, but people hardly ever said that.

Sin went round to Lydie's table and tossed her braid over her shoulder, trying for a slight air of glamour. It never hurt a kid to have a cool older sister.

"Having fun?" she asked.

"Sure," said Lydie, stowing away books and pencil case. Sin put a hand flat against her thin little back in case a hug would be going too far, and Lydie leaned into it a tiny bit. "Alan's here," she added in a tone of inquiry but with bright eyes. Sin was instantly very glad Alan had come in.

"Well, he was going up to the hill anyway, and when he heard I was picking you up, obviously he wanted to come along."

Lydie went off to grab her coat from the cloakroom, and

Sin went back to the teacher, who was standing with Alan, apparently deep in conversation.

". . . mother and stepfather died in a car accident a while ago," she heard him say in a confidential tone, and heard the teacher murmur sympathetically. "Their guardian's a little elderly. It's a challenge, of course, but Cynthia picks up a lot of the slack."

"I do what?" Sin asked brightly, deciding that she had not heard anything else he'd said.

Alan gave her a slightly wary look, and she took his arm and squeezed it to show that she was impressed. It was a good lie: the teacher won over to Lydie's side, the adroit mention of a stepfather meaning that there would never be a question of how she and Lydie were related, and neither parents nor guardian would ever be expected. Sin planned to remember exactly how he'd said it, but she doubted it would have quite the same effect.

"And you're . . ." the teacher began inquiringly.

"Alan," he said, and he shook her hand. "Friend of the family."

There were not so many hillwalkers on a weekday afternoon in October, but Sin took Alan out to a field near where the Market wagons were assembled anyway, where people would be discouraged by all the don't-notice-us charms and inclined to overlook whatever was going on without exactly knowing why.

Unfortunately, this meant that when she was setting up targets and Alan was trying out different bows, the rest of the Market decided to wander by and take an interest. Jonas started to shoot in order to impress Chiara. Phyllis came and told Alan she hoped he was eating right, and Sin had to hide her smile behind her quiverful of arrows.

"Can I borrow him for a moment, Phyllis?" she asked after she was done grinning like a fool. "I promise I'll return him. I know he'd be devastated if I didn't."

Alan gave her a reproachful look. Sin gave him a dazzling smile and a longbow.

She'd changed out of her school uniform into jeans and a bandanna. It was mostly for practicality but partly to see if being the daughter of the Market – someone who the older ones still sometimes called by her father's childhood nickname of Thea – was the role Alan would warm to rather than Sin the dancer or Cynthia the schoolgirl. It was funny which presentations of herself boys sometimes went for.

He hadn't seemed to notice, though, so she'd decided to be all business.

"This is your most traditional kind of bow," Sin said. "Not allowed at the Olympics. Pretty difficult to shoot. Best one if you want to kill people. I figured you'd like it."

"I do like a challenge," said Alan. "Though I weep for my Olympic dreams."

He turned the longbow over in his hands as if it was a musical instrument, gentle and a little curious, the same way he touched everything. Then he laid it down on the grass, shrugged off his shirt so he was in only a T-shirt, and slid on a shooting glove. He picked the bow back up again.

"Okay," he said. "Show me."

"Right," said Sin. "So – feet about a shoulder's width apart, do what you need to do to be steady."

She didn't exactly know how to position someone whose balance was necessarily always off, and she was mortified to realise she was a bit flustered, as well. There was obviously something to the way the Victorians had kept women all covered up so guys swooned at the sight of an ankle. Sin saw boys in T-shirts every hour of the day, but she'd never seen Alan in one. It struck her more than it really should have.

He wasn't coiled with muscle like his brother, but he was lean when Sin had thought he was thin, shoulders strong, back a taut arch like the bow. If it hadn't been for his leg, Sin would've thought he looked like a dancer.

Sin rested a hand on his waist and checked he was steady, fingers brushing over cotton and the edge of a hipbone. She made a mental note that it was possibly time for her to find a boyfriend.

"So you nock the arrow in the bow, like so. Firmly on the bowstring," she said, and put her palm against his elbow. "Bring the elbow of your drawing arm up high."

Alan was so much taller than she was that correcting the position of his drawing arm and trying to get some idea of his line of sight was pretty difficult. Sin had to lean in against him to do it, a bit too aware of his body against hers.

"Don't," Alan demanded, his voice tight.

"I wasn't—," Sin began furiously, and then realised that she'd been leaning her weight against someone with a bad leg. "I didn't mean to," she said quickly. "I'm sorry."

"Not to worry," Alan said, his voice a little too smooth, trying to let them slide past this moment as fast as they could. "What do I do now?"

Sin came round to his side, skirting him a little more widely than she had to. She saw him register that out of the corner of his eye and wanted to explain that she didn't want to hurt him again, that was all, but she doubted that would help.

"Find your anchor point."

"What's an anchor point?"

"Where the hand is positioned and what the bowstring draws to. Choose a point on your face," she said, and reached out to press her fingers lightly against the corner of his jaw. "Here, or the corner of your eye, or the corner of your – mouth," she continued, and was angry with herself for the pause she hadn't intended. "The anchor point is the most important thing in archery. It affects your draw length and the whole force of your shot stems from it. You have to choose your anchor point and always let the arrow fly from it."

She withdrew her hand. Alan raised his bow from point to point, his face absorbed, and Sin watched as he settled on the corner of his mouth.

"Then hold, tense." Sin ran a palm over the muscles of his back. She smiled. "Like that. And adjust aim, concentrate and release."

Alan didn't fumble on the release. He let the arrow slip smooth through his fingers, drawing his hand back and loosing the bow. The arrow just missed its target.

"That really wasn't bad," Sin told him honestly.

She was expecting either frustration or pride, but Alan just smiled.

"Could be better."

He took another arrow and strung it. This time he got it right first try, index fletch at his mouth, arms moving easy and graceful and sending the arrow in flight.

It hit the target, though just barely.

"Okay, that was actually good."

Alan smiled. There was still nothing on his face but good humour and determination.

"Thanks," he said. "Now can you teach me how to hit the bullseye?"

Alan kept practising, his draw getting smoother and smoother though his arms must have been killing him. Lydie and Toby were actually being very well-behaved since he talked to them and they seemed to feel it was a great treat to sit and watch him.

At this point Sin's role as teacher consisted of a few pieces of advice and a steady stream of insults and insinuations about how impressed Phyllis was going to be, so she sat back on the bank with her arm round Lydie and watched.

Lydie leaned into the curve of her hip. "Maybe he would like to stay for dinner," she suggested shyly.

The Market usually had a communal dinner, potluck, batches of curry, a lot of barbecues in the summer. It worked for Sin, who was a pretty basic cook. But sometimes they stayed in the wagon, just the three of them, and ate easy things to make like beans on toast. She turned over in her mind the idea of having Alan there, too.

Then Alan dropped his bow at her feet.

"I've got to go," he said, his voice tight.

"What?" Sin asked. "What's wrong?"

"Nothing's wrong," Alan snapped, and turned on his heel. Sin noticed that he was not heading for his car.

She might not know Alan well enough to recognise when he was lying. Probably nobody knew him well enough for that.

But she could always recognise a bad performance. And Alan was excellent at pretending everything was all right: if he was turning in a bad performance, then something was really wrong.

Sin intended to find out what.

She couldn't think of what she wanted first, though. Toby and Lydie came first. She ran over to Jonas and asked him to watch the kids for a minute, bring them to Trish if she was gone too long, make sure they were fed. Toby was playing with a tiny bow and looked happy, so she didn't disturb him, but she stopped and hugged Lydie and told her she was just going to ask Alan if he would like to stay for dinner, after all.

Then and only then was she allowed to run, and she ran, sure and fleet, legs carrying her in easy motion over the fields in the direction Alan had gone. There were a few fences in her way: she ran at them, sometimes clearing them, sometimes hooking a foot in them and launching herself over them without breaking stride. She knew where she was going and what she was doing. Chasing Alan was easy.

Catching up with Alan was hard, because she had no plan of action for what to do when she drew level with him as he limped determinedly beside another fence.

He whirled on her, face very pale, and demanded, "What do you want?"

"What did you think you were doing, running off like that?" Sin asked. "You should've known I'd come after you."

Alan's mouth twisted. "And of course, I can't outrun you."

"Nobody can outrun me," said Sin.

It was just the truth. But it seemed to knock Alan back a little. He almost smiled, and ran one hand roughly through his hair. It made his hair stand up on end, a glinting riot of curls.

"Cynthia," Alan said. "Trust me, you don't want to be here. Will you just go?"

"Trust you?" Sin echoed. "Aren't you, like, a compulsive liar? No, I think I'm going to stay right here."

She illustrated her point by perching herself on the fence.

Alan almost smiled again, but insisted, "You really don't want to—"

He'd been pale before, but now he went grey, his face locked in a spasm of pain. He gritted his teeth for a moment, lips skinned back, grimacing helplessly, and then he fell face forward on the grass.

Sin scrambled off the fence and on to her knees.

"Alan," she said. "Oh my God, Alan—"

He could not answer, that much was clear. He was moaning into the grass, but they didn't sound like conscious moans. They sounded like the long, guttural cries of an animal in agony.

Sin manhandled him on to his back, careless of his leg, too desperate to be careful of anything. He screamed once when she was doing it, but she was a dancer, and that meant never hesitating once you were committed to a course of action.

When she had his head in her lap, she realised that she'd trapped herself there, but it wasn't like she could have abandoned Alan while he had some sort of fit. She couldn't leave him, not like this, not all alone. So she couldn't get help.

All she could do was watch his body seizing with what seemed like hundreds of separate convulsions, shaking with another rush of pain before the first had completely passed, face turning away from her even as she stroked his hair. The terrible moaning sound seemed to be ripped right from his chest after a while. It went on and on, helpless and exhausted.

She thought it would never end, and then it did. The sky was grey with evening and Alan's skin looked as ashen as the fading light. His body was still shuddering a little with the aftershocks of pain, but the terrible strained tautness had finally gone out of it.

He blinked up at her. His glasses had gone crooked, and he looked a little confused.

"Cynthia?"

"What," Sin said, "the *hell* was that?"

Alan struggled to sit up, his arms bracing his body up, able to drag himself a little away on the grass. Sin was impressed that he'd managed it, though she was less impressed that the first order of business once he was conscious was apparently getting away from her.

Alan looked like he was considering trying to get up, but he wisely remained sitting in the grass. He wiped the sweat off his forehead, and winced even at that movement. "That was the magicians."

"The Aventurine Circle," Sin said. "They're torturing you."

Alan offered up a tired smile, as if that could possibly convince her this was not as bad as it clearly was. "Something like that. Yes." He pushed his hair back again with what seemed to be a habitual gesture. His fingers were trembling. "I'm never going to be able to make you believe you don't owe me now, am I?"

"No," Sin said, because – well, of course he couldn't.

She'd already known she owed him everything, and now here was more proof, evidence more terrible than she had dreamed. And it could have been Toby: it could have been her baby.

It occurred to her why he'd said it.

"You don't have to worry," she said, lifting her chin. "I'm not going to assault you with sexual favours. This isn't actually your most attractive moment."

Alan laughed weakly. "I imagine not."

"That's not—" Sin stopped, and swore. "How are you feeling? Why are they doing this?"

"Horrible," Alan said promptly, with the same lack of bravado he'd shown about the bow. "And they're doing this to make Nick do what they want." He sighed and rubbed the inside of his left wrist. It was the left hand that bore the magician's mark. "That's why Gerald marked me, and why Celeste thought Gerald having a mark on me was valuable. They wanted me as a hostage, so they could have a demon on a leash. Killing me would make me useless. But every time they make a demand and Nick doesn't obey them, they give me a little display of their power."

That was why things had been so quiet over the last few weeks, when Sin had been expecting the magicians to attack the Market fast and without mercy. The magicians had bigger game to go after, and once they were assured that the demon was theirs to command, they would come for the Market.

Sin should have thought of this, shouldn't have been counting Nick and Alan as allies so readily. She bet Mae, with all her plans, had thought of it.

"Does Mae know?"

"Yes," Alan said. "She guessed, so I told her everything. Plus I'm trying not to lie to her any more."

His voice warmed when he talked about her, Sin noticed. She got it: Mae was the one smart enough to guess, the special one he didn't lie to, the one he wanted.

"Aren't you angry?"

Alan frowned. "What do you mean?"

"You're being tortured!" Sin almost shouted at him. "And the demon is just letting it happen!"

It was enough to make her laugh, or scream. The magicians had actually overestimated the demon. They had thought Nick would mind about Alan getting tortured, and maybe he was displeased that his human toy was being broken, maybe he was angry, but he was a demon like all the others. So unfeeling that it didn't matter if Alan had given up everything for him, so cold that he could weigh Alan's suffering in the balance and find it nothing to affect his behaviour at all.

She called herself seven different kinds of fool for being shocked.

He was a demon. They just did not care.

"Nick doesn't know," said Alan. "The magicians give me their messages for him. I don't deliver them. I have warning of when they're going to attack, and I've managed to get away from him every time, get somewhere he can't hear or see. He has no idea what the Circle are doing."

"You crazy bastard," Sin said, in awe and horror so tangled up she could not tell which was which. "What if they decide you're useless and they kill you?"

A corner of Alan's mouth went up. "Then they really won't have any leverage over Nick at all, will they? He'll be safe. He won't do anything terrible, except to them. He'll be allied with the right people. He'll be all right."

"You, however, will be dead," Sin reminded him.

Alan seemed calm, even though he still looked sick and shaky. "I admit the situation is not ideal."

"Demons always take more than you can afford to pay," she said in a low voice, remembering Merris and her eyes bleeding into blackness.

Alan shook his head, closing his eyes. He looked too exhausted to keep them open. Sin had a sudden urge to push back his hair herself, take care of him, as if he was Lydie or Toby. He looked so lost and so resigned to it that she thought perhaps nobody had taken care of him in years.

Her care would not be welcome, though. He'd made that pretty clear.

Even when it was worn to a thread held taut with pain, his voice was still beautiful.

"Love always costs more than you can afford to pay," he said. "And it's always worth the price."

They sat together on the cool grass in the gathering evening, silent for a while. Sin had absolutely no idea what to say. She'd been right, he was crazy. Sane people did not do things like this. Sane people did not love demons.

"I don't understand," she admitted softly at last. "I don't see why you're doing all this."

"Wouldn't you," Alan asked, "for your brother or sister?"

Sin was silent. After a moment she reached out and took his hand, trying hard to make it clear it was an offer of comfort and nothing more, not shifting any closer. Alan was visibly startled, maybe even a little disturbed, but his fingers closed round hers tight all the same. Perhaps he was just so desperate for comfort he wasn't going to be choosy about its source.

She would have liked to sit there with him longer, but night was already closing in, and she could not think about what she wanted first.

"I've got to go," she started awkwardly after a pause. "The kids."

"Of course," said Alan. "I'm sorry to have kept you from them so long. Thank you."

"Oh for God's sake, don't thank me," Sin burst out, her voice rough. She didn't want to cry.

She helped Alan up instead, and he let her. He refused to lean on her, though, so she walked beside him as he made his slow, wavering way down through the fields to his car.

About halfway there Alan's phone rang, the noise stunning in the still evening. Alan fished the phone out of his pocket, and Sin was not surprised to hear his voice come out suddenly steady and strong.

"Hi, Nick," he said, and after a pause, "Well, that's right, I sent you a text. If you insist on killing people with paintbrushes, you have to get the Tube home. Those are my rules. I consider them harsh but fair." Another pause. "I didn't think that while I was gone, you'd forget how to use the *stove*."

He talked on for a little while, teasing and fond, obviously keeping up about two-thirds of the conversation. He sounded absolutely normal.

If she was Nick, Sin thought, and she found out about this lie, she wasn't sure the magicians would get the chance to kill Alan. She might do it herself.

Sin let Alan get in the car and drive away, back to the home where he would have to pretend to be tired from learning how to use a bow and nothing more. She went quietly to the wagon, thanking Trish as she went by for putting the kids to bed.

When she swung the door softly closed behind her, she found Lydie awake and sitting up in bed. There was a small radiant sphere of light held between her palms, rays dancing on the walls of their tiny home.

"Lydie," Sin said, her voice hushed with terror. "Lydie, you know you can't do that."

"It was dark," Lydie told her. She sounded guilty, though, and the light went out.

Sin crawled into her bed between theirs and curled her body round Lydie's through the sheets. She couldn't let her muscles be stiff with fear that Lydie could've been discovered while Sin was away. Lydie would notice. Lydie was seven years old. Sin couldn't let her mind dwell on thoughts of how the Market would react to a child who was showing power this strong, this young. It was bad enough to have any magical power. Then you couldn't really be part of the Market. You had to be a pied piper or a potion-maker or a necromancer.

But people born with too much power, they said, always wanted more. When their sixteenth birthday came, when they came into their real power and made their choices, the people born with too much power became magicians.

Which meant, as far as the Market was concerned, that people born with too much power were born evil.

"It doesn't matter if it's dark," Sin whispered, her arm tight round Lydie's body. "I'm here. I'll keep you safe."

5

Traitor in the Nest

THE NEXT DAY WAS SATURDAY. SIN USUALLY LET HERSELF SLEEP IN until nine at the weekend, but today she had magicians to hunt down.

She slid out from between Lydie and Toby, and asked Trish to watch out for them when they woke. She hoped they would sleep late; not dancing at the last Market had left them with very little money to get by on until next month, and Sin didn't want to owe favours. Nobody was getting Toby or Lydie's hair or teeth for any enchantments. That never ended well.

They knew that the Aventurine Circle had buried the stones of its circle under the earth of London, creating a safe space where no magic worked but their own. Mae had told the Market about Nick having to fight stripped of his magic on the Millennium Bridge.

That was what had led the pipers to the river, and Southwark Cathedral. And that was where Sin was going now.

If she could get a glimpse of the magicians, if she could follow them back and find where the Aventurine Circle lived and thus presumably where Celeste Drake kept her pearl, she could work out how to get it.

The Tube was crowded on the way with people going to Borough Market, which was good: a crowd would be good cover for a girl combing the streets.

Sin was wearing jeans and a light green shirt, more Thea of the Market with two kids to run around after and no time than a schoolgirl trying to blend in or a dancer trying to stand out. A couple of boys on the Tube tried to catch her eye and she gave them the polite smile, no teeth, which discouraged without offending. Then she looked out of the window at the fascinating dark tunnel until they rattled into London Bridge station.

She went right for Borough Market, as if she was just seeking stalls full of delicious organic food. She strolled casually down a cobbled street full of bars and flower shops, round the curve of a Victorian tavern and across the road from the steel-like wedge of an office building, through the Stoney Street entrance into the market.

This was only a pale shadow of the market Sin was used to, but there was a familiar bustle to the place that made her relax. There were green-painted fences hemming in some stalls, with other stalls set in the stone walls. Cobbled streets radiated out from the market in every direction, as if the market was the hub of a wheel and every street was a spoke. Above it all arched the stone curves of London Bridge.

Along the stalls full of bright fruit and warm bread were throngs of people. Sin watched them go by. She'd seen the magicians of the Aventurine Circle, just once.

That was enough. She'd been trained to remember people's faces since she could walk. It made people feel good to be remembered, and people who felt good paid well.

She knew Celeste Drake when she saw her.

People were clearing a space for Celeste because she was tiny and beautifully blonde in a way that meant she probably got a lot of things, including people not taking her seriously. She sailed past Sin, her white linen dress fluttering in the warm autumn breeze, without a second glance.

There was someone else with her, a short, blond guy in a white shirt with a wicker basket on his arm. He was in front of Celeste, so Sin couldn't see his face, but as she walked and studied them out of the corner of her eye, she saw Celeste's lips move. He turned slightly to catch what she said, and Sin caught the flash of an earring and the sound of his easy laugh.

They looked happy and carefree, out shopping in London on a beautiful morning. Sin was prepared to bet the boy was also a magician, and had sold people's bodies to demons as readily as the stall owners were selling oranges.

The pipers had guessed right. They must live close by.

Sin ran her fingertips along the rough wood of a stall, making sure she did not keep the same pace at all times but went slower and faster as if she was really browsing. She made herself stop in front of one stall and look interested.

"Gorgeous English strawberries," the stall owner said encouragingly.

Sin gave him a smile and he smiled back, a spark of interest in his eye. She did not want to be noticed or remembered, so she turned off the smile, quickly bought an apple and turned away.

The two magicians were no longer in sight.

Sin set her teeth into the flesh of the apple and let herself hurry just a bit, not too much: brisk steps, girl eating an apple, nothing to see here. She came out the other side of the market and saw two blond heads disappearing down the curving stone steps that led to a space signposted Green Dragon Court.

Sin counted to five and then crossed the road after them, starting down the steps as they walked by Southwark Cathedral, the building standing like a castle against the sky with a pennant flying from the top turret and windows glowing orange, blue and evergreen.

Sin followed them, still at a distance, joggers rushing past her as if their destination was far more important than hers. Her teeth were still locked in her apple; she knew she wouldn't be able to make herself swallow a bite.

The magicians went down into the shadow of London Bridge, across the path by the Thames to a huge, white boat, all silver lines and curving surfaces that reflected the gleaming of a clear sky.

A boat that had been there, but that Sin had not really noticed before.

An enchanted boat.

A demon might be after them, so the magicians were living on the river.

The two magicians came onboard, and Sin tossed the apple and finally began to run, down to the path because it was downhill. She reached the boat as its engines purred to life.

She stood close to the deck, one hand on the shining white surface. This was a piece of luck that would be unlikely to come her way again. This might be the only time she had a chance to get close to the magicians. If she climbed aboard and could get her hands on the necklace, she would have won.

If the magicians found her, she would be killed.

Sin looked at the slick, white deck and tried to screw up her resolve.

"What are you doing?"

Sin turned and was aware even as she turned that she'd started, and betrayed guilt. The woman standing in front of her had puffy ginger hair and a mouth wearing plum-coloured lipstick and disapproval. Sin didn't recognise her as a magician or see one of the messenger's tokens on her.

A civilian, then, she thought, and let go of the knife in her pocket.

But if she alerted the magicians to Sin's presence, Sin was dead just the same.

"I know the guy who owns this boat," Sin said quickly. "Just wondering whether I should hop onboard and surprise him."

The woman's eyes narrowed like doors being closed in front of her.

"I have to agree with this lady," said Alan.

Sin started again and cursed herself.

Alan was coming down the pathway from the direction of the cathedral. He looked subtly different from usual, the set of his shoulders making his shirt look more starched somehow, his mouth very thin.

"You know you're not welcome down here any more, Bambi," he said.

Sin stared at him for an instant, then glanced at the woman. She was looking intrigued.

Sin reached up and pulled out her hair tie so the waves fell down round her shoulders. She twisted one strand round her finger and gave the woman a slow smile.

"See?" she said. "Told you I knew the owners."

"You used to know my brother," Alan corrected primly. "Dad made it very clear that your acquaintance was at an end."

"You're so boring, Clive," Sin drawled. "I knew Nick would be pleased to see me."

"Nicholas isn't there," Alan informed her, with a smug little smile. "And I very much doubt Dad would be overjoyed by your reappearance."

Sin sort of wished she had bubblegum. She felt that blowing a big, pink bubble would fit right into this role.

She did without, putting her hands on her hips and shifting her stance so her hips rolled beneath her palms.

"*You* could show me the boat," she suggested, with another slow smile. "I really would love to have a look around. And I bet you're just a little pleased to see me."

The ginger lady looked shocked by how brazen Sin was.

"Not even a little," said Alan, and the woman's mouth twisted in satisfaction. "Come along, Bambi. I'll get you a cab."

He reached out and took hold of Sin's elbow, towing her fastidiously along, not bringing her body any closer to his than necessary. He looked over his shoulder as he did so.

"Thanks for keeping an eye out, ma'am."

"Don't mention it," said the woman, lifting her chin proudly.

Sin sighed. "Seems I underestimated you, Clive. I had no idea how boring you could be."

After a few minutes of being towed, Alan's pace slowed and Sin risked a glance over her shoulder. She saw the woman's retreating back, but she also saw the boat pulling out from the bank.

There was that decision made for her, then.

Sin couldn't decide whether she was relieved or disappointed.

On the whole, she was going to call this expedition a win; disaster had been averted, she had valuable new information and, well – she couldn't say it hadn't been a little fun.

She resumed facing forward, then slid a glance up at Alan. "Bambi?"

"In my defence," said Alan. "Clive."

"Just a little obvious, that's all I'm saying."

"But it worked."

"Well, you've obviously had a lot of practice, so you were able to carry it off okay," Sin conceded. "So."

"So what?"

She gave him the slow, Bambi-style smile that had scandalised the woman by the boat. "Lie to me, Clive."

One of Alan's eyebrows came up, and then he smiled a little. He put his hand into his pocket and she saw, cupped in his palm, the glint of his gun. "I was doing a chemistry experiment. I'm so sorry the noise disturbed you; I'm in some advanced classes, and sometimes when I'm studying, I lose track of time."

Sin slipped her knife out of her pocket and showed it to him. "This? It's a prop. I do a dance with it." She paused significantly. "A belly dance."

"And that sound was a car backfiring. My brother's keen on cars, you see. Don't worry. I'll have a word with him."

"Of course I remember you from the last Market," Sin said, restoring her knife to her pocket. "Who could forget you?"

"Actually," Alan said, earnest and clear-eyed, "this is my first time playing poker."

Sin laughed, delighted, loving the sunlight shining on the Thames and playing a part with someone who understood she was playing.

"What are you doing here?" she asked softly. "Were you following me?"

A few guys had followed her before and it had been shocking, frightening: they had wanted to own a bit of her without her knowledge or her permission. She had been furious.

If Alan had followed her, he'd wanted to help. She wasn't furious.

She was glad, she thought, and stranger than that, uncertain and blossoming, she was hopeful in a way that was new to her.

Sin had had very few actual crushes, seldom felt interest that survived from one meeting to the next. It was hard to take boys seriously when they were at best diversions and at worst easy marks.

She was taking this one seriously. Alan was looking down at her, grave and attentive, his steady gaze seeing a lot more than people usually did. She wanted him to see more, and to like what he saw.

"I was following someone else," Alan told her.

Sin said, "I see."

"Then I saw you, and I thought you could maybe use a hand. Though I'm sure you could have dealt with it yourself."

"Thank you." Sin made an effort, painful in a way acting usually wasn't for her, and tried to smile a casual smile. "Really, I appreciate it. If you need to go and find someone, feel free. Thanks again. Unless you'd like my help?"

"No," said Alan. "I'm all right."

He took her at her word and began to limp up the slope to the cathedral. Sin looked away automatically, across the water at the magicians' boat.

Then she knew who Alan had been following, and knew she had no head start on Mae at all.

There on the shining white deck stood Celeste Drake. Beside her and even shorter than Celeste, looking utterly at her ease, was Mae.

Sin realised that she hadn't believed Matthias when he'd warned her about Mae. Beneath all her jealousy, she'd still thought of Mae as her friend, someone who could ultimately be trusted. These days there wasn't much for Sin to rely on.

The clouds above the river were parting, sunlight rippling along the surface of the water. Mae's pink hair shone, and against her hair gleamed a knife in a circle.

The sign of a messenger. Of someone sworn to the service of the magicians.

Sin called her father as she was walking towards the Tube station and offered to come and see him. He sounded tired and abstracted on the phone – he worked too hard – and she said quickly, "I don't have to. Just thought it might be an idea. I don't want to be a bother."

"Please come," he said, as he always did. "It's no trouble at all, Thea. It's always good to see you."

Sin got back on the Tube, changing for the Circle Line to get to Brixton. It was a long walk from the Tube station to her father's house, but she had turned down lifts from him so many times that he'd stopped offering.

Usually she liked the walk all right, a time to be alone as she seldom was and think, but today she felt numb. It was all too much: Merris corrupt and almost lost, Mae a traitor, the constant threat that Lydie would betray her magic to someone else and the whole Market like a beloved but heavy weight placed round Sin's neck by someone who was trying to drown her. These days she felt like she was never able to break the surface often enough to draw proper breaths.

She walked by the shabby, brown library and up the long road past a park and many blocks of flats, taking a left until she reached the residential area with fancy houses and very few shops. There were trees along the street where her father lived, their roots cracking and disrupting the pavement but their leaves forming a soft, gold roof above Sin's head and carpeting the cement they had disturbed with layers of green, brown, yellow and the occasional spot of scarlet.

It was a nice house, she'd always thought, its windows huge rectangles of glass, the roof pointed. It looked like a house belonging to people who were nice and had no secrets. It was a bit ridiculous that there was a room in it that Dad called her room.

It wasn't her room, not really. She hadn't slept a night in it since she was a kid, before Mama and Dad split up.

Dad had kept trying to make them settle here, when Mama had never wanted to settle anywhere. Sin had always liked the house, liked her cousins on her dad's side who had taken her to the Notting Hill carnival and out dancing when she and Dad had reconciled and she was older. She hadn't been against settling down, but she had been against the idea of settling for less than a dance every month at the Market.

In the end, Dad had settled here without them.

Sin knocked on the blue-painted door, and her dad answered on the first knock as he always did, as if he was afraid she would give up and go away if he wasn't fast enough.

"Thea," he said, and put his arms round her. They were about the same height now: he wasn't very tall. "It's good to see you. You look beautiful."

"Yeah, not much has changed," Sin said, and summoned up a smile for him.

He had lived with Mama for years, so he was a bit too accustomed to play-acting. When he released her, he reached out and touched the side of her face with his hand.

"A little tired, though," he said. "You know, if you wanted to come and stay for even a week, we'd be so pleased to have you."

"I know," Sin said, and did her best to breeze through the hall into the kitchen, where Dad had been meaning to lay down fresh lino for about three years now.

Grandma Tess was in the kitchen making sandwiches. She gave Sin her usual look, disapproving in a way that reminded Sin of the ginger-haired woman from down by the river, a way that suggested she had seen all she needed to see of Sin to pass judgement.

Basically, whenever Grandma Tess looked at Sin, she saw her mother, the gorgeous, unreliable white woman who had snared a good man and refused to settle down with him, who had broken his heart.

Her grandmother didn't know about the Goblin Market, about what it meant. But her father knew, and he hadn't been able to understand why Mama would never stop dancing.

"Little bit of notice would be awfully nice," said Grandma Tess, and put a chicken salad sandwich in front of Sin: Sin's favourite, with salt and vinegar crisps on the side.

Her grandmother would have loved to have a lot of grandchildren who she could spoil rotten and understand completely. Sin thanked her.

"Let me make us all a cup of tea," said Dad, "and you can tell us how school is going."

Sin ate her sandwich and delivered her usual edited version of events, making magical references that Dad would get and Grandma wouldn't, letting neither of them know the full story.

Grandma Tess finished her tea and went upstairs to watch television, always careful not to show too great an interest in Sin's company. Sin knew she felt Dad was letting down their side by being always too transparently pleased to see Sin, when as far as they knew, Sin barely cared enough to come and visit them.

"How's work going, Dad?" Sin asked a little awkwardly, when she had run out of half-truths.

Just as anxious for something to talk about as she was, he launched into the tale of a particularly difficult client's account. Sin leaned her head on her arm, her free hand clasped round her teacup, and tried to listen attentively, the adventures of an accountant as strange to her as the life of a dancer was to him.

She woke with the light coming in the window tinted darker with evening drawing close, as if someone had mixed ink in with the air. Her dad was sitting across the table from her, studying the cold tea in his cup. He was getting really grizzled, she noticed, the silver at his temples making deeper and deeper inroads in his black curls.

"Sorry," she said softly. "I'm really sorry. It wasn't the company."

"You're not still angry, are you?" he asked her. He sounded tired.

She had been very angry, when she was younger: that he didn't see the glory of the Market, the fact that Mama had been born to dance. She'd been angry because he had left her, too, because that was what happened when you had a kid and you left someone. The kid was left, too, even though it was nobody's fault, even though Dad had always tried his best.

When Victor had left Mama, he'd never got in touch again, never showed any interest in seeing Lydie and Toby. Some guys never even tried.

Sin wasn't angry any more. Dad had been right, after all: Mama had been putting herself in danger. Mama had died. It was a lot, to expect a guy to stick around and watch the woman he loved risk her life every month for something he thought of as nothing but a thrill.

"What are you talking about?" Sin asked, and picked up what remained of her sandwich. When she bit in and chewed, it was dry, and she still felt tired and a little sick, but she tried to always eat what Grandma Tess put in front of her.

Besides, it was free food.

She swallowed and said, "I have to get going in a minute."

"You can't stay for dinner?"

Sin had been so angry she hadn't seen Dad for two years after he left, hanging up every time he called.

Mama had stayed angry until she died. Sin figured that meant Mama had always loved Dad best, which should count for something.

When Sin had started talking to Dad on the phone, and then coming to see him, taking trains and meeting at halfway points, it had just seemed cruel to mention Victor. Dad hadn't had anybody else, not ever. Sin had simply not mentioned it, and then her little omission of the truth had spun out of control, had made another role for her to play.

Dad didn't know why Sin could never stay. He didn't know about Lydie and Toby. She couldn't tell him: they weren't his kids. What if he wanted to put them in foster care, or simply leave them to the Market and take Sin away so she could concentrate on school or go to college or do any of the stuff he kept talking about, a holiday by the seaside or swimming lessons or something?

This was the only way.

When she had told him Mama was dead, he had wanted her to live with him. He'd promised she could keep dancing, that he would take her to the Market himself, walk through it with her hand in hand as they had when she was young.

She had told him she was going to live with Merris Cromwell, and that she didn't need him any more than Mama had.

"I'm sorry," Sin told him, widening her eyes. "I've got a lot of stuff to do."

Her dad rose from the table, using his hands to push himself up as if his limbs felt heavy. He went round the table to stand where she sat, and slipped a little roll of money into the fingers curled round her teacup.

"It was good to see you," he murmured. "Buy yourself something nice from your old dad."

"You bet I will," Sin said.

A week's worth of groceries was always nice.

She was already catastrophically late, so she leaned her head against Dad's arm for another few minutes, watching the light fade.

Love always costs more than you can afford to pay, Alan had said to her, his face still drawn with pain. *And it's always worth the price.*

Some people stayed, no matter what the cost. But you couldn't expect people to stay no matter what. Sin didn't know any way to make someone love her that much.

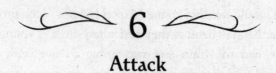

6
Attack

MERRIS WAS AT MEZENTIUS HOUSE SEEING TO THE POSSESSED that weekend, so Sin had to wait to tell her about Mae. She didn't know who else she could tell.

Being the only one who knew was nerve-racking, though. Monday morning she found herself sitting in school thinking of all the things the Market people could tell Mae that she could report back to Celeste.

By lunchtime her nerves felt strained enough that she could not bear the idea of making small talk with people who had no idea the world she was worried about even existed. She took her lunch and marched herself over to Nick's table, where he sat talking on the phone and glowering at anyone who tried to sit down.

"Got to go," he said, when Sin slid into the bench opposite him.

"Secret girlfriend?"

"Secret travelling circus," Nick said. "They're all very special to me. Particularly the Bearded Lady."

"I'm so thrilled you found love at last," Sin said. "Are you eating that yogurt?"

"Yes," Nick said, and glared.

"You sure about that?" asked Sin, since it was rhubarb custard. "If it helps, I can eat it in a sexy way."

"So can I," said Nick. Sin gave a philosophical shrug, and he continued, "Do we know each other yet?"

"It's okay, I've given it some thought. The girls at school won't think we know each other. They'll just think I want to tap your demonic ass."

Nick peeled the top off his yogurt and looked around the room with what Sin thought was a flicker of amusement in his cold eyes.

"It's true women find it hard to resist all this," he said, gesturing to his own body with a teaspoon. He slid the spoon into the yogurt and ate some, mouth curving round the metal.

"I don't know how I'm restraining myself," Sin said. "And yet."

He did have a great mouth. Unfortunately Sin found herself turning an orange between her palms and thinking of Alan, his steadfast, deep blue eyes and beautiful hands, which made her feel angry and impatient with herself, other boys' mouths and the whole world.

"Alan told me you were teaching him how to shoot a bow," Nick said, and Sin started at the name and studied Nick suspiciously in case he could read minds. He looked as blank as ever. "Can you shoot a crossbow?" he asked.

"There's no artistry to shooting a crossbow," Sin said. "You just need to know how to aim it and then put a big bolt right through someone."

"That," Nick said with conviction, "sounds like my idea of a good time."

"Well, I'm no expert, but I can teach you the basics."

Nick nodded. "Alan said you two were friends or something now," he said with what seemed to be qualified approval.

"I guess," Sin said, desperately casual. "I mean, we're friends, too, aren't we?" She laughed a little.

Nick blinked. "No."

Sin stared at him. "What?"

"I've already got one," Nick told her.

"You've already got one – friend?" Sin asked slowly.

Nick nodded. "He's a lot of trouble. I don't think I can deal with any more."

He continued eating yogurt, apparently unaware that he was talking like a crazy person. The Ryves brothers were making a bit of a hobby of rejecting Sin.

"Do you mean Alan?" Sin asked.

"Alan's my brother," Nick told her as if she was the one being dense. "You've met him. He's called Jamie."

Mae's little brother. The magician who had gone off to be with his own kind.

"That's who you're always on the phone with?" Sin asked.

Nick didn't answer. Since he was a demon who could not lie, Sin was going to take that as a yes.

"I wouldn't have thought that a demon would be overly fond of any magician."

Nick shrugged.

Sin propped her chin on her fist and regarded Nick with close attention. "And what is Mae?" she inquired. "Since she's not your friend either, apparently."

She hadn't meant to talk about Mae. She'd wanted to lay

out all the evidence before Merris, have her decide what to do.

But Merris wasn't here: Nick was, and he was one of the few people Sin knew who might not instantly condemn Mae.

There were people in the Market who would kill Mae at the mere suggestion that she'd been seen with the magicians. Sin didn't know how far Mae had gone, how tangled up with the magicians she had become, but Sin had a dead mother and a magician in the family, as well. She could understand how Mae might have messed up.

She just didn't know what she could do to help her.

Nick bared his teeth. "As far as I'm concerned, Mae's the future leader of the Goblin Market."

"Yeah," Sin said in a level voice. "I was wondering, why is that?"

"She wants to be," Nick said. "So I want it for her. And in my experience, Mavis doesn't stop until she gets what she wants."

Sin actually felt a bit better about that, the fact that Nick had apparently chosen Mae as the leader on his own rather than on orders from Alan.

"So if Mae's the heir to the Market, what am I?"

"Why should I care?" asked the demon.

"I'll tell you who I am," Sin said. "I'm the only one who knows Mae's made a deal with the Aventurine Circle."

Nick's hand shot out and he grabbed her wrist, too hard. Sin reached for her knife without even thinking about it. Nick dropped his spoon and went for his.

They sat bristling across a school lunch table, eyes locked, hands on their weapons.

Sin barely let her lips move as she said, "We can't do this here."

Nick rose without another word. The muscles in his forearm barely flexed as he pulled Sin smoothly to her feet, as if she weighed about as much as a lunch box. His other hand stayed in his pocket, where Sin had no doubt he had a knife.

They couldn't be noticed, or if they had to be noticed, they could not be followed. Sin made sure to look embarrassed and pleased as Nick stalked out of the cafeteria, sweeping her in his wake.

When the cafeteria doors slammed, she snapped the shy, anticipatory smile off her face. He dragged her into the nearest classroom, and Sin glimpsed desks pushed out of order and windows streaming afternoon light, no escape but the door behind them. She pulled out one of the long knives strapped to her back.

Nick delivered a swift, hard blow to her wrist. Pain shot up to her shoulder and the knife went flying. He threw her up against the blackboard, hand pinning her wrist to the chalk-stained surface, his body pressing down on hers so she could not reach the other knife at her back.

He looked at Sin, a lock of his black hair falling in the tiny space between them as he leaned down.

"I've got you," he said softly.

Sin smiled the sweet smile of a girl with a penknife already in her free hand, and let the tip of the blade trace the cotton over his tense stomach.

"And I've got a knife." She leaned into Nick's space, and he didn't flinch from the blade, just stood there looking down at her with his face so utterly blank and his body so tense he might as well have been made of stone. "I saw her, Nick. She was with the magicians. She was wearing a messenger's symbol. If I told the Market, they would take her apart."

There was a long pause. Sin strained, testing the strength of Nick's hold on her: his body was a solid wall of muscle. If she wanted to get away, she'd have to use the knife.

She wasn't quite ready to do that yet.

"Well, you're not going to tell the Market, then, are you?" Nick demanded.

Sin took a deep breath.

"I don't want to," she said. "I don't want her hurt. I can see how she might have gone to the magicians and got in over her head. Her own brother's a magician."

Mae's little brother. She'd met him once and found him to be the kind of guy who faded into the background, so intently inoffensive that he was barely memorable.

She'd seen him again protecting the Goblin Market in battle, palm raised and his very eyes alight with magic fire.

She'd seen his power, and how he had chosen to use it, and her heart had leaped as she thought of what that could mean for Lydie.

Only then Mae's brother had disappeared, and Mae said he had left to join a Circle of magicians.

That was a bond between Mae and Sin that Mae didn't even know about, something Sin hoped Mae would never find out. Sin had nightmares about what could happen if Lydie came into that kind of power at sixteen, if her sister went off to join the magicians.

"I don't think Mae meant to betray anyone," Sin said. "But I can't let the Market fall into the magicians' hands. And I don't know what she's going to do."

"I don't know, either," Nick snarled. "I didn't know she was doing this!"

"And this is the girl who's going to be with your brother?"

Sin asked. "This is the future leader of the Market? She's working with the magicians and you had no idea, and you're not the slightest bit concerned she might betray us all? She might betray Alan. She might betray you."

Nick's hand pinioning her wrist was pressing down to the bone. Her wrist was aching in a way that meant it would bruise later. Sin set her teeth and held the knife steady against his stomach.

"She wouldn't," Nick snarled.

"How do you know?" Sin demanded. "If you didn't know about this—"

"I know her," Nick said. "She wouldn't."

In the end it wasn't the knife Nick shied away from. Sin hesitated, then slipped it back in the pocket of her skirt, and reached out and touched the place where her knife had rested with her fingertips instead.

He broke away from her with a sudden violent movement, as if she'd tried to brand him. One minute he was there and the next clear across the room, standing at the window with the afternoon light pouring in on his bowed head.

"I don't want her to get hurt," Sin said softly. "I'll talk to her. I'll talk to Merris. I just want the Market to be safe. I won't tell anyone else, unless I have to."

She wanted Nick to look up at her, willed her voice to reach out the way she had.

I know her. She wouldn't. Nick trusted Mae.

If he'd trusted Mae, too, and was feeling bewildered and hurt, there could be comfort in that. Sin could feel better, feeling they understood each other.

"Let me make myself clear. I'm not on your side. If you do tell someone," Nick said, his voice very calm, with no hint that he ever felt anything at all, "if they turn against Mae, if they hurt her, I'll kill you."

When Sin got back to Horsenden Hill that evening, Lydie dragging her feet after the long walk from the station, Merris had still not returned.

"Have you heard from her?" Trish asked.

"No, but I'm sure she'll be back by tomorrow," Sin said as she collected Toby from Trish's tent, where Trish had the Market kids gather while she tried out recipes and kept an eye on them. Toby was playing with a couple of Elka's younger kids, but he lifted his arms up readily for Sin as she approached.

She scooped him up and breathed in the smell of his hair, baby shampoo and milk and dirt, because he'd apparently been digging holes. Even the weight of him in her arms was reassuring, and Sin could use a little reassurance.

Merris had told her she'd only be gone for the weekend.

What if this was it? a voice in her head whispered, cold and terrifying. What if Liannan had taken over, and Merris was gone?

"People are looking for you," Trish said, and Sin thanked her and quietly panicked some more.

Toby was talking in her ear, a long nonsense story about what he had done that day, small fists pulling on her hair and clothes hard enough to hurt, and Sin's thoughts were like another child's monologue in her mind, endless and insistent and devolving into a garbled rush.

What did these people want, how could she run the Market, would she have to condemn Mae to stop her trying to take control, what would Nick do then? She wasn't prepared, she thought, walking across the expanse of grass to their wagon with the sun setting and newly cool air running down her neck. The future loomed before her like the moment before a fall she felt sick and winded already.

Sin got the door of the wagon open with one hand, the arm it was attached to still holding Toby, and held it open for Lydie with her elbow.

Mae was leaning against the table that bore Sin's crystal ball. The sight of her was a shock followed by resentment: Mae looked cool and collected, her pink hair a gleaming brushed bob and her ironed blue T-shirt emblazoned with the words WHEN I PLAY DOCTOR, I PLAY TO WIN. Sin felt rumpled and tired, and her wrist still hurt.

"Mae," she said, and smiled brilliantly. "It's traditional to come into people's homes when they invite you. And when they're actually in them."

"I'm sorry," Mae said. "Phyllis said I should wait in here for you."

Sin still bet that Mae would've hesitated before going into someone else's actual house. Mae looked genuinely sorry, though, and Sin wasn't going to make an issue out of it. There were several more important issues to take up with Mae.

There was the Market to think of.

She took a tiny revenge by putting Toby into Mae's arms. Mae and Toby sent her hilariously similar looks of distress as she did so.

"I'm glad you're here," Sin told Mae, pulling off her shirt and starting to undo her blouse. "I wanted to talk to you."

"Yeah," Mae said, jiggling Toby tentatively as if she was worried his head might fall off. "Nick – said you might."

"Did he?" Sin asked. "Really."

"Hi," Lydie put in. She'd scrambled up on her bed and was

sitting in a red sea of blankets decorated with pirates, staring at Mae with big eyes.

"Oh, hi," Mae said awkwardly.

Sin didn't ask Lydie to get lost, or give Mae any help. She shrugged off her blouse and hung it up, keeping her eyes on Mae, who looked a little more uncomfortable.

She met Sin's gaze head-on all the same.

"I would never betray the Market," she said. "Or you. I want you to know that."

"I think you know I have a few reasons to doubt it," Sin said, sliding out of her school skirt and reaching for a pair of jeans.

"I was offered the earrings," Mae said. "I took them. I've got my reasons."

"Your brother."

Sin sat on her bed squashed up against Lydie's, using one hand to draw Lydie against her side and her other to roll her socks off. Lydie snuggled into Sin's side, her head butting her sister's collarbone hard, and Sin tried not to think of losing her, of how that might be.

"My mother."

Sin looked up, startled, and saw Mae's face, cold and set as it had never been before her mother fell before a magician on to bloodstained cobblestones.

"The Aventurine Circle killed her," Mae said. "I'm going to make them sorry."

Sin thought about her own mother falling, about the world going dark as the creature inside her smiled. If there had been anyone to blame but the demon, if there had been any way to take revenge, she might have wanted it, too.

"You want the magician who killed her?"

"No," Mae said. "I know who brought the Circle into the

square. I know who gave the orders. It was the leader's responsibility. I want Celeste Drake."

"We all want Celeste Drake," Sin told her, with great patience. "That's why we're here."

"We don't all have access to the magicians," Mae argued. "I do. I know that the reason the Circle hasn't attacked yet is because Gerald has been—"

"Going after Alan," Sin finished for her.

Mae stood briefly stunned. Sin could practically see her thoughts regrouping like tiny soldiers behind her eyes, and spoke before Mae found another route of attack.

"Which, I might add, we'd all already know if Alan Ryves hadn't decided to withhold the information in case it makes his demon brother start helping out the side of evil."

There was a wry twist to Mae's mouth that said she might agree on the topic of Alan withholding, but she said loyally, "He's going through a lot. And it was brave of him to go through it alone."

Sin closed her eyes for a moment. "I know it was brave."

"And you don't understand," Mae said. "I meant, I want Celeste Drake personally. I want to kill her myself. I've got a gun," she continued, the words tumbling out in a rush, as if she'd been dying to tell someone else her plan. "I've carried it every time I went to see the magicians. One day I'll get the chance to use it and get away afterwards."

Sin stood up and stretched; she couldn't help a soft, incredulous laugh. "Well. That should be easy."

Mae certainly didn't think small. Sin thought about Nick saying *Mavis doesn't stop until she gets what she wants.*

The corners of Mae's mouth turned up a little, tentatively moving towards a smile. "So you believe me."

Sin rolled her eyes. She reached out and laid a palm for an instant against the curve of Mae's cheek. "Oh, honey," she said. "What you're saying is so completely insane, I have to believe you."

Mae did smile then, dimple flashing, looking about five years old, and Sin withdrew her hand and tucked away her relief that Mae didn't mean to betray the Market, that she was still something like a friend.

It didn't matter what she felt. She had to lead.

"If this puts the Market in any more danger than it's in already," Sin said, "you should know, I'll tell everyone you're working for the Aventurine Circle. And if I do that, one of us will kill you. The pipers could make you dance out into traffic. I could knife you at thirty paces. There will be nothing you can do to save yourself."

Mae looked down at the floor and took a deep breath.

"You should know," she said, "I'm not just doing this for my mother. I'm going to kill Celeste Drake, and I'm going to take the necklace. I'm going to take the Market. There will be nothing you can do to keep it."

Sin leaned against their tiny stove, standing directly across the room from where Mae was leaning against the little table. There was barely a foot of space between them. When Mae looked up and met her eyes, Sin felt as if they should be standing ten paces away from each other, ready to duel.

There was a knock on the wagon door.

"Cynthia?" Alan said. "It's—"

"The only person at the Market who calls me Cynthia?" Sin called out. "Come in, Alan. Oh, I'm only half-dressed, but I don't mind."

"Um," Alan said. "I'm bashful. I'd be sure to blush, and I have red hair. It's not a pretty sight."

"Since Sin apparently has her kit off, I doubt anyone will be looking at you," said Nick, and he pulled open the door before Sin recovered from the shock of hearing his voice at all.

When he entered the wagon, Lydie scrambled backwards on the bed until she had her back to the wall. Nick's black eyes followed the movement.

"I didn't say *you* could come in," Sin told him, brushing by him to snag a shirt to put on over her bra.

Alan pushed gently past Nick, as if Nick was a child rather than six feet of well-armed bad temper, and went directly over to Mae, standing close and putting out his arms for Toby.

Of course Alan's first instinct was to help, and of course Mae responded with a smile of gratitude, dimpled and sweet. She leaned into him and murmured a few words, their bodies curving in towards each other. Sin shrugged on her shirt and did up the buttons, concentrating on the simple task.

If Nick wanted Mae to lead the Goblin Market, Alan probably did, too.

When she looked up, though, Alan was closer to her than to Mae. Surprise and a jolt of ridiculous happiness coursed through her: he was holding Toby; he'd probably come to hand over the baby.

He didn't, though. He shifted Toby comfortably in the circle of his arm, Toby making an approving sound at him and burrowing his face into the curve of Alan's neck. Alan looked down at her, then leaned in a little.

"You hurt your wrist?" he said, low and inquiring.

Sin glanced down at her shirt cuffs, which covered her wrists completely, and then raised her eyebrows.

"You were looking at my wrists?"

The beginnings of a smile crinkled the corners of his eyes. "I'm a lightning-fast observer. I notice all kinds of things."

Sin had a response and the move following it ready when Alan's eyes left her and turned to his brother.

"Are you going to stay in the doorway?"

Nick jerked his head towards Lydie sitting at the top of her bed, her knees drawn up. "Yeah. The kid's scared of me."

He said it blankly, as if he was talking about a chair rather than someone's feelings, and Sin wanted to hit him. Lydie might be shy, but she hated anyone thinking of her like that. She wanted to be a daring adventurer, and Sin was not about to let anyone take that away from her.

Lydie didn't let anyone take it from her, either; Sin had brought her up better than that. She lifted her chin.

"I'm not scared of anything."

"Oh?" said Nick, and drew the door of the wagon shut behind him.

Lydie took up the challenge and crept down to the foot of her bed, where she sat solemnly regarding Nick. Nick stared back at her, arms folded and eyes bottomless.

Sin stood tense. She could feel Alan standing warm beside her, the baby happy in his arms. She wanted to look at him, but she had other responsibilities: the kids came first, always.

She couldn't let them down.

If Lydie was scared looking at a demon, if she felt unsafe even for a moment, she had to be able to look around and see that Sin's eyes were on her, that Sin was there for her.

"Did you guys come here for any particular reason?" Mae asked.

Sin saw the flash of light and movement in Lydie's eyes. She caught Alan's shoulder and shoved him down as she dived for Lydie, an instant before the sound of a crash rang out through the Market.

Sin grabbed Lydie and shoved her under the bed.

"Stay down there," she hissed. "You hear me? Stay down!"

She rose to her feet, drawing both her knives. She glanced towards Alan and saw he'd gone down, Toby cradled against his chest and his gun in his hand. Nick had drawn his sword and opened the door.

Sin looked over at Mae. She had a penknife in her hand.

"Let me give you something with reach."

"No," Mae told her. "I wouldn't know how to use a long knife. I have to be able to surprise them."

"Remind me to teach you how to use a long knife later."

Sin slipped in front of Mae and followed Nick out of the door, the evening-chilled beads hanging in the doorway sliding across her face like frozen teardrops. She waited at the threshold; it was dark, the shapes of wagons grey and all the spaces in between them black. If she knew her people, they were moving quietly through the shadows.

Back in the wagon, she heard Mae speaking in a hushed voice on the phone. Sin felt a flash of exasperation with herself that she hadn't thought to call the necromancers or the pipers, then stepped off the threshold and did not stop moving. That was crucial when you were moving in the dark: you had to keep moving, like shadows, like light, always watching where you were going but never hesitating.

There was another crash, like a localised windstorm. Sin suspected that it was Ivy and Iris's wagon. She hoped the sisters had got out.

A man came towards them with his hand raised, palm up,

and Nick launched himself at him, magic streaking out before his sword like his sword's shadow made of light.

Sin stalked the perimeter of the Market, circling the clusters of wagons and pathways in between. If one magician had been wandering alone, there would be others.

There were trees on one side that protected the wagons from wind. Sin used their shadows to hide herself as she moved a little faster.

A twig ran along her face in a slow, deliberate movement, like a skeletal finger tracing a line along her skin.

Sin went very still.

The twig bit into her cheek. Her stomach turned, horror grinding on resolve, and a thin branch lashed out and curled like a whip round her arm. The tree branches rasped together and reached out for her.

The branches lifted her up off her feet. There was a sickening lurch of vertigo at the same time as the twigs stabbed into the small of her back. Wind rushed past her, and dead-leaf whispers crackled in her ears. Sin sheathed one of her knives and drew her legs up to her chest, swinging gently from the grip of those thin branches.

She reached up with her free hand to grab the branch above her, going higher up rather than trying to get down. She lifted herself up a crucial few inches and rolled in mid-air, on to the branches clawing to reach her.

They formed a shifting web beneath her feet, like a dozen tightropes trying to grab her and pull her down. She side-stepped, leaped, twisted through darkness and landed safe every time.

She could see the magician controlling the tree now, a dark shape down below.

He had his back to her.

He had his back to her because she was captured and helpless, not a threat. Balancing from branch to branch in the night air, Sin found herself wanting to laugh.

She threw a knife instead.

The magician went down with her knife in his back, felled by someone he hadn't even been paying attention to: someone he'd underestimated.

The branches went still. Sin grabbed the bough above her in both hands and swung herself up, the strain on the muscles of her arms causing a slow, good burn, and then she had her knees up on the branch and her other knife out, crouched and waiting.

Down below she could see the Market spread before her like a picnic. Ivy and Iris's wagon was the only one destroyed so far. She counted seven magicians: two already dead, three engaged by her people, one by Nick and one approaching Sin's wagon.

Sin sheathed her knife and jumped.

She grabbed one branch, then another as she tumbled down, making each one slow her fall without trusting her weight to any of them, and landed in a roll that ended with her on her feet with her knife back in her hand, racing for the wagon.

It wasn't hit by wind. It exploded into fire.

Sin wasn't even within ten paces of it when her home burst into an orange ball of flame and wreckage. Her body reacted when her mind refused to do so; she had her arm up shielding her head, fierce heat washing over the exposed skin of her arm, making the material of her shirt billow away from her back. She could smell the ends of her hair burning.

She rolled into a space between two other wagons, dark and cool, leaned her sweaty forehead against her scorched arm and let a choking noise rip out of her smoke-filled throat.

"Shh," said a voice beside her.

That brief, simple sound, less than a word, was so harsh and curt that Sin knew who it was, even before she looked up and saw the demon sitting in the dark with her.

The dying glow of the fire lit the white planes and angles of Nick's face. Shadows moved across him, striping him like a tiger crouching there in the grass. Sin lowered her hand and touched Nick's sword, lying on the ground between them. The steel was warm and slick with blood.

"They're dead," she whispered. Lydie hiding behind her golden hair, Toby who had been one year and nine months and four days old, which nobody in the world but she would remember because she had seen his birth. Her whole heart, lost in an instant of remorseless light.

"Mae's alive," Nick said.

For a moment Sin hated him for not remembering his brother first, and then hated herself for thinking of Alan at all.

"Do you think you would just know if she was dead? Why?" she asked, her voice cracking. "Because you're in love with her?"

Nick stared at her, eyes doorways into the dark.

"I'm a demon," he said softly. "I don't even know what that means."

"Then how?" Sin demanded, and then she understood.

He was a demon. A demon would know if a human was alive if he'd put his mark on her. Which would mean that Nick could tell if Mae was alive, and could tell if she was in danger. He could find her and protect her.

He could kill her, possess her and control her.

Sin closed her eyes. "Oh, Mae." Her eyes snapped open. "But she's alive. So the others . . ."

Even if Mae was alive, that was no guarantee the others were. Maybe Mae had left the wagon as soon as she'd made her calls.

"I don't know!" Nick snarled at her.

Sin bowed her head and swallowed. She didn't know what to do with hope, any more than she had known how to speak of misery.

A shot cracked through the air, not quite like the sound of a bough breaking.

Sin spun, on her feet with joy coursing through her as if there was lightning in her veins, burning and brilliant. It hurt.

"It could be anyone," she said before it could hurt too much. "Carl has guns."

She hadn't heard Nick move, but suddenly he was pushing past her, blade in hand, running towards the sound of the gun. Sin hesitated and then ran after him, through the pathways round the wagons to the other side of the hill. She was pulled up short by the dead body at her feet.

Nick was already kneeling by the body, his hand against its chest. He looked from that dead thing up at Sin, and he smiled a wild smile that made him look handsomer than she'd ever seen him.

"You can't be sure it was Alan."

"A shot in the dark, through the heart?" Nick asked. "I'm sure."

With some people it was a voice they would recognise, with some people a step in the hall. Sin guessed it was fitting that Nick could look at a corpse and see his brother's skill.

If Alan had got out, surely Toby and Lydie were safe. But

she had put Lydie under the bed herself. She had told her, *Stay down there*.

Nick rose. "Where—"

He was looking at the night beyond them, not the wagons behind them, and Sin knew failing to look both ways wasn't safe. She glanced round and saw two magicians walking towards them with their hands full of light, ready to hurl.

She launched herself at Nick, tumbling him down into the night-cool grass with hot fire scything through her hair. Nick was breathing hard underneath her, muscles coiled, ready to attack. He didn't thank her for saving him, just gripped her arm in one hand and his sword in the other.

"If Alan hadn't asked me to cut my power in half," he ground out, "in less than half, I could have killed them all."

And Toby and Lydie would have been safe, Alan would have been safe.

"Why did you give it up?"

"I'm not very bright," Nick said, and tipped her over into the grass, his body covering hers, pinning her down for a minute. He lifted his free arm, and a bright bolt of magic flew through the air, as if he'd had a knife in his hand when he hadn't. He grinned down at her in the magic light. "Lucky I'm so pretty."

Sin shoved Nick off her with a knee against his chest. She rose to her feet, missing her second knife, left in the back of that first magician.

There were two magicians, both men; Nick went for the older-looking one, so Sin went at the younger. He retreated as she rushed at him, and as she drew closer to him and he drew closer to the wagons, she saw he was even younger than she'd thought, about her own age. He had dark hair and green eyes with dilated pupils. He looked terrified.

"Listen," he whispered, low and urgent. "Listen, I don't want to hurt you."

Sin smiled her most gorgeous smile at him. "That's wonderful news! Can you tip your head back just so and expose your jugular?"

The boy magician's mouth opened. "No! Look, we've met."

"I don't recall," Sin snapped. "Maybe it's the shock of seeing my home set on fire. Perhaps that induced temporary amnesia."

She slid the tip of her knife up along the boy's stomach. She felt a twinge of panic at the thought that she might have to kill someone who wasn't fighting back.

"Sin," he said. "Where's Mae? Is she all right?"

A woman's voice sliced through the air. "What are you doing, Seb?"

"She has a knife," Seb said quickly, stepping away. He didn't stay to help either of them, backing into the shadows instead, and Sin made sure to keep watching him out of the corner of her eye even as she turned to face the real threat.

The woman was tall and lean, muscled in a way Sin would like to be one day, when she had more time to work on her routines. She came towards Sin in a series of spare, efficient movements, a sword burning magic in each hand.

"Got a knife, have you?" she asked. "I'm armed myself."

The reach of those swords was going to be a real problem. Sin looked at her knife, measured her chances and feinted. When the woman checked herself and looked for a knife that wasn't coming, Sin threw the knife from a different angle.

The swordswoman was just a hair too fast. She got a sword up to deflect the knife. Sin had thrown hard, and the sword flew from the woman's hand, but that left her with one weapon and Sin with none.

None that this magician knew about. Sin wasn't about to tip the woman off about the knife at her ankle.

She waited for a chance to duck and make it look natural, which meant standing there empty-handed as the woman advanced on her.

"Cynthia Davies, I think? My name is Helen," the woman said. "The Market's in your hands, in the absence" – her lip curled – "of your leader. Care to surrender it to me?"

"Come and take it," Sin told her.

Helen ran at her and Sin waited, waited and threw herself to the ground, curled up in a ball with her hand finally at her ankle as the sword came hurtling down towards her head and—

Stopped.

Sin grasped her knife, and only then looked up.

There was an orange line over her head, drawn on the night sky like a line beneath a sentence. The sword had hit it and stopped.

Helen was staring at a point beyond Sin. Sin followed her line of sight, expecting to see that boy Seb.

Instead she saw her sister. Lydie, running into the fray with both her hands thrown up as if she had a shield in them.

Alan was behind her, limping far more obviously than he usually did, trying to catch up with her. He had Toby in the crook of one arm and his gun trained on Helen. Helen wasn't looking at him. She had her eyes on Lydie and she was retreating, lowering her sword.

It was the worst possible thing she could have done.

There were a dozen Market people and pipers coming up behind her, Mae and Matthias among them, and all of them saw what Helen was doing.

They saw the magician refuse to fight one of her own kind.

Helen surveyed the new opposition over her shoulder, and then looked back to see Nick appear at Alan's side. There was fresh blood running down his sword.

"Time to go," Helen called out.

Matthias's bow was already strung. He let fly an arrow directly at Helen, who turned with a sweep of her sword and disappeared in a wash of shimmering light, as if she was only the reflection of a woman in a pool and someone had drawn a hand through the water.

The magicians gone, they were left standing and staring at one another. The air was full of smoke and the smell of blood.

"So," said Phyllis, drawing her dressing gown shut. "There's a magician among us."

Matthias had not put his bow away.

Sin backed up, knife in hand, until she bumped up against Lydie, felt Lydie's small, frantic hands clinging to Sin's belt loops.

"I'm sorry," she whispered to Sin. "I'm sorry."

"Don't be sorry, baby," Sin told her, then lifted her voice and spun her knife so that the Market people could not mistake her meaning. "Don't come any closer."

"Sin," said Carl, who was draped with half the weapons from his stall, a broadsword in each hand. "She's a magician."

"She's mine."

"Think a little, Cynthia," Carl said, coaxing. "If she can do that at seven, what'll she do at sixteen when the power really comes in? You know what she'll do. You know she'll be one of them."

Sin saw Mae make a small, angry movement, but there was nothing Mae could say: the whole Goblin Market had seen her brother join the magicians. They always went to their own kind, in the end.

"The issue could be shelved until she is sixteen," Alan said softly behind Sin. "Now is hardly the time to fight among ourselves."

"Now is hardly the time for divided loyalties!" Phyllis said, her voice crackling like old wood in a fire. "Iris is dead! We're not keeping a magician in the nest. It's not like this is the first time Sin has failed us. She would've sacrificed us all for the sake of that baby, last time. It's not like we don't have another choice."

Everyone looked at Mae. Mae lifted her chin, glaring back at them.

"My brother's a magician, too."

"A lot of us have magicians in the family," Phyllis said. "And the magicians all left."

Mae took a deep breath. "I don't want the leadership like this."

"But you would step up and take it if you had to," Phyllis said. "You wouldn't abandon the Market. That's what we're saying. It's Sin's duty to send the child away."

Phyllis had known Sin and Lydie since they were born. Carl, too. These were her people, the Market people, closer than an ordinary family, bound together by danger and a common cause.

Sin was amazed by how little that seemed to matter.

She was even more amazed when Matthias the piper, who she had never liked much or trusted for anything but a song at sunset, unstrung his bow with an abrupt motion and said, "Sin's not abandoning the Market. Throwing ourselves into the arms of a girl we've known a couple of months is insane."

"I have an idea," Alan said. "If she would agree to leave the girl with magicians—"

"No!" Sin snarled, wheeling on him.

Alan stood with his gun lowered at his side. His eyes were fixed on her, intent and just for a moment, pleading. She knew him well enough by now to know when he was role-playing.

She could stay at the Market with Toby. He'd keep Lydie until they could get something figured out.

All it would take was Sin convincing the Market that she would abandon Lydie. In front of her sister.

No, no, not in a thousand years, even though she loved him for trying, not in the light or the darkness, not for any reason. Lydie could not be allowed to doubt, ever.

"She's mine," Sin repeated.

Alan lied more easily than he told the truth, but she was a performer: she knew there was always a choice between lies and truth, that it was a balancing act. Alan might not know what was too important to lie about. She did.

Carl looked away, at the ground. Elka covered her mouth with the back of her hand. None of them spoke up when Phyllis stepped forward.

She said, "You are not welcome back here. Not ever."

Sin had banished Alan from the Market like this, three months ago.

She looked at Mae, who was biting her lip and still looking angry. Sin could tell them all about Mae's messenger's earrings, about Mae's demon's mark. She knew she could create enough uncertainty to get Mae banished, too.

"My brother's a magician," Mae said, before Sin could say a word. "If she has to leave, I'll leave, too."

But that would leave the Market with no one.

"Phyllis is right. Your brother's gone," Sin told Mae. "I'm keeping my sister."

Sin bowed her head, turning to the urgent grasp of Lydie's hands. She bent down and scooped her up. Lydie wasn't so heavy, and her thin arms went round Sin's neck so tight Sin thought she could have hung on all by herself.

Sin turned her back on the Market and leaned her cheek against Lydie's hair, looking out at the spread of London at night, thousands of lights like the glittering points of knives.

Alan spoke again, quietly this time and not trying to persuade anyone. His voice was still lovely.

"You can come home with us."

7

Lie to Me

ALAN AND NICK WERE LIVING IN A BLOCK OF FLATS IN Willesden. Nobody was speaking in the car as they drove, and the kids fell asleep on either side of Sin. Sin felt tired enough to fall asleep herself, but she had to think.

The Tube station at Willesden Green was only six streets away. She could still get Lydie to school. Thank God Lydie and Toby were both dressed warmly. Sin curled up to sit on her cold feet and tried to calculate how long the money Dad had given her would last. She was going to have to buy shoes.

By the time they parked, it had started raining.

"Nick," Alan said in a meaningful tone.

"I can carry you," Nick told Sin flatly.

Sin raised her eyebrows, making sure they both caught her expression in the mirror. "I'd rather walk."

She shook Lydie, not too hard, so Lydie was just wakeful enough to stumble along with Sin's hand on her back and not enough to start panicking. She left Toby zonked out and drooling on her shirt.

Nick strode on ahead, possibly not thrilled by Alan offering their home as a refuge to three strays.

"We won't stay long," Sin told Alan in a hushed voice.

Alan, bereft of any current opportunity to help someone, had already got out his keys. He was looking at them and not at her, so Sin looked away at the reflections of streetlights glinting on the wet pavement.

"You can stay as long as you like."

His voice was as warm and certain as it had been on the hill, just for her, but when she glanced up, he was still looking at his keys.

"The kids can have my bed," Nick offered, his voice abrupt. Sin would have thought he was being kind if he had not added pointedly to Alan, making it clear where his concerns lay: "You sleep in yours."

"Of course," Sin said, before Alan could respond. "Thank you."

Lydie blinked in the fluorescent lights of the hall and the lift, looking bleary and lost. Sin shifted Toby so she could offer Lydie her hand, and her sister grabbed on to it, small fingers tugging Sin insistently down with every step, as if Sin was a balloon that might float away from her.

Alan lived up on the top floor. There was a walkway to their door, with a wire mesh instead of a fourth wall. The wind and rain blew through it at them, and the cement beneath Sin's feet was rough and wet.

When Alan opened the door and flicked on the light, the wooden floors looked yellow as butter. There were battered cardboard boxes full of books in the narrow hallway and beyond that a little kitchen with crumbs on the counter. Sin was profoundly and deeply thankful for this, a roof over her head, somewhere like a home where Lydie and Toby could feel safe.

"Shall I show you your new room?" Alan asked Lydie, offering her his hand, his voice back to being persuasive now, small and tender as Lydie's clinging fingers.

He held the door of Nick's room open for them and Lydie went in eagerly, her whole small body aimed like a missile for the rumpled blankets and sheets of the bed. She hit it face first.

The bed was too narrow for three, and Toby and Lydie needed sleep. Sin tucked them up, murmuring reassurances she was almost certain they were too sleepy to hear. She touched their heads, safe together on one pillow, Lydie's fine, blonde hair and the warm, round shape of Toby's scalp beneath his curls. She didn't let herself do anything else that might wake them up, just rose and slid out of the door to see if she could rob a couch cushion.

Alan and Nick were in the kitchen. Nick was leaning against the kitchen sink, his arms crossed, and Alan was cleaning off the counter.

"—cannot believe you said that," Alan said.

"It's simple," Nick told him, sounding bored. "You're crippled. So you sleep in a bed."

"It was still very—" Alan glanced up from the counter. Colour rose to his cheeks in a flash flood of embarrassment. "Hello, Cynthia."

"Hello, Alan," Sin said. "Hello, Nick."

Nick did not look fazed in the slightest. "I was just telling Alan—"

Sin raised her eyebrows. "I heard."

"And as I was telling Nick," Alan said, "I'm fine."

"Nick is right—" Sin started.

Then she stopped as she saw a change pass over Alan's face,

like the dark shadow of something coming just below the surface of still waters.

"Okay then," Alan said, a touch too lightly. "If you're both so keen on me sleeping in my own bed, I guess I'll go and do that now. We have an early start in the morning – Lydie's school is pretty far off."

He had obviously done this before, lied and taken himself out of Nick's sight. He'd obviously got away with this before.

It was Sin's fault he didn't get away with it this time.

She said nothing, just stood there and tried to cope with the realisation that Alan was going to be tortured in the next room, and she could not even go to him lest his brother find out it was happening.

Alan moved past her.

Faster than even she could move, Nick was blocking the door.

"Why does Sin look like that?" he demanded. "What's going on?"

"Nick," Alan said, his voice fraying like a rope about to snap. "Get out of my way."

Nick filled the doorway edge to edge.

"No."

"Nick," Alan said. Then he screamed between his teeth, a strangled terrible sound, and fell forward on his face.

Sin lunged and grabbed one of his arms, slowing his fall so he did not land as hard as she'd feared he would.

Alan did not seem to notice the impact as he fell. He gave another low cry, trying to curl in on himself and failing to do even that, his body shuddering out of his control.

Sin slid to her knees, dragging Alan's head and shoulders

into her lap. The floor was hard wood; she could at least stop him hurting himself. Alan gave another low scream, cut off as if he was strangling himself.

"Shh," Sin said helplessly. "You're all right. I've got you. I'm right here."

As if that would matter to Alan, but she could think of nothing else to say.

There was movement in her peripheral vision. She looked up into the drowning black of the demon's eyes.

"What is happening to him?" Nick demanded.

Alan let out another awful choked sound, shaking so hard it was difficult for Sin to keep hold of him. Nick recoiled as if someone had hit him, someone strong enough to make him feel it.

"What—" he ground out.

"Shut up," Sin told him. "I need to help Alan."

"Help him, then!" Nick's voice was becoming almost impossible to understand, as if someone was using the wrong instruments to play a familiar song, and the melody was coming out fractured and strange. "What can I do? There has to be something I can do!"

"I'm just going to be there for him," Sin said. "And you're just going to shut up."

Alan moaned, the sound ragged and terrible. Nick was silent.

"Shh," Sin said again. She stroked his hair and felt Alan's hand clasp her wrist, his skin fever-hot. He made another cut-off sound, and she realised what he was doing, in the midst of agony.

He was trying not to wake the children.

Sin wanted to cry. Instead she held fast to her control, and to him.

It went on, and on, and on. She had the thought that she would never have let anybody else comfort one of her family, that she would have reached out, and wondered if the demon cared too little to do even that much.

She looked at Nick again, over Alan's head.

He was crouched on the floor and trembling in sharp bursts, like a whipped dog. She saw his hand, reaching out across the floor towards Alan, then forming a fist and hitting the floor instead.

He did not seem to notice he was bruising his hand, any more than he noticed her looking at him. His devouring demon's eyes were fixed on Alan.

He might care, then, Sin thought. In his way. But he wasn't human, and his way wouldn't do Alan much good.

"I'm here," she told Alan, again and again. "I'm here."

It might be a comfort to know someone human was here for him, at last.

Her knees were aching by the time Alan finally went limp and boneless in her arms. For a moment the thought that his heart could have simply given out, that he could have just died, sent sick fear coursing through her, and then he tried weakly to sit up.

Sin helped him, her arm round his shoulders, and Nick acted, grabbing hold of both Alan's arms and almost throwing him into one of the chairs by their small, round kitchen table.

"Now," Nick said. "Tell me what's going on."

Sin slipped in, eel-swift, to block Alan from Nick's view. "Leave him alone. Have you no pity?"

Nick put a hand to Sin's throat, forcing her head back. The demon's attention was on her now, his eyes glittering.

"Don't stand between me and my brother," he said softly. "And no."

"Don't touch her," Alan commanded, his voice thin and hoarse.

Nick released Sin's throat and stepped back, until he was behind the counter, as if he did not trust himself not to lash out unless there was a barrier in his way.

Sin didn't trust him, either.

"She knows what's going on," Nick observed. "Obviously. How many people know? Why did you lie to me? Why do you always lie?"

"It's in my nature," Alan said in a low voice, and then more clearly: "I didn't want you to get upset. There was no point in telling you."

"No point?" Nick echoed.

"No," said Alan. "There's nothing you can do. It's just Gerald demonstrating his power over me. He wants you to be upset, so when he comes to you with demands, you'll do what he wants."

Alan had decided not to mention that there had already been demands, Sin noticed. She turned towards Alan, joining him in this conspiracy almost without a thought. She bowed her head as if she was fussing over him, making sure Nick could not see her face.

Her eyes and Alan's met in perfect understanding.

In his nature, indeed.

"And you didn't think I should know this," Nick said.

"I didn't feel like giving him the satisfaction," Alan returned.

"He was trying to keep it from everyone," Sin added. "I happened to see him have another attack, the day I was teaching him archery up on the hill. If I'd thought it would do you any good to know, I would have told you."

Perfectly true, as far as it went.

She looked up to see if Nick was buying it. He was standing with his arms braced on the counter and his head bowed.

"What are we going to do?" he asked, and then louder, his voice furious: "What's the *plan*?"

"Oh, well," Alan said, his voice gentle and tired. "That's the problem. There isn't one."

"What do you mean, there isn't one?"

"Think about it, Nick," said Alan. "I can't make a plan. If there was a plan, I couldn't know it. Gerald could torture it out of me any time he liked."

Nick's shoulders bunched as his brother spoke. His head stayed bowed.

"What are we meant to do, then?" he snarled. "Just sit and wait until he comes with his demands? Or until he pushes you too far and kills you?"

"The second would be preferable," Alan said. "I won't have you a magician's slave."

"Why not?" Nick demanded. "What does it matter? I was one before."

"That was before you were mine," Alan said. His voice was steadier now. "Nick, if I do die. If it happens, I hope it won't, but if it does, it's all right. I'll feel all right about it if I can leave you safe behind, with Mae and Jamie. It will be like leaving behind a life's work. Do you know something? I remember snatches of things before you came, bits and pieces about my mother. But as far back as I can think in a straight line, from that point of my life to this, there's you, and wanting to take care of you. That's what I remember. It's all right."

Nick did look up, then.

"I remember my life, before you," he said, his voice chilly and distant. "Don't make me live like that again."

"Nick," Alan said.

"Nick," Nick repeated viciously. "What was that, in the beginning, but some baby name you used because you heard Olivia call me Hnikarr. A demon's name in a child's mouth. Until you turned it into the biggest lie you ever told. Nicholas Ryves. As if there was such a person. As if I was a person. Who do you think I'll be, when you die?"

"I think you'll be Nicholas Ryves," said Alan. "You made that lie true for me. You've answered to the name, every time I called. I know who you are."

"Do you know what I am?"

Demon, thought Sin, but she did not say it. Even Alan did not speak, just shook his head and waited.

"I can't make a plan," Nick said slowly. "I can't save anyone. All I can do is kill. I'm a weapon. And if I can't be your weapon, I'll be someone else's."

"What are you going to do?" Sin asked.

Nick tilted his chin, baring his throat to Alan for a moment, as if that was a response.

"Be careful," Alan murmured, as if it was.

"You're one to talk," Nick said. "For nine minutes tonight, I thought you were dead already."

He sounded perfectly calm about that, but he had counted the minutes. Sin couldn't quite put the two things together, not in a way that made any sense.

Nick turned his eyes to her, blank but still demanding, like staring into an abyss that stared back. Sin met his gaze, refusing to let him read anything from her face again, and his eyes bored into her for a moment.

Then he turned away. He left the kitchen, and a second later, the door of the flat slammed shut.

Alan got out his phone and called Mae.

"I think," he said, "you might want to expect a guest fairly soon. Let me know if your Aunt Edith sees him and calls the cops. I'll come and bail him out eventually. Yes, Cynthia and the kids are safe here."

He raised an eyebrow at Sin. She shook her head.

"She's already asleep," Alan said without missing a beat. "Yeah, it's been a long night. I'll let her know you want to talk to her."

He turned the phone off.

"What do you think Nick's going to do?" Sin asked.

"I don't know," Alan answered. "I'm trying not to think about it. If I don't know, I can't tell Gerald. Besides, it's only fair for Nick to have some secrets, considering my – entire life."

"Yes," said Sin, thinking of how she'd thought the demon might lash out, even at Alan, the way Nick's hand had felt at her throat. "You're certainly the problem child."

She sagged against the kitchen table. Alan could see through any show she might put on. There was a certain freedom in knowing that, in simply stopping.

She was so tired.

"You really should take my bed," Alan said. He gave her a beautiful, plausible smile. "You've had quite a night of it. You need your sleep."

Sin didn't mention what Alan had gone through tonight. Instead she backed away from the table, going for the sitting room and the sofa there, and paused at the kitchen door to say, "I do need my sleep. That's why I don't want an angry demonic alarm clock going off at me."

"I can handle Nick," Alan told her.

"No doubt," Sin said. "I can handle the floor."

Alan got up and limped over to her. The limp wasn't usually so obvious, but then, he must be even more tired than she was. Sin looked away so she wouldn't have to see it, closing her eyes and leaning her head against the door frame.

When she opened her eyes, she saw that had been the wrong thing to do. There were faint, bitter lines round Alan's mouth.

"Some horrible things have happened to you tonight," he said in a level voice. "I'd just like for you to have a bed."

"And what about what happened to you?" Sin asked. "Oh, that's right. I forgot. You don't think that counts, because it's you."

She stopped leaning and backed away from him, through the door into the other bedroom. She crooked her finger at him and summoned up a smile. "We can share. I don't mind."

She moved backwards without a glance behind her. She might not have the Market any more, but she was still dancer enough to move gracefully, no matter where she was. She backed up without missing a beat until the backs of her knees hit the bed, and then she sat.

When she looked up, Alan was standing in the doorway.

"I do mind," he said.

"Right," Sin said, and her fragile calm broke like a rope snapping beneath her feet. "I wasn't offering anything more than sleep, you know."

Alan went scarlet to his eyebrows. "I didn't think you were."

"I wasn't," Sin snarled, and she leaned her head in her hands. She wanted to cry, but her eyes felt like hot hollows in her face. She hadn't cried in a long time.

She heard Alan crossing the room, never able to be light on his feet. He sat down on the bed beside her and touched her arm, just brushing it with his fingertips, as if he didn't want to presume.

"Cynthia," he said. "Okay."

"I wasn't," Sin insisted, and was almost sure she was telling the truth: she was so tired, and she might want comfort, but that was no way to get it. She ground the heels of her hands against her closed eyes until they hurt.

"Cynthia," Alan repeated, putting so much effort into his beautiful voice that it cracked, the whole façade cracked, neither of them quite good enough at their roles to make them true. "It's okay."

"What's okay?" Sin demanded. "Nothing's okay. I let the Market down. I should have known that since getting to you wasn't working, they would come after us. I should have worked it out!"

"I should have—" Alan began, but she interrupted him fiercely.

"They're my people," she said. "Not yours. I was the one who knew Lydie had magic, and I should have protected her. I was meant to be a leader, I was meant to take care of her and I failed!"

She still could not cry, but she was shaking suddenly, hard, bone-jarring shaking, her whole body betraying her. Alan took hold of her elbow carefully, always gentle, and Sin turned to him blindly and locked her arm round his neck. She buried her face in his collarbone, gritted her teeth and shook and shook.

"Cynthia," Alan murmured, and rocked her for a little while, stroked her hair. She could feel it going electric with static, curls rising up to wrap round his fingers. She wished she could tie him down somewhere, keep him just like this, just for her. "Cynthia."

She let him go and leaned back, stretching on to his pillow. She kept hold of his arm, pulling him towards her. "Come here," she said. "Lie to me."

Alan lay down beside her, a little awkward pulling up his bad leg on to the bed. His hand in her hair wasn't awkward, anything but, fingers slow and light as the rays of the moon on her skin, drawing a curl back from her cheek. She reached up and took off his glasses, snapping the earpieces closed with her teeth, and smiled at him as she slid them on to the bedside table.

He was gorgeous by moonlight, hair and skin turned a hazy golden colour, his eyes starlit-night blue and so sweet, so deep, pools you could drop your heart into and lose it forever.

"Cynthia," he murmured, fingers still brushing her cheek, making her shiver. "I'm not lying."

Sin closed her eyes and tucked her cheek into the curve of his neck and against his pillow.

"Yeah," she whispered. "Just like that."

8

Burning Wishes

SIN WOKE WARM AND SAFE, THE MORNING SO EARLY THAT THE rays of light falling across the bed just seemed like paler shadows. She had a hand curled round the front of Alan's shirt, anchoring him close beside her. The blankets were heaped over her, Alan's breath was slow and regular against her hair, and Sin felt no inclination to move whatsoever.

She tugged Alan a little closer. He made a drowsy inquiring sound.

Sin gave a sleepy hum in response.

Her hum wavered and died away in her throat when Alan's fingers brushed her ribs. She hadn't really registered before that her shirt had ridden up, but she did now.

Alan's hand slid along her side, moving smooth and sure from cloth to skin. His gun-calloused fingers lingered at the hollow above her hip, and Sin realised that Alan had definitely woken up with a girl in his bed before.

She rolled a little towards him, easy as a cat being stroked, and at that point Alan woke up all the way, yelped and fell out of bed.

Sin would've laughed, except for the small, stifled sound Alan made when he hit the ground.

She levered herself up on her elbows and said sharply, "Are you all right?"

"Fine," Alan bit out, white round the lips, and she hated his stupid leg for ruining something that should have been ridiculous and warm. If it hadn't been for that, they would both have laughed; if it hadn't been for that, she would have noticed him before, the same way the other girls who had been in this bed must have.

"Your leg," she began. "Is it—"

"Cynthia, *leave* it!" Alan snapped.

There was something furious and humiliated about the tight line of his mouth. If she had been another girl, someone who hated his leg less, he wouldn't have been this embarrassed.

He grabbed at the bedpost with unnecessary force and hauled himself gracelessly to his feet. Sin closed her eyes, imagining how it would be if she knew her body was guaranteed to fail her.

"I apologise," Alan told her stiffly.

Sin blinked her eyes open. "What?"

Alan was staring with great interest at the wall. "I didn't know it was you," he said. "Well, I did know it was you, but I was half-asleep, and—"

Sin blinked again as the fact that he was being a gentleman about not quite groping her sank in. She began to smile.

"That's all right," she said, and rolled back on the pillows, making a space. She glanced up at him through her fallen hair and asked, amused and inviting, "Are you getting back in?"

"Ah," Alan said. "No. I have translations to do. And you—"

He reached out, then, not for her but for the blanket, which he pulled up over her shoulder. "Cynthia," he said. "Just rest."

Rejection number one hundred and fourteen – but who was counting – should have stung more, but his voice and the way he drew up the blanket were gentle, and she could stand to get more sleep.

Sin cuddled in under the covers. She was asleep again almost immediately. She stirred automatically every now and then, her hand reaching for the kids, but as soon as she surfaced from sleep, she knew things were taken care of for now. For now, she could rest.

Every time she woke she glanced over at the little desk by the window, where Alan sat with an old scroll and a sheet of notepaper, occasionally scribbling something. His face in the morning light was serious and absorbed. The sound of the pencil on paper was like a whisper, shushing her back to sleep.

The last time she woke up, her eyes snapped open to the sound of Toby fussing.

Alan was standing up, hip propped against the desk, the baby in his arms.

"Shh," he said, commanding and coaxing at once, his voice very low. "Shh. Let your sister sleep a little longer."

Toby stared at him, mouth working doubtfully for a moment, then decided to grab for Alan's glasses and laugh. Alan echoed the laugh back at him, the sound turning into music and the sunlight pushing warm, gold fingers through Alan's red hair.

It was a revelation.

Alan mattered. He meant something to her, and that meant he could hurt her. Considering the evidence so far, it meant he was going to hurt her.

This was another terrible problem, on top of all the others.

She had no idea what she was going to do, but she could sleep for just a little longer.

She hadn't slept like this in more than a year.

She woke up with the demon hanging over her, blank eyes on her face.

Sin whipped a fist round hard, aiming for his stomach. He grabbed her wrist, and she twisted and sat up in bed. "What do you want, Nick?"

"Mavis on the phone for you," he said, and dropped his mobile phone on her pillow.

"Mavis?" Sin asked.

"Definitely not," said Mae. "Smack Nick around a little for me, would you?"

"Anything for a friend."

"So I was wondering what shoe size you are."

Sin rose from the bed, unwrapping the sheets from round herself as she did so. She realised only when she saw Nick's raised brows that she'd unwound them slowly, with a little dramatic gesture. She raised her eyebrows back at him and turned her back.

"I don't understand."

"Look, all your stuff got burned to ashes last night," Mae said. "I've got a ton of clothes and things I'm going to bring over. Also I'm going to buy you some shoes."

"I don't want charity," Sin said flatly.

"It's practicality," Mae volleyed back. "We're allies, right? Allies need to be able to leave the house. For that you need shoes. So tell me your shoe size, because I'm financially irresponsible and if you don't, I'll buy a whole bunch of different size shoes."

"Mae—"

"I'm in the shop," Mae said. "I'm getting ready to waste the world's shoe resources!"

Sin told Mae her shoe size and hung up. She was going to have to work out a way to pay back Mae, as well.

She turned back to Nick.

"Thank you for the phone," she said. "And for letting us stay."

"Alan's letting you stay," Nick said.

"Okay," Sin said. "Why aren't you at school?"

"Why aren't you at school?" Nick echoed.

"Uh, my uniform burned up. When my home exploded into flames."

"So did mine," said Nick. "When I tossed a lighter into my wardrobe. Tragic, really."

Sin rubbed the centre of her forehead. "Where are Toby and Lydie?"

"Alan has the baby, and he brought the girl to school. He went by to pick up Mae and they're coming back here to make some sort of plan."

"What sort of plan?" Sin asked apprehensively.

"I don't know, I'm not any good at plans," Nick said. "Well, I've got a stage one: kill some people. After that you've lost me."

"Stage two, kill some more people?" Sin asked. "Stage three's a bit of a mystery to me, as well."

There had always been Merris to think of strategies and long-term goals. There had always been things Sin had to deal with immediately: she'd never really thought about making plans. She liked to act.

But where was Merris, and what was she supposed to do now?

Mae could make plans. But Sin loved the Market more. She knew she loved it more, and that meant she should be able to do something.

"I'm going to practise the sword," Nick said. "Since stages one and two are all I can manage, I'd better get them right."

"There's somewhere we can practise?"

"Roof garden."

"Give me a second," said Sin. "Can I use your phone again?"

Nick shrugged and made for the door. He only paused to say, "See you on the roof."

Sin sat on the bed in her sports bra and jeans, and made calls to all the pipers, potion-makers and occult bookshops in London that she knew.

She'd always looked down on dancers who danced outside the Goblin Market. They had no partners, no fever fruit, nothing to safeguard people outside the circles if the dancers got possessed, and nothing to offer the demons when they came.

Sometimes demons took their lives. Sometimes they would be satisfied with hurting the dancer, sharing one of their bad memories, tasting human pain and trying to plant a doubt or a desire in them so one day the demon could persuade them into possession.

It was a terrible gamble.

The money was good, though. Sin had always thought dancers who went it alone were greedy.

Maybe they were just desperate.

One woman asked her if she was sure, her voice trembling slightly. Sin told her she was quite sure.

She might not know how to plan. But she could act.

She had to sit for a minute after she made the last call, her arm linked round her knee. She tried not to think.

The phone went off in her hand. She answered it automatically.

"Nick?" said a strange man's voice.

"Who is this?" Sin demanded.

The line went dead.

There was a roof garden on top of Nick and Alan's building. A roof garden where they grew cigarette butts and concrete.

Sin bounded up the couple of steps to where Nick stood outlined against the chilly, steel-blue sky. He'd pulled off his shirt and thrown it on the ground; Sin noticed the flex of muscles in his arms and chest as he feinted, lunged and withdrew. They'd lost a good dancer there.

They'd lost a better one with her. Sin cast off her own shirt and began to warm up wearing jeans and her sports bra, doing some shoulder rolls and ankle circles, and then started on hip flexes. With her knee on the floor and her arms over her head, she pushed her hips forward and counted heartbeats.

When she switched to a calf stretch, Nick tapped her on the back of her knee with his sword. Sin glanced at the talisman, glinting and swinging from his bare chest, and up to the challenging curl of his mouth.

She grinned back and he swung, and Sin bent over backward on her palms to avoid the blade. It cut through the air, the edge skimming an inch above the line of her hips. Sin rolled away as Nick's sword lifted, and then dodged as he swung. She went weaving around the silver blur of his blade, rolling over and under it, capturing it in the arch of her arms and leaping over the bright barrier.

"Stop dancing around," Nick said, baring his teeth at her.

She let her arms dip low, crossed at the wrist, as the blade flashed forward. She caught the blade just above the hilt, just before the point touched her stomach.

She grinned back at him. "I never do."

They disengaged and she spun away; he lifted the sword and she swung out from it, her fingertips on the blade as if it was her partner's hand. The cold air felt good against her hot skin now, and her muscles were all singing to her.

Nick advanced on her, bringing his sword up and around. Sin did a split and sprang back to her feet when the sword had already passed her. She retreated a step, and the inside of Nick's arm hit the small of her back.

He stopped and looked down at her, as if he had only just noticed she had turned his sword practice into their dance.

There was a flash above them, almost like a spotlight. Standing out against a pale, empty sky, with not a cloud or a murmur of thunder, was a brilliant, silent stitch of lightning.

They both stood staring at it for a moment, their faces lifted.

"Did my phone ring while you had it?" Nick asked.

Sin said, "Yes."

"I have to go," Nick told her. He disengaged and went for the steps down to his flat, sheathing his sword as he went.

He left Sin with his shirt at her feet and her head tipped back to stare at the sky.

Only a magician could send a sign like that.

She was still staring when Nick's phone went off in her back pocket.

Sin answered warily, waiting for magicians, and got a reminder that she had plenty of problems that were all her own.

The woman at the occult bookshop, the one with the

worried voice who'd asked her if she was quite sure, had clients lined up for her already.

"You don't have to do this," she said.

Sin said, "I'm on my way."

She met Mae and Alan coming into the flat.

Mac frowned. "Is this no-shirts festival day?"

"Every day with Nick is no-shirts festival day," Alan said absently, but he was frowning, too. "Where are you going?"

"I'll tell you later," Sin said. "If you could look after the kids for just a few hours, I'd really appreciate it. This is important."

"Of course," Alan said. "But what's going on? Do you want one of us to come with you?"

Sin smiled, bright and swift as light glancing off water. She knew how to fake confidence until she could make it true. "I hope you're not suggesting I can't handle anything on my own."

She refused to look at him, because he saw too much, and she didn't want him to see that she was scared. She got changed, kissed Toby, thanked Mae for the clothes and asked if she could borrow some money to buy a Tube ticket.

She bought a one-way ticket. No sense being wasteful: she might not be coming back.

The bookshop was several streets away from Tottenham Court Road station, not far from the British Museum. There were streets around it with wide sandstone flagstones, filled with sunlight. The sun was almost a winter sun, though, bright but not warm, and as Sin walked up the street, she found herself shivering. She had chosen a gauzy white skirt of Mae's that slipped down her hips a little too much, and a white tank top. She was a performer. She had to look the part.

Customers didn't want to see a real person, one who could get cold.

Few people were interested in seeing a real person, of course. A boy whistled as she stepped off the pavement and crossed the road to where the bookshop stood, its door painted dull green and lightbulbs glowing in black iron frames through the huge glass window.

"Girl," he said. He was white and wearing expensive clothes and talking what he obviously imagined was ghetto slang. "You are *fine*."

"Boy," she snapped, "I know."

She did not spare him another look. In a second she was pushing open the bookshop door, which was heavy against her palms, and moving through the dim and dusty interior of the shop. There was a little cardboard sign that said BARGAINS at the top of some stairs, with an arrow pointing down drawn on it in red marker. The steps down to the cellar were golden yellow wood and looked polished, but they creaked under Sin's feet and felt very shaky.

In the cellar there were four women. Sin remembered the bookshop owner, a South Indian woman with tired eyes and a green shirt. She was arranging amulets on the floor.

Of the other three women, two were wearing very nice jewellery, and one of the jewellery wearers had salon-sleek, highlighted red hair. Well, they had to have money to afford this.

"This is Sin Davies," the bookshop owner said. Her name was Ana, Sin recalled.

Sin just smiled at them, beautiful, mysterious and silent. She held out her hand for the chalk.

"I hope the amulets are all right," Ana said.

"They look fine," Sin murmured. There was a pack of

coloured chalks in the woman's hand. Sin took it gently and selected a sky blue one.

The chalk squeaked and crumbled as Sin set it to the floorboards. She traced round the amulets, down the lines of communication that translated demons' silent speech, and the big circle that would keep her and the demon trapped. She did it over and over again. There couldn't be even the smallest space for the demon to escape.

In the end she was left with a useless nub and sky blue dust all over her hands.

She stood and looked round at Ana and the three women, drawn together like a coven.

No, she told herself. They were an audience. It was time to perform.

Lots of dancers cried and got the shakes the day before a Market night, but nobody ever let the audience guess. Sin lifted her arm, arched above her head as if she was wearing a spangled bodysuit and opening a circus show.

She kept the red slip-ons Mae had bought her, even though she probably could have danced better with them off. For luck.

She stepped into the circle.

The drums of the Goblin Market were her own heartbeat in her ears. The Market was in her blood and bones. It didn't matter where she was: she could dance a Market night into being.

And the demon would come.

She danced and made the fall of her dark hair the night, the drape of her skirts the drapes on the Market stalls. The swing of her hips and the arch of her back were the dance. Nobody could take this away, and nobody could resist her.

Come buy.

"I call on Anzu the fly-by-night, the bird who brings messages of death, the one who remembers. I call on the one they called Aeolos, ruler of the winds, in Greece; I call on Ulalena of the jungles. I call as my mother called before me: I call and will not be denied. I call on Anzu."

The dark cloud of her hair veiled her view of the room for a moment after she was done.

When that brief darkness had passed, there was already a light rising. There was a sound between a crackle and a whisper.

Sin felt as if she was standing in the ring on a giant stove, and someone had just turned it on.

The flames rose, flickering and pale. They seemed hotter than the flames at the Market.

The demon rose as if drawn into view by fiery puppet strings. Anzu was trying to mock her and scare her at once, Sin saw. His wings were sheets of living flame, sparks falling from them and turning into feathers.

He was wearing all black, like the dancer boys did at the Goblin Market to contrast with the girls' bright costumes.

Fire and feathers were raining down on her, and she didn't have a partner.

Anzu tilted his head, feather patterns shining in his golden hair. She felt all the things she usually did when standing with a demon: the cold malice, the abiding fury. There was something else today, though: a kind of startled curiosity that left her startled in turn.

"What are you doing here?" Anzu asked.

"I'm here for answers," Sin said in a level voice, and kept her head held high. "As usual. I will not take off my talisman, and I will not break the circle. Other than that, you can name your price."

"Is that so," said Anzu. He looked out over the flames at the little wooden cellar, the open books on the tables with their pages curling as if trying to get away from him, and the faces of her three customers. "I don't think you know what a prize you have bought," he told them. "This is the princess of the Goblin Market, their heiress, their very best. Throwing her life away for a song."

The women looked at Sin in a way she did not want. She was meant to be a beautiful tool for them. They weren't paying her to be a person.

Sin knew the demon was only trying to provoke her, but she could not help her own anger, and the curl of Anzu's lovely predator's mouth let her know he could feel it.

"Not for a song," she informed him. "For a price. What's yours?"

"Let's put ourselves on an equal footing, shall we?" Anzu's smile made it clear how much she was degraded, how far the princess of the Goblin Market had fallen. Sin's rage burned, and Anzu's eyes gleamed. "Three true answers in exchange for three true answers. Doesn't that sound fair?"

"Agreed."

Merris had always said Sin wasn't good at looking ahead. Well, let it be so. She chose to act, give the customers what they wanted. She would think about the price later.

The woman with the red salon hair was the first to speak, her voice ringing out, obviously that of a born organiser.

"Does my husband love somebody else?"

Anzu looked over at her face. For a moment his eyes did not reflect otherworldly lights, but the ordinary lamps of this ordinary room; for a moment his gaze was warm.

"No," said the demon. "But he stopped loving you six years ago."

The woman's faint beginning of a smile shattered. Anzu's savage pleasure coursed through Sin's veins like poison.

The next woman spoke, the one without jewellery or salon hair. Her fingernails were bitten down to the quick.

They saw what happened to everyone else, but they always thought the demon's answers would be different for them. They never seemed to learn that the truth was always cruel.

"Will they find out what I – what I did?"

The woman's voice was a thread that had become knotted, a twist in her throat.

"Yes," Anzu answered. The woman sagged as if she had been dealt far too hard a blow, but that wasn't enough for Anzu. "But you asked the wrong question," he continued relentlessly. "Will they find out tomorrow? Will they find out after you die? You'll never know when."

He gave her a smile as brilliant as a lit match hitting petrol. Then his attention swung to the last woman, who had real diamonds at her ears but rather a nice face. She looked uncertain under the demon's attention, and Sin thought for a moment she might decide to be wise.

As always, desire was stronger than wisdom.

The woman took a deep breath and asked, "Did she forgive me before she died?"

Anzu's cruel delight washed through Sin, like the cold rush of an ocean wave with knives in it.

"No."

The last woman began to cry. Anzu turned away from them all, making it clear he was bored. He shook back his hair; a cascade of sparks becoming feathers drifted through the air, like a flurry of golden autumn leaves.

He wasn't actually all that good at showmanship, Sin thought. He relied far too much on props.

"And now, dancer," Anzu said, his eyes on her alone. "Now it's my turn."

He lifted a hand. He couldn't touch her, not while she wore her talisman and kept within her lines, but he wanted the shadow of his hand on her, talons curled, a looming threat.

Sin lifted her own hand, fingers curled to mirror his, and made a dance of it. She'd danced with one demon already today. She could dance with this one, too. They walked in a circle within a circle, the shadows of their hands touching on the firelit wall.

If she didn't answer every question with absolute truth, he had the right to kill her.

"What happened to you, to reduce you to this?"

Sin laughed at him. "Nothing reduces me unless I let it."

"You haven't answered me."

"Hold your horses, demon. I will."

It was none of his business. But it was just possible that, along with wanting to trap her, he was interested. She had been summoning him for years.

"The Market found out that my sister is a – that she has strong magical powers," Sin said. "Very strong. She couldn't be allowed to stay. And I couldn't let her go, not to the magicians. She's mine. She and my brother stay with me. And they need to eat."

"The princess in exile," Anzu said. "That must hurt."

"Is that a question?" Sin demanded.

Anzu laughed. The flames of the demon's circle leaped and danced with the joy of hurting her. "No. Don't be so impatient. I am letting you off easy, you know. When and where did you last see Hnikarr?"

"You're not letting me off easy," Sin said. "You just have more to think about than possessing one dancer. Like revenge. I saw him less than an hour ago, at his home. I'm staying with him. We were training together."

"Is that what the kids are calling it these days," Anzu mused.

Sin smiled at him scornfully, and Anzu's mouth twisted, showing nothing but darkness beyond his lips, no more teeth than a bird had in its beak.

"Last question pays for all, falling dancer," he said. "Are you in love?"

Sin flinched, her hand pulling back on reflex as if they had touched and he had burned her. Anzu lunged at her, but Sin was too well trained to fall for that trick. She stood unmoved and stared into the demon's eyes, shimmering with light and shadows but ultimately empty.

He was beautiful, a dazzling gold mirage amid the flames, and he conjured a vision of another demon standing just this close to her, shadow-black hair falling into a face like a sculpture and a chill in the air all around them.

Beautiful boys had stood looking into her eyes before. None of them had ever touched her like the sight of someone at the window with her baby brother, trying to make sure she got to rest a little longer.

"Well?" the demon whispered, calling her back from a certain smile in the sunlight to the crackling flames and his bleak eyes.

Sin wrapped her arms round herself.

"Yes," she whispered back. "I am."

Anzu grinned. "I thought so."

The demon was dwindling, the flames of the circle winking out, and Sin said, "It's not who you think."

Even Anzu's wings were going dark, so she could hardly see them against the black of his clothes. The only light left was that of his hungry, watching eyes.

"No?"

"No," said Sin. "I don't think demons are very lovable."

Anzu said, "I think you're right."

Then he disappeared, down into darkness. All that was left was a chalk circle on the floor, and the echo of his last laugh from the walls.

Ana the bookshop owner counted the money out into Sin's hand. One of the women stirred, as if she would have liked to protest and say she hadn't received what she wanted, but she did not speak.

Nick's phone rang in Sin's pocket as she was going up the steps, and she answered it.

"Cynthia," said Alan, and the human world came back in a warm rush, the performance over.

Sin gripped the phone tight. "Hi."

"Nick said you had the phone. Toby's sleeping, and Nick and Mae are both here, so I thought I would go and buy some books that might help us and collect Lydie from school. Can I pick you up on the way?"

"Yes," Sin said. She left the shop and sat on the pavement, refusing to let her legs collapse underneath her, making herself sit gracefully, her skirt in a pale pool around her. "I'm outside a bookshop now. Come get me."

9

My Mother's Daughter

Sin had been worried Alan would notice something was wrong. She had not been expecting him to be distracted by his own obvious delight, filled with a kind of hushed awe, like a child ushered into a sweetshop and told he could have anything he wanted if he would be quiet.

"These are real Elizabethan spell books. It was an amazing age for magic, you know."

Alan ran slow, tender fingertips down one book's spine. Sin had a little flashback to the morning, and then put herself on notice. She might have had a revelation, and she might even go so far as to admit this behaviour was adorable, but she was not prepared to develop a full-on nerd fetish.

She smiled up at him, and was fairly sure she pulled off mysterious rather than besotted.

"You're not one of those crazed conspiracy nuts who thinks Shakespeare was a magician, are you?"

Alan's face lit with his smile in return. "Some people might say the theory isn't crazy but the only way to explain Shakespeare's extraordinary time management."

"Some people might be crazy," Sin said, dancing backwards with a volume in hand. "Just a thought!"

She raised her voice a touch too loud, and Ana the bookseller looked up and caught her eye. Sin fell silent and tried not to think about the cellar, where the smell of balefire must still be lingering. She looked back at Alan, wanting his smile, but he was looking at the shelves.

Sin went and sat on the warm radiator in the corner, tucked up behind the shelves on New Age spirituality, and breathed in and out. She wished she could do some actual exercises, but doing the splits in a bookshop was bound to attract attention.

She just sat with her head bowed for a little while, then got up and went to find Alan.

He was standing with his hip propped against the bookshelves, rescuing a book from a high shelf for a tiny brunette with glasses.

"Anything for a woman who likes Poe," he was saying, which Sin could have done without hearing: She could already tell from his attentive stoop and his smile that he was flirting.

Sin slinked her way to his side with all due haste, and slipped an arm round his waist. "Hi," she said throatily, tipping her face up to meet Alan's slightly startled eyes.

"Hi?" he said, as if he had some reservations about the word.

His shoulder was at exactly the right height for her chin, Sin discovered, as she rested it there and beamed at the little brunette.

"Hey, I'm Cynthia," she said. "You looking for something? You should let us help you!"

The girl got the message and gave a small nod. "No, I think it's in another section. Thanks anyway."

She looked a bit disappointed. As well she might: Sin really doubted that any of the other sections had bookish redheads.

"What was that about?"

With anyone else, Sin might have been able to say, "What was what?" and convince him of her innocence. But lies didn't work on Alan; she knew better than to play a player.

She disengaged from him and kept her eyes downcast, suddenly scared he could see right through her.

"Can't waste time dilly-dallying," she said. "We're on a mission."

She was extremely grateful when Alan did not pursue the matter. He went back to browsing instead, and it was not long before he was ready to buy his books and go.

That gave her time to think.

He'd been flirting with the little brunette. She'd seen him with Mae, too, recalled with sudden, vivid clarity a time when he'd taken off his talisman and put it in Mae's hand, the long line of his fingers gently closing Mae's over the necklace.

He'd never once flirted with Sin.

Why should he, though? The same night he had almost stroked Mae's hand closed, Sin had spat in his face.

There was an alternative theory, of course. She might not have given him any encouragement back in the day, but she had been throwing herself at him for weeks now.

He'd had plenty of chances to flirt with her. If he'd been at all interested in doing so.

Sin got into the passenger seat of the car, and when he slid into the driving seat, she said, "So did you pick up Mae in a bookshop?"

She was so smooth.

She tilted a teasing smile towards him to make it seem more like a friendly question. He smiled faintly back.

"I met Mae in a bookshop," Alan said. "If that's what you mean."

"I just wondered if that was how you rolled. Finding dates in bookshops. New one on me."

"Well, I do work in a bookshop," Alan said. His voice was warm and relaxed, a little puzzled, but he hadn't turned on the engine. Sin wondered if that meant something.

"Time management," she remarked. "Like Shakespeare."

"'We are time's subjects, and time bids be gone,'" Alan said, his voice slightly different, touching the words gently the way his hands touched books. She thought it was a quote. "Well, that," he continued, his voice back to normal. "And it is an easy way to find girls who read."

"Right," Sin said.

Girls who were smart.

"Girls who I'd have something in common with," Alan went on. "Something to weigh in the balance before they meet Nick."

That last part wasn't quite a joke, Sin noticed.

"Not that much in common," she said. "Since they wouldn't know about demons, or magic, or the Market. Ever tell any of them?"

"No," said Alan. "That's why – that's why I thought Mae was so perfect."

Sin looked across the tiny, unbridgeable space in the car between them. Alan had turned his face away.

"She came to us to save her brother," Alan said. "I could – I could understand that. She found out about everything because of her brother. I didn't draw her into anything. And I could help her."

Sin's voice went sharp. "Oh, so it's vulnerable women?"

"No," Alan snapped. "Mae's not—"

"She's not," Sin said. "And you wouldn't like it if she was. But you, with Nick and that mother of his, with kids? Has anyone ever loved you without needing you?"

The question exploded out of her. Alan didn't even turn his head.

"My dad," he said. He drew his wallet out of his pocket and flipped it open.

Sin peered at the photograph tucked into the plastic slip. It was an old picture, with a white curl at one corner. It showed two kids, Alan thin and inquisitive-looking under a mop of hair, a very short Nick and Daniel Ryves standing braced with his arms over his chest. Sin remembered him a little, a big, burly guy with kind eyes. Everyone had liked him.

"He looks like Nick," Sin said. "I mean, Nick stands like he did."

Alan slid a single look over to her, but it was enough. She was surprised to see that she'd somehow said the right thing.

"Yeah," he said. "Yeah, Nick does."

"And your mother?"

"I couldn't help her," Alan said. "She died when I was four. I remember how the world was when she was alive, how normal everything seemed, how warm and safe."

"So, normal girls." Sin paused. "And what were you going to do with Mae, after you saved her?"

"I was hoping she would love me," Alan said.

He was back to staring out of the window.

"She didn't?"

"It wasn't her," Alan said. "It was me. Like I said – she was perfect. She's strong, she can handle anything about this world, she can handle Nick and I can . . . I can read people. I can manoeuvre them. She liked me a little. There was some hope. But instead of being honest with her I lied to her for Nick, without a second thought. She was everything I'd been dreaming about, that I thought I could be happy if I found. She was the girl I could have had a normal relationship with, the girl I should have been able to trust. She was perfect. Which means there's something wrong with me."

Sin nodded. "Did you think you were just going to change back?"

To the kid he'd been when he was four years old, like someone in a fairy tale waking up from a long sleep. As if it worked that way.

"I think," Alan began, and stopped. "I feel as if I made a bargain. When Nick and I were kids. I wanted, so badly, for him to belong enough in the human world. Not to be human, but to be happy, to have people around him be safe and for people to love him. If he doesn't have a soul, I thought – I wanted to give him mine. I feel as if I did."

"Do you regret it?" Sin asked. "For Mae?"

Alan stopped looking out of the window. He didn't look at her, either. He looked straight ahead, and turned the key in the ignition.

She caught the small smile all the same.

"No," he murmured. "But like I said. There's something wrong with me."

They peeled away from the pavement, finally leaving that bookshop behind them.

"I think you're all right," Sin told him. "I mean, you know, irredeemably messed up, but in a charming way."

Alan laughed. "Thanks."

"I'm glad we made friends before my entire life collapsed round my ears, though," Sin said. "I don't want to be your latest little kid in danger, or kitten up a tree to be rescued, or whatever. Speaking of which, here's my half of the money for the books."

She plucked a ten out of her sports bra and held it out to Alan between two fingers.

Alan almost drove into a wall.

"Watch it, I don't want to be rescued from a car crash!"

"Where did you get that?"

"Oh, I mugged someone."

"Cynthia," Alan said, his voice twanging like a string about to snap. Anyone else would have had to guess or at least have made her confirm what he already knew, but not this boy. "You could have been killed."

"Nah." Sin waved her hand. "She was an old lady. Feeble."

"Seriously," Alan said.

"Seriously," she said. "You're the one who wants to look after everyone he meets. Don't tell me I can't look after my own family. Don't you dare."

Alan looked briefly exasperated before he tried to look persuasive and patient.

"I want to help you."

"And you did," Sin told him. "And I appreciate it. But I don't like it. I can't bear owing someone as much as I owe you, not for long. I'd rather take some chances."

"Surely I can be concerned that you've decided to adopt a job that kills half its practitioners in their first year."

"Yeah," Sin said. "Be concerned. Knock yourself out."

"You ever think that you might be taking on too much, when other people would be happy to share the load?"

"I'm sorry," said Sin. "Is this the inhabitant of number one, Glass House Lane? Sir, I think you should consider putting down your stone."

Alan nodded. "You make me think of a play."

Sin thought that sounded very promising. She seemed to recall that Shakespeare had said a lot of things vaguely along the lines of "We should date".

"Yeah?"

"Dryden wrote a play called *The Indian Emperor*, the sequel to *The Indian Queen*."

"Oh, Alan, this had better not be going to any gross 'you're so exotic' places."

"No," Alan said, very fast.

"Good," Sin told him firmly.

"There's this bit in it with a princess being threatened by the villain with death or, um, a villainous alternative. And the princess tells him to get lost, of course." Alan turned the corner cautiously, making their way out of the borough. "She says, 'My mother's daughter knows not how to fear.'"

She had been right before. He did have a special voice for quoting.

"Oh," Sin said.

"When you were standing in front of the Goblin Market," Alan said, "with your sister behind you, I thought of that line."

"That sounds like a pretty good play. You have it at home?"

"I do," Alan admitted. "Why?"

Sin raised her eyebrows. "I thought I might read it."

"Really?"

He didn't have to look so surprised. Sin felt uncomfortable and irritated again, felt as she had for years at the mere mention of Alan Ryves.

"I *can* read, you know," she snapped. "I'm not stupid."

"I know that," Alan snapped back. "I was stupid."

It was a strange enough admission from him that Sin found herself tilting her head to look at him from a different angle. "Were you?" she murmured. "How?"

"I thought you were exactly what you choose to appear as in a certain context," Alan said. "I should have known better than that. Me of all people."

In a certain context. At the Goblin Market.

And then there had been the battlefield, where he saved her brother. There had been the school, where they looked at each other, and because they were playing different parts than they usually did, they both saw that they were playing a part and maybe saw each other for the first time.

No sooner had she seen, but all this had started.

"Why do you keep calling me Cynthia?" Sin demanded. She knew that this was no way to make him come around to seeing her the way she wanted him to, but she couldn't help it. She wondered if this was how he felt when he got reminded of his leg. "I know you used to do it to annoy me, because you wanted to make it clear you thought it was a dumb name and being a dancer wasn't something you took seriously. But if things are different now, why do you keep calling me that?"

"Well," Alan said. "I mean, the Market people who knew you as a kid call you Thea. And they call you Cynthia at school, and Sin for a stage name. Cynthia has all those names in it. Why would I want to pick just one?"

Sin thought back to quite a few guys who had told her solemnly that they wanted to "get to know the real you". As if they deserved a prize for wanting one colour and not a kaleidoscope.

Of course, none of them had been as interesting as this liar.

"Okay, Clive," she murmured.

"I'm glad we have that sorted out, Bambi."

They reached Lydie's school in okay time, though Alan had to park on a bit of pavement broken up by the roots of a tree.

"So you're not normal," Sin said. "You want to take on crazy burdens, and you lie all the time, and you think you might not have a soul. You're terribly strange. And you thought going after normal girls would work out?"

The car was still, but Sin's side was tipped slightly towards Alan's. His voice was wary.

"What are you saying, Cynthia?"

"I'm saying, try someone terribly strange."

Alan glanced at her, and Sin moved as if that was her cue. She unwound from her car seat and towards him, her hand on his shoulder, his face tilted up to hers. His eyes were very wide.

"Try me," Sin suggested softly, and bent towards him.

Alan turned away an instant before their lips touched, and stared determinedly out of the window. "Cynthia," he said, "we've been through this."

She was frozen, hovering over him for a minute. Then she scrambled back to her own seat and stared out of her own window.

"Right," she said. The school doors were pushed open by the first rush of kids and Sin repeated herself, woodenly, as if there was a chance he hadn't heard her before. "Right."

Sin would have thought she'd be thankful for any distraction, but she wasn't feeling any significant gratitude about having to get out of the car after twenty minutes of waiting and collect Lydie from the infirmary.

"She had a headache," the nurse said. "She seems anxious about something."

Sin got into the back seat with Lydie for the drive home, which was a reprieve, and she and Alan put on a wonderful show for Lydie about their marvellous bookshop adventures all the way there.

Lydie was looking slightly more cheerful as they took the lift up, which meant that of course they could hear Toby screaming through the front door.

Sin put her shoulder to it and pushed it open as soon as Alan's key turned, running in and grabbing him from Mae's arms. Toby reached out insistent arms as soon as he saw her, twining round her neck like an octopus assassin who specialised in strangling his victims. He bawled a couple more times in her ear, hoarse barks like a seal, rubbing his snotty face on her neck.

"Oh thank God you're here," Mae said devoutly, collapsing against the wall. Her face was a brighter pink than her hair. "I hate kids. No, Toby, I don't mean it, please don't start crying again. They're fine from a distance. Lovely! I love them. From a distance."

"He just needs to be changed," Sin said, bearing him off to do just that.

Behind her, she heard Mae say faintly, "Oh my God."

When she came out, Toby balanced on her hip and regarding the world beyond her shoulder with a distrustful air, she heard Alan in the sitting room reproving Nick for not helping Mae.

"I tried," said Nick, who was stretched out on the sofa reading a magazine. He had found a shirt somewhere, Sin noticed. "He cried a lot more when I was in the room. I think babies are like animals. They can sense my demonic aura of evil."

"I want a demonic aura of evil," Mae muttered, still looking traumatised.

"Too bad, Mavis, it is all mine," Nick told her. "So I can't babysit."

"It would be irresponsible to leave you with Toby if you upset him," Alan said thoughtfully.

Nick gave him a brief smile. "That's why you're my favourite."

"But it would be irresponsible not to do something about this demonic aura of evil," Alan continued, still thoughtful. "I mean, as part of my ongoing quest to acclimatise you to human ways. I think I'm going to offer your services as a dog walker to the neighbourhood."

Nick looked up warily from his magazine.

"You know Mrs Mitchell doesn't like to leave the house, Nicholas," Alan said. "And she has those twin toy poodles. It would be a good deed."

"I can smite you," Nick grumbled. "Any time I like."

Mae and Alan were the ones who did the best research, so after a quick discussion, Nick and Sin went off to start dinner. It soon emerged that Nick was better at it, so Sin was delegated to chopping vegetables.

Which would have been fine if she hadn't been afraid of dropping the knife on her baby sister's head. Toby was settled happily, pretending to read with Alan, but Lydie stayed with Sin, clinging to her skirt. It reminded Sin of the way Lydie had been after Sin had come back from Mezentius House, once Mama was dead.

"Do you want to help me with the cooking?" she asked.

Lydie pressed her face against Sin's hip. "No," she said, muffled. "I'm fine here. I don't want to be any more trouble."

"Why is she scared now?" Nick asked, sounding bored. He was making white sauce for the lasagne.

"There could be *magicians* looking for me," Lydie told him in aggrieved tones.

"I'm a demon," said Nick. "You've heard about me, haven't you? How I can make someone's insides boil just by wanting it? Demons are supposed to be humanity's worst dreams come true."

"Nick," Sin said warningly.

"So you don't have to worry about magicians," Nick continued calmly. "They're not scary. Not compared to me. And if they come, I'll kill them all."

Sin made a meaningful gesture with her knife so Nick could see it. He shut up.

When Sin had to run to the bathroom for toilet paper to use as kitchen towels, though, Lydie did not follow her and trip her up. Instead she elected to stay in the kitchen. Sin heard her saying in an interested tone, "How many people have you killed?"

Kids.

She came back in time for the educational lecture about dumping bodies. Sin hoped she was not in for another talk with Lydie's teachers about her marvellous but disturbing imagination.

After dinner it was Mae who saved Sin from having to look at Alan. She suggested that Sin try on all the clothes she'd brought, in case some of them didn't fit.

Most of them fitted pretty well. Sin was vaguely surprised.

Mae, lying on her stomach with Lydie on Alan's bed playing fashion critics, with a book open and ignored before her, grinned. "They're mostly my mother's clothes," she said and her grin faded. "Annabel was skinny like you."

Sin smoothed her hands down a white tennis skirt.

"I have money now," she said. "Are you sure you want to—"

"Yes, of course, like I'm ever going to stop eating and fit into them," Mae said. "I want you to have them. They look good on you."

Sin looked at her brown eyes and wondered how rich you had to be, how sure the basics were always coming your way, before you felt comfortable giving without counting the cost and demanding a lot from the world.

Demanding a lot from the world could otherwise be thought of as ambition, which was a pretty desirable quality in a leader. Sin shoved the thought viciously aside.

No matter how far Sin might be from the Goblin Market, she wasn't going to surrender it to Mae in her head.

Sin pulled another garment out from Mae's bag and saw it was a deep blue silk robe with the price tag still attached.

"Mae!"

"I happened to see it when I was shoe shopping," Mae said. "It reminds me of the red robe you used to have. It's gorgeous, you're gorgeous, you should have it."

As if it was that easy.

"Thank you," Sin said, slipping it on. She climbed on to the bed as Lydie clambered off to investigate the bag.

Mae jostled Sin's bare leg with her jeans-clad one. "Think nothing of it."

"Is Merris back yet?" Sin asked, now their heads were close together and they could speak quietly.

She wished she could take it back as soon as she'd said it. Mae would have told her right away if Merris had returned. Sin knew better than this.

She just couldn't help wanting Merris to come home, in a desperate, pathetic way, as if everything would be okay, then. When she knew it wouldn't change anything.

"No," Mae said, and stared fixedly down at her open book. "This is about the enchantments laid on magical objects," she continued after a moment, surging ahead with resolution. "There's a chapter about breaking spells meant to be unbreakable. Like, for locks, or magical chains, or—"

"Jewellery," Sin said.

Mae smiled. "Yeah. Celeste Drake's pearls. The suggestions are to break the thing surrounding it. Like if a magic lock's on a treasure chest, stove in the top of the chest instead. Or if the magical object's locked on a person – you can kill them. It should come off, then."

Sin leaned her head against Mae's. "Ah."

"That works for me," Mae told her, voice hard. "It really does."

Sin kept her head by Mae's, speaking low and tracing the vein running along the inside of Mae's arm. "You should know," she said. "I don't want to take your revenge away from you. But I will. Getting that pearl could get me back into the Market. It could even get my sister accepted. If I get the chance to take it, I will."

"Then you have two good reasons to get it," Mae whispered in her ear. "But I have three."

They both had the Market to gain. Mae had a mother to avenge and Sin a sister to protect.

Mae's third reason came to Sin like a dark cloud on the horizon, changing the whole landscape into something dim and menacing.

Of course. Mae was carrying a demon's mark. She was being watched and controlled.

That pearl, the barrier to the power of demons, meant Mae's freedom.

"Why'd you ever take that mark?" Sin whispered back. "Did he make you?"

Mae stared at Sin. "How do you know?" she whispered.

Sin shrugged, her shoulder pushing against Mae's. "Nick told me."

"Did he?" Mae shut her dark eyes. "It was my idea. I wanted him to. I asked him to. I just wanted to do something. At the time, I was feeling helpless and I had to do something. If I did the wrong thing, it's up to me to fix it."

Sin raised her eyebrows, even though Mae could not see her do it. "*If* you did the wrong thing?"

"Another demon was coming for me," Mae said. "Anzu."

Sin's body was lying alongside Mae's, so there was no way for Sin to hide the sudden tension that ran all through her muscles. Mae opened her eyes.

"You know him?"

She remembered Anzu's smile today, as she had told him she did not think demons were lovable. She'd had a moment to collect herself, though, and that was long enough for her to be able to put on a show.

Sin twisted her hair round her finger and gave Mae a jaded smile. "Honey, I know them all."

"Then you know why, if any demon was going to have their mark on me," Mae said, "I wanted it to be Nick."

"You trust him?"

Mae hesitated and drew back to meet Sin's eyes, her gaze level and serious, to show how much she meant it. "I trust him."

"Well," Sin said, her hand still on Mae's arm, "that makes one of us."

"It doesn't matter, does it?" Mae asked. "No matter how I feel about him, nobody should have that kind of power over me. So I'm going to get the pearl, and nobody will have power over me again."

"So," Sin said, and rolled away from Mae, lying on her back and staring up at the ceiling. "Consider me warned."

Mae left. Sin stayed and watched Lydie play dressing-up for a while, making sure she seemed all right, and then she put her clothes back on and returned to the living room, where Mae and Alan were sitting on one sofa together. Sin looked away to see Nick lying on the other sofa, back to his magazine.

"You might help," Mae told him.

"I wish I could," Nick drawled. "But I find reading so challenging."

Mae directed her accusing glare at the magazine.

"I'm really just looking at the pictures," Nick said, and smirked. "They're very . . . absorbing."

Mae jumped up off her sofa and snatched the magazine from his hands. "Nick, there are children here!"

She spared a moment to actually look at the magazine. Sin was able to see the cover.

It was about cars.

Nick propped one elbow on the back of the sofa, pulling at his own hair. He gave Mae a slow smile.

"I know," he murmured, his voice a dark, conspiratorial whisper. "Scandalous."

Mae flushed slightly and hit Nick on the head with the magazine.

Sin gestured for Nick to get his legs off the sofa so she could sit down. He scowled and complied, sinking low against the sofa cushions with his magazine.

"Give me back my phone."

"Sorry," Sin said, forking it over. "Thanks for it. And thanks for letting us stay another night. We'll be out of your hair soon."

"It's fine," Nick muttered. "Alan's always bringing home strays to bother me."

Mae glared. "Hey."

"You annoy me less than you used to," Nick told her, and then after a pause, "Still quite a lot, though."

"I wish I could say the same," Mae said. "The annoyance just grows and grows."

"Toss me a book, Mae, I'll help," Sin offered, and Mae turned away from Nick and did so.

After wrestling with Elizabethan spelling for a while, Sin looked over at Nick. Lydie was sitting at his feet, staring intently. Nick was reading his magazine, apparently oblivious to his devoted suitor.

"You said demons are meant to be humanity's darkest dreams come true," Sin said.

"It's a theory. Alan tells me them," Nick said.

"But," Sin said, "don't you come from, you know, hell?"

"We're demons," Nick told her, glancing up from his magazine. "Not devils. I know exactly as much about hell or heaven or where I come from as you do."

"But demons don't die," Sin said. "So you'll never know anything else."

"No."

"If we go to a better place—"

"Then I can't follow any of you. I presume I go back to the demon world when this body dies," Nick said in a soft snarl. "But for now I'm here, and I don't want anywhere better. Here is fine."

He looked at the other sofa, then turned back restlessly to his magazine. Sin looked at him and felt almost shocked. It had never occurred to her that Nick could be happy.

Here in a tiny flat, getting white sauce on his leather wrist cuffs, lounging around reading a magazine with his brother and Mae close by. This was what the demon wanted.

Heart enough to make a home for a demon, Sin thought, her eyes straying to Alan again, and she hated herself for the abiding little ache of longing.

She was very flexible, so she could have kicked herself in the head with relative ease, but she doubted it would help.

That night Sin told stories to Toby and Lydie until they were asleep, and slept on the floor by their bed, borrowing a sofa cushion to use as a pillow. The next day Alan had to go to work and Nick had to go to school. Sin spent her time walking with Toby through Willesden, going through charity shops finding clothes for Lydie and Toby and even a uniform for herself, though it was two sizes too large. She bought the cheapest phone she could find.

She spent the afternoon checking out the prices of flats and the cost of day care. She had just enough for a deposit.

When Merris came back, she'd see that Sin had managed without her.

Alan called the house and offered to take a break from work to collect Lydie. Sin turned him down, but said it would be great if he could sit in the house and eat a sandwich or something while Toby took his nap.

"Then I can go and get Lydie myself," Sin finished.

"It's really no bother," Alan began.

"And I really want to do it myself," Sin said.

It hadn't been a bad day, Sin thought as she walked up the street to Lydie's school. She'd got a lot done.

She was a bit late, so she wasn't surprised to see Lydie already outside the school.

She was extremely surprised to see that Lydie was with a tall, dark boy. Every muscle she had went tense.

Then he turned, and she saw his profile.

It was that boy Seb, from the night of the attack. It was a magician.

Sin drew her knife and charged, hitting their linked hands so Seb's grip broke. Then she wheeled on him.

"Lydie," she ordered. "Run."

"Watch out," said Seb, hands lifting. Her knife was at his throat: she could kill him before he threw magic. She was almost sure.

He didn't try to throw magic. He wasn't looking at her.

He was looking over her shoulder, Sin realised, and she spun an instant too late to do anything but see Helen the magician, a burst of white light and then nothing at all.

10

The *Queen's Corsair*

S IN WOKE SLOWLY TO THE SENSATION OF A FLOOR LURCHING beneath her. She was grateful for the feeling. It warned her as she slowly returned to consciousness, and she did not have to open her eyes. She knew exactly where she was.

In the hands of the magicians.

Aboard their boat.

Sin did not allow herself to move, and tried not to let even her breathing change. There was a rug beneath her, soft and possibly fake fur, and both her wrists were secured with a chain. She tested them, easing her hands in tiny increments so it would look like the involuntary movements of sleep, trying to make sure the chains would not even clink.

She could move her hands with relative ease. But she couldn't get them out.

Her talisman was burning against her skin. Sin paid very little attention to that: in the lair of the magicians, of course there would be magic and demons.

There were other people breathing in the room, at least four people.

Having absorbed all that she could pretending to be unconscious, Sin opened her eyes.

She was lying on a fluffy white rug. The chains on her wrists were twined round a table leg, and the table leg was fastened to the floor.

There was no way to use that to escape, then, but she worked the chains further up the table leg so she could crouch rather than lie on the rug. She was able to manoeuvre her hands so they rested on the tabletop, in a futile pretence that she was not chained.

Her prison was a beautiful sitting room, decorated with antique chairs with fragile, golden legs, large, square mirrors and small, round windows. There were six magicians and one messenger in the room.

Lydie was not there.

Three of the four people sitting on the antique chairs, Sin knew. One was Gerald Lynch, the former leader of the Obsidian Circle, which had joined up with the Aventurine Circle a couple of months ago. He was looking at her when her gaze fell on him, his eyes grey and watchful, but almost as soon as their gazes met, he leaned back in his chair and his eyes looked lighter, blue and almost friendly, as if he bore her no ill will and had not a care in the world.

He did not look like a man who missed being in power, or resented his new leader. He looked relaxed, his sandy head tipped back and his legs crossed at the ankles. He looked utterly harmless.

Gerald put on a show better than any other magician Sin had ever seen.

On Gerald's right sat a grey-haired woman in a twinset and pearls. She looked like nothing so much as a very efficient secretary, death to improper filing personified. Sin didn't know her name.

On Gerald's left was Celeste Drake. The leader of the Aventurine Circle was small and fine-boned, a dove of a woman. Until you noticed her clear, cold eyes.

What Sin mostly noticed was the pearl, dull black in the white hollow of her throat.

The safeguard against demons, the leadership of the Goblin Market, was in the room with Sin, and there was no way on earth she could reach it.

Sin spared a glance for the other magicians: Helen was standing up against one wall, looking over at Sin. Their eyes met for a moment, and Sin could not read her expression.

Seb was standing against the other wall, his dark head bowed, and there was a boy at the far end of the room, curled up in a window seat. He was turning over an object in his hands, something that Sin could not quite make out but that kept catching the light.

And then there was the last person in the room, the person Sin had been trying not to see, the way she might avoid the eyes of someone she knew well in an audience, lest they catch her eye and she lose her nerve.

Phyllis, who had run the chimes stall since Sin was born, with her kind smile and her grey hair always getting tangled up with her earrings, who had such a fondness for Alan. Who knew where Lydie went to school.

Phyllis's hair was getting tangled with circle earrings with knives in them now.

Mae had been right.

There was a spy at the Goblin Market.

She flinched and looked at her hands when Sin looked at her. Sin looked away.

Her survey of the room complete, Sin looked back at Celeste. Celeste smiled at her, the smile sweet and as quickly gone as sugar dropped in hot water.

"Welcome aboard the *Queen's Corsair*, Cynthia Davies," she said. "I have good news. We're going to let you live."

"That is good news," said Sin. "Where's my sister?"

"And we're going to let you go free," Celeste continued. "Now you've been exiled from the Market, you're not a threat any more, are you?"

Sin smiled. "Unchain me and find out."

Celeste leaned forward in her chair. "You're not much of anything any more. But you did protect one of our own. We don't forget things like that."

"My sister isn't one of yours," Sin snarled. "Where is she?"

"We'll bring her to you in a moment," Celeste said. "And when we do, I want you to tell her that she will be staying with us. That this is the best place for her, the only place for her, and you don't want her to live with you any longer. Tell her she belongs with her own kind."

Over Celeste's shoulder Sin saw the boy, Seb, flinch. He didn't look at Celeste or at Sin, though. He just kept staring at the ground.

For her part, Sin kept staring at the pearl. She did not want to meet those cold eyes.

"We do not usually take in children so young, but considering how gifted she is and how terrible her circumstances are . . ." Celeste shrugged. "There is absolutely nothing you can give her, is there? Except this. Make the parting easy, and be sure she will be treated well. She's going to be a great magician. You should be proud."

Sin's lip curled. "Maybe she can start killing innocent people before she hits ten. Wouldn't that be something?"

"If you gave her up to the magicians," Phyllis said in a low, rapid voice, the voice of a woman making excuses, "then you could come back to the Market."

"Your concern for the Market is very touching," Sin murmured back.

"You should do as we ask for her sake," Celeste continued gently. "But if you don't see that, you should do it for your own. You should do it for your baby brother. What will happen to him if we kill you?"

Sin spared a moment to be deeply and terribly thankful that she had left Toby safe with Alan.

"I know what will happen to Lydie if I abandon her," she said. "I won't do it."

Celeste's hand twitched a little, a touch of pale magic glinting on the surface of her pearl. She did not lash out, though. She stood instead, straightening her skirt.

"You're not important enough to sit around arguing with, Cynthia," she told her, with a pitying smile. "You can have some time to think about how little this show of bravado will get you. When I come back, if you're still being stubborn, I'll give you to the demons. They took your mother, didn't they? Think about that."

She headed for the door, making a small gesture, more waving them forward than beckoning, for the others to follow her.

Phyllis was the first to leave, getting out of Sin's sight as fast as she could.

"You two stay and watch her, okay?" Gerald said. He crossed the room towards the boy in the window seat. "Okay?" he repeated gently.

He reached out a hand to touch the boy's shoulder; the boy drew away without looking at him.

Gerald reacted so smoothly it seemed like it hadn't happened, nodding as if he'd received confirmation of his orders and looking at Seb.

Seb nodded almost automatically, then glared at Gerald's back as Gerald went for the door.

Gerald didn't catch the look, but the grey-haired woman beside him did.

"He's not good for much else besides standing guard, is he?" she said, her voice cutting through the air. Seb's face turned, a red mark rising on his cheek as if she'd slapped him.

"Leave him be, Laura," Gerald advised as he and the woman – Laura – left the room.

Helen, the magician with the swords, lingered for a moment by the door. She didn't look undecided. She looked as if she'd never been anything but absolutely decisive in her life.

"I spoke up to save you, dancer," she said abruptly. "Don't make a fool of me."

Then she ducked out of the room. The boat lurched as she crossed the threshold, but she didn't falter for an instant.

Sin was left with the two magician boys. Which was better odds than she'd had before.

"Looks like it's you and me, Seb," she said, and lowered her voice just in case a pretty girl in distress might appeal to him. She could use that. "And you," she added to the boy in the window seat. "I don't think we've been introduced."

The boy turned away from the window.

All of Sin's breath was scythed out of her throat.

He unfolded from the window seat in a leisurely fashion, in slow, deliberate movements, and every movement sent a chill down Sin's spine, like a ghost drawing a cold finger along the small of her back. He was slight and not tall, but that didn't matter: it just made her think of elves as they were in the oldest stories, alien and terrible, child thieves and traitors. His eyes were silver coins, whatever colour they had once been drowned in shimmering magic, and his face was a perfect blank.

Sin's sense of dread built, as if the finger tracing her spine had become a claw. The thing between his palms, the thing he was turning over and over as if it was a familiar and favourite toy, was a gleaming-sharp knife. There were carvings on the hilt, and the blade looked too sharp to be real.

Worse than that, as he turned to face her head-on, she saw the demon's mark set along the sharp line of his jaw. It was a dark and wavering brand, an obscene shadow crawling on the boy's porcelain-pale skin.

"You don't remember me?" he asked. "I'm Jamie."

For a moment Sin could not accept it, her head filled with buzzing like far-off screaming. She did not want to accept it, that this was the sweet, forgettable boy she'd met at a barbecue, that this was Mae's only family, her beloved brother.

If Mae's brother could turn into this, what would they do to Lydie?

Whatever expression she had on her face at that moment, it made Jamie laugh softly. He came towards her, tossing the knife from hand to hand. The blade made a whining sound in the air, like a hungry dog.

"Ring any bells?"

"Sure," Sin said, and did not let herself strain against her bonds, did not try to scramble away, as he drew closer. "Your eyes used to be brown."

His eyes were shimmering and bright, pools of pure magic. They looked awful. He looked blind.

His mouth formed a crooked smile, something that might have been almost sweet without those eyes and that knife. All the other magicians looked so much more normal, Sin thought, the claw of horror raking up her spine again. What had he done to himself?

He sat at the other end of the table from her, still smiling. There was a tiny dimple on the cheek above the demon's mark.

"True," he said, and she almost couldn't remember what she had been talking about. He looked even more amused, as if he could read her mind. "I'm a whole new man."

Maybe he could read her mind. She couldn't know.

Jamie tossed his knife up into the air and then caught it again.

"Imagine your baby sister turning out like me."

"Oh, I am," Sin breathed.

"Then you should do the right thing," Jamie advised. "Think it over. It will all come clear."

The boat rolled. Sin's stomach was rolling, too, but she didn't think there was any connection. Jamie checked his watch.

"How long are the two of us expected to stay here watching a chained-up girl with no powers?" he asked in a bored voice.

The question brought Seb's bowed head up for the first time.

"I don't know," he answered. He seemed to be choosing his words with difficulty. "But I'm – I'm glad they did. I want to talk to you."

"I got that from all the knocking on and waiting outside my door," Jamie drawled. "Here is some information about me you may not know. When I want to talk to people? I give them subtle hints like opening the door."

He slid the blade on his knife closed and put it in his pocket. Then he slid closer down the table, towards Sin and away from Seb.

Even though Seb had had his head bowed and his eyes determinedly fixed on the floor while Celeste and Gerald were in the room, Sin had received the impression that he was terribly, guiltily aware of her the entire time.

Neither of the boys seemed aware of her now.

Seb was looking at Jamie, green eyes intense, like a man on a mission. Jamie just looked bored.

"I've been thinking a lot, since we came here," Seb went on. "Now that all the things that used to matter – school and stuff – they don't matter any more. Everything's changed."

"I know," Jamie said in a serious voice. "At school, you were the one with all the power, and you made my life miserable. And now I'm the one with the power, and you want to be friends. Isn't it funny how that works?"

"That's not it," Seb burst out, and bit his lip.

"That's not it? You don't want to be friends?"

Seb hesitated. Jamie laughed.

"It doesn't matter," he said. "I don't care about how tortured you are about killing or your pathetic lack of power or anything else going through your mind. You may have finally worked out what you want, but I don't care about that, either. Because I don't care about you."

Given Seb's rapt attention, drinking in those terrible white eyes, Sin could work out what he wanted, too.

So the beautiful prisoner-in-distress routine was unlikely to work, then. Just hell.

Careful not to let her chains rattle, Sin drew closer to Jamie.

"I know that," Seb said. "But—"

"Would you care for some advice?" Jamie asked, his voice full of mock pity. "There is a reason following someone around and drawing little pictures" – he sneered at the word, and Seb flushed a painful red – "is so very unappealing. You lose sight of the fact that the object you're viewing from afar is a person."

"I know you're a person!"

"You don't know anything about me. In fact, I sort of doubt you know anything."

"I know some things about you," Seb said. "I could get to know more. You could get to know me."

"Tempting!" Jamie exclaimed. "No, wait, that's not the word I mean. What's the opposite of that?"

Normally, it wouldn't have taken Sin so long to notice someone's body language. But there had been the knife to distract her, those awful eyes and the demon's mark.

Jamie's thin shoulders were hunched up, his fingers always on the curl towards fists. Every muscle he had looked tense.

"I realise I don't deserve a chance," Seb said. "But I wanted to say – I wanted you to know that I want one."

Jamie blinked, which was the first not entirely negative reaction he'd had. Sin was horrified witnessing the whole scene: she didn't want to think about magicians having painful crushes, or feeling anything. They were the enemy. She didn't want to see this.

She was grateful for how distracted they were, though. She could reach out and touch Jamie.

Seb looked away, obviously embarrassed, as if he hadn't meant to reveal that much desperation.

"Why should I care what you want?" Jamie asked eventually.

"Well, you and Gerald don't seem to be getting on so well lately," Seb said awkwardly. "I thought – you might want someone who would be on your side."

The way Jamie was standing changed in a way that might have meant there would have been a change in his eyes, if they had still looked like human eyes.

"What do you mean by that?" Jamie asked in a soft voice.

"Well," Seb said again, awkward and hopeless. "If you felt like I do – no, I don't mean that. I mean, if you're lonely here."

"And you were doing so well, too," Jamie said. "I don't care about being lonely. But you're right. I'm not getting along with Gerald. I don't like it when people tell me what to do, and the whole Aventurine Circle seems to have an opinion on how I should behave. I could use an ally."

Sin saw the wariness in Seb's eyes, but he took a step forward all the same.

"What do you mean by an ally?"

"I mean someone who will support everything I do," Jamie answered, with a faint, unpleasant smile, "and do everything I say."

Seb took another step forward. Jamie stood. The knife in his pocket, which Sin had just managed to get her hand on and draw out a few crucial inches, tumbled neatly into her palm.

Jamie didn't seem to notice. He reached out his hand and Seb hesitated, then jerkily offered his hand in return.

"Then it's settled," Jamie said, still smiling that smile. His fingers slid over the inside of Seb's wrist. Seb shivered, and Jamie's nasty smile spread. "Sweetheart."

There were steps outside the door. One was someone in heels, Sin thought. Seb jerked away at the sound, as if he'd been caught doing something indecent. Jamie didn't seem to care.

"Here it is," Celeste's voice said.

Sin couldn't see her, because she was standing behind Nick.

He stood at the door like death waiting to be invited in, all in black. It made his face look white as a skull.

"You're late," Jamie snapped. He clicked his fingers, and Nick walked slowly, reluctantly, forward over the tilting floor.

Sin realised this wasn't Nick's ordinary pallor. He was a demon in a human body: being trapped in a vessel over running water was like being slowly tortured for someone possessed. There was no way he would be here willingly.

He was here, though, and coming like a dog to heel.

When he reached Jamie, he went down in a crouch by the table. His eyes flickered over Sin, not even seeming to register her.

Jamie reached out and twisted the cord of Nick's talisman round his fingers. Sin saw the leather bite deep into the side of Nick's neck.

"Don't be late again," Jamie commanded softly. "Or I won't let you go back. Understand?"

Jamie's hold on the talisman forced Nick's head back, his face tilted up to Jamie's. The strange light of Jamie's eyes shone reflected in Nick's blank, black gaze.

Nick lowered his eyelids and nodded.

"Turns out when a demon marks a magician," Celeste said from the door, her voice rich with satisfaction, like a cat in the process of drinking the cream, "it doesn't give the demon any power over the magician at all. Rather the opposite, in fact. Isn't it marvellous?"

It couldn't be true, Sin thought. If Gerald had control over Nick already, he wouldn't have bothered torturing Alan.

"Marvellous for me," Jamie agreed, his tone as silky as hers. "Since he's mine, and I don't feel like letting the rest of the Circle enjoy any of his magic. I guess you shouldn't have killed my mother."

"Jamie, do we have to go through this again?" Celeste sounded impatient. "Helen has apologised. And she was only a human."

"I know, I know," Jamie drawled. "But it's the little things. Don't you agree?"

"Make sure it behaves at the party tonight," Celeste ordered. She turned on her heel and left.

Jamie let go of Nick's talisman and leaned back along the table, putting his weight on his hands behind him.

"You heard my fearless leader, Hnikarr," he said. "This party is going to be her little show of strength to the other Circles. I want you to stay in the ballroom like everyone else, so I can show you off. And I want you to be on your best behaviour. No more magically throwing people down the stairs. That is naughty."

"I understand," Nick grated out, as if he was having difficulty speaking at all, or as if he was too sick to talk much.

Sin felt sick, too, sick at the thought that this was how magicians treated their friends. She wanted to do something, to hurl the knife she had just stolen at Jamie's head, but she couldn't do a thing to help Nick, and if she tried, she would only make sure she couldn't help herself.

"Atta boy," Jamie said encouragingly. "That's what I like to hear. See how nice the world can be, when one of us is just the obedient slave of the other?"

Nick said nothing, but his lip curled in a soundless snarl.

Jamie smiled at him brightly, then got up. "Well, come on," he said. "We have to get ready for the party."

Nick uncoiled from the floor and rose, passing Jamie and making silently for the door. The boat lurched a little again, and Nick had to catch himself against the wall.

He had not acknowledged Sin's presence in any way.

"You coming?" Jamie asked Seb.

Seb was looking at the floor again, but when Jamie stopped in front of the other boy, Seb lifted his eyes slowly to Jamie's face.

"We're supposed to guard her."

"She's chained up," Jamie reminded him. He reached out and touched Seb's arm.

Sin couldn't see Jamie's face, but she could see Seb's. They could all hear the breath he drew in and could not let go.

"I thought," said Jamie, "you were going to do what I wanted from now on."

When Jamie left the room, Seb went after him.

Sin unclenched her fist round what she had been terrified for ten minutes one of them would see, or Jamie would miss. The magician's knife gleamed safe in her palm.

She handled it with care, and let out a deep sigh of relief as the blade cut through the chains attaching her to the table leg with as much ease as if they were string. Then she unwound the chain from round her wrists and the table and stretched it out on the floor. She chose her spot and cut the length of chain exactly in two.

Then she wrapped the ends of her two new chains round

both wrists, leaving them dangling so she could strike out in either direction at any time. She sheathed the blade and tucked it in her jeans pocket.

She was a dancer, so she made it to the door without more than the softest jangle of chains. She stepped outside to begin the hunt through the magicians' lair for her sister.

End the Party with a Bang

S IN WALKED THE CORRIDORS WITH A SOFT TREAD, TRYING TO MAP out the enemy's terrain. The boat had not looked this big from the outside. That might be magic, and it might just be perception.

Magic or not, it was a pretty fancy boat. There was nice furniture in every room Sin peeked into, smooth wood everywhere, sometimes bare, sometimes painted white. She would not have known she was on a boat if it had not been for the rocking on the water and the curves to the corners in the rooms. She went by a window once and saw the Thames, the buildings of London not so far away.

Far enough.

She went down two broad, shallow steps and saw glass doors leading into a vast, dim room. She didn't think a boat, however magically enhanced, could have more than one room like this one. It was clearly the ballroom.

She went inside. There were spindly white chairs arranged round the edges of the room, and when Sin looked up, she saw rafters. She went through another set of double doors, these ones wood instead of glass, and saw a smaller room with the same high ceiling. There was a long table set for dinner, lilies in tall vases hanging their heads above china and crystal glasses.

An alarm began ringing through the boat.

Sin moved fast but not too fast, keeping her walk smooth so the chains would not rattle. She went through the door on the other side of the dining room, up some narrow steps into a dark corridor. She stopped outside four doors and heard voices or movement, then at a fifth door she heard nothing.

She pushed open the door and found Seb with his head in his hands.

Seb jumped to his feet. He and Sin stood staring at each other.

"Get in here," Seb said in a level voice. "And shut the door."

Sin stepped inside and shut the door. His room was small, just a bed, a little wardrobe and a desk with a green sketchbook on it.

If Sin struck out with one of her chains now, it would be very hard for Seb to dodge. She was pretty sure she could knock him unconscious in less than two minutes.

"We could break the window," Seb said, locking his door with shaking hands. "And you could jump in the river."

"What would your new boyfriend think of you helping me escape?" Sin inquired.

Seb turned back to her, his mouth twisting. "He doesn't have to know."

"I'm not leaving my sister."

"They're not going to hurt her," Seb told her in a low, strained voice. "They're going to hurt you! I don't want to see anyone else hurt. You have to go."

"They're not going to hurt her?" Sin asked. "Like they haven't hurt you?"

Seb was silent.

"Do you have any family?"

Seb cleared his throat, a painful sound. "No."

"If you did have a family," Sin said, "if you had someone who loved you better than life, and who wanted more than anything to keep you safe, would you want to be left here?"

She heard steps coming down the corridor.

There was a wavering smile on Seb's face, an expression that he seemed to be wearing because he did not know how else to respond. "There's no one who loves me," he said. "Get in the wardrobe."

Sin climbed in, folding herself up small over a tangle of socks and shoes, and Seb shut the wardrobe doors firmly after her. She was in a tiny black box, the only light the yellow line where the wardrobe doors met. She could still see Seb.

He sat back down on the bed and put his head back down in his hands.

He wasn't a good actor at all. Sin could see his shoulders shaking, his whole body caught in a fine, continuous tremor. This wasn't a boy used to the extremities of life and death, even if he was a magician.

She tensed her legs for a spring, and drew the magic knife out of her pocket.

"Sebastian," Celeste's voice said sharply from the door. "The girl—"

She stopped. Seb looked up from his hands.

"I'm sorry," he said roughly. "What?"

There was silence. Then Sin heard a click of heels as Celeste walked over to Seb, and a flash of blonde hair and black skirt as she sat on the bed beside him.

"You shouldn't have left that room," she said.

"I'm sorry," Seb said again, very stiffly, and Sin began to think this might work. If he seemed terrified and guilty all the time, he didn't have to act. "It was – Jamie asked me if I wanted to talk."

"I see," Celeste said. "Sebastian, you're going to have to give that up."

Seb went deep red and traumatised-looking, as if someone had dipped him in tomato sauce and was about to continue with other strange forms of torture. Sin thought he might actually have forgotten he was hiding a fugitive in his wardrobe.

"I don't know what you're talking about," he muttered into his chest.

"We're very glad to have James in the Circle," Celeste said. "He's very talented, and I do hope he will become an asset to our side, but he's obviously extremely volatile. And I wouldn't describe him as a team player. It's not all about having the power, you know. It's about going the distance. I wasn't the most talented magician of my generation. But I cultivated relationships, and I did not burn out. Don't worry about your magic, Seb. Focus on your commitment to the Circle."

Sin wished Celeste was not being kind. She would have bet Seb didn't get a lot of that.

She didn't want to think about the chances of Seb deciding to commit to the Circle and open the wardrobe doors.

"James is a very troubled young man," Celeste said. "I hope he can learn to rein himself in, but I've seen a lot of gifted young magicians fall from grace. I wouldn't want to see you go down with him."

Seb still looked overcome with horror and shame at being spoken to like this, as if he could not deal with the fact that she knew, but he looked up at her last words.

"You don't know him. He's really good," Seb said. "He was always such a good guy. I was pretty awful to him. A bunch of us were, but it was my fault. He had the power to hit back at us, but he never did. That's what he's like."

The leader of the magicians put a hand on Seb's shoulder.

"And then he got tested," Celeste said. "And you see what he's like now. Maybe you'll be the special one in the end, Sebastian. I think you could be, but you have to try harder. You can't do things like leaving that girl unguarded.'"

And then she drew her hand away, giving him just a taste of approval with a promise of more later, if he could manage to deserve it. Sin saw Seb's eyes skid to his wardrobe, and she clutched her knife.

"I could guard the – the little girl," Seb volunteered hesitantly. "Where is she?"

"You can help us find the missing girl," Celeste told him, sounding annoyed. "The party's about to start, and I want everything in order."

"What if she's gone into the river?" Seb asked. "That's what I would have done."

Celeste stood up and moved out of view. After a moment, Seb rose to join her. Sin heard Celeste's voice, clear and cold, as their footsteps echoed down the corridor.

"Then you will have to think of another way to make up for your failure."

Sin did not dare move while the magicians searched the ship for her. If she ventured out, she was bound to betray herself.

Of course, staying where she was, she had plenty of time to think about how Seb might betray her.

She stayed put despite her doubts about how long his

courage would last and despite her longing to act. This was her best chance, and that meant it was Lydie's best chance, as well.

She counted the seconds as if she was doing exercises and had to hold herself in position, so her mind would not play tricks with time. She lost count a few times, but she knew she waited in the dark for well over an hour before the noises outside dulled and centralised, concentrated at a spot a little way away.

Sin assumed they were getting ready for their party. The question was, would they want Lydie there or not? Would a scared child be a trophy or an embarrassment?

She wished Alan were here, or Mae, someone who could make a plan.

The only thing Sin could think to do was go and look.

So she pushed the door cautiously open with her foot, gradually so it did not creak, listening for every sound. She slid out of the wardrobe like an eel, magic knife at the ready.

She missed her throwing knives so much.

The corridor was empty. Sin slipped along it and down the stairs, then waited with her hand hovering over the door, her other hand clasping the knife and her breath snared painfully in her throat.

There was no sound directly beyond the door. Sin just touched it with her palm, and the door slid open a little, then a little more.

Beyond the door was the dining room with no lights on, the dimness illuminated only by the glow of lights at the top of the far wall.

The ballroom and the dining room had obviously been one vast room recently transformed into two. The wall that divided them was built only so far. The large wooden rafters ran along the vaulted ceilings of both rooms without a break.

There was a supper laid out on the table now, tiny sandwiches in rows like soldiers and jellies gleaming like jewels. Sin eyed the chairs pushed neatly in under the table; their carved wooden backs looked sturdy enough.

Sin closed the blade on her knife and tucked it securely under the wire of her bra. She could not risk it falling out of a pocket.

She charged forward, taking a running leap at the chair and then launching herself from the top of the chair back, somersaulting into the air. Behind her the chair rocked on two legs before falling back on all four.

Her hair flipped into her face, air rushing round her but none in her lungs, every burning molecule of her aware that if she fell, the crash would bring the magicians in the next room running.

The backs of her knees hit the rafter. She latched on and swung like a pendulum until she could get a grip on it with her hands, then grasped the wood and pulled her weight up until she was lying flat against the rafter. She found herself breathing a little hard.

There was no time to be lying around, though. She turned, her body almost tipping off the slender beam and the world swimming crazily in her vision for a minute, until she was on her front. Then, face down, nose pressed hard against the wood and her fingertips lightly curved round the edges, she began to wriggle her way down the rafter into the other room.

Chandelier lights refracted in her vision, brilliant and blinding for a moment. Heat and noise rushed up towards her like a blow. Sin swallowed, closed her eyes and held on for a moment.

When she opened her eyes, she could see, though blurry yellow after-images danced in front of her, like the mocking stars round a concussed cartoon character's head. She began to slide slowly along the rafter again.

The scene below her was like a play seen from terrible seats, with hot, glaring spotlights in Sin's eyes and a riot of colour and activity below. For a moment the people below her looked like splashes of paint on a palette, all mingling together in a vivid blur.

Then the colours coalesced into shapes. She could make out the magicians of the Aventurine Circle. They were all, as far as she could see, wearing white. There was Helen, bright and straight as a blade in a white silk suit, and the woman called Laura in a simple white dress.

Celeste Drake, wrapped round and round in ivory gauze, was making the rounds with Gerald behind her. They nodded at and shook hands with everyone they saw, engaging them in brief rounds of conversation. They did it very well, Sin thought. One of them always managed to make the magician they were talking to laugh.

At no point did Celeste and Gerald ever touch. The first Market after Mama was dead and Sin was back from Mezentius House, Merris had taken her around and shown her to everyone as the heir apparent. Sin hadn't done half as well as Gerald was doing now, but the whole time Merris had kept her hand on Sin's arm, steady and sure, anchoring her.

Seb was leaning against a wall, shoulders hunched beneath his white T-shirt. He looked ready to run if someone spoke to him.

Sitting on one of the fragile chairs as if it was a throne was Jamie, surveying the company with the scorn of a spoiled young prince and the eyes of a mad soothsayer. His gleaming white clothes matched that bright, opaline gaze. The only dark things about him were the demon's mark crawling on his jaw and the demon crouching at his feet.

Nick was in position to spring for throats, and looked as if he would have liked to. He was wearing the battered black clothes he'd been wearing earlier, but the effect was good, like the black pearl at Celeste's white throat.

Sin had to admire Celeste's showmanship. The Aventurine Circle stood out radiantly against all the other magicians, an army with a weapon in plain sight.

Their weapon, the Rottweiler at the spoiled young prince's feet, was glaring people away. Jamie was the only magician who did not have to make nice with the members of other Circles.

Occasionally he grabbed a handful of Nick's black hair and yanked his head back to address a few words to him. Sin saw the strained line of Nick's throat and the curl of his mouth when his head went back. He never answered Jamie.

They sat alone until the door of the ballroom opened and Mae walked in.

She was in white, too, a shimmering dress tight as a bandage with her shoulders rising bare from the wrapped material, and wavering slightly in some of the highest heels Sin had ever seen. They seemed to be made entirely of glass and silver threads.

Mae pulled it off the same way she pulled off her pink hair, brushed now into shining perfection, looking ridiculous, appealing and dignified all at once.

Mae's faith in herself was as towering as those heels, and so she could walk into a nest of magicians not even able to run.

Oh, you brave, dumb tourist, Sin said to her silently.

Now she had two girls to get out of here.

When Mae reached Jamie, she went and stood by the side of his chair like a sentinel.

Sin's fingers bit into the edge of the rafter, splinters sinking into her skin. Mae couldn't fake much. She certainly wasn't faking this, the way even her face bent towards Jamie's was loving, her neck a protective arch above him.

What if it was real? Sin thought with a sickening lurch. It felt for a moment like she was going to fall off the rafter, even though she hadn't moved. What if she'd left the Market, no matter how temporarily, in the hands of a traitor?

Mae loved Jamie, she could see that much. If it was Lydie, so affected and addicted by magic, Sin didn't know what she would do.

She couldn't even really think about it. When she tried, the idea turned into a nightmare, a black cloud she could not hold on to or deal with but that diffused itself around her mind and made everything dark.

People approached Jamie, then; they approached him through Mae. Mae smiled and shook hands, held brief conversations. She was acting in a way Sin could only describe as sophisticated.

Sin guessed it was a trick Mae had learned from her mother or a formidable headmistress or someone else in her rich world. She wished she could learn how to do it, and doubted she could pull it off. The best acts needed conviction behind them.

After yet another person had left, Jamie leaned back further in his chair and said something to Mae. Mae hesitated for a moment, then slowly left Jamie's side, one hand clinging to the chair back, as if it was the only thing keeping her afloat and it was being inexorably drawn out of her reach.

She clenched her hand into a fist when she finally let go, and offered her other hand to Nick. Nick glanced up at her and then stood, very slowly.

Once he was standing he loomed over Mae, tall, dark and sinister like a villain in a pantomime about to crush an innocent, but he seemed like a villain who had forgotten his cue. He just stood there, and his complete lack of action looked almost like helplessness.

Mae stuck her hand out further, persistently. When Nick turned his own hand palm up, moving as slowly as if he was a robot with rusting joints, Mae laid her fingers across his palm. He used her hand to draw her body in close against his.

Moving gradually into the centre of the room, they started to dance. Mae's skyscraper heels at least made her closer to Nick's height than she usually was, so she could meet his eyes comfortably.

Sin couldn't see either of their faces, but there was a solemn atmosphere about the moment, the song playing fainter than any of the other songs before. Nick's hand was at Mae's gleaming white waist, and her hand was gripping the shoulder of his black T-shirt.

The assembled magicians were staring.

Jamie stopped slouching and got up, slipping easily through the crowd.

Sin decided it was about time for her to go as well. There were a lot of people here, but none of them was Lydie.

She squirmed slowly back along the rafter, creeping backwards rather than forward. She had a moment where she misjudged, not seeing where she was going, and found her leg sticking out into space. She pulled it back slowly, re-anchoring herself and refusing to panic, then risked a glance down.

Apparently none of the magicians had been looking up just then.

Reaching the other room was such a relief, the dimness and relative quiet like being submerged in cool water after the hot lights and having to watch dozens of people act out a hundred strange scenes. Sin let her eyes shut for just a moment, and breathed out.

When she opened her eyes, she saw someone moving in the darkness below.

Adrenaline chased chills up her spine, straightening it and preparing her for action. The person below was wearing a long garment with a hood. She couldn't tell if they were male or female, but Sin could get the jump on them, and that was all that mattered.

Then she caught the movement beneath the cloak, the very slight giveaway.

Sin let go of the rafter and stretched out an arm, wrapping just enough of the chain round her wrist round the rafter. She launched herself into space, the chain reaching its limit and her feet hitting the chair back at the same time so the impact was shared.

Sin unwound her chain carefully and leaped lightly on to the ground. She barely made a sound, only a very faint jingle, like faraway bells.

He turned.

"What are you doing here, Alan?" Sin asked softly.

Alan pushed the hood back, curly hair ruffled and looking almost black in the dim lights.

"Rescuing you?" he suggested with a small, wry smile.

"I appreciate the thought," Sin said, smiling back.

"I'm lying," Alan told her.

Sin raised her eyebrows. "I'm shocked."

"I came to bring you these," said Alan. He drew out two

long knives, one in each hand. "I know candy and flowers are traditional, but . . ."

"I'll call them candy and flowers," Sin said. She took one in her right hand; it was a beautiful weight. "This one's Candy."

"Nick sent me a text message saying they've got Lydie in a cabin away from the main living quarters, the first door across the deck."

"Nick," Sin said, tensing. "Alan, do you know—"

Over Alan's shoulder she saw a flicker of movement, and the magician at the door, backing away. There was no time to think, so she didn't. She already had the knife in her hand.

Sin threw. The magician caught her knife in the throat and crumpled.

She and Alan went towards the door and stood together at the foot of the stairs. Sin bent and pulled her new knife out of the body. Alan picked the end of his cloak up from the floor and offered it to her. Sin accepted the swathe of material and cleaned the blade carefully.

"Nice cloak. Where'd you get it?"

"There was a magician in this stylish thing," Alan said. "And now he's in the river. I imagine he could use some company."

Sin nodded. "You dump the body. I'll get Lydie."

"Meet you on the deck?"

He stood in the doorway, regarding the body with serious attention. He spoke casually, his mind obviously already on getting rid of the magician, trusting her to do her part.

She knew where Lydie was. She couldn't wait to go and get her.

She did pause for a moment before she headed up the stairs. She rested her hands against Alan's shoulders, met his eyes steadily and kissed him on the cheek.

"Thanks for coming," she said.

Then she ran up the stairs to find her sister.

Sin just kept going up, chasing through corridors and up stairs, until she opened a door and found herself on the deck. The wash of cool night air was sweet on her face, the lights of the city bright against the deep, dark blue of the sky.

Across the deck a door swung open. Jamie emerged, holding Lydie's hand. Lydie was stumbling and obviously scared, her fair hair tossing in the wind.

Sin threw one of her knives at Jamie. The magician lifted his free hand and the knife went clattering on to the deck, as if some invisible fist had struck it down in midflight.

Jamie thrust Lydie in front of himself. His unearthly eyes blazed over her little sister's head.

Sin did not throw her other knife. She advanced on Jamie, shaking the chain out from round her right wrist. The end of the chain hit the deck with a rattle.

"Wait," Jamie said.

"No," Sin told him, and lunged. The chain spun through the air and Jamie dodged backward: it only caught him a glancing blow on the head.

Jamie gasped aloud, the sound trembling with pain, and Sin whirled to hit him again before he could retaliate.

The invisible hand of magic caught her chain and held it suspended in mid-air, like a curtain between them.

"Stop," Jamie said, his voice still shaky. "Now."

Sin was very close. She could duck under the hanging chain and stab him. She moved fast enough that she was pretty sure his magic wouldn't stop her in time.

But he'd used his magic to stop the chain, not hit out at her.

"Why should I?" she snapped.

"I fought for the Market once."

"And now you're part of the Aventurine Circle, and you treat one of our allies like a dog."

Jamie flinched at the reference to Nick, and Sin followed up on that advantage.

"He told me you were his friend," she said, moving forward. He stepped back, but she saw his fingers tighten on Lydie's shoulder, and that only made her more furious. "And you're using him as a power source."

"What else do you want me to do?"

"Uh," Sin suggested, "*not* use him?"

"I haven't taken the Aventurine Circle sigil, which lets you get the stored power from their circle of stones. Gerald has a new mark that allows all the magicians to exchange power between them, and I haven't taken that, either. Using Nick was absolutely the only way I could avoid taking the marks. Having him, and more power than anyone else, is the only reason they let me stay."

"And why do you want to stay?" Sin inquired.

Jamie looked down at Lydie's head. "To help."

"Forgive me if I think you might have another motive," Sin said. "I can see you're brimful of magic right now. Everyone at the Market knows how magicians kill more, the longer they're in a circle. The appetite grows by what it feeds on – the craving gets worse and worse. If you were safe, if the circles were gone, would you give up all the magic the demon gives you? Could you give it up?"

Jamie kept looking at Lydie, and not into Sin's eyes, but he did answer her.

Low and soft, he said: "No."

At least he sounded ashamed.

"So you'd rather enslave a friend than give up power," said Sin. "And you expect me to believe you want to help?"

"I came and sat down beside you with a magic knife in the pocket nearest to you," Jamie said. "Either I want to help you, or I'm kind of dumb."

Sin hesitated. "I don't know you that well. You could be all kinds of dumb. What I know for sure about you is that you're a magician. Power runs through your veins, more essential than blood. You can't tell me you could give it up."

"No," Jamie answered, his voice stronger this time. "I can't."

"Nick trusted you, and you're using him," Sin said. "Maybe you hate the other magicians. But power obviously comes first with you. So I can't trust you."

"That's true," Jamie said. "But you can pick up your knife. I hope you will take that as the goodwill gesture it is, and not the chance to chop my head off, which . . . it also is."

Sin walked across the deck to her other knife. She scooped it up in one movement and wheeled back round to Jamie.

With both knives in her hands she felt calm again, the sound of them slicing air like a lullaby in the dark. She held her arms crossed, poised to kill anything that hurt her family.

She allowed herself to look at Lydie.

Lydie was being brave, taking short, panting breaths but not crying. She stared at Sin silently, her eyes huge, and Sin nodded at her and saw she was being held quite gently, and quite far away from Jamie. As if she was a peace offering, and not a shield.

Sin tucked one of her knives into the belt of her jeans, so she had one hand free.

"I'll give you your magic knife for my sister."

"Done," said Jamie. He took his hands off Lydie's shoulders and flung them up to catch the knife Sin hurled, at the same second Lydie threw herself at Sin.

Sin checked Lydie's rush and pushed her sister behind her. "Stay calm," she said. "I've got you."

She kept her gaze steady on Jamie, who was holding the knife tight in one hand without opening it.

"Thank you," Jamie said. "It's my lucky charm. I don't mean that in a serial killer way."

"You have a lucky knife, but you don't mean that in a serial killer way?"

"That's right," said Jamie, with a little smile. "I'm harmless, I promise."

She didn't believe he was harmless for a second.

Since she had got to know Alan better, she had been thinking about different sorts of acts.

This boy, with his hunched-in shoulders, his flood of so many words it was hard to pay attention to any of them, he was camouflaging himself.

Since he'd been living a normal life while secretly a magician up until a couple of months ago, camouflaging himself must be second nature to him.

"Whose side are you on?" Sin asked directly.

"My own," Jamie said. "And my sister's. I promised her I would help you."

"And how do you intend to help me?"

Jamie grinned at her. "Like this," he said, and made a sweeping gesture.

The whole boat rocked with the wave that went shuddering through the river.

"Jamie, you might want to think about taking it down a

notch," Alan said. Sin saw him from the corner of her eye, gripping the door frame so he didn't fall down.

"Everyone's a critic," Jamie muttered. He repeated the gesture, this time in miniature.

The river moved, nudging the boat gently but inexorably towards one of the riverside walls. There was a flight of shallow, slimy stone steps set in the wall. They were the most beautiful things Sin had ever seen.

Jamie's forehead was creased with concentration, his hands moving in short, careful gestures as if he was embroidering some priceless silk.

The boat edged forward, and forward, and then finally reached the steps. There was a small crunching sound as the boat rocked against them.

"I'll hold it," Jamie said. "You can go."

Sin ran forward to the rail of the deck, Lydie's feet pounding beside hers. She heard Alan limping after them.

She heard Celeste Drake's voice from the doorway Alan had just left.

"Leaving so soon?"

Sin spun and threw her knife. Or she meant to. It did not even leave her hand, staying rigidly in place as if she had stuck it in a block of ice rather than throwing it through the air.

There were three men behind Celeste, Sin saw, and then recounted. There was one man she didn't know, and there was Seb, who might or might not be on Celeste's side, and shoving viciously past them both was Nick.

"Come here," Jamie commanded, beckoning.

"I am *trying*," Nick snarled, and the magician Sin didn't know went for Nick with his hands full of black light.

"Hey!" said Jamie, and made a gesture that sent the man reeling back a step. Nick closed in on him hungrily.

Celeste snapped a look over at Seb, who shrank back, then at Sin with her knives and Alan with his gun out. She had both her hands raised, palm up. On anyone but a magician, the gesture would have looked like surrender.

On a magician, it was a threat.

"Go ahead," Celeste said. "Shoot me. Stab me. If you're both quite sure I won't have time to hit that child before you do."

Sin did not look away from Celeste's hands. She could not afford to.

Now they had turned, Lydie was in front of her, pressing with the urgency of terror against her legs. Sin saw Celeste's eyes narrow, measuring the distance between them.

In a far-off way, she noted the sounds of Jamie and Nick fighting the magician. There was the sound of a sky turning savage above them, a grumble rising too fast into a snarl.

Nobody could use magic in the Aventurine Circle's territory but them. Except that Jamie was part of the Circle, and Nick was Jamie's.

Despite this, Sin knew that Celeste, and the man fighting Nick and Jamie, were both wearing the magician's mark Gerald had invented, the one that let magicians channel the power of all the magicians in their Circle who wore the mark. And Celeste would have been formidable on her own.

Sin felt Alan tense beside her. They both knew a shot was their best chance, but if Celeste was enchanted to withstand a shot, there would not be any other chances.

There was a short, sharp crack.

Celeste staggered forward. Sin seized the moment to grab

Lydie and shove her over the side, on to the steps. Lydie's hand closed on the chain round Sin's wrist for a moment, clinging.

"Lydie, go!" Sin yelled, and twisted back round.

In the doorway stood Mae, holding a gun in both hands. She was wavering slightly in her high, high heels.

Celeste Drake had not been enchanted to withstand gunshots.

She lay sprawled on the deck. The gauze of her long dress fluttered in the rising wind, a pure white shroud with a dark red stain marring it at the centre.

The storm rose so fast it was like an eclipse. For a moment Sin could not see, but she stumbled forward anyway, fumbling in the dark. She went down on her hands and knees on the deck where she guessed Celeste's body lay.

Lightning flashed. Mae was looking down at Sin, her face all shadows and pallor, as if she instead of Celeste had died and become a ghost.

Sin's gaze dropped to Celeste, to the hollow of her throat where the falling rain had already begun to pool. Her throat was bare. The pearl was gone.

Mae had won, then.

"C'mon," Nick said, his own opponent dead behind him. He gave Mae a solid push, and she almost stumbled and fell on to Celeste's body. Nick dragged her past Sin and Celeste to the side of the boat, then let go of her so he could help Alan over.

Mae tried to climb over after him by herself and started cursing.

"Stupid dress, stupid shoes—"

"*You're* stupid," said Nick, and scooped her up bodily in his arms. He held her over the rail and Alan grabbed her hands and pulled her on to the steps to safety. "Now you," Nick said.

Jamie leaned against the ship rail. "No."

"Oh my God, you're both stupid," Nick snarled. "Do you want to die? Because if you stay, you will."

Alan limped to the top of the steps as fast as he could and Sin saw Lydie, a tiny figure against the dark-torn sky, come rushing to him.

That was what snapped Sin out of her paralysis. Too late.

She had scarcely uncurled from beside Celeste's body when they all heard, clear even accompanied by the sound of the storm, a lot of footsteps coming up the steps.

Jamie's eyes met his sister's. For a moment Sin thought that would be it, that they would all just run.

"We'll see," said Jamie, and lifted his hand.

The boat was torn away from the side of the wall as if Jamie had ripped a piece of paper off a notebook. Sin made an enraged sound, Mae and Alan and her sister suddenly just black dots almost disappearing against the grey sky, almost entirely lost to her.

"Don't—," she began, advancing on Jamie, and he spun towards her with his eyes blazing white.

Blackness blasted her vision as she was knocked off her feet and across the deck, rolling and hitting the other side of the boat. The door opened. There was a shallow shelf on this side of the boat, with rope coiled upon it. Sin rolled under it.

She would be half-hidden by its shadow. Unless someone looked too closely.

As a dozen magicians burst on the scene, though, it was clear that at least for now all their attention was focused on Celeste's body.

The sword-wielding magician called Helen went down on

her knees beside Celeste. It gave Sin a strange feeling to watch the woman touch Celeste's hair, as pale a blonde as her own. She wondered if they had been related, sharing that as well as a Circle.

Some of the magicians looked truly grief-stricken and horrified. There were others, not just magicians but messengers, among whom Sin spotted Phyllis, who simply looked scared.

Gerald stood at Celeste's feet, his head bowed and his hands clasped for a moment. When he looked up, Sin could read nothing on his face.

"Jamie," he said, his voice as unruffled as his expression, mild and calm. "Perhaps you can explain this to me?"

"The Market people came for the girl and her sister. We were attacked and overpowered," Jamie said flatly.

The storm had quieted into a dark muttering in the sky, which seemed muffled by the blanket of clouds that made the whole world dim. The glow of Jamie's magic gaze seemed like the only light in the world, and that light was a terrible one.

"Perhaps you can explain this to me in some way I might believe," Gerald suggested, his voice even softer than before.

"It happened like I said," Jamie insisted. "They came. And Celeste died."

"And you, with the demon's power, you couldn't do a thing to stop it?"

Gerald almost smiled.

Jamie said, "Maybe I could have."

That shocked Gerald, Sin noticed, sending a jolt through him that seeing Celeste dead hadn't. Now Jamie was the only one who looked calm, standing on the deck with a ring of people around him whose murmurs were turning louder and fiercer than the dying storm.

"She let my mother die," Jamie continued. "She wasn't my leader. You are."

"Is that so?" Gerald asked. "And how am I supposed to trust you, if you would stand aside and let one of our own die?"

The sky was so thickly overcast, everyone's skin looked grey. Gerald took a step forward.

He loomed over Jamie, his shadow falling over Jamie's face and quenching the glittering light of his eyes. The boat lurched on the river, and Sin felt cold hit her skin. She twisted round and saw trails of dark water snaking across the rail, over her own body, towards where Gerald stood.

"Where's Celeste's pearl?"

"I don't know," Jamie whispered.

"You let a fellow magician be killed. You let the symbol of the Aventurine Circle be stolen. You realise that I should execute you."

Four glistening black lines of river water crawled their way up Gerald's trouser leg, trailing from his shoulder to his right hand. The water wrapped round Gerald's fingers, which he lifted to Jamie's face.

"I could drown you in an inch of water," Gerald said.

Threads of water touched Jamie's face, sealing his mouth like a transparent gag. He glanced around for support, and then water criss-crossed behind his neck and held him in place.

"He isn't lying," Seb said. "Everything happened just like he said. He couldn't have saved Celeste. Neither of us knows where the pearl went."

Nick stepped up behind Jamie, and the water dissolved into silver smoke.

Gerald's hand stayed uplifted, wreathed in the smoke.

"It was a risk, taking you into the Circle at all," he said. "Now a magician is dead. Give me a reason to trust you."

When Jamie spoke, he was gasping for breath a little, his face wet as if he had been crying.

"We were friends once, weren't we?"

A flicker crossed Gerald's face, like the flicker of lightning behind dark clouds, not illuminating or changing anything.

"I thought so," he said, and he sounded a little sorry.

"Doesn't that mean anything?"

Gerald shook his head regretfully. "Not enough, Jamie."

"Well," Jamie said, "it means something to me. I don't want to leave the Circle, and I don't want to fight you. So how about I make you an offer?"

"What's the offer?"

"What means most to you, Gerald," Jamie murmured. "Power. What if I offer you my demon?"

Nick was suddenly the centre of attention.

The storm was dying away, but there was rain falling now. Nick had his arms crossed over his chest, shoulders bunched defensively under the wet material of his shirt.

"Jamie," he said, in a tight voice, "I'd prefer it if you didn't."

"Nick," Jamie said, "I really am sorry."

Gerald, alone of the magicians, was still looking at Jamie. "You mean it?"

"Forgive me for Celeste," Jamie said. "Trust me again. And we have a deal."

"Jamie!" Nick snarled.

Jamie rubbed a shaking hand across his wet, pale face. "I'm sorry," he said. "But you're not like me. What is it that they say, that demons are made of fire and humans are made of earth? Magicians are made of need. We're born human and we become something else, like earth turning into sand without rain. We become something that needs power. You can't understand, because you're not like me. But they are."

His brilliantly shining gaze cut through the murk, swinging from Nick back to Gerald.

"I want you to give him your mark."

Nick strode forward and Sin was certain, almost certain, that he was about to commit violence rather than obey anyone. Gerald glanced at Jamie and either decided to trust him or decided he could not pass up the opportunity to have the power obviously flooding through Jamie's body.

He held firm, hand still uplifted, but making no move to halt Nick's rush.

Nick stopped and grabbed Gerald's arm. His teeth were bared in a snarl. Sin had seldom seen expressions marked clearly on Nick's face, but this one was clear. He badly wanted to kill Gerald.

He wrenched up Gerald's arm and pressed his mouth against the inside of his wrist.

Gerald convulsed, making a thin, agonised sound that made Sin think that Nick had ripped open the veins of Gerald's wrist with his teeth. She could only see the bow of Gerald's back, arched taut in pain, and Nick's blank, black eyes over Gerald's wrist.

When Nick let go of Gerald, the magician fell to his knees. The other magicians were drawing back from him, a murmur of distress and unease rising. Only one moved forward: Seb, coming to stand at Jamie's shoulder.

Jamie looked at Seb, looked at Gerald kneeling on the ship deck and smiled.

Sin's last moment of hope died as she saw Gerald climb to

his feet and meet Jamie's gaze with his own eyes turned fierce silver, brimming with magic.

He raised his hand and a bolt of lightning sliced through the sky, wrapping round the silver ring on his finger and shimmering with contained light.

"I think the Aventurine Circle can learn to follow this symbol instead," he said, his voice echoing, trembling on the point of laughter.

The magicians in white all knelt even as he spoke, and Gerald turned to Nick.

"Hnikarr," he said. "I have a little test for you."

"The power isn't enough?" Nick snapped.

"Nothing's ever enough," Gerald told him. "Kill her."

Sin flattened her body against the deck as if she could escape being seen, and then realised that it had not been her Gerald was speaking of at all.

He was pointing at Phyllis.

She stood there in a growing circle of space as magicians and messengers alike scattered away from her. She looked suddenly very alone, her shoulders bent more than usual under the burden of fear.

"This woman's worthless as a spy," Gerald said. "She might have handed us a magician, but her first loyalty is to the Goblin Market. Now she finally has a use. I want to see you kill her on my orders."

Phyllis had handed over Lydie to the Aventurine Circle.

But she had done it to get Sin back to the Goblin Market. Sin had known Phyllis all her life.

Nick had known Phyllis since he was five years old.

Sin had thought that no magician could have so complete a dominion over a demon, had thought that some of it at least must be Nick choosing to ally himself with Jamie, had thought she didn't know what in order to prevent herself being overcome by despair and fear.

Despair and fear came just the same, crashing through all the fragile barriers Sin could put in their way.

She could not see Phyllis's face, only Nick's, and it told her nothing.

"Do it slowly," said Gerald.

Nick lifted a hand, and Phyllis started to cry.

He did it slowly.

When it was done, Phyllis was a crumpled heap on the deck. Sin's bones were aching from being curled up so tight on the slick, wet boards, the freezing press of her knives imprinted on her palms. The magicians had gone in to celebrate further, Gerald and Jamie walking in brilliant-eyed accord, Seb close by Jamie's side. The only things left on deck besides Sin were the demon and the dead.

Nick watched as Sin rolled out from her hiding place beneath the shelf. He did not speak to her.

She did not know what to say to him, who had been made the Aventurine Circle's slave, who had been betrayed by his friend, who had just killed someone without pity or flinching. There was blood in Phyllis's bedraggled grey hair, but none on Nick's hands.

They just waited together as the boat drifted slowly to the side of the river, until they reached the steps up to the street.

As they left the *Queen's Corsair*, rain was still falling, through the darkness, into Celeste Drake's open eyes.

12

Look on the Tempests

TOBY AND LYDIE WERE SLEEPING BY THE TIME NICK AND SIN GOT back. Sin lay down on the bed for a while with her arms wrapped tight round Lydie, just the same.

Then she got into the shower. Her wrists were sore from the weight of the chains, and the muscles in her back were screaming. Being drenched in cold water after performing acrobatics hadn't been particularly good for them.

The shower had amazing water pressure, though, and the hot points of water drummed relief into her skin. She emerged feeling a little better, drying off and leaving her hair a damp knot at the back of her neck. She slipped into the blue robe Mae had bought her, the silk cool against her heated skin, and was grateful for that little comfort.

When she entered the living room, she saw Nick must have told them already. There was a pall hanging over the whole group. Alan looked white and strained, so close to ill Sin wondered if it was bad for his leg to be out in the rain. She didn't know, and she didn't know how to ask.

Mae was shivering, her naked shoulders covered in gooseflesh, in long, continuous shudders, as if she had not stopped shaking since they came inside.

Nick was at the window, watching them both.

"I don't think you quite realise what you've done," Alan was saying to Mae as Sin paused on the threshold.

"I did something I had to do," Mae told him, lifting her chin. "I'll take the consequences."

"Like you took the gun?" Alan inquired. "And I don't need to ask who gave it to you. Do you remember when Gerald's first leader was alive, someone he didn't like any more than he liked Celeste? I came in shooting, and the magicians panicked. Gerald didn't panic. He didn't create light, either, didn't try to calm anyone down or offer advice. He lay down on the floor and let things happen until Arthur was dead, just as he wanted. All the members of Gerald's original Circle were enchanted to withstand gunfire. He knew you had a grudge, he gave you a weapon that couldn't harm anybody who was on his side and he did the same thing he's done before. He let things happen until Celeste was dead, until everything was just as he wanted. You gave him just what he wanted."

"You think I don't know that? He gave me just what I wanted," Mae told Alan fiercely. "He gave me a clear shot at Celeste. I took it. I'm not sorry. I wanted revenge, and I wanted to hurt the Circle. I did, even if Gerald doesn't realise it yet. The Market can't depend on its leader any more; well, neither can our enemies. We're on equal ground again."

Alan put his hand up to his forehead, trying to press worry lines away. "And you didn't think of mentioning any of this reasoning to us? You didn't think that taking a gun from Gerald Lynch was worth a mention?"

"A funny thing happens when you don't trust people with your plans, Alan," Mae said distantly. "They don't trust you with theirs, either. If you came to me for help, I would do anything I could to help you. If it came down to it, I would die for you. But I have absolutely no obligation to be honest with you. We both know that."

"Yeah," Alan said, sounding quieter suddenly, even though his voice had not been loud before. "We do. I'm sorry, Mae."

"You just wanted to make sure I knew what I was doing," Mae said dryly. "Well, I mostly sort of do. Trust me."

Alan said, "I try."

He got up from the sofa, moving awkwardly enough that Sin could see how tired he was. Of course, he would have been the one to put the children to bed when they got home.

She slipped silently backwards into the shadows, letting him go to his bedroom without having to deal with yet another person he felt he was duty bound to help out.

When the door of Alan's bedroom swung gently shut, Sin stepped back into the living room.

Mae and Nick both had their backs to her. Mae had turned her chair slightly, and Nick had come to sit at the foot of her chair, as she'd seen Nick sit at the foot of Jamie's and Alan's. It seemed to be a thing with him.

"I'd ask how you're feeling," Nick said. "Except I'm scared you might tell me. And terrified you might cry."

"I'm not going to cry."

"I'm overcome with relief."

Mae took off her chandelier earrings, which she placed in a glittering heap on the arm of her chair. She kicked off her high heels and curled up in the chair, as if Nick's cool voice was a comfort to her, as if she could relax now.

So nobody was going to be making any plans tonight. Like Sin, nobody had the faintest idea what to do next, and everyone was tired.

"I'm okay," Mae told Nick. "I didn't like doing it. I thought maybe I would, this time, but I'm never going to like doing it. And that's sort of a relief. Because if I hated it, even this time when I thought I wanted revenge, I'm always going to hate it. And that will make me look for other ways to get things done."

"The killing way usually works for me," said Nick.

"Because it's the easy way," Mae said. "And it gets easier every time you do it, which is the scariest part. I'm not going to plan an assassination again. But I felt like this had to be done. I learned from it, and I wanted it to be me who did it."

Nick did not respond, which Sin personally would not have found consoling at all.

"Do you remember," Mae asked, "what you said to me, the first time I killed someone?"

"Ah, the sweet, rose-coloured memories of our youth," Nick drawled. "Good times, good times."

Mae snickered. There was another long silence.

"Well done," Nick said eventually.

Mae leaned her head back against her chair. "Thanks."

Well, whatever worked for Mae. Sin went to lie down and hold her sister for a little longer. She had Lydie back safe. That was the only bright spot of her night so far.

Nick's bed was not made for three. Sin, balanced on the edge and determined not to disturb Lydie or Toby, couldn't manage more than an uneasy doze that was broken by hearing voices in the hall. Specifically, Alan's voice.

"Where are you going, Nick?"

"My new master gave a whistle," Nick answered curtly.

Sin got up quietly and walked to the door, opening it in time to see Alan's stricken face.

Mae grabbed Nick's wrist, and Sin noticed that Mae looked pretty stricken as well.

Sin thought for a bitter moment that Mae didn't need to be so very upset, not when she'd got her revenge, got the pearl and thus got the Market, not when Alan thought she was so perfect.

"Take care of Jamie. No matter what he's done. Please."

"Do I have a choice?" Nick asked. "Personally, I was considering tipping him over the side of the boat and hoping there was a lost shark in the water below."

"Nick, swear to me."

Nick backed away from the stark, desperate emotion on Mae's face. She didn't let go of his wrist, though, keeping her gaze fixed on him as if she could hypnotise him into doing her will through sheer persistence.

"I swear," Nick said abruptly, and Mae let go.

Nick went for the door and slammed it after him.

Mae's determinedly set shoulders slumped a little. "I'd better get home. Can I borrow a jacket? I left my coat with the magicians."

"Sure," Alan said gently, and ushered her into his room, presumably to select one.

The door slamming had made too much noise. Sin spun at the sound of stirring from the bed and saw Lydie, her hair rumpled and her eyes unfocused.

"Hey, baby girl," Sin whispered, going over to the bed and sitting on the edge so she could ease Lydie back against the pillows. "Hey."

"Sin," Lydie murmured. "I'm sorry."

Sin tucked Lydie's hair behind her ear. "None of this was your fault."

"None of it was your fault, either," Lydie whispered back.

"Yeah, I know," Sin said, and kept stroking her hair. She spoke clearly, so Lydie would understand, so that she would know Sin could never resent her for any of this. "And I'm not sorry. Here we are together, right? I'm not sorry about anything. It could've been much worse."

A hot drink was in order, Sin thought once Lydie was asleep again. She went into the kitchen and found Alan sitting at the table. The only illumination the room offered was the moon shining through the skylight.

"Coffee?" she asked.

He glanced up at her and smiled. It was a really lousy effort. "Yeah."

Sin turned on the kettle and occupied herself getting cups and going on an epic teaspoon quest. For once Alan seemed to have nothing to say, no enthusiastic digression about books or questions about her feelings.

Sin had no idea what to say, either. She made the coffee, the chiming of the teaspoon in their cups the only sound in that dark kitchen.

"Here," she said, offering the cup over his shoulder.

This time when he glanced up at her, he didn't even try to smile. He looked so lost that Sin moved instinctively, putting his cup down on the table and touching his hair.

Alan went very still, as if he was stunned that anyone might reach out and comfort him. Then he shuddered, a fraction of the tension going out of his shoulders, and pressed his face hard against the inside of her wrist.

It lasted for only a moment, and then he lifted his head, pulling away. Sin turned to the counter and picked up her own cup of coffee.

She was making for the door when she heard the sound of the chair being pushed back.

"Cynthia," Alan said.

Apparently Sin was a glutton for punishment, because she turned round. They stood together, Alan leaning against the kitchen wall, and Sin might really have to speak to someone about these masochistic urges, because she found herself taking the one step closer necessary to touch him.

Alan put his arm round her neck immediately, drawing her in. Sin put her head down, resting her forehead against his collarbone to avoid any further acts of madness. He smelled familiar and comforting, like steel and gun oil. He stroked her knotted hair.

"I was really worried about you," Alan whispered in her ear.

Sin was startled enough to look up. It was a terrible mistake. Alan was very close, glasses catching glints of silver in the moonlight, eyes troubled behind them. It would be easy to pull his head down an inch closer.

"Yeah?" Sin asked roughly.

She held her body taut. She could control it: she was a dancer. She wasn't going to shake, and she was not going to make a fool of herself again.

Alan's hand stroking her hair went still. His fingers curled round the nape of her neck. He closed his eyes and kissed her.

At the first touch of his mouth Sin dropped her coffee cup, hearing it break and not caring, and slid both her arms round his neck. He kissed her and kissed her again, mouth warm, curls sliding through her fingers, body pressed against hers. She kept losing track of her hands, but she knew where his were, one at the small of her back keeping her close. She was so happy, warm all at once and filled with delight, and he kissed her soft and deep and slow, then pressed a light kiss on the side of her smile.

They stumbled into the kitchen table.

"Oh my God, are you all right?" Sin asked, breaking the kiss. Alan nodded, and Sin slid on to the table to eliminate that problem and drew him back by her grip on his shirt. "Thank God for that," she murmured, and kissed him again.

"Wait," Alan said, and tried to step back.

This proved impossible when Sin did not let go of his shirt.

Alan looked down at her and said, "I'm sorry."

"That's all right," Sin said patiently. "I think I can be persuaded to forgive you if you come back here right now."

"No," Alan told her. "I'm sorry. I'm – I'm really sorry. I apologise. That was very wrong of me."

"What? Why?" Sin demanded.

Alan gestured at her. It was usually something she liked, seeing him talk with his hands, but right now she could think of about a hundred things she'd rather he be doing with his hands.

"I realise after tonight you probably think you owe me even more than you did before, but I've tried to explain to you that it's not like that. I don't want you to do anything because you owe me. I also realise that I just sent you rather a mixed message and as I've said, I apologise. I'm disgusted with myself. I shouldn't have done it, I shouldn't even have been tempted, and I'm so terribly – I'm so sorry."

"Wait, *what*?" Sin asked. "You think this is about owing you? My God, that's insulting. I'm a Market girl. You don't think I know better than to keep making the same offer over and over again?"

Alan seemed at a loss for words. Sin felt delighted and calm. So that was why, then. She looked up at him, looking so worried and trying to do the right thing. His hair was ruffled crazily.

"And here I thought you were supposed to be so smart," Sin said. She tugged him down sharply; he wasn't actively resisting any more, so she managed it. Then she let go of his shirt and laid her palms on either side of his face, smiling up at him. "Fool," she whispered. "I love you."

Alan jerked back. Sin was left with empty hands.

His body had actually recoiled, as if she'd shot him. His chest was rising and falling hard.

"What is it now?" Sin asked, and heard her voice waver. She almost hated him for doing this to her again, for being able to make her so happy and taking it away. "You don't have to say it back, you know. I realise the idea is new to you. Just – turn it over in your mind. See what you think."

His mouth curled into a sneer, too much like an expression that belonged on Nick's face, and Sin thought, *Raised with a demon*. She felt hollow inside.

"See what I think?" Alan repeated, his voice cold. "I think it's ridiculous!"

Sin pulled her robe tighter at her throat. "Okay," she said. "I think I'm done here."

"About when did this great romance start?" Alan inquired. "Was all that looking as if you wanted to be sick every time you saw me walk some sort of clever cover? What do I have to do to get you to stop, smash my kneecap with a hammer? I bet that would do it."

"I wouldn't bother," Sin said. "I thought we were past this.

Do I have to remind you that until five minutes ago you assumed I'd throw myself at someone a hundred times as if I was merchandise that could be used to settle a debt?"

"You were the one who leaned in to kiss me and told me how very grateful you were in the same breath," Alan said. He had the absolute gall to look distraught, as if it was his heart being thrown aside as if it was rubbish. "Tell me, what else was I supposed to think?"

She had said that. She tried to put herself back into that skin, only a few weeks ago, tried to feel what she had felt before her heart had changed.

"I wasn't offering love, then," she said, and he flinched at the word. "I don't offer that as payment for anything. But that doesn't matter. You've already made up your mind about me. What you want is someone like Mae to love you, someone normal and white and perfect. You see me as something the real people come and watch as if they're at the zoo, and the idea of me having feelings is ridiculous!"

"Yes," said Alan. "The idea of you having feelings for me is ridiculous."

They stood staring at each other across a moonlit foot of space, both of them standing in shadows and the square of light under the skylight between them.

So there it was, the truth laid out between two liars at last. He thought she was too shallow to love anyone. He'd kissed her because he thought so little of her, thought she was a toy. He was just like everyone else: he believed the role.

"Something else you always thought about me was that I was stupid," Sin said at last, her voice shaking. "Well, you were right. I can't believe how stupid I've just been."

It was cowardly to use the kids as a shield, but just for that moment she didn't care. She ran into the room where they were sleeping and curled up by their bed, burying her face in the sofa cushion she'd slept on the night before so she could cry into it and be sure no one would hear.

In the morning Alan was gone. Sin couldn't spend time worrying whether he had just gone to work early or if this meant she should clear out before he came back. She had to get Toby to his new day care, and Lydie and herself to school.

The Tube had delays on the Northern Line, and that meant once she had delivered the kids she was late for school. She got off at her station hurrying, her hair floating in a static mass around her head from the shoving fight she'd had through the crowded carriage.

She was really not in the mood to meet Mae outside.

Mae's hair was shining and straight. Her T-shirt reading I'M NO MODEL LADY – I'M THE REAL THING, unlike Sin's charity shop uniform, fitted her perfectly. And Sin was tired of trying to be above all that.

"What do you want now?"

Mae recoiled at her tone. "I was just wondering when you were coming back to the Market," she said frostily.

"What?" Sin asked. "Are you graciously inclined to allow me back in? Might want to deal with being a tourist leading the Market before you make any rash decisions."

"What?" Mae asked. "Wait."

Sin didn't have time to wait, but she stopped in the middle of the street all the same, the early-morning traffic of London buzzing all around them, and watched Mae's brown eyes go wide.

"Sin," Mae asked carefully, "do you have Celeste's pearl? Because I don't."

"I saw you—" Sin began, and remembered how dark it had been, in the storm. She'd seen Mae so close, and seen Celeste's throat bare. She'd just assumed.

Mae nodded. "I thought you had it. And obviously, you thought I did."

Mae's subdued manner the night before suddenly made more sense.

She still looked subdued, actually, and hurt on top of that.

"Would you hate me?" she asked suddenly. "If I had it?"

Sin looked her over, shining hair to expensive sneakers, and back to her eyes. "Yeah," she said, and then smiled. "But not for that long."

Mae's dimple flashed out in return. "Good to know. Not that either of us is likely to get the pearl any time soon."

"You sound like you think you know where it is," Sin said slowly.

"Who was the one person on that deck we can't trust?" Mae asked. "I don't want to think it – but it would make sense for Seb to take the pearl. He could use it as proof he's on the magicians' side if his loyalty is called into question. He'd be able to show he kept the pearl safe."

Sin thought about Jamie the magician, who had put Nick in the Circle's hands, who looked as if he had pearls for eyes. She thought of Nick the demon, and Alan the liar. Alan who worked for his own agenda, and did not care how cruel he might be.

Who was the one person on that deck we can't trust?

She wasn't sure it was that simple. But Mae's argument did make sense.

"Could be," she said finally. "I'm late for school."

If Mae was right, even if she wasn't, the pearl was as far out of their reach as it had ever been. Exactly as far, if it was with a magician, aboard a boat.

Neither of them had an invitation there now. Mae becoming a messenger, consorting with the magicians, firing that gun – it hadn't got her the pearl. Sin could be sorry for her.

She wasn't sorry that Mae wasn't leader yet.

Sin didn't have a terribly convincing cover story worked out. She mumbled about a family emergency and wished she'd thought to call the school earlier. The headmistress had given both her hair and her baggy uniform a look that nicely combined disapproval, distaste and disbelief.

It was Sin's own fault. She was all off balance, and her performance was substandard at best. She got through it somehow and went to class.

They were studying a book about a woman who was all angsty about her husband's dead wife. So far Sin liked the dead wife best, though because she was a girl and the most interesting character, Sin had dark suspicions she might turn out to be evil.

She did not air her suspicions. She kept her head down, hoping questions about the Gothic tradition would not hit it.

She needed to pay attention and catch up, but she could not keep her mind off the question of the pearl. If Mae was right and Seb had it, the person with the best chance of getting it from him was Mae's brother. Sin had to act first.

She tried to think of anything she could possibly do, and tried not to think of anything else.

There was a knock at the classroom door. Sin jolted out of her reverie so hard she almost knocked her book off the desk; only her fast reflexes saved it.

Ms Black walked over to the door and opened it.

"Hello," said Alan, and as soon as that gentle, courteous voice hit Sin's ear, she hurt her neck looking round. Alan was wearing a suit jacket and had his hands clasped, a particularly solemn and responsible look on his face. He seemed older somehow. "I'm a social worker the hospital assigned to the Davies family?"

"Oh," said Ms Black, and shot a quick, guilty look at Sin.

"You heard about the incident?" Alan asked, as if quietly grateful to have a fellow adult who understood the situation and could sympathise with him. "I'm sorry to disrupt your class—"

"Oh, no," Ms Black said. "Not at all."

Alan gave her a grave smile. "I'm afraid I must ask if I can take Cynthia Davies away from her studies. There are some forms at the hospital that require her signature. Routine, of course, but without them . . ."

"I understand completely," Ms Black said.

Sin shoved all her books into her new bag at once and was rising to her feet before Alan murmured, "Thank you."

There was a little park a few streets away from Toby's day care. Sin told Alan to drive there. They could talk, and she would be close enough to get Toby even if the talk went wrong.

They didn't speak much on the way. Sin leaned her forehead against the car window and hushed feelings of excitement trying to clamour within her. She'd been happy too soon last night.

The park was basically a bit of grass and trees fenced around, but at this time of day it was deserted, and that was good enough. They sat on a rise of grass between trees and a path. Alan was a little awkward sitting down. Sin forced herself to watch and keep her face impassive.

When they were sitting down, Alan turned to her. "I'm sorry for being such a jerk."

They were not touching, and Sin lowered her head so she wasn't looking at him. "Okay."

"I'm really sorry," Alan said. "I can't – I can barely believe I acted that way. I've thought about someone saying that to me for years. I had it planned out in my head. Which is pathetic, I know. It went a hundred different ways."

Sin bowed her head. "It was just never me saying it."

"Well – no," Alan said.

Sin laughed past an obstruction in her throat. "Oh, keep going," she said. "You're doing *so* well."

"I never imagined you," Alan said quietly. "My imagination's not that good. I never thought that was possible. Even when I started to want it."

Sin raised her head. "Just so you know? First time you've made that clear."

"Right," Alan said. He looked pale, and Sin realised she could finally, tentatively, start to be happy again. "I'm really messing this up, then."

"Yes," Sin told him.

"I'm not very good at human emotions," Alan said. "I know that's creepy. I have an aunt and cousins, and a few months ago I tried to get back in touch with them. I thought we could have a blissful family reunion, and it didn't – it didn't quite work out that way. I keep thinking of human love as something from the picture books my mother used to read to me, something fixed in pastel colours. Something sure."

"Something perfect?" Sin asked. "Like Mae?"

Alan looked startled. "But I told you how it was with Mae. I told you I lied to her, and I couldn't make myself stop, and I couldn't make myself be sorry enough."

"Here is a tip for you about romance," Sin said. "If you tell a girl another girl is perfect, that's the bit the first girl tends to focus on. Also, telling a girl another girl is perfect is really dumb."

"Thank you," Alan said. "I need all the help I can get." He paused. "Also, Mae is not perfect."

Sin looked up at him from under her eyelashes. "And me?"

"I don't lie to you," Alan said. "I lie *with* you."

Sin stopped looking up at him from under her eyelashes and burst out laughing.

Alan went red. "So I've just realised how that came out. Uh."

Sin laughed and laughed. She had to cover her face with her hand and laugh into her palm, leaning into Alan a little.

"Oh, Alan Ryves," she said. "You're such a fantastic liar. You are the smoothest con man of them all. Who could resist that silver tongue?"

Alan laughed and leaned closer, his shoulder solid and warm against hers. "I was all set to grovel," he told her. "But now I've lost my concentration." He paused. "I really am sorry," he continued softly. "I might be messed up, but I shouldn't have taken it out on you. I want – I want to be as good to you as I know how."

"I'd like that," Sin said, in a low voice. "I want to be good to you as well. Your leg—"

Alan flinched so that their shoulders were no longer touching. "You don't have to say anything about it. You were right, things have changed. I was wrong to bring it up."

"No," Sin said. "You were wrong to bring it up like that, but all the things we were yelling about are big. They matter. So I want to say: it's a big deal, but it's not a bad thing. And it's not ever going to be a deal breaker."

She took a deep breath and stared at her knees, her legs swimming in the grey flannel skirt. She wanted the conversation to be over. She wanted to be as good to him as she knew how. But she'd had enough of misunderstandings.

"Do you see any deal breakers for you here?" she asked. "In the long term? Because I was thinking about – the long term."

She looked up at Alan, lifting her chin and being the princess of the Market, not afraid to look anyone in the eyes. Alan had gone still.

Then, slowly, he smiled. It was like the smile he'd given her at the Goblin Market, the time she'd thrown him the fever blossom. It was better this time: it was just the two of them, and the knowledge that all the parts they played would be seen through.

"I don't have deal breakers," Alan said. "I look on tempests, and am never shaken."

"Shakespeare?"

His eyes brightened. "You know the poem?"

"No," said Sin. "I know your quoting voice."

"Oh," Alan murmured. He leaned forward. Sin leaned forward, too.

She smiled at him, their faces so close he probably couldn't see the smile. "I'm not like other girls," she whispered, and she thought he could hear the smile in her voice. "You can't just have me for a Shakespeare quotation. I thought you were meant to be a charming devil."

"It's true," Alan said. "I am quite the wordsmith."

"So?" Sin slid his glasses off and threw them gently on to the grass, and then leaned closer.

"There are so many reasons I want to be with you," Alan said. "But I know the most important one."

She leaned her forehead against his. "Yeah?"

"You being brave and beautiful and smart is nice, obviously," Alan said thoughtfully. "But it's not important. Not compared to the future we have together in a life of crime."

"You make a good point."

"Conning people out of their savings," Alan said. "Forgery. Blackmail. Selling property on Mars. We could have it all. You with me, Bambi?"

Sin pushed him back on the grass and leaned over him, her hair falling on each side of his face. The whole world was small and quiet, the sun filtering through her hair in gold and red.

"Clive, I was with you from 'I'm a social worker'."

She laughed down at him. He rose on one elbow and caught her mouth and kissed her, slow and warm as sunshine, and Sin could be happy. Nobody was going to take this away.

When they left the park to pick up Toby, Alan held her hand. Sin could move with any partner, and she focused so she did not outmatch his step. An elderly lady with a terrier gave them a second look, because they were obviously together. Sin just smiled at her, and after a moment, the old woman smiled back. They passed on.

Alan charmed the day-care supervisor, of course. Sin rolled her eyes at him behind the supervisor's back.

"I'm naturally charming," he told her in the car. "I can't help that."

"I don't have your way with words," Sin said. "So I'm just going to go with a quick response. Ha!"

Both times they got out of the car, when they stopped for Lydie and when they got home, Alan reached for her hand. Sin rested against his side despite the difficulty of balancing Toby and measuring her step with Alan's: she liked being there. The contact made everything seem real.

It also made things clear to Nick and Mae, who were both in the flat. Mae's eyebrows went up, and then she grinned.

Nick's eyes narrowed.

Neither of them said anything, because Mae was occasionally tactful and Nick was always Nick. Sin changed into a T-shirt and jeans, Alan made dinner and everyone discussed how to get the pearl back.

"I'll kill Seb and take it from his body," Nick suggested.

"Your plan is always killing, Nicholas," Alan said. "It worries me. I want you to have many goals. What if he didn't take it?"

Nick shrugged.

"What if he did take it, and hid it?" Alan pursued.

"What are you going to do with the pearl, if you do get it from Seb?" Sin asked, on an impulse.

Nick looked at her steadily. "I'm going to give it to Mae."

So there was yet another way for Mae to win. Sin met Nick's eyes and wondered if he was bothered by the new development of her and Alan, or if this was just Nick being himself. It was hard to differentiate between Nick being deliberately offensive and his everyday personality.

She did think there was something tense about the line of his shoulders that wasn't usual.

"I don't want to win because you just hand the prize to me," Mae said, outraged.

"Fine," Nick said. "Then I see only one fair way for you to settle this. You girls will have to wrestle."

Mae and Sin glanced at each other. Sin grinned. "Fine by me. I'd win."

"I don't know," Nick drawled. "She's tiny, but she's bad-tempered. Plus, she comes up with strategies. I suggest one that involves oil."

"Thank you, Nick. If you insist on being no help at all, you can do it quietly," Mae told him.

"I think you're very helpful, Nick," Lydie put in worshipfully.

Mae smirked and turned back to the map of the boat she'd sketched out with a little input from all of them, and which she had accidentally got a bit of ketchup on.

Sin had caught Mae's look of doubt at Alan when the leadership of the Market came up. She'd also noticed that Alan didn't say anything.

There was no way to tell from the map where someone might choose to hide a pearl, and no way for Nick to go back right now. Gerald had told Jamie to get rid of him. The Aventurine Circle was in upheaval, and the last thing they needed around was a demon.

Until they had another use for him. Until they had someone else to kill.

That didn't stop everyone from talking about it until Toby was passed out with his head on the table, and Sin had to get up and put him and Lydie to bed. It took a few stories to get Lydie down, and when she came out into the hall she saw through the open door Mae sitting on the sofa watching TV and Nick sharpening knives at the window. The was no Alan in sight.

Which meant Alan was probably alone in his room. Sin figured he might want some company.

"So, Alan and Sin," Nick said.

On the other hand, Alan probably had a book. He could wait for just a little while. Sin drew closer to the door.

Mae lifted the remote and clicked off the television, easing backwards with one arm along the sofa back and her head tilted to look at Nick from a new angle.

"What about them? How are you feeling?"

"You know I don't like it when you ask me such personal questions, Mavis," Nick said. "Be a lady."

Mae made an unladylike gesture. Nick had his head bent over the whetstone and knife in his hands, his hair falling in his eyes, but he must have caught the gesture reflected in the glass of the window. He gave a half smile.

"Does it bother you?" Mae asked.

"Bother me?" Nick repeated slowly, as if he was speaking in a foreign language. Sin supposed he always was. "I didn't expect it," he said finally. "And I usually do expect that kind of thing. It's strange. If she's using my brother, I'll make her sorry."

"Sin wouldn't do something like that," Mae said.

"Is Sin really your big concern?" Nick inquired. "What about Alan? I always thought you two would – I thought he liked you."

"Not enough," Mae answered softly. "And I didn't like him enough, either. We've both known that for a while. The only one who kept insisting that it was going to happen was you."

Nick did not look up from sharpening his knife, and this time he didn't smile, either.

"Because you wanted to give me to Alan as a reward or something equally horrible," Mae said.

"Maybe I thought you'd be a good reward."

There was a long pause.

"This is me staring at you in disbelief," Mae said eventually. "Just so you know."

"Don't talk to me about what I know. You know about how humans feel about each other. Alan knows better than I do, anyway. I get that I don't know. I *know* that I don't know. I wanted something good for both of you. I wanted you to be happy."

"Well, you got it wrong," Mae said, her voice growing more gentle. "But that's pretty normal for humans, too."

"Everyone in this world does seem to spend all their time getting it wrong." Nick stopped and tested the sharpness of the knife with his thumb. "Everyone in my world, too."

"We get things right in this world," Mae said. "Every now and then. You get things right."

"Every now and then," Nick responded, almost under his breath. He laid the whetstone down on the windowsill. "Why would Alan go for Sin?" he asked, and outrage spiked hot in Sin's chest. She wanted to fly into the room and hit Nick until he was bloody, until she realised exactly how furious and bewildered Nick sounded. "Alan doesn't even like new people."

Sin couldn't see Mae's face, but she saw her hand clench on the sofa cushions, in a movement that looked partly like frustration and partly like prayer, as if she was imploring the sofa gods for patience.

"Sin's hardly a new person."

"It's new for her to be this *close*," Nick argued.

"You don't think Alan likes people to be close? He obviously likes Sin to be close. And Alan likes new people just fine," she told Nick. "He liked me and Jamie from the first minute, and he'd known us a few days when he let us move in. He wants people to be close. The minute you found out he had other family, he dragged you off to Durham and tried to bond with people he barely knew."

Nick stood up. His face was not quite as expressionless as usual; there was a hard edge to his mouth, of anger or just possibly distress.

"What are you saying about Alan?" he demanded. "That he wants people to be close too much? Is Sin going to hurt him?"

"I trust Sin. And I'm not saying anything about Alan. I'm talking about you, and this thing you do."

Nick took a step toward, the sofa, not as if he wanted to be closer to Mae but as if he was advancing on her.

"What do you mean?"

"I remember reading your father's diary," Mae said. "I remember how you said that Alan didn't like being left alone, when what you meant was that you didn't want to leave him. It's okay if new people upset you, if you're wary about them getting close to you or your brother. Don't shove what makes you uncomfortable on to Alan. They're your feelings, and once you admit that, you can deal with them."

Nick was still for a moment, considering.

Then he said, "All right."

Sin could not see Mae blink, but she knew body language. The way Mae's head was suddenly held, frozen for a fraction of a second, meant that Sin would have bet a week's rent that a blink had happened.

Apparently the demon was not always this amenable during his lessons about emotions. Colour Sin shocked.

"I remember things too," Nick said. "I remember when you and Jamie were living with us, when Alan had a demon's mark and I wasn't talking to him."

236

"You were so unhappy." Mae did not sound as if she was reminiscing, but as if she was giving Nick information.

Nick came a few steps closer, no longer advancing like an enemy, but prowling forward just the same.

"Once I woke up and Alan was screaming from the dreams demons were sending him. I went to him, but you were already there. Do you remember that?"

"Not really," Mae answered. "I tried to do whatever I could."

"You were comforting him, and I thought – I thought that after his mark was taken off, he wouldn't want to go to Durham. I thought he would want to stay with you. But he didn't want to. He went back to the people he thought could be his family, the people he was surer of."

Nick reached the sofa, going on one knee in the sofa cushions, one hand on the sofa back where Mae's arm lay. He was arched over her, his back a curve, hair in his eyes and his eyes utterly intent.

"So tell me, Mavis," he murmured. "Who wanted to be with you?"

He reached out and touched her face, turning it towards his. Mae turned her face up to his, the ceiling lights touching her profile with gold. For a moment Sin thought, *Good for them*, and that maybe tonight, for just this one night, everyone in this little home could be happy.

Before their lips met, Mae turned her face away.

"Nick," she said in a low voice. "Don't."

Nick went tense all over. The bow of his back, with his face bent towards Mae, suddenly looked a great deal more sinister. "Why not?"

Mae tilted her face up again, this time defiantly. She did not move out of Nick's shadow. "Leaving aside the fact that I actually do have more pride than to let you say, 'Oh, well, I might as well have her' the moment it seems like Alan doesn't want me after all, as if I have no choice in the matter, as if I'd put up with being passed around like a parcel—"

"That isn't how it is," Nick snarled. "Just because I was trying not to stand in the way—"

"Leaving that aside," Mae said, powering on determinedly over Nick's voice until he shut up, "there's the mark. And that makes the idea that I have no choice in the matter far too close to the truth."

Nick glared down at her. "You asked me to put that mark on you!"

"I know I did," Mae said, her tone level.

"Don't lie to me." Nick's voice was suddenly loud, suddenly so angry that it struck Sin it went right through being an order and crashed into becoming a plea. "You wanted me before the mark. I know you did."

"I know I did, too," Mae said again, in just the same way, and then her voice went softer. "But feelings change."

Nick stared down at her, eyes boring into her face. "No," he murmured, his voice low and sure. "You still want me."

"What does it matter?" Mae asked bleakly. "I don't know how my feelings would have changed without the mark. I trust you not to use the mark against me deliberately, but we don't know how much the mark affects me without either of us knowing it. We do know it makes me want to please you, to do what you want. I can't risk becoming some sort of satellite to you. I don't want to lose bits of myself. I want you, but I don't want to be yours. I want to be mine. And what about you? What do you want?"

Nick drew his hand away from her face as if her skin had burned him. "I don't understand."

"Sure you do," Mae said. "You can't just reach out and snag the parcel as it goes by. This is the human world, and I'm a human. I know that you're not one. But I need you to say something to me. I need to know."

"What use is it?" Nick demanded. "Since apparently I'm being punished for doing what you wanted."

Mae launched herself up from the sofa. Nick had to stand up in a hurry, or she would have head-butted him in the face. He swung away from the sofa, looking like a caged animal about to start pacing, and Mae crossed her arms over her chest. There was a sheen of tears making her dark eyes gleam.

"It's not about punishing you," Mae said furiously. "It's not about you at all. It's about me, it's about staying myself. But if I'm able to get the pearl, well, then maybe I'll want to hear what you have to say to me."

Nick went still. He had not considered the pearl this way before, Sin thought, and she thought, too, that he might be surprised Mae had.

"So what you need is the pearl."

"What I want," Mae said, "is for you to come to me after I get the pearl, and tell me what you want. And if you don't want anything enough to try and put it into words—"

She shrugged in a jerky movement and went for the door. Sin flattened herself against Alan's bedroom door, about to slide in, but she heard Mae's last words loud and clear.

"Well then, Nick. Don't bother."

Once she had slipped into Alan's room she leaned back against the closed door and gave him a smile.

"So your brother disapproves of me."

"Of course," Alan said, looking up from his book and smiling at the sight of her. "You're obviously going to break my heart."

It didn't sound entirely like a joke, and Sin didn't know what to say, so she went over to the bed and kissed him. Alan pulled her down close, his hand at the back of her neck. After a few minutes Sin drew back so she could climb on to the bed. She got in on the left side, his good side, and whispered into his ear, "Obviously, that is my plan."

"It's just clear to everyone I don't deserve you," Alan said. "But don't worry about it. I'm going to lie and scheme and kill to keep you anyway."

"That's all right, then," Sin said. She drew her mouth along the line of his jaw. "Why don't you close your book?"

Alan did not do so. "It's very interesting."

Sin smiled against his skin. "So am I."

"The most interesting girl I know," Alan murmured.

She'd heard that before, with "beautiful" instead of "interesting". She liked it better this way.

She wasn't crazy about the way Alan pulled away from her a little and looked at her seriously.

"I don't want you to take this the wrong way," he started, which was a beginning that never ended well. "And I want to be honest with you."

"You don't have to be," Sin said. "If you lie, I'll know what you mean."

Alan reached out and touched her face, and looked at her as if she was a kaleidoscope, showing all her different colours, and he liked them all.

"I'm being terribly selfish right now," he said in a low voice. "Cynthia. You know I'm as good as marked for dead."

Sin's hands curled into fists, her nails cutting into her palms and stinging, the way tears stung when you refused to let them fall.

"I know," she said.

"The Circle's a mess right now," Alan continued. "But it won't be a mess forever. They'll find a way to use Gerald's mark on me. Or they'll just kill me."

"We'll get it off," Sin said.

"We'll try," he returned. "But that's the thing. I don't want to act like I only have a few days to live. I want to act like I'm not going anywhere. I don't want to go anywhere. I want us to take our time."

"Oh, just great," Sin said. She kissed him again to show him that he could wait around being romantic all he wanted. She would still be there. "You'll be sorry when I move out."

"You're still—?"

"'Let's not rush things, Cynthia,'" Sin said in an imitation of Alan's voice. "'Let's just move in together.' Yes, I'm moving out. You can come over and cook me dinner now and then, though."

"Sounds fair."

Sin settled lower down, against the rise of the pillows. "For now you can read to me."

"I'd like that," said Alan.

He sat up a little to rearrange the pillows, then pulled them flat rather than pushing them against the headboard, Sin's head sliding down on them. Alan leaned over her and kissed her, arched over her, one hand running along her ribs, fingers trailing warm over her thin T-shirt. Sin's breath came short as the kiss went deep and it didn't matter, breathing seemed like a faraway irrelevance compared to shivering under Alan's mouth.

241

"I would, you know," Alan murmured into the kiss.

Sin gave a soft interrogative sound, which was as good as he was getting right now.

"Lie," Alan answered, kissing her again.

"Scheme," he added after a moment into her ear, and kissed the place at the edge of her jaw. Sin arched up underneath him, and his fingers touched the slice of skin between her shirt and jeans.

"And kill," he whispered against her mouth, and kissed her breathless again.

"That's good to know," Sin told him when she had to break away, her heart drumming in her ears. She turned her head to the side, saw Alan's free hand still holding his book and started to laugh softly, looking up at him. "You're keeping your place."

"Of course. I'm going to read to you." Alan smiled down at her. "In a minute."

After quite a lot longer than a minute, he did. Sin put her arm round his stomach and rested her cheek against his shoulder and listened to him. He'd chosen something he thought she would like.

She did like it. She was simply happy, in a way she hadn't been in a year and more, in a shining, certain way. She hid her smile against his shoulder and went to sleep.

When she woke up in the early morning, she was cold because she was lying on top of the covers and she was alone.

Sin stretched and rose from the bed, straightening her wrinkled clothes and yawning as she padded out into the hall. She saw Mae in the sitting room, curled up on the sofa in a ball and fast asleep. She hadn't left after all.

Sin was smiling as she opened the kitchen door.

Nick was sitting on one of the chairs, hunched forward with his elbows on his knees, his hands hanging empty in front of him. Something about the way he was sitting made Sin think he had been there for a while.

But not all that long. The blood on the table and on one of the other chairs, sprayed over the floor, was not quite dry yet.

There were two knives on the table. Sin knew them, had seen Alan throwing them once at the Goblin Market. Nick must know them, too.

They were Alan's knives.

She could see very clearly what had happened. She wished she couldn't. She wished she could just stand there in the doorway and shake and demand to know what was going on.

But she knew, as well as Nick did.

When the mark that could torture him or kill him or do anything to him that Gerald of the Aventurine Circle wanted had made Alan get up and go God knew where, Alan had forced himself into the kitchen.

To stop himself from leaving, to delay himself just a moment, he'd put a knife through his hand and held himself pinned to the table for the time he needed to leave them a message.

The words were cut deep into the surface of the table, deeper than they needed to be, as if Alan was desperate to show how much he meant what he had written.

I love you. Don't come after me.

13

Dark My Light

"**I**'M GOING AFTER HIM," NICK SAID.

It made Sin blink and shook her out of paralysis into movement. She wasn't certain how long she had been standing there, shivering and staring at the blood and words.

She moved forward a step and found her body had betrayed her, making her wobble. "We don't know where he is."

Nick stood up, pushing his chair back violently.

"I know where Gerald is. And I'm going to gut him slowly until he tells me what he did with my brother."

Sin looked up at his black eyes.

"All right," she said. "We'll go together."

She left before he could argue with her, running back to the room and shoving on her shoes, grabbing up her knives. She got one look at the dented pillow where Alan had slept beside her that night and had to swallow down terror and panic, but she didn't let herself falter. She ran right back out to the sofa, where she shook Mae awake.

"Wha—" Mae said, her eyes still blurry with sleep. Sin felt

a moment of envy that Mae didn't know, and pity because she was going to tell her.

"Alan's gone," she said. "Nick and I are going to get him. Please will you stay with Lydie and Toby?"

Mae was awake in an instant, reality doing the job of cold water, her whole face changing. A slight crazed look about her eyes suggested she would much rather deal with a whole band of killer magicians than two kids, but she nodded at once.

"Of course," she said, and squared her shoulders.

"Thanks," Sin told her, and ran. In the hallway she ran right into the solid wall of Nick's back. "I'm coming with you," she reminded him furiously.

Nick didn't say anything, but he let her follow in his wake as he slammed through the door along the wire-mesh corridor and down the cold stairwell. He was moving fast, but Sin could do that, too.

They found themselves out in the chill of an autumn morning, shivering by the side of the road and looking at the empty space where Alan and Nick's car had been. Sin glanced at Nick.

"Can you just – send yourself there?"

"No," Nick snarled. "Because my stupid brother convinced me to give up the best part of my power for nothing."

He wheeled, a furious but contained movement like an animal in a cage, and stalked down the street.

Sin followed. "Are we stealing a car?"

It seemed like a good idea to her, but she hoped Nick knew how to do it. She suspected he did.

Over his shoulder, Nick said, "I've got another car."

The car was parked a few streets away. Sin would never have

picked it out as Nick's. It was a sleek, silver thing, gleaming like the surface of a polished gun and expensive-looking.

At any other time, Sin would have had questions. Now she slid into the passenger seat as soon as Nick turned the key in the door. The black leather of the seat slid beneath her jeans, butter-soft and sinking, and Sin's guess was that this was an old car lovingly restored.

She remembered seeing a car this colour in Nick's garden this summer, but she would never have thought he could do so much with it in such a short time.

She hoped it went fast.

The engine purred into life, and she found that it did. Nick, grim-faced behind the wheel, seemed to be taking street corners very personally. Sin gripped the dashboard and waited, watching the city pass by in a blur until they reached the river.

Then all there was to do was follow the Thames through Bankside until they found the magicians' boat.

Sin was on the riverside, and she wasn't driving. She watched the river with such intensity that her eyes burned.

"There!" she said, and pointed.

Nick followed the progress of the boat down the river, and at the first opportunity he took a sharp left on to London Bridge. Car tyres screeched around them, horns blaring and wheels spinning, and Nick stopped their car by driving it into the bridge railing.

Sin was braced against the dashboard already. She lowered her head and tried to absorb the impact as it slammed through her body, then shoved open the car door and staggered out. On one side of her was Tower Bridge, framed golden against the light, and on the other was the glittering far-off city and the

246

hundred sparkling red eyes of the OXO Tower. They swam in front of her eyes.

She stood still for a moment, staring straight in front of her, trying to will the dizziness away. Between massed rows of box-shaped office buildings with box-shaped windows there was another building, almost hidden. The piece of it she could make out looked like a white door surrounded with light. Sin focused on it until she could see properly again.

Then she turned to Nick and found him standing on the bridge railing.

He jumped.

Sin rushed to the rail and saw the boat passing in the river below, saw its pristine whiteness marred by the dark shape of Nick landing on the deck. In the wake of the boat as it moved were two white lines cut into the black water, ripples spreading to form bird's wings, like a swallow leaving as winter came. In a moment the boat would be gone.

Sin vaulted on to the broad steel strip that lay on top of the marble rail and dived like a swimmer.

She landed like an acrobat, like a dancer was taught to land, in a ball, rolling off the impact and ending the roll on her feet.

On her feet, on the deck of the *Queen's Corsair*, a boat where the whole Circle was waiting for them. And they had no plan, neither of them even knew how to make a plan, all they had was this driving rage and the need to find Alan, to save him at any cost.

Nick had landed like a cat on his feet, braced, and Sin didn't like to think about how much that must have hurt. His only concession to the pain was standing still for a few seconds.

Then he was moving again, going for the door, and Sin followed him. To hell with plans.

Down the flight of stairs they went, and into the corridor, where they met their first magician.

It was the grey-haired woman, Laura.

Sin knew something was very wrong, so wrong she could not even put it together in her head, when Laura stepped aside for Nick and Sin with a smile.

Nick stormed on without a sign he had noticed, but Sin had noticed. They passed Helen next, and she stood to one side with her head bowed. Not one magician tried to stop them on their way or even seemed surprised to see them.

When Sin glanced back over her shoulder, she saw the magicians they had passed were following them at a distance, in procession like mourners following a hearse.

Nick did not look back. He just strode on, apparently oblivious to everything, down the corridors and the steps until he reached the glass doors of the ballroom. He shoved both open, and they broke with a crash like music and thunder.

Inside the ballroom was most of the Aventurine Circle, all except for the magicians following in Nick and Sin's footsteps, and Jamie. Seb was there, and the look on his face made Sin go even colder.

All the other magicians were tense, almost standing to attention. Gerald was chatting to a couple of still and silent magicians as if he was attending a soiree.

He turned after a moment, a well-mannered host recognising two new guests. He nodded at them, tall but basically unthreatening-looking, his voice mild and pleasant.

"Cynthia Davies? I never expected to see you here again, but – out of the frying pan, straight back into the frying pan, as the saying doesn't go. Of course, you're welcome. And Nick.

Always a pleasure." Gerald smiled. It was a genuinely nice smile. "I admit I was expecting you."

Nick drew in a breath. Even that sounded like a snarl.

Sin discovered she'd stepped back from him, as if his fury was a black aura pushing people away without their conscious will.

"Where is he?" Nick asked. Hearing his voice was terrible, the sounds mangled and flat, like the sound of an animal being flayed alive and still roaring for blood. "Where is he?"

The other magicians drew back. Gerald's smile did not even flicker.

"The thing is," he said conversationally, "I can't let the other Circles think the Market can run around assassinating magicians without consequences, can I?"

Oh God. Gerald had given Mae a gun for more reasons than one.

He knew the entire Circle would believe Alan had killed Celeste. He'd framed someone he knew he could publicly, terribly punish any time he wanted, and thus win over Celeste's supporters.

Sin whispered, "What have you done to him?"

Nick's voice rose, something between a howl and a whine. "Where is he?"

"Come now," Gerald said. "Since you let him be tortured instead of performing the very simple tasks we requested, I didn't think it would be too much of a blow."

"What are you talking about?" Nick demanded. "Where is he?"

"Nick didn't know," Sin said. "Alan told him you hadn't made any demands yet. Alan didn't want him to know."

She wondered dully what Gerald had done with the body.

She was sure he'd killed Alan slowly.

"We lied to you," Sin told Nick. "Gerald asked for things. Alan told him you wouldn't do them."

Nick laughed, a horrible cracking sound. "I would have – I would have done anything."

Gerald looked briefly disconcerted, but a second later he was smiling again. "Now you'll do anything because I tell you to," he said gently. "Alan was of no further use to me. And this was so much fun. I can't wait until you see."

"See?" Sin asked.

Gerald nodded towards the double doors that led into the dining hall. Nick did not spare him another glance. He wheeled and went for the doors.

Sin followed him, forcing every step. She couldn't not look, and yet she knew that whatever lay beyond those doors, she did not want to see.

Nick threw them open. The sound rang out through the ship.

The dining hall was cleared of its table and chairs, cleared of everything. It was just an empty room, with the morning sun casting gold rays on the wooden floor.

There was something glittering in the middle of that bare floor.

Alan was standing at one of the windows, the sunlight turning his hair more gold than red.

Everything was very still and quiet in the room, nothing but the sound of them all breathing. Sin slowly realised what the metal thing on the floor was: it was Alan's glasses, broken and twisted out of shape.

Alan turned slowly from the window to face them.

Of course, it wasn't Alan any more.

The sunlight was warm on the face she loved, lingering on planes and angles, brightly caught in the curls of his hair.

Sunlight could not touch the flat black of his eyes, cold openings into another world.

The world slipped away from Sin, lost a second time. She was terribly cold in that sunlit room, shaking with it, and there was no one to put his arms round her now. The room was filled with the demon's silence.

That thing worse than death, that thing every dancer feared worst of all, the word never spoken, meaning lost and lost forever.

Possession.

Sin heard something break the silence and realised it was her, her ragged breaths turning into gasps. She put her shaking fingers to her lips, trying to cut off the sounds, and found streams of tears running down her face. She pressed her hand hard against her mouth and tried to stop crying.

The demon in Alan smiled.

14

Pouring Away the Ocean

S IN FORCED HERSELF TO STOP CRYING. SHE CHOKED BACK THE frantic sounds that wanted to erupt from her. They hit the back of her throat hard and burned on the way down.

She couldn't stop looking at the demon, though, and she still had not the faintest desperate idea what to do.

When Nick moved, she realised she had been braced for him to move all along, body tensed to cope with whatever Nick was about to do while her eyes were fixed on Alan. She didn't know what horror Nick was about to unleash, what storm of fury was about to descend on all their heads. Her survival depended on being prepared and reacting fast.

She was not prepared for Nick to turn round and leave.

She tore her eyes away from Alan's face, which was the same face and yet so different, still and smooth as a mask with that faint, horrible smile superimposed on it, like an obscenity scrawled on a gravestone.

Nick was already walking through the ballroom, magicians scattering out of his way. He didn't seem to notice them at all.

Not until Gerald stepped in his path.

"I think we need to talk."

"No," Nick said indifferently. "I think we're done."

He looked up at the rafter Sin had crawled along two nights ago, and the big chandelier that looked like an expensive ice sculpture.

It burst into flames.

Nick raked his eyes along the walls, and lines of fire scored burning claw marks everywhere he looked.

It took an instant for the ballroom to become an inferno, the roaring and hissing of the flames drowning the magicians' screams.

"How dare you?" Gerald demanded, his voice ringing with command. "Stop!"

Nick hesitated, his whole body vibrating like a bowstring pulled too tight. Then Jamie came running through the burning doors. His eyes were shining mirrors that reflected the flames.

"Nick," he said. "I swear I didn't know he was going to do it."

Gerald's face darkened. "I don't find the demon's hurt feelings of much interest. He's going to repair the damage he did to my boat."

"No, he's not," Jamie returned. "I have first claim on the demon. He can go."

He looked up at Nick, his body strained and his face imploring, as if Nick would allow a magician to comfort him, as if he could betray Nick and then still act like he cared about him.

He was spun round by Gerald's voice, cracking like a whip and crackling with magic. "I am your leader!"

"I don't care," Jamie said, and shoved Gerald with magic glowing in his hands.

Gerald rocked back, eyes incredulous and furious. His expression said that Jamie would pay for this moment of defiance.

Jamie said, "Leave him alone!"

Nick's eyes slid over the struggling magicians as if he didn't know either of them, and cared less. Then he turned and walked calmly away through the flames.

Sin could chase Nick or stay in a nest of magicians that was on fire. She went after Nick.

She was running up the stairs to the deck when the boat lurched sideways and hit a wall. She grabbed for the banister and caught herself before slamming face first on the steps, almost yanking her arms out of their sockets. Then she was on her feet again and running for the deck. There was smoke rising all around her, still thick on the deck, and the crackling was everywhere, like a thousand demons laughing at her.

She chased Nick through the smoke and fire to the wall he'd wrecked the boat against. There were steps here, too, and she ran up a few of them before she realised why the smoke and fire had seemed like the whole world.

The river was burning. Winding under Tower Bridge like a crimson ribbon, lighting up the London Eye as if it was a wheel of torment in hell.

"That's running water," Sin whispered in a voice destroyed by sobbing and smoke.

"I don't know how the body bore being on the water that long," Nick said. "I can cope much better than the others can. I don't have anyone fighting inside. The magicians must have transported it there specially, because they knew I'd come to them first thing. They wanted me to see."

Sin ran up the steps and drew level with him. He wasn't

running. He was walking casually by the riverside as the flames raged and people screamed in the streets.

"I mean, how are you doing this?"

He didn't seem to hear her. "I don't see why they bothered," he said flatly.

The heavens above them were roiling and dark with storm clouds, the smoke from the burning river rising like ghosts into the sky. Sin could hear the shriek of ambulances and the wail of fire engines, and she wondered how many people had been added to the list of Nick Ryves's victims.

She didn't know if this was a demon's version of adrenaline, performing impossible acts under the influence of panic or grief, or if she was seeing Nick go mad.

Sin was keeping pace with Nick, but she thought of Jamie and Seb, and she looked back at the boat.

She did not see it, because when she looked, all she saw was the shape standing behind her wreathed in the smoke, against the scarlet glow of the river and the black clouds.

Sin drew in one shuddering breath.

"Nick. He's behind us."

"Of course. It wouldn't want to stay on the boat for long," Nick said dispassionately.

Sin looked back, as unable to help herself as anyone who had loved and lost and been offered the chance to see their loved ones again, no matter what the consequences. People always looked back in hell.

The demon returned her gaze, standing under an unlit lamp post. He'd been much closer when she looked an instant before.

"Nick," Sin said in an urgent whisper, and looked round again.

The demon was standing directly behind her, his face near enough to hers to kiss. The burning river was reflected in both his eyes, turned into trails of blood in two black mirrors.

Sin swallowed down a scream and forced herself to look away. She felt the demon's presence like a cold shadow on her back.

"Nick, he's following us."

"That doesn't matter," Nick said.

"Yes, it does! Listen to me—"

Nick stopped and looked at her, and he had demon's eyes, too, blood on blackness. Sin stopped cold.

"Shut up," said Nick. "Or I'll kill you. Nothing matters now."

Sin shut up. She wasn't going to get into a suicidal conversation with a demon; she wasn't going to think about what she had lost; she wasn't going to look behind her.

She was going to keep walking. She was going to endure, through this city turned into hell, and she was going to get back to the children, who would be helpless without her.

She kept all her promises to herself but one. She did look back.

Not too often on that long, nightmarish walk through fire and darkness as the fire in the city and the shadowed daylight began to die, but often enough. She looked back and saw Alan's face, pale as a dead thing, watching her with endless amusement.

As soon as Nick turned the key in the lock, Sin pushed her way through the door, and Mae barrelled out of the bedroom.

"What happened? Where's Alan?"

Of course, Mae would expect them to come back with Alan

alive, Alan safe, because she had been brought up in a world where magic meant fairy tales.

"Alan's possessed," Sin said, the inside of her throat burned and razed with smoke, her voice too broken to break any more. She didn't even resent Mae for that lovely, stupid belief, just felt a distant kind of pity.

She stepped past Mae and realised she could stop moving at last. She leaned against the wall.

And she realised Mae was suicidal and crazy, because she ran forward and tried to hug Nick.

Nick backed into the door, moving as sharply as if Mae had weapons and he was an ordinary human being, the kind of person who would see weapons and panic hard enough to back himself into a corner.

His body hit the door, and Mae got her arms round his neck.

"Nick," she said against his chest, too short to even get his shoulder. "I'm so sorry, Nick."

Nick's hands balled into fists and his head ducked slightly, as if it might bow. He could accept the hug or he could hit her.

Then Sin saw his spine straighten as he recalled he wasn't human, and he had another choice.

"Mae," he said, in the flat voice he had been using since Alan had turned round in the morning sunlight. "I want you to get out."

From a hundred nights at the Goblin Market, Sin knew the feel of magic thick in the air. She knew the feel of little magics, like fireflies landing on your skin, and powerful magic like wind roaring in your ears. She knew the feel of magic twisting and turning dark.

She knew at once that when Mae stepped stiffly back and away from Nick, it was not of her own free will.

"Nick," Mae said in a horrified gasp, her hand going to the demon's mark near her throat.

Her feet took another jerky step back, and Nick was able to move past her, down the tiny hall and away from them both.

He had no right. Sin drew her knife with shaking fingers, and it slid out of her hand like an escaping snake, striking the wall.

"Nick," Mae said, and her voice was not a gasp any more as she started to believe the immensity of this betrayal. Her voice was furious.

Her feet dragged forward, one pushed after another, clumsy as a puppet. She tried to get a purchase on the walls, her hands scrabbling, until they were forced down to her sides.

She turned her head even as her hands fumbled for the lock on the door.

"I won't forgive you for this," she said.

Nick was not even looking at her. "I don't care."

The door slammed behind Mae. Sin looked at Nick, and he shoved past her and went into the kitchen. She stood in the doorway and watched him.

"That was—"

"Inhuman?" Nick pulled out a chair and threw himself into it. "Imagine that."

"Cruel," Sin told him.

Nick bared his teeth at her. "That's what we are," he said. "Do you want to know what possession feels like?"

Sin couldn't answer him. Her mouth had gone dry. She went and stood with her back against the kitchen counter, her hands gripping it, because having a physical support and something to hold on to was all there was to comfort her.

"I know enough about possession," she said eventually, her voice paper thin and dry. "I was with my mother every day until she died."

She tried not to remember the echoing white passages of Mezentius House, the sounds of screams from the other rooms. She tried not to remember when the screams were coming from her room, how scared she'd been the demon would hurt her so she couldn't dance any more, how her mother's body had twisted like a prisoner's on the rack and changed, so terribly fast. Her beautiful mother.

Oh God, Alan.

Sin clutched the countertop as hard as she could, until her bones ached. She could not fall apart. In a minute she would go to the kids.

No, in a minute she would go to the bathroom and wash away the traces of ashes and tears. They couldn't see her like this.

"You don't know about possession like I do," Nick said. He sat at the table with his head bowed over his arms, staring down at his knuckles. His voice was measured, utterly cold. "You don't know it from the inside."

"Stop," Sin said.

"No," said Nick, calm and pitiless. "First you slip in and they're fighting so hard, they can't believe such a thing has happened to them. So you torture them. You crush them and they scream inside their own heads and you laugh at them, because nobody but you will ever hear them again."

Sin closed her eyes and measured her breaths, in and out. She wasn't going to think about Alan, she wasn't going to break down. She had the kids to think of.

"Second, they start to beg, and that's funny. You hate them

so much, for no reason except that they're human and they've been sucking up all the warmth of the world for years without thinking to appreciate it. You want them to crawl to you. And then you torture them some more. Because it's so much fun. Third—"

"Third, they want to make a bargain," said a new voice, as flat as Nick's but not as smooth, the words jerky, not quite pieced together, in a way that reminded Sin of the way Mae had moved when Nick forced her to the door. As if it wasn't her body.

As if it wasn't his voice.

She opened her eyes and saw Alan's body lounging in the doorway, with an easy grace Alan had never possessed. He was standing in a little pool of ashes, looking like he'd been swimming in that burning river. Ash covered his clothes and made a filthy halo round his head.

He gave them both a sunny smile.

"Usually it takes a few days before they get around to the bargaining," the demon continued. "But you may have noticed, your boy's quick. Such an interesting mind."

Nick's head had reared back. He looked more nightmarish than the other demon did, his eyes black holes in a mask so white it blazed.

"Do you want to know why bargaining with demons almost never works?" the demon asked. He strolled into the kitchen, moving in fluid, easy strides.

Seeing the loss of the limp she'd always hated was almost too much for Sin. She wanted to be sick.

He circled Nick's chair, but Nick sat there like a stone. The demon roved over to Sin. She pressed back hard against the counter.

"How about you, princess?"

That was what made her realise what should have been obvious long before. Of course, what other demon had served the Circle so well that he deserved a reward like this? What other demon wanted revenge like he did?

What other demon would have followed Nick home?

"I don't know, Anzu," Sin said between her teeth.

"Humans are so rarely eager to offer us what we want," Anzu murmured, the curve of Alan's mouth like a scimitar. "Everything."

He was standing very close now. She was glad he smelled like ashes and blood, not like guns.

"But your boy, your Alan—" Sin flinched, and Anzu's smile broadened with delight. He pushed his face closer to hers, as if he could scent out weakness. "*Alan*," he repeated, but she didn't let him see her flinch again. "Well. That's exactly what he offered. Not like Liannan's deal, sharing a body for privileges. Just unconditional surrender. His voice, free access to his mind, a promise not to fight, total cooperation."

She made herself breathe in measured, controlled breaths. She held her body still and did not speak, and Anzu lost interest in her, moved away and back to his real target.

"Interesting how quickly he gave up, don't you think?" he asked Nick. "Really, it's as if he was used to being the slave to a demon already. As if he never had a soul to call his own."

Now that Anzu had turned away, Sin moved quietly, heading for the bathroom. She was going there to wash her face; she had always intended to do that, it was nothing to remark on.

As soon as she was in the bathroom, she slid the lock on the door closed, even though she knew it would not keep a demon out.

261

She leaned against the bathroom door, fished her new phone out of her jeans pocket and called Mae. The phone rang and Sin was still in control, she was, but her body felt as if it had been frozen in those moments where Anzu leaned close, and now it was turning to water. Her legs simply would not hold her up. She slid, the door still at her back, to the cool tiles of the bathroom floor.

When Mae answered the phone, Sin said, "You have to help me."

"Anything," Mae said. She'd obviously been crying; she was no good at modulating her voice to conceal it, but a stuffed nose didn't impair Mae's determination at all. "I'm so sorry, Sin. I'm so – Alan was one of my best friends. Anything I can do, I will."

"He has a plan," Sin whispered, and wiped her brimming eyes with the back of her hand. "Anzu's the one possessing Alan. And he's here, he's gloating to Nick, he can talk. Alan gave him his voice, he's not fighting him at all."

Mae's voice was choking up even more. "Oh God, Sin. God."

"But you know why he's doing it," Sin said. "You see."

Her manipulative liar, her endless schemer, did not do things without a reason. He was managing his own possession.

"He's buying himself time," Sin said. "The body will last longer if he doesn't fight. He's buying us time, to save him. He's got a plan."

Even saying the words, mentioning the possibility of saving him, made her feel dizzy. It was a fairy tale, it was ridiculous; everyone knew possession was a death sentence. Everyone knew it was worse than that.

"Sin," Mae said, her voice gentle, "if he's got a plan, Anzu knows it by now. Alan's plans won't work any more. He can't scheme his way out of this one."

She had known that, really, all along. The blinding realisation of what Alan was doing had dazzled her for a moment, that was all. The thought that he was still somewhere in there hoping had made her hope, too.

But there was no hope.

Sin leaned her head back against the bathroom door. "I know," she said. "I know."

Mae said, "We have to think of a plan ourselves."

15

Brothers in Arms

THE KNOCK ON THE FRONT DOOR CAME ALMOST IMMEDIATELY after Mae spoke.

"Mae," Sin said, low. "Are you at the door?"

Just as low, though the demons were not there to hear her, as if Sin's fear was infecting her, Mae whispered, "No."

Sin cut off the call, leaned her forehead against the phone and boosted herself to her feet. She shoved her phone into her pocket, unlocked the door and threw it open so hard it hit the wall, because otherwise she would have stayed cowering in the bathroom.

A moment later, she wished she had.

She'd stepped out between the possessed bodies of the people she loved. Anzu and Liannan were standing in the hall. They had been looking at each other, but now they were both looking at her.

Liannan stood there with the red hair streaming down her shoulders snarled with ash, a bright, sharp smile on her face.

"Merris?" Sin whispered, because it was not night yet. It was daytime even if it was daytime in hell, and that was who should be in this body.

And Merris answered, black starting to bleed from the ash in her hair, staining the red and spreading.

"Thea," she said, using the Goblin Market nickname for her instead of the severe "Cynthia" she usually preferred.

Sin felt a great bound of hope in her chest, as if she could fling herself into Merris's arms like a child and expect to be saved, just like that. As if it could be that simple.

But Merris's hands had nails that glimmered strangely sharp, and there was still red in her hair and a wild strangeness to her face.

"Liannan?" Anzu asked, and he sounded uncertain.

"I'm here," said Liannan, her voice changing again, lifeless and flat, all the humanity leached out. "But it is technically her turn."

"Technically?" Sin whispered.

Liannan smiled. "Our boundaries are more fluid these days."

"It's disgusting that you have to sully yourself like this," Anzu said.

"I don't know," said Liannan. "All that screaming gets tiresome after a while, don't you find?"

Sin wouldn't have thought she could look away from Liannan lest she miss a moment when she might turn into Merris, but she found her head turning helplessly to look at Alan's face.

"No. I enjoy it," said Anzu, and used Alan's mouth to smile. "Especially now."

Liannan moved past Sin, her hair brushing whisper-soft against Sin's shoulder, and stood beside Anzu. She reached up and drew her fingernails down his cheek, deliberately drawing four bleeding lines.

"I do not think this was a particularly good idea," she said. "The city's on fire. So I see he's taking it well."

The trails of blood moved across Alan's face, drawing a pattern as if the demon was going to play noughts and crosses in blood across Alan's skin. Then a shadow fell across the blood.

Nick stood in the kitchen doorway, his hands on the door frame as if he was blocking the way.

There were three demons standing close enough to reach out and kill her, and the kids were only a door away.

"Liannan," said Nick, "you're not welcome here."

"But the city's burning," Liannan said. "It's beautiful. I know you're put out that Anzu stole your pet, but we are all together at last. Let us cheer you up. Let's take your bad mood out on the humans. We could go to the Tower of London and get those executions started again."

Nick stared at her blankly. Liannan turned away from Anzu and towards him, reaching out a hand. He didn't flinch back, and she didn't touch him: he'd known she wouldn't. They were comfortable together, with the ease of long familiarity.

"I'm sorry, too," Liannan told him. "Alan was lovely. But he's gone now. Let's go out and choose you a new one."

"Why don't you get out?" Nick asked. "You're boring me."

"We could—"

"I have a headache tonight, dear," Nick drawled. "I didn't ask you to come. I could have gone to find you any time in the last month, Liannan, but I didn't. Can't you take a hint? I don't want you here."

"I want to talk to Merris," Sin said into the silence after those words.

The demons looked at her, as if they were distantly surprised she dared to speak at all. Anzu moved towards her, and a warning, animal impulse at the base of Sin's spine told her she was in danger.

"No," said Merris. "Don't touch her."

She reached past Anzu and took Sin's wrist, and Sin let her despite those lethally pointed nails. Merris drew her into the sitting room, leaving the others out in the hall.

Merris sat down on the sofa, gracefully crossing her legs. Her whole body looked younger, Sin saw with a dull sense of shock, her legs strong, their muscles taut. Dancer's legs.

"What is it you need, Thea?" Merris asked, and her voice was gentle, for Merris. It would have been reassuring, aside from everything else.

Sin sat on the very edge of the sofa and uncurled her hands from their fists.

"You've changed," she said softly.

"Well," Merris said, and smiled a small, secretive smile. She did not look at all displeased. "I suppose I have."

"You've been away from the Market a long time," Sin said. "Were you at Mezentius House?"

"At first." Merris's tone was dismissive. "I put a friend of mine in charge there. I was not going to simply abandon my responsibilities."

Her hands had been veined but strong once, gnarled at the back like old tree trunks but still moving gracefully to express herself. They were smooth now. Sin had liked Merris's hands the way they were. The Market had been safe in Merris's hands. Sin had, as well.

"What about the Market? Were you just going to leave it up to Mae?"

"Oh," Merris murmured. "She's come out on top already, has she?"

She did not sound in the least surprised. Sin gritted her teeth.

"She hasn't come out on top. I've been thrown out of the Market, but they haven't chosen her as a leader. They all thought you were coming back, and I want to know what's going on," she said between her teeth. "I thought – you said Liannan was whispering to you, and you had to silence her, and now you're letting her out during the day!"

Merris smiled faintly. "I started whispering back. We started whispering to each other. When I was young, I was a dancer."

Sin nodded.

Merris raised an eyebrow. "Oh, you've heard the stories. But you never saw me dance. I was better than your mother ever was, I was better than you ever will be. I danced in Goblin Markets around the world. The most beautiful songs played in the Goblin Market today, Cynthia, they were written for me. Do you want to know why I was so good?"

In Mezentius House, Sin had thought about not being able to dance any more. She'd pictured being hurt, being wrenched out of the world she knew, and when she'd escaped unscathed, she found it even harder to look at Alan, or anyone else who couldn't dance.

She'd always known that she would have to stop dancing one day, but something about Merris's voice made her picture it now: more than half her life, not able to dance a real dance, the true dance, under the lights of the Market.

Merris said, "I never cared about anything else. And then it was over."

The word *over* was crushing in Sin's mind for a moment, and then she thought, *Never? About anything else?*

"I had to find something else to do, some other way to be part of the Market," Merris said. "And I found a way. I founded Mezentius House, and I made the Market bigger and brighter than it had ever been before. But when I went away with Liannan, I went dancing. And I was better than ever."

"It's the demon," Sin got out. "But I'll get the pearl, and I'll bring it to you. I will."

"I'm going to go round the world," Merris said. "I only have so many nights to do it, but I'm going to visit every Goblin Market there is, and dance one more time. If you could do what you loved best in this world, would you let anything stop you?"

"Yes," Sin answered. "If people needed me."

"And that's what has always been wrong with you," Merris said tenderly. "That is why you will never be a true artist. But you come so close. I cared about the Market, I cared about turning a profit and building up the magic, but I was never able to care much about any one person. You were different. You almost reached perfection, but you were never quite disciplined enough. The children, your school, those visits to your father – oh, I knew about those. You were never focused. Not enough to sacrifice everything else. You were such a disappointment. But somehow, I don't know how it was, exactly. Somehow I cared more about you than I ever did about anyone before."

Sin turned away, back hunched, trying to bear the onslaught of the words. She felt the touch of Merris's hands on her face, smooth and young, and looked up into demon eyes.

"If I'd had a daughter, I would have wanted her to be like you," Merris murmured. "But just a little better."

It wasn't Merris's fault. She was possessed, and a lie could not pass her lips any more than her eyes could change back to grey.

Sin had tried, as hard as she knew how. She'd never wanted to disappoint Merris. She'd always tried to balance in a place where she could be both like her mother, beautiful and carefree, and like Merris, the ideal leader.

All these performances, and nobody had ever really appreciated them except one person, and now he was gone. Alan was gone and Merris was going, and Sin knew the only thing she could do was protect what was left.

Sin swallowed. "Will you go back to the Market?" she asked. "Will you check that everyone's all right? Will you talk to Mae? Please."

Merris stood up from the sofa. Sin did not dare look up, in case she saw Liannan intent on going dancing through flames and death. She kept her head bowed until her neck ached.

She felt Merris's lips touch her forehead, gently.

"For you," she said, "I will. But I won't stay."

Sin looked up into those black eyes. "I'll get the pearl," she promised again. "I'll bring it to you. You'll see, then. The demon will be quiet, and everything will be the same as it was before."

Merris smiled, pitying and a little scornful. "Child," she said. "That never happens."

She left, her back straight, her body strong and lithe and young. Sin watched her go and told herself that she would get that pearl, she would, and once the demon was silenced, Merris would come back.

She tried to forget the kiss goodbye.

"I'll go with Liannan," Anzu said from the hall, and Sin looked round to see Nick grab his arm.

"That's not Liannan right now," Nick told him. "And you're staying here."

The door closed behind Merris, and Anzu rounded on Nick. "Oh, I am, am I?"

Nick's eyes narrowed. "Yes."

"Great," Anzu said. The air seemed to glitter around him, molecules crystallising with his icy rage. "What do you do for fun around here? Oh, wait, don't tell me, I know!"

He spun and slammed open a door. Sin was on her feet with her heart in her throat and her knives in her hands before she realised that he had gone into Alan's room and not Nick's.

She sheathed her knives immediately. She couldn't show concern, she couldn't give him the idea that it might be fun to play with Toby and Lydie. She had to hope he had forgotten or was at least uninterested in the fact that they were there.

Anzu emerged from the doorway again almost at once. He was carrying a sword.

Sin had forgotten they'd stowed all Nick's swords in there, away from the kids.

Alan had never had the balance to use a sword effectively, and seeing him wielding a blade with such careless ease was as surprising as seeing his smooth, easy new walk. The sword shone in the dim hallway. Its point was aimed at Nick's heart.

"Come on," Anzu said softly.

The steel edge pierced the cotton of Nick's T-shirt, just touching. One shove of the blade, and Nick would be spitting blood.

Nick moved, not backwards but sideways, drew his sword

and brought it round in a tight, vicious circle. Anzu only just raised his blade in time to meet Nick's, and there was a ring of steel that echoed through the little rooms.

Sin couldn't see Nick's face as he followed up on his strike, moving in and forcing Anzu's blade back.

"Let's take this outside."

She could see Anzu's face, though, savage and hungry and gleaming with a terrible kind of triumph, though Sin didn't know what he thought he'd won. He spun and almost swaggered through the door, blade dangling carelessly from his hand. Nick followed him.

As soon as the door shut, Sin leaped into the hall and to Nick's bedroom, scrabbling for the doorknob and shoving at the door with her elbow in a burst of panic.

Lydie and Toby were on the bed, curled up tightly together, asleep. Mae had made sure they got dressed, and Sin hoped she'd fed them, too. She couldn't tell if Mae had washed their faces, because both of their faces were grimy again already, screwed up and covered in dried tears.

They must have heard some of what was going on outside. They had been so good. They hadn't made a sound.

Sin hated to wake them.

Maybe, since they were asleep, she could go outside and see what was happening. Just for a moment.

She shouldn't do it, Sin thought, wiping her sweaty palms on her jeans. But Alan was in there, trying to hold out, helpless and watching all this. What he must be feeling, fearing his own hands would strike down his brother.

She knew it was a mistake, but she made it. She closed the door softly so she wouldn't wake the kids, grabbed her keys and dashed out of the door.

The demons were duelling in the roof garden, circling and striking, blades catching the light of the sinking sun in a blinding rain of blows. Anzu was dancing round Nick, taunting, making a game of this, and Nick was feinting and dodging.

Nick was trained, but Alan had made sure his brother's power was limited. Sin suspected it might be less than Anzu's power.

Sin ran down the cold passage lined with wire mesh and then up the steps. She knelt on the highest step that would still be out of view, poised like a sprinter ready to leap.

The sunlight bathing him could not alone account for the gold of Anzu's hair and skin. Even the bones of his face looked different; he was changing Alan's very bones because he felt like it, turning his face into something sharp-edged and beautiful and terrible.

He seemed angry.

"What I want to know is what's wrong with everyone?" he demanded, dealing Nick a blow that, if Nick hadn't parried it, would have cut his head clean off. "Liannan cooperating with a human, sharing with her, running around doing the human's little *errands!*"

The way he spat out the word had added vehemence because it was punctuated by another savage stroke of his sword. Nick met the stroke, his arms and shoulders braced. If Sin hadn't known enough to measure the impact of that strike, she would never have guessed how hard Nick had just been hit.

"And as for you," Anzu exclaimed, disengaging and spinning in a furious circle. Nick met each of the blows, blocking them, parrying them, but not making any attacking moves of his own. He was like a stone, looming dark and comparatively still. Next to Anzu, he looked like a statue in a graveyard. "You," Anzu said with loathing. "Having a temper tantrum about your little pet? You make me sick."

Nick's shoulders bunched, muscles moving differently than they had before, engaging with the sword now. Sin knew the look of someone turning their body into a weapon.

She was not surprised when he lunged at Anzu. Anyone human would have stumbled at the sudden onslaught, and Anzu had to retreat, but he did it fast, almost gleefully, almost dancing back.

Nick delivered a series of punishing hits so close together they didn't look like a series but like one continuous, monumental effort to batter Anzu to pieces. Anzu was only just keeping up, only just able to defend himself, and he looked delighted about it.

Nick wasn't lacking power; he had been holding back. For a moment Sin didn't understand why he should do that, why he would want to spare Anzu, and she thought about a demon's loyalty to its own kind.

Or maybe he had realised what she had, after Anzu started talking. Maybe he knew his brother was trying to hold out, and he was trying to spare the body.

She wished she knew. She wanted to be sure, but all she was sure of was that Alan was being tortured, and that he would never in a thousand years have wanted to hurt his brother.

If it came down to a choice, she had to try and protect Nick.

Nick did not look especially in need of protection. Anzu was still dancing backwards, the body changing like a mood ring, all shifting colours and bones. He seemed to be trying to alter the body into something entirely new, into air and light.

He stepped off the side of the building, pivoting into nothingness, and landed on the rooftop of a building yards away. He stood on the smooth, grey slant of the roof, staring across the space at Nick, their gazes locked and mirroring each other, a void reflecting a void, nothingness going on forever.

Nick jumped, a spring that a human wouldn't have been able to make. If Anzu was barely connected to his human body, Nick was using it to the fullest extent he could. He was a thundercloud of muscle and magic, fighting a lightning bolt. Anzu kept laughing and they kept moving, halting for a moment with swords locked at the crest of the roof.

They went down the other side of the roof caught in combat, even their silhouettes against the sky slipping away from her.

Sin judged the distance and then bounded to her feet and ran, building up steam for the jump, all the muscles in her body coiled and burning to prepare for the effort.

Her hurtle through the air was a brief moment of terror, wind and hair whipping into her eyes and leaving her blind. Then her knees hit the very edge of the roof, viciously hard. She felt her jeans and the skin of her knees both tearing, but she ignored the sting and, crouching low, made her way up the slope of the roof.

The sound of swords clashing filled her ears before she saw them again. Anzu was not even sweating. Nick was, his T-shirt clinging damp to his collarbones. He was breathing hard, but he circled Anzu without a hint that he might relent or pause. His mouth was set in a grim line.

"We can go duelling through the rooftops of London," Anzu said. "We could cross blades on top of Westminster

Abbey. No human could catch us. No human could stop us, no matter what we wanted to do. You were stranded out here with the humans, isolated and in chains, but we are both here now. There's no need to crawl for them any longer."

Nick was crouching like Sin, not to hide but to attack. Locks of wet hair were falling in his eyes and he was panting, but his teeth were bared in something like a savage grin.

It occurred to Sin that they might both be enjoying themselves. She might just be trying to throw herself into the middle of some deadly, inhuman game.

"And as for that pet of yours," Anzu went on, raging and exulting at once. "He couldn't fight you like this, could he? He was even more worthless than an ordinary human. He was broken, and useless, and pointless."

He punctuated each of his descriptions of Alan with a slash, face alight with triumph. Nick dealt him another series of hard blows for an answer, bearing down with his superior weight and strength, and Sin waited for the moment when one of them would stop using their magic to fuel their fight and simply use it to lash out.

It didn't happen. Anzu betrayed himself by flinching under the barrage of blows, his parry vicious but wavering a little, almost uncertain.

Nick knocked him back with another blow.

"I'm your brother," Anzu shouted. "Not him!"

The next blow of Nick's sword brought Anzu to his knees. Nick drew his blade slowly, lightly, along Anzu's throat. Anzu was still wearing an awful half smile, as if he thought this was all part of a game.

"You're right," Nick said, his voice utterly emotionless. "This isn't like fighting Alan. He's human and weak and broken, all the things you said. And Alan would have cheated by now. He would have won."

Anzu stopped smiling. Nick crouched down, his face close to Anzu's.

Cold as ever, Nick murmured, "I know my brother when I see him."

Sin sat on the sofa and hated herself. Nick had had the situation under control. Of course he had. There was no need for her to be running around like a fool, trying to protect a demon!

Once she'd seen that Nick could handle himself, she had turned round and gone back, but it was too late. She had no time to wake the children and make her escape. Both the demons had come back almost as soon as she did.

Worse than that, Nick had gone into Alan's room and slammed the door. Sin had not the faintest idea what he could be doing there, but she did not appreciate being left out here alone with Anzu.

Anzu did not bother her. He seemed not to notice she was there. He just stood staring out of the window, arms crossed over his chest. The sun was setting, throwing red banners over the buildings and crowning them with light. It almost looked like the city was burning again.

For a while Sin sat, waiting for him to do something and reproaching herself for her own stupidity in not running when she could. She would almost deserve whatever the demon decided to do to her.

At last she began to believe he would stay put. There was still no sound from Nick's room, where the children were.

Sin tried to make herself relax. She had to be strong to get the children out at the very next opportunity that arose. She would not be so weak as to let the chance slip out of her fingers a second time.

She couldn't relax. She wished something would happen, a disaster, anything she could deal with so she wouldn't have to think.

Failing that, she wished Nick would get out of Alan's room so she could go in there and look at his stupid guns and books, put her head on the pillow they had shared last night and cry.

With nothing she could do, all Sin could think of was Alan. He was locked up in his own body, dying slowly, watching all of this.

She knew what happened to a possessed body. What Nick and Anzu had been saying today was not news. Demons loved to boast in their dancing circles of how they made humans suffer, trapped in bodies that started to fall apart so fast, trapped in a corner of their own minds and screaming.

She had spent hours talking to her mother, trying to comfort her even though she knew that Mama could never respond to her touch, never answer her again.

Alan would go through that, all of that, but even more slowly, and he might have to see people he loved hurt at his hands.

Sin looked across the room at Anzu. He was not using much magic now, and he looked almost like Alan again. She could look at his red hair curling against the collar of his shirt and the solemn lines of his profile, as if he was absorbed in thought, and she could almost think it was Alan.

But it wasn't. It would never be Alan again.

She was on her feet before she realised what she was about to do, walking softly until she reached the window and the demon.

She stood beside him and thought of Alan trying desperately to survive a little longer, as if she or Mae could possibly hope to save him. She shut her eyes, the setting sun painting the darkness behind her eyelids scarlet and gold.

Sin put her hand at the back of his neck and drew his head gently down. She kissed him on the mouth.

The demon let her do it.

"I'm right here," Sin breathed. It felt like Alan was close for a moment, even though he wasn't. "Hold on."

16

They Have to Take You In

S IN WOKE TO EARLY-MORNING LIGHT STABBING BETWEEN HER eyelashes. She was wedged in the corner of the sofa, and she cracked her neck to get out the crick in it, stretched and realised that she had fallen asleep with a demon two doors away from Lydie and Toby.

She wrenched herself off the sofa, flooded with horror, and met a demon's eyes.

"Anzu's not here," Nick said.

Sin closed her eyes for a brief moment of pure, deep thankfulness, and then she went for the door. She'd been stupid long enough.

"What are you doing?"

"I'm getting Lydie and Toby out of here."

"I see," Nick said. "Well, that makes sense. Alan's no use to you now."

"What do you mean by that?"

Nick was in yesterday's clothes like she was, and he looked as if he'd slept less than the few hours she'd finally caught sitting up on a sofa, but his voice was very clear. "Oh, I don't know. You openly despise Alan for years, and then suddenly you're homeless and friendless and you discover a burning desire to go out with him? That's awfully convenient."

"I'm sorry," Sin said. "Are you still cranky because you've lost your pet? Tell me, do you think that you'll be over it soon? How long does it take to replace a really good pet – was Alan special enough to wait a week before you get a new one?"

Nick moved in close to her, tall and strong enough so simply doing that seemed threatening, and Sin held one fist clenched and positioned to punch him in the stomach.

"I never called him that."

"I never called him a meal ticket, either."

"And yet the evidence is against you."

"What about you, Nick?" Sin demanded. "Isn't the evidence against you? I know your kind don't have the same feelings as humans. I know you think of humans as jokes, as pets, as playthings. You threw a tantrum and you fought a duel, you lashed out; that's what demons do. They don't care! I don't know how you felt about Alan. You don't know how I felt, but I can tell you, and it doesn't matter whether you believe me or not. I loved him, and he's as good as dead, but I still love him. If there were any way to save him, I'd do it, if there were any bargain to make, I would make it, but there is nothing I can do and there is no time. I love Toby and Lydie, as well; they're my first responsibility, and I have to get them away from danger. If Alan was here, he would understand, because he did anything he had to do to protect you. Now shut up and get out of my way."

She shoved Nick aside. He didn't stop her, and she made for the door.

She was stopped at the threshold by his voice. "Did you tell Alan?"

"Tell Alan what?"

"How you – what you thought of him," Nick said roughly.

Sin looked at the painted wood of the door frame. "Yeah."

"Good," Nick said. "He would've liked that."

She didn't know what to say in response. She bowed her head for a moment, then went to get the kids.

Lydie was awake. When the door opened, Sin saw her freeze and clutch Toby tighter. Then she recognised Sin and sat up.

"I'm so sorry," Sin said. "I should've got you out earlier, but I'm getting you out now. Give me Toby and grab your things."

Lydie threw herself off the bed and began stuffing all their loose clothing in the bag Mae had given them. Sin lifted Toby in her arms and he started to fuss, cranky and scared. Sin rubbed his back and tried to soothe away the low, continuous whine.

"Want to give me that bag?"

"No," Lydie whispered, and then more firmly: "I've got it."

Sin gave her a smile. "Then let's go."

She was calculating as they left the bedroom: the money she had would keep them in a hostel for a few days, and by then they would have a flat. She'd just have to make another appointment to dance, and fast.

The important thing was that they would be safe.

The front door opened before she could reach it, and Anzu stood in the doorway and stared, horribly close to her. Nick strode into the hall to her side, and even though it might pique Anzu's curiosity, she was glad to have him there. Lydie immediately hid behind him.

"What's going on?" Anzu asked, sounding faintly puzzled.

"They're leaving," said Nick. "Get out of the way."

Anzu did not move, and, somewhat to Sin's surprise, he did not look at Nick.

He looked at her instead.

"Why are you leaving?"

"I don't think this is the best place for Toby and Lydie to be right now," Sin said honestly.

"Why not?" Anzu asked. "I have no interest in hurting them. What use are they to me? I don't take bodies under sixteen. None of us do."

Toby was full-on wailing now. Sin could not fight with him in her arms. She did not even dare raise her voice, but no matter whose body he had, at that moment she would have loved to kill Anzu.

"He's scared of you," she pointed out, and tried to control her voice, give a performance that would get her by him. "He's scared of both of you," she added, glancing at Nick. "And even if you don't mean to hurt them, they might get hurt in an accident around you guys."

Anzu gave Toby a considering look that had her baby cringing back, whimpering into Sin's neck.

"They might get hurt in an accident any time at all," he said softly.

Sin did not let herself react as if it was a threat. "That's true," she said. "But it's more dangerous around demons. Since you have no interest in us—"

"I didn't say that." Anzu smiled, lazy and malicious. He reached out a hand and touched Sin, trailing a finger along her arm, too close to her baby brother, then letting his hand fall away. "I have no interest in them."

Demons only ever touched people for one of two reasons. Sin's stomach did a slow roll of horror.

But she had no time for horror.

"Well, I am fairly interesting," she murmured, determinedly calm. "But I have these children to think of."

"Oh, they can stay, too," Anzu told her carelessly.

He could afford to be careless: she had her two vulnerabilities out in the open, and if she provoked him or Nick did, it would be the easiest thing in the world for Anzu to take revenge.

Sin caught Nick's eye and tried to convey that to him. She had no way of knowing if her message got through to him, but he stayed perfectly still as she stroked Toby's hair, desperately trying to hush him. Anzu could crush Toby's skull like an eggshell and still have Lydie's life to bargain with for her good behaviour.

She had to get the kids out, before he stopped thinking of them as a minor inconvenience to put up with and started thinking of them as leverage.

"I really think it would be best if I took them away. You can't possibly want them here."

Anzu touched her arm again, this time not lightly. He did not mind how tight he grasped, or if it hurt her.

"Have I been unclear? You're not leaving."

She had very little choice, then, except to do the one thing she had promised herself she never would, and to beg for help.

"No," said Sin, holding her head up, keeping her voice perfectly serene. "I'm just going to drop the kids off somewhere else. Then I promise you, I will come back."

She moved forward, calm and sure, not allowing her self-possession to falter for a moment and projecting the absolute conviction that he would step out of her way.

And he did, moving back until he hit the wire mesh wall.

He stood against it, black eyes intent. At that moment he looked like nothing so much as a bird of prey escaped from its cage, burning to return to the hunt.

"Where are we going?" Lydie asked when they were on the Tube, in one of the old trains with fuzzy orange benches rather than separate seats. Her voice was a bit muffled because she was pressing her face into Sin's arm.

It was hard to say the words because it still seemed unreal that she was doing this, the thing she had tried so hard to avoid doing for so long. But if she could do it, and she had to, she could say it. "I'm bringing you to my father."

"Jonathan?" Lydie asked, surprising Sin, though she supposed it was natural Lydie knew. Mama had talked about him a lot, which Lydie and Toby's father had hated. "Is he nice?" Lydie inquired, sounding a little afraid.

"Yes," Sin said firmly. "Yes. He's very nice."

Lydie seemed to be trying to burrow her way into Sin's side.

"Maybe I should stay with you. Toby should go to your father, of course, because he's only little. But maybe I could help."

Toby turned at his name and helpfully pulled Lydie's fringe.

"Thank you for offering, but I'd only be worried about you and do stupid stuff," Sin said. "You understand what's happened to Alan, don't you?"

Lydie nodded, head-butting Sin in the arm.

"I want you guys safe," Sin whispered as their train rattled into Brixton.

It was a long walk to the house, and they had to sit down on the pavement a few times. A blonde woman gave Sin a silent, reproachful look as she passed them, obviously thinking Sin was the worst babysitter in the world.

The fallen leaves along Dad's road had been rained on and had turned into soggy, solid brown banks.

Sin held on tight to Lydie's hand so Lydie couldn't slip, and they made their way through the gate and knocked on the blue-painted door. At this hour of the morning, Sin figured Grandma Tess would be catching up with the news and Dad would be in his home office. It was fifty-fifty on who would go for the door.

When the door opened, it was both of them. Grandma Tess was on the stairs, but Dad was at the door, right in front of her.

Sin was shocked to find herself shaking.

"Thea, honey," Dad said. "What's wrong?"

"Whose are those children?" Grandma Tess asked from the stairs, her voice accusing, and Sin had had enough.

"They're mine!" she shouted, and then stopped, horrified at herself. She had meant to come here and bargain and beg, Toby and Lydie's safety depended on it, and instead she had started by yelling on the doorstep so all the neighbours could hear. "I'm sorry," she said immediately, squeezing Lydie's hand. "I'm sorry for yelling. But they're mine."

Dad was looking at Lydie.

"They're Stella's," he said, soft and a little sad. "Aren't they? Come in."

"Stella's?" Grandma Tess said from the stairs.

"They're mine," Sin said fiercely. "My brother and sister. This is Lydie, and this is Toby."

"Come in," Dad said for the second time. "All of you."

Grandma Tess beckoned, Dad stood aside and Sin came in. She had to bump against Lydie as she came, Lydie orbiting her like a small, anxious moon round a planet until they both stopped at the foot of the stairs.

"Your name's Lydia?" Sin's grandmother asked.

"Lydie," Lydie said firmly.

"Your face is a sight. Who's been looking after you?"

"Sin looks after us," Lydie answered, chin up. "Sin looks after us *very well*."

Which was not at all the speech Sin had trained her to give if anyone ever came asking. That speech included vague references to Merris as their guardian; it shamed Sin that a sister of hers had such a bad memory for her part.

"Well," Grandma Tess said, and held out her hand. "Let's get your face washed. I still have some of Thea's clothes from when she was your size. Would you like to find a pretty dress?"

She descended the stairs, and after a moment's thought Lydie accepted her hand.

Grandma Tess had liked Sin best when Sin was Lydie's size, when Sin's parents were still together and she could fuss over her and fix family meals and expect more grandchildren.

"Thea, give me that child, I don't know what way you think you're holding him," said Grandma Tess, and took Toby in her arms. Toby looked uncertain for a moment, then made a grab for her glasses.

Sin had not expected Grandma Tess's desire for more grandchildren might outweigh everything else.

Behind her, Dad asked, "Why didn't you tell me?"

Relief washed away, and there was nothing left but this moment she did not know how to escape. There were no demons watching. Lydie and Toby were upstairs and did not need to be reassured.

"I'm sorry," Sin said, staring at the shadowy stairs, not wanting to look round and see his face. "I thought – I thought you never had to know. I thought it would be best for you, and I know I hurt you all those times I wouldn't even stay for dinner – but I had to be with them, I was all they had, I was responsible. I didn't have anything more fun to do. I did care about you. I did. I'm sorry."

She felt him touch her shoulders, gently, and turn her round. He touched her face with soft hands, accountant's hands that had never held a knife or a gun, and she realised she was crying.

"My brave girl," he said. "You should have told me, so I could have helped you."

"Could you keep them?" Sin asked. "I'll come back, I promise. I'm going to get a flat. I can take care of them. It's just I don't know how to keep them safe, and I don't know what else to do, but I'll make them safe. Can you keep them for just a little while?"

"Of course," Dad said. "But you're not getting a flat. Cynthia, you're sixteen years old! They can stay with us. We'll all live together. You're safe now."

She inched forward. He was the same height as she was, but she could stoop down and put her head on his shoulder, his shirt warm and woollen against her cheek, and suddenly he was the father of her childhood again, the still centre she and Mama had whirled around, the anchor without whom Mama had drifted and been lost.

It was that easy, then. She would never have believed it. Dad had left and Victor had left and now Merris had left, too, and Sin had not known how to count on anyone but herself. If she had come to Dad after that time in Mezentius House, they could all have been safe in this house for a year.

It would all have been so easy. But she wouldn't have known all she could do, if she had done that. She was her father's daughter as well as her mother's. She could be her own anchor.

And it was too late to accept help for herself now. There was a demon waiting.

"I can't stay with you, Dad," she whispered into his shoulder. "The kids wouldn't be safe. There's a demon and – and he's out, he has a body. There was this guy I loved and now this demon has him and I don't know what the demon wants with me. I have to go."

"I can't let you," Dad said. "I'm your father. It will be all right."

Sin put her arm round his neck and held on for a moment. Then she drew back, and she drew her knives.

"You're a tourist. You can't defend yourself. And think of Grandma Tess, and the kids. I can get myself out of danger, but I can't put you in it."

He was a tourist, but he'd loved a Market girl. He did not start or back away from the knives. He just stood staring at her at the foot of the stairs in his lovely house, where she was so glad, so painfully glad that he would be keeping the kids. He looked miserable.

"Thank you," she told him. "Thank you so much. I'm so sorry."

"You have nothing to be sorry for," Dad said. "Nothing at all."

The kids would have gone crazy if she had left without telling them, so they had to say a last goodbye on the doorstep. Sin was desperate to be gone by then. She didn't know how patient Anzu was going to be, and she dreaded leading him to them, and dreaded almost as much leaving them and thinking about what the demon would do next.

But at least she would be with Alan, for all the good that would do. At least she could be with him at the last, the same way she'd been with Mama. He would not be lonely or scared when he died, not if she could help it.

"Nick will take care of you," Lydie offered at the door, wanting comfort for Sin and to be comforted as well.

"I'm sure Nick will do his best," Sin lied, holding her tight. "But I can take care of myself."

On her way back alone, she thought that she could return to the Market now. Merris was not going to stay, Lydie was safe and they wouldn't want a young tourist in charge at a time like this. She might be able to win the Market right now.

Then she remembered Anzu's air when she left, the way he had looked like a hunting bird. She could not let him come hurtling down from the sky to attack the Market. If she was his target, she had to be alone.

And she didn't even know if she had the energy to win the Market back. She was so tired.

Her shoulders slumped, but as the train rattled through a space of open air, her phone buzzed in her pocket. She dug it out.

"Sin," Mae said. "A messenger just called me. She says she wants to meet, and she has an important message for me."

There was no point asking Mae if she might refuse to see the woman. Sin knew Mae well enough by now to know that.

"I'll see her with you," Sin said.

Mae sighed. "Thanks. I don't want to meet her at my aunt's house. Aunt Edith might come back unexpectedly. Do you think maybe a hotel—"

"Don't be stupid," Sin said. "Tell her to meet you at Nick's place."

There was a brief, taut pause.

"I don't much feel like seeing Nick," Mae told her in a brittle voice.

"I don't care," Sin said. "You don't know what this

messenger has to say to you, but one thing we both know: it's always best to seem strong. You want back-up, and what's better back-up than a demon on your side? Personal stuff doesn't matter. What matters is this: do you want to lead?"

"You know I do," Mae snapped.

"Do you want to lead well?"

"Of course I do!"

"Do you want it more than your pride?" Sin demanded.

The train went back into the underground even as she asked the question, and whatever reply Mae would have made was lost.

Sin knew Mae well enough by now. She was pretty confident that continuing on her way back to Nick's was the right way to go.

There would be no time to rest. She hadn't really expected it.

A boy sat on the seat across from her, eyeing her with something between hope and speculation. Sin bared her teeth at him.

"Don't even think about it," she advised, and closed her eyes and felt the train thunder beneath her, carrying her inexorably to her destination.

As Sin opened the door to Nick and Alan's flat, she heard a strange woman's voice. Sin tried to push the door open quietly, but the door to the sitting room was open. She found Nick, Mae and the messenger all staring at her as she came into the hall.

The woman was not quite a stranger after all. Sin recognised her from a few Market nights, when she had bought expensive trinkets.

The only trinkets the woman was wearing now, though,

were her earrings. The silver knives in silver circles, the token of a messenger.

Sin supposed it was a sign she was here on business.

"Sin Davies," the woman murmured, as if she had the advantage over her.

Sin raised her eyebrows.

"Jessica, isn't it?"

She gave her a dazzling, cursory smile, which the woman returned. Jessica had dark hair and an expensive suit, and she looked like a businesswoman who helped with charities in her spare time.

In what was left of her spare time after she was done carrying messages for the magicians.

Mae was sitting in the armchair, which she must have moved so it was as distant from both sofas as it could be while still being in the same room. She was regarding the messenger with a remote air, like a queen.

Nick was sitting in the other sofa, scowling across at the messenger. Anzu was not there.

Nick said, "You're just in time."

"For what?"

"To hear me finish delivering my message," Jessica replied. "Which Nick seems to find so amusing."

"It's the way you tell it," Nick assured her.

"Apparently Gerald wants me to meet him," Mae said in a colourless voice. "He says he wants to make a bargain with me."

"Anything to oblige Gerald, of course," Nick said. "What can I do for him? Does he want to borrow a cup of sugar? I'm afraid I'm all out of brothers. He took my last one."

Nick's voice had grown colder and harder as he kept speaking, every word like a stone being hurled.

"He doesn't want anything from you at all," Jessica said, smiling sweetly at him. "If he did, he'd just order you to give it to him. And you'd have to do it, wouldn't you?"

Nick glared at her. Jessica was looking at Mae and did not even seem to notice.

"He wants Celeste's pearl," Jessica told Mae. "He has something to offer you in return. Something he thinks you'll be very interested in. He wants to meet you this evening to discuss it."

So Gerald thought Mae had the pearl. Since Sin had come to the same conclusion herself at first, she felt she could hardly blame him.

But what did he have to bargain with, and why did he want to bargain when he could just try to take? Did he want to make a bargain with Mae, who he must presume was the new leader of the Goblin Market, in the same way he'd tried to make a bargain with Merris? Did he want them to promise they would leave the magicians to their killing and never help another tourist?

Sin's lip curled as she watched Jessica. Mae would never go for it.

"Something I'll be interested in?" Mae repeated inquiringly.

"How interesting!" Nick said in a savage voice. "Do you have any useful hints, or are you trying to entice me by being a woman of mystery? Mae's not going to meet Gerald anywhere."

"Mae's not going to be spoken for," Mae told him. "Mae can speak for her own damn self. What will Gerald do if I don't go?"

Jessica shrugged. "I imagine he will come to find you."

And if he did, he'd find Mae's aunt or the Market. Sin could see the wheels in Mae's brain turning.

She could see Mae was curious.

So, apparently, could Nick.

He stood up from the sofa and said, his voice rolling through the room like thunder in the sky, "You're not going."

Mae's eyes narrowed. "Don't you dare try to stop me." She sat glaring up at him for a moment, then turned deliberately to Jessica and said in a cool voice, "Excuse me. If I'm meeting Gerald, I'm going to have to settle matters with this demon first."

Jessica waved a hand giving permission. Mae turned with such vehemence her shoe squeaked on the floor, and made for the door. Nick followed hard on her heels.

The shouting started about an instant after the door to the hall banged shut behind him.

"Pardon me," Sin said, and slipped out after them. "Do you two mind keeping it down? There's a messenger in there listening to every word you say!"

"Then you take a turn getting this through his thick head," Mae said. "I'm going. It's the best thing for the Market, to find out what he wants right away. It's the best thing for all of us."

"I agree with you," Sin said.

Mae flashed her a grateful look, and Nick glared at them both. "And it hasn't occurred to you that Gerald won't be pleased when he finds out you don't have the pearl?"

"He won't believe I don't have it if I don't come," Mae said. "And then he'll come for me. The only thing to do is talk to him, and find out what he thinks he has to offer."

"What if he gets annoyed by the fact you don't have the pearl and *kills you*?" Nick shouted.

"Jamie won't let him kill me," Mae said.

"What if he kills both of you?" Nick raged. "What am I meant to do, then?"

Mae stepped in close to Nick and shoved him furiously

hard. Nick did not brace himself against the blow. His back hit the wall. He did not react much at all; he just kept that dark, intent stare on Mae.

"What do you mean by that?" Mae demanded.

Nick hesitated. There was a click in his throat, as if it was dry, as if he was out of words.

They waited, and he wasn't.

"I was fighting Anzu up on the roof yesterday," he said at last. "I could see all of London. I'd just beaten Anzu, and it wasn't any good, it didn't make any difference, Alan was still gone. And I thought about setting the river on fire again. I thought about setting the whole city on fire, and watching it burn. I was angry enough to make it happen. But then I thought of you and Jamie."

His voice was expressionless. Mae stared at him, her eyes suddenly beseeching as well as furious, and Nick looked away from her and stared at the floor.

"I want to burn the world because Alan is gone," he said. "I want to destroy everything I see. But you mean something to me. I will not destroy the world, because it has you in it."

Nick crossed his arms defensively over his chest. They were all silent for a moment.

Mae said, in a voice trying far too hard to sound practical, "Also, Liannan took half your power, so you probably couldn't destroy the world if you wanted to."

"I don't know about that – I set the river on fire. I could set the city on fire. I could give destroying the world a good try. I was never really sure how much power my brother left me, but it seems like it was more than I thought. It seems like he gambled on me one more time. So you see," Nick said, soft and menacing, "you and Jamie are all that is protecting the world from me. You should think about that before you throw both your lives away."

Mae looked shaken. "You mean something to me, too. But that doesn't mean I forgive you. And it doesn't mean I'm not going. I am."

"Then promise me something," Nick said. "Promise me that if things get bad, you'll let me handle it."

There was another pause, during which Sin saw Mae think it over.

She finally promised, "I'll let you have first try."

They returned more sedately than they had left. Jessica had an air of slight amusement as they filed in.

"We're going," Mae announced. "All of us. Where does Gerald want to meet?"

"At the Monument, six o'clock," Jessica replied.

Sin was startled. She carefully did not look at either of the others, lest she betray that fact.

The Monument was not part of Bankside. It was outside the Aventurine Circle's circle of power. Other people could use magic there.

But Gerald had control of a demon, and Mae had no magic at all. He obviously wasn't afraid of anything the Market could do.

"We'll be there," Mae said, with barely a pause. "And you don't have any hint of what this bargain he is offering might be?"

"Hey, just the messenger," Jessica said. "Not even that for long."

"And what do you mean by that?" Sin asked.

Jessica looked across at her. "Haven't you heard?" she

inquired. "I suppose the exile's always the last to know. Merris Cromwell left a necromancer in charge of the House of Mezentius. And the new leader of the Goblin Market is a tourist." Jessica's coolly amused gaze slid to Mae, standing still as stone, and back. "I heard she says that anyone who wants to join the Goblin Market – necromancers, pied pipers, potion-makers, messengers – can join. They'll be just as good as the Market people, they can travel with them if they want and there will be no private deals between Market folk or keeping any particular magic for themselves." Jessica shrugged. "Who knows if it will last? But I thought it was worth looking into. I'm getting tired of the magicians' games."

So Mae was being referred to as the new leader of the Goblin Market, as if she had won by default.

Even worse, Mae was not denying that she wanted to overturn Sin's Market into chaos, in a time of war. She couldn't trust the people they had, let alone a pack of necromancers, carrying their dead bodies around with them wherever they went; potion-makers, who used God knew what ingredients in their potions; or pied pipers who would pipe you down the river literally for the joy of the song.

Worse than any of them, worthless messengers who had been reporting back to magicians their whole lives.

The worthless messenger eyed Sin, looking a little amused. "Don't say you're upset, my dear."

"Actually," said Sin, "I wasn't planning on talking to you again at all."

17

The Knife That Would Cut Through Anything

MAE LEFT ALMOST AS SOON AS THE MESSENGER HAD, SAYING she had to make preparations for the meeting with Gerald. Sin suspected that Mae simply wanted to get away from her, and told Mae they'd follow her.

She had a lot to say to Mae, but first there was something she had to ask Nick.

"Where's Anzu?"

"I let him go and try to find Liannan," Nick said. "He was angry that you left, and I knew she would be long gone by now. Neither of us were ever able to find her when she didn't want to be found."

It was a relief, a reprieve, not to be faced with Anzu right now. But Sin knew you had to pay for most gifts in the end.

"So he won't find her," Sin said. "And he'll come back angrier than he left."

Nick nodded, inscrutable as ever, betraying not the slightest worry about what Anzu might do when he was angry. On the whole Sin thought that was better. She could imagine it well enough on her own.

"Well, we'll have to deal with that when it happens," she said. "Let's go before he comes back."

She had to deal with the Market, and then the magicians, and last of all the demon.

The Market was not, as Sin had uneasily feared, in ruins.

It was under construction.

She and Nick could hear the hammering from halfway up Horsenden Hill. The ringing floated up into the clear, blue dome of the sky like bells.

Sin lengthened her stride and Nick fell slightly behind, obviously not seeing the urgency of the situation at all. He seemed totally unmoved when they reached the crest of the hill and saw the new wagons. Some were brilliant with fresh paint in the sun. A couple were wooden skeletons, planks bare and spaced out like the yellowed ribs on the skeletons of extinct animals in museums.

She recognised almost everyone who was there, milling around, whether they were helping with the construction or fixing food or – as a lot of them seemed to be – standing around talking in unhappy knots.

Mae was on the ground, hands cupped round her mouth so she could yell something up at Sin's friend Jonas, who was standing on the roof of a half-built wagon rolling his eyes, as if what she had to say was not significantly helpful. He caught sight of Sin and called out, "Sin! You came back."

Mae turned and strode across the sunlit grass, beaming.

"Hey, Sin," she said. "What do you think?"

"You invited necromancers to live with us?"

Mae blinked. "Sin, we needed more people. Confusion to the enemy, right? They won't know what messengers to use, they won't know exactly who's with us or how much magic they have when they attack. Besides, this is the right thing to do."

"To invite necromancers to live with us," Sin said, just in case Mae had missed that point before.

"Yes!" Mae said. "They're all on our side. They're not magicians. We can use all the magic and all the help we can get, and the Goblin Market should be a place where we can all live and work together, not just one night a month."

"And you're the authority on how the Goblin Market needs tearing to pieces, why exactly?"

"Who else is there?" Mae demanded. "What would you do?"

A young potion-maker Sin knew called Isabella yelled out to Mae about where to put something. Mae glanced round.

"Coming! Excuse me, I'll be right back," she said. "You," she added, addressing Nick in a cold voice, as if to prove to both herself and him that she truly had not forgiven him. "You're a demon, right? I seem to recall something of that sort. If you have to be here, go and make yourself useful."

Mae stared stonily at Nick. Nick stared back, his face a blank wall, but after a moment he walked towards one of the wagons under construction. Mae glared after him and then went running off to Isabella.

Sin was left standing alone at her own Market, with nothing to do.

"Sin," said Carl the weapons master, breaking away from one of the murmuring knots of people. "Thank God you're here." He hesitated. "Where's the—"

"Lydie's with my father."

Carl's face cleared. Sin's father was a tourist, after all, not one of them. "That was the right decision. And now you can be here for us. That tourist's got completely above herself, and she's running wild. Some of those necromancers arrived with stinking bodies in their cars."

Confusion to the enemy seemed to be leading to confusion about who the enemy was.

"Nobody's happy," Carl murmured conspiratorially. "Look around."

She looked at Jonas trudging by with his tools and fresh wood in hand, wearing a scowl caught between uncertainty and anger, and she realised that most of the core Market people, the real Market people, were feeling that uncertainty and anger. They were feeling abandoned enough that they would put their trust in what was familiar. Merris was possessed and abandoning them. Mae was a tourist dragging chaos in her wake.

Sin had arrived without a magician in tow. They knew her.

She wouldn't even have to try and win them back. If she started giving orders, they would obey.

It was a stunning realisation. Even more stunning was the second one.

She didn't know what orders to give. "Everything stay the same!" was probably not a good idea, given that the magicians could attack at any moment.

And given that the magicians could attack at any moment, having more people in place to fight started to seem like a better idea.

Sin caught sight of Matthias, piping beside one of the wagons shining with new paint. There were tiny objects floating

301

in the air all around him: hinges, nails and several small screwdrivers.

She excused herself to Carl and headed over to him.

"Hey," she said. "Got a minute?"

Matthias lowered his pipes. A dozen nails dropped lightly to the ground and lay sprinkled and gleaming in the grass. "Not really."

Sin inclined her head to the wagon. "You moving in as well?"

"Oh, yes," said Matthias. "Nothing in the world I want more than to live with you miscreants in all this racket."

"Why are you helping, then?"

Matthias, raising his pipes back to his lips, paused. "If people are so massively misguided as to want to live with you," he said eventually, "they should be allowed." He paused again. "Besides," he added, "with the new regime, I thought I might bring my parents to the next Market."

"Your – what?"

"My *parents*," Matthias repeated irritably.

Sin had never thought of Matthias as having parents. She supposed it was logical, most people had them, but Matthias liked music so much more than people, she would hardly have been surprised to learn his father was a flute and his mother a music stand.

With the new vision that came from being jolted into a new way of thinking, Sin watched him push back his hair and noticed that despite how gaunt and worn he was, he was probably still in his early twenties.

She wondered if there were young necromancers, too.

"Your parents would have been welcome any time," she said.

"Oh, yes," said Matthias. "Anyone with money's welcome. And if they happened to hear a joke about pipers stealing children, well, where's the harm?"

Sin didn't make piper jokes herself, because it would be insane for a dancer to annoy her musicians. But she'd heard them. "That bothers you?"

"Only the fact that they're stupid," Matthias snapped. "What the hell would I do with a pack of children anyway? My landlord doesn't allow pets. But my parents don't need to know about it. They gave up a lot for their piper son. I accidentally stole their voices when I was a kid, and they think the Market is this place of – of *celebration*. They don't need to come here and see me sneered at."

Sin chose her words with care, because she was not sure how to respond to what Matthias was saying, but she had asked to hear it. He deserved a thoughtful response.

"You think all this will make that better?"

"I don't know," Matthias said. "But the Market spoke, and my people came at their word. And I'll play for them. Or I would, if you would stop asking me ridiculous questions."

"Just one more," Sin promised. "I guess you've changed your mind about who should lead the Market?"

"Is the leadership still in question?" Matthias asked. "If it is, I think you should let us know. A lot of people might be very interested."

He raised his pipes to his mouth with an air of decision and resumed playing. Sin opened her mouth, and he raised one eyebrow in a manner that suggested he would not be impressed if she spoke, and the nails rose from the grass, hanging in the sky like tiny stars.

Sin turned away and saw Nick and Mae standing side by

side. They looked a bit funny together, Sin thought, Nick tall and grim and Mae so short, with her bright, silly hair.

They didn't look like they were having a funny conversation. Sin started over to them.

"I won't do it again," she heard Nick say abruptly as she came into earshot.

"You're damn right you won't," Mae told him. "If you do, I swear, I'll find some way to kill you."

"Hi, guys," Sin greeted them, with the carefully assumed air of someone too preoccupied to pay much attention to other people's conversations. "Were you talking about Gerald's little message?"

Immediately Sin could see Mae's brain turning possibilities into a checklist and ticking them off. "No, but I was thinking that Seb has the pearl, and wondering why he hasn't handed it over. He has to have it, because none of us do. If I had it, I'd be wearing it and using it to rule the Goblin Market."

"You seem to have appointed yourself leader anyway," Sin remarked.

"Well, I don't have it," said Nick into the ensuing silence. "And I don't feel the Market has done anything terrible enough to deserve me as its leader, though my face would look amazing on the money. But if Seb has it, I'll kill him for it. And then I'll give the pearl to Mae."

Mae met his gaze coolly. "I've told you I want to get it for myself."

Nick turned away, and Mae watched him go for a moment, then fixed her eyes on the construction of one of the wagons.

"All of our fuss over that pearl," she said in a brittle voice. "And it looks like neither of us is going to get it."

"Looks like," Sin murmured. "I didn't want it for me

anyway. I wanted it for Merris. I thought it could help her fight back the demon." She paused. "Not that I didn't also want to win."

"I wanted to win, too." Mae's hand went up to touch her talisman, and then the place where her mark lay beside it. "And I wanted the pearl for me, as well. So I could fight back the demon."

Sin took a deep breath and shoved envy aside.

"I'm sorry Nick did that to you. If I was you, I'd be sick about it. When I saw him do it, I wanted to kill him. But he said he wouldn't do it again."

Mae sighed. "Yeah."

"You don't believe him?"

"I believe him; he can't lie," Mae said. "It just doesn't matter. I don't want him to be holding back from controlling me. I want him not to be able to do it. When he can just make me turn round, make me do what he wants, make me think or feel whatever he wants, even if he never does again, how the hell am I meant to be around him? Let alone . . ."

"Let alone what?" Sin asked gently.

Mae set her jaw. "There's something I want to tell him," she said, not looking at Sin but at the wagons she had ordered built. "Something he probably won't understand. But I want to tell him anyway. I can't, not when we're like this, but I thought if I could get that pearl . . . I thought maybe I could." Mae tried to smile. The expression folded in on itself. "Pretty stupid, right?"

Sin, who could smile on command a hell of a lot better than Mae could, did so. Her smile made Mae smile back, just for a minute, but for real.

"Oh, I'm not all that surprised. You never met a ridiculous

305

challenge you didn't like. Which is not to say it's not stupid, mind you."

"Thanks," Mae told her, and made a face. "Your support means a lot to me." She shoved her hands in her jeans pockets. "You don't – uh, you don't seem altogether thrilled by the plans I have for the Market."

"That would be because I'm not."

"Merris came to see me today," Mae said. "She said you sent her. Thank you."

Sin felt the practised smile slip off her face. "It doesn't seem to have done much good."

"None of this would be happening if Merris hadn't given me the nod and let me put it all into motion," Mae said. "I'm – I'm sort of in charge, because nobody else wants to do it, but they wouldn't have let me do any of this if Merris hadn't spoken to them. That's down to you."

"I'm thrilled."

"Merris didn't seem to think my ideas were too bad," Mae offered, almost tentatively.

"I'm not Merris, am I?" Sin returned, and softened slightly at the look of dismay on Mae's face. "I wouldn't leave."

"So," Mae said, still looking wary. "If you don't approve of what I'm doing, are you going to do something about it?"

Was she going to stage some sort of coup? Maybe, if she had had a plan of her own, if she had not promised a demon she would deliver herself into his hands and promised her father she would come home safe.

"Sure I'm going to do something," Sin answered. "I'm going to go with both of you tonight. And I'm going to ask if you'll send some Market people along ahead of us. We could use the back-up."

Mae's eyes shone. "I was already planning on it."

"Good," Sin said. "Because the asking was going to be pretty much a formality."

They both laughed a little, and then stood silently together for a little while more, watching the new Market rise around them.

The Monument to the Great Fire of London was a looming shape against the evening sky, looking like a tower for the villain of a story. The lights of London touched on the golden urn high at the top of the column, making it shimmer and then dim.

They had to walk a few steps down the incline to get there from Monument tube station.

"You know, we could've driven here," Sin remarked. "If you hadn't insisted on driving into London Bridge."

"It's true what you see on the news," Nick said. "Teenage guys are a menace on the roads. Reckless drivers. Speed demons."

Sin noted the glints on top of a grey office building, on the roof of another building with a glass front. The archers were in place.

She looked back to Nick, who was walking in the middle, between her and Mae. The line of his shoulders made her think of a high stone wall, a scribble of wire mesh at the top, surrounding a prison nobody could ever escape. He looked like he wanted to kill someone.

They went round the pedestal bearing its sculpture of angels watching human misery, to the other side.

The Aventurine Circle stood in a group at the foot of the Monument.

Sizing up the enemy, Sin saw signs of dissension in the

ranks. About half the Circle was there, and about half of those present were wearing the Aventurine Circle's usual pale clothes. The other half were wearing ordinary dark or colourful clothes, and nobody was standing very close to one another, shoulder to shoulder as they should have with companions they trusted.

Helen the swordswoman was wearing white and had an air very similar to Nick's about her.

Gerald was wearing clothes that were a combination of both light and dark, and his mood seemed to be shifting even as he stood there. Looking at him made Sin think of Matthias the piper: it came as another shock to realise that Gerald was very young as well.

Celeste had threatened him into joining her Circle, and now she was dead and he was leader of a Circle that barely knew him, that could hardly be expected to respect him. And he had lost Celeste's pearl, not only a powerful magical object but the leader's token of power in the Circle.

As they drew closer, Sin saw that Gerald was toying with the ring on his left hand, an obvious sign of discomfort.

An uncertain leader could be unpredictable. Gerald had invented the mark that delivered Alan into his hands. He was too clever and he had too much power over Nick: if he was feeling backed into a corner, he could be even more dangerous.

Sin noticed where Nick's attention was fixed. He did not even seem aware Gerald existed. He was staring, murderous intent clear in every line of his body, at Seb.

His look seemed to clear a space around Seb, the other magicians unobtrusively drawing away. Seb stood on the grey cobbles, looking very alone.

He'd been looking as unsettled as Gerald, but strangely,

Nick's cold stare seemed to calm him. He squared his shoulders and glared back at Nick as if he would have a chance fighting him. There was hectic colour in his face now, as if he had a fever, and a reckless glint in his green eyes.

The glint died and his eyes went flat as Gerald said, "Mae, always a pleasure. Come to make a trade?"

"That depends," Mae said. "I'd like to know what this thing I'm trading the pearl for is. The one I'm supposed to find so interesting."

Gerald smiled at her, though the smile was strained at the edges. "Well, here's the thing," he said. "If I thought Nick had the pearl, I would have just ordered him to hand it over. I thought it might be Seb, who is coward enough to grab at anything that looks like leverage, but I offered Seb the same trade as I'm going to offer you. I really think he would have taken it, if he'd had the pearl."

The glance he cast Seb was dismissive. Seb shot back a look of such open loathing Sin was shocked: no magician was going to survive who displayed such hostility to his leader.

"I don't have it," Seb ground out.

"I believe you, Sebastian," Gerald replied lightly. "I think Mae here has it. And she has a weakness."

Gerald gave a smile; the corner of his mouth twisted as if he wanted to rip the smile off his own face.

"Everyone has a weakness," he continued. "Either you destroy your own weakness, or people use it against you. I think this qualifies as me doing both."

Gerald turned abruptly away from them, bowing his head, and made a swift gesture.

Laura and another magician, both in dark clothes, stepped apart.

Jamie was crouching at the base of the Monument, back to the white fence surrounding it. He was in chains.

Sin had known he would pay for defending Nick. She had not dreamed he would pay as much as this.

For a moment Sin could not even feel sorry for Jamie. She just felt stunned.

If Seb had the necklace, he would have given it to Gerald in exchange for Jamie's life. She was sure of that.

So who in the name of God had the pearl?

All Sin knew was that she did not.

She looked at Mae, and saw that Nick had grabbed her arm.

"You promised," Nick murmured, low so only Mae and Sin could hear. "You promised me I could have first try. And I promised you I would take care of Jamie. Let me."

Mae's whole body was as taut as a bow, taut with the longing to fly to her brother, but between her teeth she said, "Fine."

Nick stepped forward. Sin looked at Jamie, his thin, bowed back and the expression he wore on his face, trying to look brave, and she was sorry for him, then.

"Tell me, Mae," Gerald said. "Where have you hidden the pearl?"

Mae looked at Nick. It was a nasty moment for Sin to remember that Nick couldn't lie.

"You won't kill him." Nick's voice rumbled in the centre of his chest, lower than his usual tone. She thought it might be his version of uncertainty.

Gerald stopped toying with his ring.

"Watch me," he said softly.

It was obvious that some of the other magicians were

uneasy. Helen, who had put the sword through Jamie's mother, looked like she wanted to be sick.

Sin had to wonder why they cared. She'd seen them set fire to her home, which could have had children in it, and then she remembered the way Helen had been with Lydie.

They thought magicians were the only real people in the world. They didn't want to witness their leader killing one of their own.

Gerald was making a bad mistake. He would regret this.

Regret wouldn't save Jamie. Sin didn't dare move. Nick was as unmoving as stone.

The one who moved was Jamie. Crouched there with the white stone of the Monument towering behind him, the Latin inscribed on it making it look like the tallest gravestone in the world, he looked small and helpless, his mouth trembling.

Sin saw that only one of his arms was chained. The other was free.

Between his skin and his sleeve, she saw a glint of metal.

The magicians thought that Sin had disappeared with the magic knife, the only weapon that could have cut her chains. They didn't know that Sin had given it back.

What this called for was a diversion.

Sin stepped forward, tossing her hair over her shoulder. "What if I have the pearl, Gerald?" she asked in a ringing voice. "I don't care what happens to Jamie."

"If you have the pearl," Gerald said, and advanced on her, "I doubt you're bright enough to have hidden it. We can just take it."

A lick of fire burst from Gerald's fingertips, turning into a rope of light headed straight for Sin.

It veered off into the sky abruptly when Gerald, the most

recent in a long line of men who had underestimated Sin, had to dodge back from an arrow.

"Do you ever get tired of being wrong?" Sin asked as the magicians scattered, looking to the roofs.

None of them were looking at Jamie, as oblivious to him as the passers-by along the dark road, making for the Tube and unable to see their little enchanted space.

Jamie brought the knife down with a crash on his chains.

The knife hit his chains and stopped as if it was made of plastic.

The magicians had not been fools enough to chain up a powerful magician with anything but chains that were enchanted themselves to resist magic. Sin froze in horror.

Everyone was looking at Jamie again now. The magicians murmured, a half-pitying and half-satisfied sound rippling from head to head. Gerald glanced back over his shoulder and laughed, light and mocking, as if at a stupid child.

Across grey stones and a dark sky, gold glinting far above him, Jamie's magic-pale eyes narrowed to glowing lines.

He brought the knife back round, its blaze blurring the air round it, its hungry whine louder than ever.

Jamie launched himself to his feet, stumbling forward, free. The chains fell clinking to the base of the Monument.

Jamie's left hand lay, severed neatly, palm up on the grey stones.

A trail of blood blazed scarlet behind him as he staggered forward, and several magicians stepped up to help him and then stopped themselves.

All but one.

Seb lunged forward and grabbed Jamie, both of them hurtling past Sin and landing practically at Nick's feet. Sin glanced round and saw Nick on his knees, snarling something and touching Jamie's arm. The blood stopped spurting from the horrible space where his hand had been, and they were all three crouched on the cobblestones, shirts covered with a vivid mess of blood. Jamie was sobbing, low and hoarse.

Sin and Mae exchanged looks. Mae had gone bone white, but as Sin met her eyes, she nodded once, slowly.

Both of them drew their knives and stood protectively in front of the boys.

The sight of weapons galvanised Helen. She drew her sword and went for Sin, who parried the sword with one knife, then cut in at Helen's ribs with the other. Helen only just managed to leap back and deflect the strike.

A blaze of magic flew at Sin from another magician's fingers, and she had to throw herself back out of its path. She smelled the ends of her own hair burning.

All around them, arrows were let fly. Mae had hurled herself on the ground to escape them.

Helen attacked again, delivering a strike so hard that Sin held her knives crossed one in front of the other so both knives absorbed the impact of the blow, jarring the bones of her arms to the elbows. Sin saw another magician's hands brighten and she ducked and dived, sliding on her belly on the cobblestones and snatching Helen's ankle, pulling her foot out from under her.

She couldn't keep dodging, she thought as she rolled and sprang back up. She could hold them off for maybe two minutes longer.

Nick rose from his crouch, and there was no more light glancing on the Monument.

The storm rolled in low. It felt as if the city of London had been swallowed at a gulp by some vast, hungry beast.

"You took my brother," the demon said, and his voice echoed against that dense, dark sky. "Now you've crippled my friend. There is almost nothing else in the world you can do to me, and absolutely nothing else you can bargain with. All I want is to tear you to *shreds!*"

Lightning hit the Monument and travelled down and down, enveloping the whole stone column in a shimmering blanket of light. The light chased down the column to the ground in seconds, and when it hit, it hit two magicians.

It didn't hit Gerald.

He said, "I command you not to hurt any member of my Circle. And I don't think Jamie is in any state to counteract my order."

A shudder passed through Nick, as if he was trying to ripple out of his own shape and become something else, anything else so long as it could leap at Gerald and destroy him.

Gerald's lips curled.

Then his face was obscured.

The piping started, eerie and low, as if it came creeping with the mist over the broken cobblestones from the lightning strike. Every loose shard of stone began to rise, dancing in the air and then being hurled at the magicians.

The pipers of the Goblin Market were hidden on the rooftops, in the mist. The magicians had nothing to fight. Sin almost laughed in triumph, and then had to whirl out of the way of Helen's sword, jumping in mid-air and twisting. She didn't have to be better than Helen. She only had to be faster.

Then she looked round to check on Jamie. He was unconscious in Seb's lap, Mae on her knees beside them. The wound where his hand had been was nothing but smooth skin, and his face, gilded by lightning, was grey and still.

Sin spun into engagement with Helen, making her knives a blur, almost dancing, going for the quick cuts to Helen's arms and legs, holding her off and distracting her so she would let Sin move. She hurtled right into the path of Nick's sword.

Nick checked his swing just in time and threw himself at her. Sin tumbled down to the cobblestones with Nick on top of her as Gerald's latest fireball whizzed over their heads.

Nick took his weight on his arms, braced on either side of her. She was extremely grateful: it left her with enough breath to hiss, "Jamie's in shock or worse. We have to get him some help! How much magic do you have left after healing him and causing a storm?"

Nick hesitated.

"That much, huh."

"Enough," Nick growled, and a dark cloud fell like a curtain. The little light remaining in the sky went out.

The bells of St Magnus the Martyr pealed out from below in a rush of music that ended in a deep clang, like another, closer thunderclap.

Mist and storm cloud met to make their little stretch of cobblestones a square of impenetrable smoke. It bought them enough time to scramble to their feet, dash to collect the magicians who were on their side and run.

~ 18 ~

Reaching Through the Dark for You

THEY TOOK JAMIE TO THE GOBLIN MARKET. IT WAS ACTUALLY very helpful to know where you could go to find all the potion-makers.

They did not let the older members of the actual Market know they were bringing magicians in, but Sin did get her friend Chiara to help.

Nick and Mae went outside, Sin presumed to fight where they would not disturb Jamie. Sin stayed in the wagon with Chiara and a potion-maker called June, helping them mix up concoctions for pain with fever fruit as well as willow bark. Someone had run for one of the pipers, and a girl carrying an ivory-inlaid pipe played a song to soothe care away.

The song was like one of those shells in which you can hear the sea turned inside out, the pearly inside of the shell as much part of the music as the soft sound of a private ocean. Everything seemed all right while she played.

And then she stopped.

"Well, I suppose I can see why the pipers might be a bit

useful to have around," Chiara whispered grudgingly. "I still can't stand the necromancers, though."

June and Sin exchanged grins over a pestle and mortar, and the piper began another tune.

Eventually, though, she was tired and they had done all they could do, and Jamie started to stir. They had made sure he was not in any pain, but nobody could replace that gaping emptiness at his wrist. His arm lay on top of his blanket and their eyes kept falling to the place where his hand should be.

He didn't start screaming when he woke. He made a little, painful gasping sound. Sin had to lay her own hands flat on the table to stop them shaking.

"Hey, Sin," he said, his voice a thread.

She tried to make hers gentle and reassuring. "Hey, Jamie."

"Thanks for getting me out."

"You got yourself out," Sin told him.

Jamie's mouth was pulled out of shape for a moment, but he managed to say, "Yeah." There was a pause. "Is – is my sister, Mae, here? Is Nick?"

The others could not seem to even look at Jamie, so Sin had been appointed spokesperson. "They'll be back soon."

"Oh," Jamie said, forlorn. "Oh, thanks. That's good."

He turned his face away on his pillow. He looked all of eight years old swallowed up in blue blankets, alone in a strange place with strange people, hurt and scared.

Sin marched out of the door and almost fell over Seb, sitting on the top step. She bit back a curse, closed the door and walked down the two steps of the wagon so she could stand on the ground and face him.

"Get in there," she ordered.

Seb stared at her, looking startled to be spoken to. He

looked as if he had been a thousand miles away and having a nightmare there.

"He doesn't want me in there," he said. "He hates me."

"Yeah?" Sin asked. "How do you figure that?"

"He's told me that he hates me?" Seb answered. "Seven times."

"Ah." Sin thought this over for a moment. "Well, get in there anyway. I saw you two making your lunatic pact to be evil boyfriends."

"That wasn't real," Seb said. He dropped his head so he was staring at his fists, clenched against his knees, and not looking at her. "He only suggested it because he didn't trust me to be on his side without it. He doesn't like me."

"What does that matter?" Sin inquired, as Seb made a noise that sounded like it was going to become a protest. "You're in love with him, right?"

Seb looked horrified and embarrassed and ashamed all at once. Sin had no time for it.

"You're the only person here he knows. He's surrounded by strangers and he's badly hurt and his whole life is going to change because of it. So it's simple. Do you want to be there for him or not?"

Seb squared his big shoulders and stood up.

Sin smiled at his back. "That's what I thought."

She was delayed following him up the steps by the others, seizing the chance of his entry to leave. When Sin got to the door, she found him standing across the room from Jamie's bed, arms crossed over his chest.

"Hey," he said awkwardly.

Jamie smiled. It was a very faint effort, but it looked real. "Hey, Seb. Sorry if I got you into trouble."

Seb looked at the ground. "I was in trouble anyway."

"I didn't help," Jamie said. "I'm sorry about dragging you into my evil schemes with my masculine wiles. I didn't realise, um, the force of my own wiliness. I don't actually use my wiles a lot."

Seb could not seem to help smiling, though his smile was still directed at the ground. "You just had to ask. I didn't do anything I wouldn't have done anyway."

"Oh," said Jamie.

"I've known you since we were fourteen," Seb informed him. "You didn't fool me. And I knew the evil schemes were never going to be as evil as all that. But that doesn't – Jamie, that doesn't matter. How are you doing?"

"Great," Jamie said.

That made Seb look up. "Great?" he echoed blankly.

Jamie smiled. It was brighter than the first smile, even though it was shaky. "Yeah," he said. "I think this is going to be really good for my street cred. Don't you think I'd look cool with a hook?"

Seb laughed and immediately looked horrified at himself, then stole another glance at Jamie and laughed again.

"Nah," he said. "You never look cool."

He ventured to push himself away from the wall of the wagon and approach Jamie's bed. When Jamie blinked up at him and did not yell for him to get back, he sat down cautiously.

"I could maybe draw you with a hook?" he offered. "So you'd know what it would look like."

He pulled a tiny pencil and tinier notebook out from his jeans pocket and glanced at Jamie for approval. Jamie, still looking terrified and small but a little steadier, nodded.

Sin heard voices outside and stepped back, closing the door

so whoever it was wouldn't ruin the moment, and saw Mae bearing down across the dark fields with Nick behind her.

As Sin watched, Nick drew level with Mae and said something to her, too low for Sin to hear, and Mae whirled round and punched him in the face.

"What was that?" Nick asked.

Sheer horror at what she had done crossed Mae's face for a split second, only to be submerged in the rising flood of rage.

"I'm serious," Nick said while she shook. "What was that? Don't punch people with your thumb inside your fist like that. You could break your thumb that way."

"Don't make fun of me," Mae cried. "Don't you dare. I trusted you. I trusted you to keep Jamie safe! What were you doing? How could you let this happen?"

"What was I doing?" Nick demanded. "Oh, standing idly by. What else would I be doing? Since I have absolute power over everything in this world. I thought it would be fun to watch Jamie get hurt. I'm just sorry I missed seeing Alan get possessed!"

"You probably didn't miss much," Mae shouted back. "It was probably just like all the times you possessed people yourself. They had families, too."

"You don't have to tell me I deserve what happened to Alan," Nick snarled. "I know I deserve it. I've possessed people; I've killed for thousands of years and I never cared about it. I could never even imagine regretting it. But I can now. I'm sorry now. Does that satisfy you? I'm sorry now. I'm sorry about Jamie. I would have done anything to stop him getting hurt, but I couldn't do anything. I'm sorry, and it doesn't matter at all."

"I appreciate it, though," Jamie called out.

His voice was completely audible through the wagon walls. Mae and Nick both looked round. Sin, at the door, gave them a little wave.

"We can hear you," Seb contributed helpfully.

"Could you maybe come inside and yell here?" Jamie asked. "I'd – I'd like to see you."

Mae charged for the door. Sin stepped aside, off the wagon steps and into the night-damp grass.

She didn't want to go back inside. This wasn't her tragedy. She hardly knew Jamie, and what she did know she did not much like. He had traded in Nick's freedom, no matter how good his intentions.

She didn't want to see Mae cry and try to fold Jamie against her, the space where his hand should have been a terrible obstacle between them. The two people in there were people who loved Jamie: he deserved to be surrounded in love now, in the darkest night of his life.

"Nick too," Jamie called out, his voice muffled and a little wavering.

Nick, came at the magician's call, not glancing at Sin as he went by. It was impossible to see from his blank face what he felt at the order.

He had to do whatever Jamie said, and Jamie had betrayed him. But Nick was sorry Jamie was hurt.

Sin did not understand the ways of magicians and demons, and she did not know where else to go. She didn't want to ask anyone in the Market for shelter, and now that she was alone with her thoughts, she could not help but think of Alan, of how he would never be rescued like Jamie.

Sin turned away from the wagons and towards the fields, through deep night and wet grass to the place where she'd taught Alan to use the bow. She sat cross-legged in the middle of a field, hands clasped and arms stretched out, and looked at the lights of the Market, not her home for the first time in her life. She was so glad Lydie and Toby were safe, but she was used to them always being there, always being a worry and a comfort and company.

Now it was just her, alone in the night, with nothing she could do and nobody to depend on her. She couldn't think of a way to stay strong for another minute.

Sin laid her head down on her arms and cried.

She looked up after a while, shoulders shaking, because the Market was bred in her bones though it had cast her out, and she knew when a chill running down the back of your neck meant nothing and when it meant a demon was near.

Anzu was sitting very close. He was watching her solemnly, black eyes wide, like a child who did not understand what she was doing. He reached out a hand to touch her face. When his fingers came away wet with tears, he smiled, as if wondering at the gleam in the moonlight.

"Come here," he said.

Sin shook her head dumbly. But this was what demons did; they came when you were weak, when you had nothing left to lose and no way out of your pain.

"Come here to me, like you did before," Anzu said, soft, coaxing her, and he put an arm round her and drew her in close.

It was Alan's body and not Alan's body, it was Alan and his murderer. Sin wanted to hold on and she wanted to kill him. In the end she just cried, thinking of sunlight in this meadow and Alan smiling as he missed a shot, thinking of all she had lost, and lost forever.

"That's right," Anzu whispered. His low, cold voice chased

another shiver down her spine as he stroked her hair with Alan's hands. "You can pretend I'm him."

Sin woke curled up and chilled in the wet grass, the morning drawing yellow and blue fingertips across a clear, grey sky. There was a demon standing over her, his arms crossed.

"Ready to go back?" said Nick. "Jamie's sleeping. Mae wants to be alone with him."

"What about Seb?"

"What about him?"

"What's he doing, do you know?"

"I really don't care," said Nick. "Stalking Jamie from a bit further away, I imagine. It's his hobby." He looked at Sin, stretching out the kinks from sleeping in her field, and his mouth twisted. "You'd better come along. Anzu will be expecting us."

They welcomed the exchange of the damp Tube station for a rattling old carriage with worn seats.

"Thoughts?" Sin asked eventually.

"Anzu seems pretty taken with you," Nick said. Sin wished that he had a tone other than enraged or non-committal. "I think that's why he's sticking around. That and, of course, to torture me."

"Should I be concerned?"

"Not especially," said Nick. "He always treats his pets pretty well. Much better than I did."

That effectively killed that conversation. They made their way back silently to the flat, and Sin waited as Nick got out his keys. She heard nothing in the flat, but that didn't mean Anzu wasn't there waiting, silently in the dark, with the infinite patience of demons.

She was listening for Anzu's silence so intently she almost did not register the slight noise. Her instincts saved her; her hands were on her knives before she knew why they were there. Nick, who had pushed open the door, was an instant too late drawing his sword.

The magicians were waiting for them. Sin leaped back as Laura sent a bolt of black fire shimmering from her hands. It hit Nick head-on and he stumbled, going down to his knees. Sin ducked down and darted to his side, her hand under his elbow, and tried to get him up. Then a crow launched itself at Sin's eyes from the ceiling, and she spun away from Nick, throwing her knife like a javelin and pinning the bird against the door frame.

The illusion changed and the magician turned from bird to man, slumping on the threshold, and black fire came from two directions. Sin threw herself down on the dead body.

While she was down there, she retrieved her knife. When she rose to her feet again, she saw that Nick had fallen and was slumped against the door, his face slack and young and defenceless.

It had been that easy for the magicians to get the jump on them. It would be this easy to die.

There were four magicians left alive in the flat, Sin saw. She should leave Nick and run, but Nick was Alan's little brother, the person he loved best in the world. Nick was her ally.

Sin stepped over and in front of Nick with both knives at the ready.

She deflected one fireball and hit the wall hard, jarring her arm up to the shoulder. She thought Laura was the leader of this expedition. If she could just get to Laura—

One of the other magicians crashed into her hurt shoulder,

his burning-bright fingers sending a sizzling line of pain up along her arm. His hand pinned her wrist against the wall, and her fingers convulsed open. The knife slipped from her numb hand and clattered to the floor. Sin lunged at him with her other knife, driving it home, but her aim was off and the knife stuck in his rib.

Black fire exploded behind Sin's eyes, and she slid down the wall. She hit the floor too hard, cracking her forehead against it, and watched three sets of feet approach as blood rushed in her ears.

One set of feet exploded in ash and bones. Darkness washed over Sin's vision, and her hand clenched on the ash carpeting the floor, trying to force herself up and into consciousness, trying to understand what has happening.

Dimly, she saw Laura's heels moving past her eyes, the sound of the shoes echoing in her ears. She could not even lift her head, could not tell if she was saved or dead.

Darkness rushed back to stay, and the world was gone.

Sin's head throbbed. Her arm was red agony, but the darkness had receded enough for her to be able to sit up, her palms sliding in ash and blood. The magicians were long gone, though one had left a charred shadow on the wall.

Behind her, Nick said, "Am I supposed to be grateful?"

Sin turned her head slowly, and saw Nick sitting up against the open door, one leg drawn up and an arm round it. There was blood on the side of his face, streaking vivid red from his black hair.

Anzu was crouched in the doorway, between Nick and the dead body. There was a smudge of blood and ashes on his cheek.

Sin was fairly certain that, unlike Nick, the blood on Anzu's face was not his own.

Anzu shrugged in answer.

"I'm not," Nick said. "You took my brother. There is nothing you can give me that will make up for that."

There was a silence. Anzu glanced over at Sin, almost as if he expected her to say something, to disagree with Nick. Sin just stared at him, silent as a demon. She could not feel grateful either.

Anzu turned his gaze back to Nick.

"He left you, you know."

"What?"

"Your precious brother," Anzu said. "We don't lie. You know I am telling you the truth he never did. He left you a thousand times. He used to lie in bed daydreaming about he and his father driving off, getting away from you when you were a nightmare child with black button eyes. He used to not be able to sleep because he was scared of you! He worked with his leg hurting, and he thought about how much easier the struggle would be if he didn't have to feed you and your mother. He knew Mae preferred you, so many girls preferred you, and he resented you for that. He would get in the car and drive away and leave you for ten, fifteen minutes, driving out of the city never to come back, until he turned round. He meant to leave you. You took his life, and you took his chance at love, and he hated you, and he wanted to leave you!"

Nick swallowed, the flex of his throat terribly obvious and almost vulnerable with his head tipped back like that.

"But he didn't leave."

"No," Anzu said. "But he wanted to. He should have. If he had, he'd still be alive, wouldn't he? I didn't kill him. You did. He would have lived, without you. He would have had a life, if only he hadn't wasted his time trying to love something that could never love him back."

Nick laughed. It was a truly horrible sound, with nothing human in it, echoing off the cement and the prison wires on the walkway. He sat against the door because he was too hurt to get up, bleeding beside the body of a magician and the body of his brother, and laughed a cold, awful laugh as if he was at the point of madness, as if he was on the edge of despair.

"Who knows?" said Nick Ryves, with nothing at all left to lose. "Maybe I did."

He turned his face away from the demon in his brother. Anzu stared at him, furious and disgusted, and lifted a hand to hit Nick, as if too angry to simply strike out with magic.

He raised his right hand to hit Nick, and his own left hand shot out and grabbed his wrist. Protecting his brother.

Nick looked round. Sin shot to her feet, which a moment ago had seemed impossible, and all the blood rushed dizzily to her head, the world spun in a sickening whirl and she did not care.

"Alan?" she whispered.

Anzu looked down at his hand as if it had betrayed him, and then his gaze turned inward, thoughtful, almost dreamy, as if he finally had something to look forward to.

"Oh, you're going to be very sorry you did that," he whispered in Alan's stolen voice, and Sin knew it was for their benefit. He left Nick's side, turning his back on him, and went over to Sin. "Say it again," he commanded her.

She was not going to endanger herself by refusing the demon when he was furious. But Alan was in there. She would not throw his name in his face.

She looked into his black eyes, the crackling magic changing him, and tried to look past it all.

"Alan," she said softly.

Anzu gave her a charming smile, bright and brilliant as stage lights.

"No."

19

Mavis to the Rescue

ANZU DISAPPEARED THEN, LIKE A GHOST AT DAWN, LEAVING A shimmer in the air. Sin put out a hand to steady herself and then pulled it away, too late: she had already made a bloody handprint on the wall.

Nick eased himself to his feet and passed his hand over the magician's body. It sparked, like the glints of fire in banked coals, and turned into more ash.

Neither of them spoke about Anzu, and what revenge he might be taking on Alan's body. It would do no good. There was absolutely nothing they could do about it.

The sound of a door opening made them both go for their weapons, with what Sin suspected was a mutual sense of relief. Anything was better than thinking.

It wasn't a magician. It was Mae. She had dark circles under her eyes, but she looked fairly calm.

Mae looked round at the hall, decorated with ashes and blood.

"I love what you've done with the place."

329

"What are you doing here?" Nick demanded.

"Well," Mae said. Her fingers played with the strap on her messenger bag, plucking at the strap so hard her knuckles were a little white, but she kept her head tipped back and looked Nick squarely in the eye. "I hit you. But you controlled me, so I'm glad I punched you," she continued, and twisted the bag strap round again. "But I'm sorry I blamed you. I know you did everything you could to protect Jamie."

Nick said, "Why are you here?"

"Oh," Mae said. "Yes."

She stopped fiddling with her bag strap and squared her shoulders, a habitual gesture of hers, trying to make herself larger than she was. One small girl, wanting to be able to take on the world.

"I came here so you could look at my face."

Sin often had trouble reading Nick's expressions, or being able to tell whether he had an expression at all. This one was pretty easy, though. He stared at Mae as if she was insane.

"What?"

"I know," Mae said. "It's pretty big of me, especially considering what an enormous jerk you are. But I'm a giver."

"I think I may be missing a subtle human nuance here," Nick told her. "What exactly are you trying to give me?"

"Emotional support," Mae said firmly. "You said once that my face made you feel better. And I know that you are feeling worse than you ever have in your life, and I know it won't help much. But in case it might help a little, I wanted to be here. For you. I thought you might want that, too."

"I want," Nick began violently, and then checked himself. "I don't want to hurt you," he said. "I want to – I want to *not* hurt you."

"That's good," Mae said, almost gently.

"Is it?" Nick asked. "It's different from how I've wanted other people. I don't want to hurt you, but at the same time I do. I want to hurt everybody, all the time. I told you. I meant it. I want to burn down the world."

He meant it. The dark promise in his voice made Sin flinch where she stood in the doorway, not quite able to look away. Mae didn't flinch.

"You don't have to hurt me. I can just be here. I'll talk at you, or if you don't want me to talk, I'll read a book and you can sharpen your weapons." She paused, and when Nick didn't speak, she said, still in that gentle-for-her voice that wasn't quite gentle, "Or I can go."

Mae waited another minute. Then she nodded her head, shifted her bag strap into position with some finality and turned away.

"No," said Nick, with an effort. "Don't go."

Mae turned back to him and smiled slowly. It was a hell of a smile, dimples deepening and dark eyes turning warm. It made her beautiful for a moment, even though she wasn't.

That was what made Sin turn away at last. She remembered being that happy, wildly, stupidly happy, happy in spite of everything. She didn't want to hate Mae.

She went into the kitchen, closed the door and made herself a cup of coffee. She sat at the table and tried not to think about what she had lost.

She was slumped over her cold coffee, half-asleep, when the touch landed between her shoulder blades and found her suddenly alert, panic flooding her system with adrenaline. Like a prince waking a princess with his touch.

Like being that princess, and waking to find your prince a monster.

Alan stood under the skylight, and aside from the black eyes it was Alan, just like Alan, with none of the sinister beauty of a demon altering his very bones.

It was Alan, but he was so changed. The line of his mouth was thin and despairing. The pale morning filtered through the skylight was stark and unforgiving, illuminating every trace of pain.

There were grey locks threaded among the red curls she had run her hands through, and he looked so tired.

Sin jumped up from her chair, horror coursing cold through her veins. One of her hands gripped the chair back so she would not reach for him, and her other hand grasped a knife.

And then like a cloud passing away from the sun, Anzu stood before her, every inch radiating bright, awful, demonic beauty.

"So I've had a thought," said Anzu.

Something about his voice made Sin blink past the brilliance of golden hair and careless menace, and she realised he was on edge. Apparently torturing Alan hadn't been fun enough for one day.

She reached for her other knife.

"They both abandoned me," Anzu told her. "Hnikarr promised us bodies, and then he changed and took it all back, and I thought I'd take revenge. I'd take his little pet and he'd be furious and he'd come around, be like he used to be. I thought Liannan would help me. But she's set on some voyage of discovery with her body, and Hnikarr, he won't – nothing's like I thought it would be."

"Sorry to disappoint you," Sin murmured, her whisper poison. He sounded like a child, a murderous child bewildered that pulling the wings off flies had not given him everything he wanted.

Only the flies were Alan: the toy he had taken to spite Nick, the toy he was breaking, was Alan.

"So I think we'll just go away together, you and I," Anzu said. "Somewhere lovely, with mountains. Do you like mountains? I do. The others like their humans so much. Hnikarr thinks being human, being loved, is so wonderful. I'll try it. I can have it, too. You can love me."

"No," Sin exclaimed. "I can't."

There it was, truth as harsh and simple as a demon's, and she braced herself for his reaction.

He brushed it off. "I'll do nice things for you," he said. "Then you'll love me."

"That's not how it works!"

"Why not?" Anzu demanded.

Sin's palms pressed into the hilts of her knives. There was a restless, fierce brightness about Anzu that seemed as if any moment it would explode into violent delight or violent despair. Or just violence.

She wanted to ask *Why me?* but she knew why. He was lonely, in his demonic way, and she was there.

And Alan wanted her. Demons did tend to gravitate to the loved ones of those they possessed, because they could possess them next more easily and perhaps also because they were familiar, because the body still yearned towards them.

In the midst of horror and fear, Sin was almost happy. She hadn't been sure of exactly what she meant to Alan. He'd never said. He'd said so many things, but not that.

If he could reach through a demon to her, though, that must mean he loved her a little.

"It won't work," Sin said. "Because you disgust me."

She shouldn't have said it, but the memory of how Alan had looked moments before with the skylight shining on the threads of grey in his hair rushed back and overwhelmed her. She stood, staring Anzu down, and when he stepped in towards her, she lifted her chin and waited for whatever was coming.

Anzu hovered over her, golden in her vision like a gilded bird of prey about to strike. Then he touched her, fingers in her hair, pulling like talons, too tight.

"I'm tired of being alone," he whispered. "I want you with me. Come to me like you did before – at the window, when you said you were here. I want you to mean here for me, not him. I want that for me. Tell me what I have to do to get that."

"I can't give you that," Sin said. "I didn't mean to give it to Alan. It isn't something you decide. And I'm not going anywhere with you."

The hold on her hair went tighter, pulling her head back. "Why not?"

"I have a family," Sin said. "I won't leave them."

"You might not have a family for long." Anzu leaned in close enough to kiss her, and Sin turned her face away. He breathed, soft against her cheek: "Think about that."

Sin relaxed all her muscles deliberately, made her body soft and yielding and exactly what he wanted it to be, as she knew so well how to do. His fingers loosened in her hair, and she turned towards him.

When he saw her face, it was his turn for all his muscles to go tense.

Sin stared at him coldly. "This is supposed to make me love you?"

"Maybe you will," Anzu said. "If you're all alone. You'll have to love me, then. Who else will there be?"

"Me," Sin told him. "I'll be there. You can't make me become something I don't want to be. And you sure as hell can't make me love you."

"Sure as hell," Anzu murmured, and smiled, drawing even closer to her. The smile hurt to look at, and then it hurt when he touched it to her ear and she felt his lips curve and the faint hint of teeth. "How sure is that?" he asked. "I live in a place of eternal pain and cold, and now I have been abandoned even there. I won't be alone here. I'm going to have you."

"No," Sin said, keeping her voice even. "You're not."

"I really shouldn't have let those children go, should I?" Anzu asked musingly. "But there are so many ways to have power over you."

He kissed her under her ear, lightly, as if they were lovers and he was teasing.

"There are plenty of other ways to change your mind. Ways that will hurt Hnikarr, too. And I would so love to do that. There's that girl Hnikarr seems so taken with, or the little magician, of all the perverse things for him to take a fancy to. The girl is your rival, isn't she? Would you like me to kill her?"

"No," Sin said, her skin crawling and cold under his mouth.

"I'd like Hnikarr to be unhappy," Anzu said, almost dreamily. "I would like for him to be alone. But perhaps you're willing to bargain for the girl's life?"

Sin thought of Mae dead. She closed her eyes and apologised to her friend. She would have fought to defend her, died to defend her if she had to, but this was different.

"No. I'm not currency."

"I wonder who I have to kill to convince you," said Anzu, and kissed her.

It was a swift, intense thing, like being made the centre of a storm, those talon-feeling fingers tilting up her chin. His touch stung and the kiss burned: there was nothing of Alan in it at all.

Sin drew one of her knives and lunged, a swift thrust upward at his throat. The blade sliced through nothing more than coloured shadows and smoke. Anzu disappeared like mist in the sun.

He left her standing in the kitchen with her blade drawn, and no enemy she could possibly fight.

Sin blundered out of the kitchen, not able to stay there for a moment longer. She hit her shoulder hard against the bathroom door and noticed distantly that things had come to such a pass that she was being clumsy.

She'd had some vague thought of washing her face, but she didn't. She found herself just standing in the bathroom the same way she'd stood in the kitchen, feeling helpless and sick.

She climbed into the bathtub, back against the edge and her knees drawn up, cool porcelain propping her up on all sides. She rested her forehead on her knees and breathed in and out.

There was a sound in the hall. Sin's head snapped up.

Nick was standing at the threshold of the room, arms up to grab the door frame. The black of his eyes were two chasms, the abyss looking back at her with intent to devour.

"I won't have him going after Mae or Jamie," Nick said. "If Anzu's taken a shine to you, can't you play along for a while?"

She should have thought of Nick overhearing. This flat was too small, the walls too thin. She should have known.

He prowled into the room, every movement he made a

promise of violence. Sin thought again of Anzu, wearing his stolen body so lightly, like a weapon carelessly flourished. He could kill you, barely meaning to.

Nick looked like he would kill her and mean it with all his heart.

"And how exactly do you suggest I play along?" Sin snapped. "You want me to cuddle up to the thing murdering Alan?"

"I don't care what you have to do. I want them safe."

"You still want to protect Jamie, even though he has control over you. Even though he gave Gerald control over you."

Nick gave a small shrug.

"You already had to murder a woman," Sin said, and tried not to think of Phyllis's blood pooling with the rainwater on the deck. "What terrible things will you do for them next?"

"I've done terrible things for a lot less reason," Nick said. "I don't mind."

"I do mind," Sin whispered. "There are some roles you can't play, without changing who you are. I can't do this."

"Alan's been possessed. The magicians are coming after us. Anzu wants revenge badly enough to go after Mae and Jamie. Is this the time to start having moral issues, when you could help?"

"I know who I am," Sin snarled back. "I know how far I can go. And from there we just have to deal with the mess."

Nick glared at her, then away. He met his own demon's eyes in the mirror.

When he moved, he moved to get into the bath, sitting on the edge, swinging his long legs into the tub. She didn't notice his eyes, then, but that he moved like she did, like a dancer, making even something ridiculous like this look graceful. She felt a sense of kinship with him, a remembered flash of feeling from a year ago and more, before all this change and love and pain, when they had just been dancers together.

He stared down at his hands, held clasped tight round each other between his knees, as if he didn't trust himself not to hit something.

"Alan would have liked that," Nick said roughly. "Having someone he could trust to do the right thing."

Sin leaned against Nick's leg, desperate for any comfort.

"I don't think you're doing the wrong thing," she said. "I think you're doing the same thing. You're doing what you can. Alan would be proud."

"I don't want to think he would be proud," Nick snarled. "I want him *back*."

His body was warm against hers, simple physical contact all the comfort he could give her. It wasn't comfort for him, she knew that, but he was providing comfort for her despite that. For his brother, because she had meant something to Alan.

Sin bowed her head. "Me too."

She finally admitted to herself that despite her lack of certain vital demonic information, she'd got it right the first time, when she had liked Nick Ryves. He tried really hard, he loved his brother, and in the end, at this last extremity, she could count on him.

She saw Mae at the door, sleep-rumpled, her eyes wide. Sin reared backwards, realising how very bad this must look, and realised a moment later that backing off must have looked much worse.

Another realisation came gradually: Mae didn't look jealous. She was smiling.

She said, "Here's what we're going to do."

20

The Thief of the Pearl

THE MORNING HAD GONE FROM PALE TO BLAZING. THE SUN WAS burning a hole in the sky, yellow darts piercing far and away across the stretch of blue, and it had turned into one of those autumn days that left everyone squinting in the light but remained cold.

Sin was putting Matthias in charge of the night shift of the Market guard. The piper was a strangely good archer.

"The bowstrings sing to me," he told Sin and Mae absently, oiling a string. "Your voices, however, I find consistently annoying. Run along."

"This is some fine, fine respect you're showing two people, one of whom will undoubtedly be your future leader," Mae said.

"People who can sing have better things to do than lead," Matthias shot back. "In any case, if I had a vote, I'd vote for Sin."

"Your support is very much appreciated," Sin purred at him, in the throaty stage voice that could make a man's head turn at ten paces.

Matthias made a face and Sin laughed at him, touched his sleeve and passed on with Mae at her side.

Sin's heart was unexpectedly lifted by the sight of the Market with reinforcements, the addition of the other magic users making the Market bigger and stronger. Now the Market was harder to hide but better in a fight.

And that was the plan.

She would never have done it. Even if she had wanted to try, she would've expected a disaster. But Mae had believed in it, and accomplished it. For this moment, with Mae's plan before her, with something to do at last, Sin was able to be grateful and not resent her.

She was startled to see Mae giving her a slightly wistful look.

"Matthias *loooves* you."

"Matthias thinks I'm a waste of space with no singing voice and thus no purpose in this world."

"But he still *loooves* you," Mae said. "With all the extra O's. I'd like to have heart-stealing glamour."

"You'd have to be taller," Sin told her.

Mae poked her in the side. Sin laughed and looked around for Nick. They needed to go soon.

She didn't see him for a moment; then she caught sight of him sitting at one of the tables beside Jamie, looking over maps. Everyone in the Market was conspicuously avoiding the magicians. Jamie and Seb weren't going to be able to sleep here another night.

Jamie looked serious and absorbed in his task, like a conscientious child doing homework. Nick was leaning on one elbow, shirtless and seeming almost too bored. Sin was attuned to the sight of a performance that wasn't quite good enough.

Her eyes went, not to the hand pulling roughly at his own hair or the fact that he was wearing nothing on top but his talisman and his wrist cuff, but to Nick's other hand, flung with too much carelessness across the table, fingers curling a fraction of an inch away from the conspicuous stump of Jamie's arm.

Nobody would put their hand there by accident.

When the shadowy hand appeared at the end of Jamie's arm, Mae stopped dead, her hand suddenly clutching Sin's.

The hand wavered between mirage and reality before their eyes, insubstantial as the reflection of a hand in water, giving no idea of bones or blood or sinews. It seemed to tip towards the real while they watched, as if Mae's silent, breathless hope gave it life. The fingers seemed as if they were actually resting against the rough-grained wood of the table, though the hand was white and still as a dead thing.

Colour flooded it as Nick closed his own hand into a fist, and the fingers stirred against the wood.

Jamie, who had been doing a very poor job of pretending he didn't know what was going on for several minutes now, let himself look up. After that bowed and almost vulnerable-looking blond head, the black demon's mark and his glittering white eyes gave Sin a shock.

He still scared her a little. She had grown up dancing for demons, but magicians had always been the enemy.

Jamie blinked those magic-bright eyes and seemed vulnerable again, for the instant it took to blink.

"What's this?" he asked, and his voice trembled.

"It's a hand, you idiot," Nick snapped. "You were missing one."

Jamie closed his eyes. "Nick. Magicians have – they've killed hundreds of people for this kind of power, and you just keep pouring it out, and I can't rely on it."

"Yes, you can."

"I can't be any more addicted to it than I already am," Jamie said slowly, as though he'd rehearsed this, and then waited for a cue Nick obviously had no intention of giving. "Think about crack!" Jamie added, clearly struck by inspiration. "Yes! It's like I'm a crack addict, and you're my friend the drug dealer who gives me crack for free, and I know you're just trying to be a good friend, but every time I think, 'Wow, this crack might be a little bit of a problem for me,' you're there to say, 'Have some more delicious crack.' Am I making sense?"

Nick stared. "Hardly ever in your entire life."

"Okay, well, it has to stop."

"Fine," Nick said, turning his face away.

"Not the friend thing," Jamie told him, sounding a little anxious. "Just ease up on the magic crack."

"You're weird," Nick grumbled, but he turned his face back to critically examine the new hand.

"You're weird," Jamie returned. "As soon as this whole magical war is over, I'm going to make us some friendship bracelets, and we will wear them everywhere because we are best friends."

He gave Nick a beaming smile.

"Drop dead," said Nick, and Jamie looked serenely pleased.

Sin noticed that Seb, standing about ten feet away in the shadow of one of the new wagons and doing what she felt could possibly be described as lurking in Jamie's vicinity, did not look pleased at all.

She walked over to the table and examined the list Jessica Walker had drawn up of all the properties Celeste Drake and the Aventurine Circle owned. It had seemed very lucky that Jessica had that list at the time, since the Market had been very wary about letting messengers join them: magic parasites who had nothing to give back. The messengers had been able to show them that information was always useful.

If only it had been more useful in this case.

"Seb is brooding about your proximity to a half-naked guy," she remarked.

Jamie looked startled, and then grinned. "Oh my gosh, Nick. You're not wearing a shirt! This must be one of those exciting days ending in Y."

"Don't call him over here," Nick said. "You can do better."

Jamie called out, "Seb, come and help out with our list of the Circle magicians."

Seb immediately started over to them, and Nick muttered, "You are so weak."

"I don't know what you mean; I'm just being nice," Jamie said. "It's nice to be nice."

"I wouldn't know," said Nick.

"Let's go over some things," Mae suggested, striding over to Jamie. She did not touch the new hand, but she kept stealing glances at it, looking away quickly every time she did so, as if she feared it could not bear the weight of her gaze. "So. A team of magicians was sent after you and Nick."

"They didn't get us," said Sin. "So they'll either try again, or they'll go for the obvious next step. Another attack on the Market."

"So we don't let them make the next move," Mae said. "This calls for a little pre-emptive self-defence. We go after them instead." She pulled roughly at a handful of pink hair, a gesture Sin was pretty certain that Mae was unaware of and also pretty certain she had picked up from Nick. "Of course, our attack plan would look a whole lot better if we had any idea where the hell they are."

"They abandoned the *Queen's Corsair*," Jamie said. "Gerald knew it was too easy for the Market to find now you know about it. Plus Nick set it on fire."

He got the same look saying Gerald's name as he did whenever he was caught by the sight of his own missing hand and sat looking at the space where it had been for a few minutes.

He looked down at his new hand now and smiled a rueful, crooked smile.

"You can check off every property on that list," Mae said gloomily. "Isabella just came back from the bolthole by the Tower."

Sin gave her an inquiring look. Mae hadn't said she was sending scouts out to Celeste Drake's properties.

Mae met her eyes with a level gaze, glanced at Nick, then leaned forward, frowning and suddenly intent, as if Nick was a mathematical equation she was bent on solving.

"What?" Nick said at last. "Do I have something on my face besides good-looking?"

"What if we're thinking about this the wrong way?" Mae asked. "Gerald didn't just inherit a leadership from Celeste. He inherited the Obsidian Circle from Black Arthur first."

"Did Black Arthur have any property in London?" Sin asked doubtfully.

Mae was a tourist, so perhaps she didn't understand that it would be very unusual for a magician to live anywhere near another Circle's territory.

"Yes, we know he did," Mae said, giving her that cool look again. "He has a house in Knightsbridge."

"I found out I was a demon there," Nick remarked flatly.

He offered nothing else. Sin hesitated, then beckoned to Chiara. Chiara slid a wary look at Jamie's shimmering-magic eyes, but she approached.

"Pass the word to the pipers and the necromancers that we have another location to stake out."

"Whatever you say, boss," Chiara murmured, and left.

It was Sin's turn to meet Mae's eyes with a level stare.

Jamie threw down his pencil. The noise made Sin turn to him, and when she did, she saw determination on his face.

"I'd like to talk to you and my sister," Jamie said. "Alone."

Sin looked at Mae, who looked as puzzled as she was, and then nodded slowly.

"Before we go," Jamie said, and lifted the new, magical hand to the light. Sunlight wrapped his fingers like five golden rings.

"It looks almost real," he said, a little wistful. "But it's not. Come on, Nick."

Nick drew in a deep breath, and in that moment, in the space between a demon's breaths, they all saw the hand dissolve, becoming transparent first so the light shone through it and it seemed as if the magic was becoming light itself.

Then the magic was gone.

Jamie nodded, drew his wounded arm against his chest and turned away.

They left Nick and Seb, with Nick looking bored and Seb looking as if he was nursing a wistful daydream about punching Nick in the face, and went to Ivy's wagon.

The new wagon looked forlorn. So many of Ivy's books and maps had been lost with her sister, but there were maps of London out on the table and notes in Ivy's large handwriting.

She wouldn't disturb them. Sin had seen Ivy having a fight with Matthias, who had pestered Ivy by crankily demanding why she did not know sign language until she was driven to scratch out on her slate in capital letters: I LIKE THINGS TO BE WRITTEN DOWN.

So they had the wagon to themselves and the curtains drawn down, creating a dim, wooden cavern for Sin, Mae and Jamie to meet alone.

Sin was sitting in the lotus position on one side of the table. Mae sat opposite her, elbows on the table among the maps.

At the head of the table, Jamie reached out his hand and held it cupped over the small candle that stood in the centre of the sea of maps. The candle sparked under his fingers and burst into a long, thin stream of light. When Jamie drew his hand away, twin reflections of the candle flame danced in the magic-iced mirrors of his eyes.

"Ladies," he said, "I want to make a bargain with you."

Mae frowned and laughed at once, wrinkling her nose at her funny, puzzling baby brother, but Sin could not help seeing him as a magician first. She had no problem taking Jamie seriously.

"What do you want?" she asked, and at the serious sound of her voice Mae's face changed.

"If I can talk magicians from the Aventurine Circle into joining the Market," said Jamie, "I want you to let them."

"You want to let the Aventurine Circle killers into my Market?" Sin asked. "And what do you offer in return?"

"If one of you says yes, and the other says no," Jamie answered, "I'll support the one who will give me what I want. As leader of the Goblin Market."

Jamie's voice was serious. He did not look at his sister, but

Sin did. In the flickering candlelight, Mae looked shocked and pale. She didn't seem able to speak.

Sin could. "Tell me, magician. What is your support worth?"

Jamie put his hand to the top button of his shirt and flicked it open. There, in the hollow of his throat, lay the black pearl.

He smiled, almost apologetically, the kid whose best trick was camouflage, who had dived forward in a moment of darkness and taken the pearl off a dead body, who had worn it through imprisonment and the imminent threat of death without saying a word. Who nobody had suspected.

"My support's worth a lot."

"So I see," said Sin. She'd been raised in the Market, and she knew the moment to strike a bargain when it came. "All right," she said, and almost smiled at his nerve; he was more like his sister than she had ever dreamed. "I'll do it."

His sister was still paralysed with shock, but she pulled herself together long enough to say, "Not Helen."

Jamie tilted his chin in the same stubborn way she did. "Anyone who will join."

"She killed our mother," Mae hissed.

Jamie flinched, looking small and easily hurt for a moment, and then straightened up again.

"They've all killed someone's mother. Maybe I would have killed someone's mother, too, if the demon had never come to my window, if we'd never gone to Nick and Alan. I don't know. I just know I don't want revenge. I want to offer them a way out."

"I want revenge," Mae said, her hands in fists on the table. "I do."

Jamie's voice was unyielding. "Then I want Sin to be the leader of the Goblin Market."

There was a silence. Sin searched for triumph, and found herself quietly terrified instead. The Market would be in revolt against this idea – magicians in their very midst – and it was already in chaos. How would she be able to balance this, and dancing and school, and Toby and Lydie at her father's house? Mae would not be there to help her, to offer any new ideas. Mae would be cast out and betrayed by her own brother.

"What if it was me, Mae?" Jamie asked. "What if they were all me, in some other life, and they made the wrong decisions and just kept making them? You'd want to save me."

Mae looked at his face for a long time and then sighed.

"You're crazy," she said. "But I love you. I'll do it, too."

Jamie smiled at both of them as they sat, stunned and quiet, staring back at him.

"Then I'll leave you guys to it," he said, and reached behind his own neck. After a moment of fumbling, he got the necklace off and rose to his feet. The black pearl swung over the table for a moment, like a pendulum.

Then he dropped it into the centre of the table, in a gleaming, candlelit pile directly between them.

"Whatever decision you two make, I'll support it," said Jamie. "It's completely up to you."

He said nothing else. He left the pearl he had so dearly won, the magicians' symbol of great power, lying on the table, and went out of the door.

This was the Market's symbol of power now.

Mae and Sin's eyes met in the shadows, over the candle flame, and held. Neither of them looked away.

Hours later Nick came to the door with the news that a

necromancer, spying through the eyes of a crushed dead bird, had seen Laura, Gerald's second in command, going up the steps and in through the door of Black Arthur's old house.

So they knew where the magicians were. They had almost all the things they needed to attack.

All but one.

21

The Last Answers to the Last Questions

S IN AND NICK WENT INTO THE FLAT, WALKING CAREFULLY. SIN hardly knew what she expected, but when they opened the door, they saw all the lights were out, the ashes on the floor and walls lost in shadow. They moved through the grey, silent rooms of the flat, not speaking, until they had covered every inch and they were sure Anzu was not there.

Sin glanced at Nick, but as usual his face revealed nothing. She covered her eyes and tried to pull herself together, be the perfect performer and present herself just right.

She headed for the kitchen where Alan had first kissed her, going straight for the kitchen table, and slid on to it.

She heard Nick's footsteps, echoing in the hush, coming from the hall through to the kitchen towards her. She found herself unable to raise her head and look at him.

She knew he was standing very close. She could feel the warmth of his body, almost resting against her legs. She sat very still.

"Alan," said Nick, the name and his voice a shock in the quiet room. It felt as if he had uttered a curse.

Sin looked up then, unable to help herself. Nick was staring down at her with those devouring-dark eyes. She shivered, not able to help that, either. The shiver almost turned into a shudder; she felt alone and cold suddenly, stranded far from human warmth and held transfixed by the demon's regard.

"I know," she whispered. "I won't let him down."

Nick's face was a blur of black and white before her eyes, too close to make anything out. The feel of him this close was like sensing the approach of a dangerous animal, his breath hot on her face as chills raced through her body.

He took a breath that hitched in his chest, not ragged but torn clean in two, and that sign of pain made him reality rather than nightmare. She lifted her hands and touched him, his shoulders solid and warm against her palms.

Nick dropped a rough kiss at the corner of her mouth and cheek. He'd never been clumsy with her before.

"Good luck," he said in her ear.

They both heard the tiny, traitorous sound as the door creaked open. For a moment Nick's arms went round her hard, the lines of his body suddenly prison bars, but Sin yanked herself free.

She strode into the hall and met Anzu coming in the door. It was such an ordinary human thing to do, coming home, and he was so unmistakably something else. His hair was vermilion, his skin bone white. All his vivid colours betrayed the fact that there was poison lying just beneath his surface.

"Anzu," she said, and gave him her best smile, like both hands held out to welcome him.

A returning smile lit that face, so lovely, so cruel, and so changed. It was strange, seeing a demon look pleased.

Of course, he had said he was lonely. And demons always told the truth.

"My dancer. Is this a greeting for a lover?"

Sin's lips curled in real amusement. "This is a greeting for someone I want to make bargains with. I'm always the sweetest to customers."

Demons appreciated the truth. Anzu looked at her with a glint in his eye that was not quite warmth but that might have been had he been human, like the reflection of fire in a glass.

"What do you want?" Anzu asked, his voice almost indulgent. "And what do you have to offer me?"

"She's not the one making an offer," Nick said from the doorway. "I am."

The room filled with nothingness, none of them moving or making a sound. Sin did not even want to breathe and disturb the moment.

"I made a bargain with you and Liannan once, that I would give you bodies," Nick continued. "All I want to do now is keep it."

Anzu's lips curled in a sneer. "I have a body."

"Now, now," Sin said, coaxing the reluctant buyer like a good Market girl. "Hear him out."

"That body won't last," Nick informed him dispassionately. "You're tearing it to pieces."

"Your brother won't last," Anzu snarled, and went for him in a rush.

Nick put out a hand and took him by the throat. Anzu halted.

"Your brother won't last," he repeated, his voice soft and hateful.

Nick nodded. He drew his thumb lightly over Anzu's jugular vein; Sin couldn't tell if it was a gesture of affection or a death threat. "I know," he said, voice just as soft. "The body lasts for such a short time. That's how it is for all demons. Except me."

"How nice for you," Anzu spat.

"It could be you," said Nick. "How about it? I can make it so you have a body for a long, long time."

Anzu backed out of Nick's hold, wary as a wild animal being offered food.

"Why would you want to help me?"

"For Alan," Nick said. "Because if I had a soul, I would trade it for his. And because I would like to keep my word."

Anzu looked at him for a long moment.

"I don't need anything from you, traitor," he said at last.

"Anzu," Sin murmured. "You don't want to go back to the demon world, do you? If he wants to help, let him. He owes you that."

"He betrayed me," Anzu said. "I spent long, cold years dreaming of his pain. I will not have my dreams taken away. Why should he be the one to escape? Why should he be happy?"

"You said you wanted to know what it was like," Sin said. "You could be happy, too. If you never had to go back to the demon world, and you had company."

Sin looked at him with passionate appeal, as she'd looked at a hundred audiences, trying to show she cared and thus make them care, too. This performance mattered more than any other.

"Take the deal, and I'll go with you anywhere."

She reached out and did not quite let her fingers touch his bare arm. She figured a demon would prefer that.

In any case, that was what her instincts told her to do. Always leave them wanting more.

She held her body curved beside his and kept her posture relaxed, as if she wanted to be there.

Demons seeking bodies came to windows and tempted humans. Well, Sin was the best performer the Market had. She could tempt anyone.

This demon had been cold and lonely for a long time.

Sin swayed towards him, warm and close.

She whispered, "Please."

Sin had not known what to expect from Black Arthur's house. This was the magician who had put a demon in his own child, the shaper of a future they had all been forced to live in, the villain of the piece who had died in the first act. She had never laid eyes on him.

The house was just a rich person's house. It had windows vast and shining as shop windows, as if the rooms were stages to display their wealth to the audience of the world.

Sin could not see inside the windows from her position on their neighbour's roof, though she did think if these people were all as rich as their houses suggested, they could take better care of their gutters. She was lying flat on the grey-shingled slope, listening to the cars purr by on the street, waiting for the ordinary noises of early morning to be broken by something strange.

All she could make out from her place was a sea of grey roofs spread out below them. The city seemed far away to Sin, a different and safer world.

But not her world.

The song came, soft and thrilling and lovely. The music

went rippling down the street like a river. Sin had always thought that Market music was more beautiful because it was secret, but it sounded even better out in the open.

Down below, people's heads were turning. Then they started to follow, moving to the sound of the song, pouring out of their houses in dressing gowns and business suits, dancing to the piping.

That would be enough to make the magicians come to the windows, and enough to make them afraid. They didn't know how far the pipers' power over these people would extend.

Nor did Sin, actually. When she had inquired, Matthias had said, "I could pipe them into the sea," and added, "Hadn't you heard? Pipers steal children." When she asked for him to stop talking nonsense and children's stories, he had laughed and walked off, piping already. She'd found her hand tapping a rhythm before she recalled that she danced to no tune she did not choose.

As far as the magicians were concerned, pipers might well be able to pipe people into the sea and steal children, and create an army to fight them.

Sin heard something else, too. She heard the rustle through the bushes in these houses' front gardens, the sound of dragging bodies through the grass in the back, and she knew the necromancers had sent every crushed piece of roadkill, every frozen cat curled beneath a bush, every drowned dog with a bloated belly in the Knightsbridge area staggering towards the magicians' house.

The railings running along the houses burst into blue flame that the potion-makers had assured them would burn hot and fast, and that the magicians would not be able to put out.

Sin heard the front door of the house slam open, heard the commotion in the garden and felt fiercely proud.

Now that the Goblin Market had come out of hiding, they were more powerful than the Circle had ever dreamed.

Sin rose cautiously, still crouched, and saw Nick rise on the other side of the roof. They gave each other a nod and a flashing smile, and then Sin tucked herself into a ball and rolled easily, head over feet, until she reached the magicians' roof.

She stood at the edge of the roof, testing it, and jumped. She caught the gutter with both hands as she fell, swinging easy, and found the windowsill with her feet. She rested her toes against the sill, and when there was no sign of it giving way, she knelt down and tested the window. It was locked.

Sin sighed at magicians and their apparent conscientiousness about home security, and stretched back up on her tiptoes to grab the gutter again. She flexed her back and locked her legs together, making herself a pendulum, gathering force and speed.

She crashed through the magicians' window feet first. Her shoes and jeans caught most of the damage, though she felt the swift, hot sting of a cut opening on her cheek as she landed on a wooden floor amid broken glass.

She had as much luck with the room as with the window. Which was to say none.

There was a magician in it, a young man drawing a circle, obviously wanting more power before he joined in the fight outside.

Well, she'd brought the fight in to him.

Sin drew her knives and threw one as the magician leaped to his feet and deflected the knife with a shimmer of magic rising from his palm.

Sin did not risk throwing her other knife. She eyed him warily. He eyed her back just as warily. Throwing knives always got people's attention, but she would have preferred to see him a little more relaxed, a little more certain he could beat her. She could've used that.

Instead he threw a pale fireball at her, and all she could do was dodge.

She dodged and ducked, making a bigger production of it than she had to, trying to draw his eye with unnecessary movement. She used fancy footwork in the mess of shards and gleaming splinters of glass, silver sweeping in her wake as she lunged and retreated meaninglessly, making battle a dance.

His eyes went to her feet for a second. Sin threw herself forward and slid her knife up under his ribs, a sure and swift killing blow. He doubled over against her, his blood spilling hot on her hands, and Sin pulled her knife out and stepped away so his body fell heavily on to the floor. There was a sickening crunch as if he'd broken his nose, but that hardly mattered now.

Sin jumped over his body and went for the door, out into a long hall full of dusty pictures. She ran under a chandelier in the shape of a dream catcher, the carved crystal hanging dull and dim, throwing open every door in the corridor as she went.

She could hear running feet and slamming doors, and did not know which sounds were her allies, intent on the same task as she, and which the magicians running to fight them.

When she opened the next door, one opposite a charmed tapestry inscribed with rings, crowns and jewels, it didn't matter.

The room beyond was vast, with a vaulted ceiling and a

glossy wooden floor that bore twelve of the most perfect summoning circles Sin had ever seen, the lines of communication that translated demons' silent language into speech straight and true, the circles within circles smooth. There were pairs of circles overlapping each other, like dancers' circles, as if to make more room for the demons. Even the circles not currently occupied gleamed with subtle fire, with a shimmer like the reflection of the magical stones for which the magicians' Circles were named.

The circles with demons in them were brimful of brimfire, and the demons inside them were negotiating with the magicians. Sin saw Gerald, Laura and Helen, their faces almost obscured by flame, intent on the demons.

Sin put her hand into her pocket and took out a beacon light, so small it was like a glowing pearl in her palm. Then she closed her eyes and crushed it in her fist.

Light erupted from her hand as if she held lightning trapped in her fingers, the shuddering shock of brightness painting the insides of her eyelids with violent yellow streaks.

Sin opened her eyes.

She'd given the signal. Everyone who could come would be coming soon.

Not soon enough, she realised, as she saw Gerald's face.

The fireball only just missed her as she threw herself on to the ground, tumbling head over feet and landing crouched behind more balefire.

It might be a good cover for her, but she didn't want the magicians to have any more power.

"Thalassa, who loves the sea by night and drowning by night better," Sin shouted. "I dismiss you!"

Name the demon, and you controlled it. The balefire

screening her began to ebb and dim, and as she performed another roll she shouted another name.

"Mafdet the clawed, I dismiss you!"

She couldn't keep this up. Where was everybody?

"Amanozako the blade-eater," said Jamie from the door, as if she had called him with her need. "I dismiss you."

Gerald stopped hurling fireballs at Sin. For a moment all he did was look at Jamie, standing in the doorway with Mae at his shoulder. Jamie was wearing the clumsy hook they had got him because they didn't have time to make anything better.

There was blood on it.

The pause gave Sin a moment to look at Gerald. He looked terrible in a way that went beyond the battle her Market had brought to him. He was very thin, attenuated as if his own flesh was being eaten away from the inside out. This was no smug villain, Sin thought. He looked like a torture victim.

He cared about Jamie. She'd known that much before, that they must have been friends at some point, that Gerald had believed in him.

He'd killed and schemed and sacrificed his friend for power, and look what good it had done him.

Jamie seemed to see the same thing Sin did. He paused with his hand uplifted, as Gerald had, and he looked sorry.

There was a commotion in the corridor. When the door opened again, there were more magicians behind it.

Sin's hand closed convulsively on the handle of her knife.

There was light like a starburst in the corridor, and the sound of steel. Sin could see heads falling from view, magicians being cut down, and a path being carved out.

Into the room with the other magicians came a band of

Market people and pipers, necromancers and messengers, and in the lead Nick Ryves.

Nick had his sword out, blood running down the steel. He moved so Mae was between him and Jamie, shielded as much as she could be, her pocketknife clasped in her hand. Jamie's hand and hook were suddenly shimmering like his eyes, his whole body obscured by a haze of power.

"Gerald," Jamie asked imploringly. His face was pinched and pale, full of dread. "Will you surrender? Please."

Gerald laughed at him.

"We can all live," Jamie continued as if he had not. "Give me the leadership of the magicians, and you can go in peace. You can live."

There was a stir among all the magicians, as if they had not expected Jamie to ask for this.

"You want my Circle?" Gerald demanded, and then laughed again. "I told you, didn't I? I always told you, no matter how much power you have, you'll always want more."

"I want the Circle to join the Market," Jamie said softly. "You could, too, if you wanted."

"I swear you could," said Mae, who always had her brother's back.

Gerald laughed again, the sound scraping Sin's ears like a shriek. "You're such an idiot," he told Jamie. "You're a child, and you're dreaming. Even if I wanted to try, it wouldn't work."

"I'm going to try," Jamie said. "But I wish you could live."

Jamie advanced, nobody else in the room moving, magicians and Market all still because nobody was quite sure what was happening any more, and everyone knew that one move would throw them all into bloody chaos.

Jamie kept coming. Nick and Mae followed behind, not at

his side, not openly threatening, but in a silent promise of defence. Gerald watched Jamie come, and watched Jamie beckon to Nick.

Nick leaned in towards Jamie, black head bowed deferentially, and Jamie's eyes flashed with a fresh wave of magic.

Jamie had hoped Gerald would surrender. Sin had not until she saw Gerald, and then she had thought that perhaps, just possibly, it might be so, that Jamie's dream could come true, that they could all walk away from this with clean hands.

"Kill him," Gerald ordered his magicians. His voice was deliberately emptied of emotion, not like a demon's innate lack of human emotions, but as if he had human emotions and had poured them away. "Kill Jamie, and the demon is mine alone to command."

He threw a slash of magic at Jamie, like a black lightning bolt. The air froze in front of Jamie's face, ice absorbing the lightning and falling into glittering shards on the ground.

"You think so?" Nick asked.

He pushed Jamie aside and walked forward, taking one step, then another, across the polished wooden floor and into one of the overlapping magicians' circles.

"Stop," Gerald commanded, and Nick stopped. Gerald's smile spread.

Jamie opened his mouth to speak.

"What are you going to do, Jamie?" Gerald asked. "You gave me control over it, too. I can say 'stop' and you can say 'go' until we tear the thing to pieces between us. But you won't, will you? Because you care about it, and I don't."

He reached out a hand towards Nick.

It felt as if the room had turned into a desert, the heat scorching and no moisture in the air, with silence all around.

Nick went blazing white, and so did Gerald's eyes.

Gerald advanced on Jamie, and light rose between them like a path for them to follow. They both walked the path to each other, and it seemed like the desert winds howled.

But it wasn't wind. It was magic, called not only by Jamie and Gerald but by all the magicians, filling the air with sound and light.

A magician with a crew cut, built like a soldier, threw himself into their midst and caught up Mae. Mae sliced her knife across his arm, and Sin grasped his hair and slit his throat.

The sound of the pipers was lost under the howl and hiss and whine of magic everywhere, and there was no time to look to Jamie. Nick was on his knees, going paler and paler until he was grey, as if he was being leached of blood instead of magic.

"To Nick!" Mae commanded the Market, someone else's blood red in her pink hair.

Sin ran, faster than anyone else, to stop Helen before she reached the demons' circles where Nick was kneeling. She threw herself against Helen, pressed close so the reach of Helen's swords was no advantage at all, and steel met steel.

Sin parried, thrust, dancing as close as she could, as light and dark tore at the edges of her vision and there was screaming under the sound of magic.

She slipped in blood and fell, Helen's sword biting into her side.

With a peculiar clarity in that moment, she saw the clear beads of sweat on Helen's brow.

Helen said, "Pity to kill you."

Falling didn't have to mean ruin.

Sin hooked a foot round Helen's ankle and twisted away

from the sword, back on her feet. "Wouldn't it be, though?" she panted. "I'm gorgeous. I don't think I'll let you."

She was wounded, and she didn't know how badly. She could feel the blood flowing warm down her belly, and through eyesight going blurry she saw Mae standing in front of Nick alone, with two magicians bearing down on her.

Sin spun away from Helen and threw her knife at one of the magicians going for Mae. She threw a glance like a prayer at Jamie, and found him still on his feet, eyes still alight with fire.

So were Gerald's.

"It seems we're about even," Gerald remarked, his shirt scorched by magic fire but his skin whole beneath.

Jamie laughed. "Well, you must hate that," he said. "Isn't the whole point to have more power than anyone else? Isn't that what my life was worth to you? Isn't that worth everything?"

The highest window in the room, curved on top like a window in a church, broke into a thousand sharp pieces as the second demon entered the room.

Jagged splinters of glass slid along the floor to mingle with the gleaming ice.

Anzu, who had landed directly in the middle of the summoning circle beside Nick's, looked around with a wild, bright smile.

Nick looked up at him.

Their eyes met as the markings of the circle burned with rising fire, burned high, burned hot, sparks flying upward into that vaulted ceiling.

"Poor Hnikarr," Anzu murmured, his amusement plain. "You don't have much power left for anyone, do you? Here you are, crawling and begging. Aren't you?"

"Yes," Nick said, between his teeth.

Anzu smiled, malice written all over his face. "I love it."

And Gerald blasted power at Jamie like a lightning flash and a shock wave combined. Jamie went flying across the floor, hit with a bang that rattled the boards and dug his hook into the wood as he tried to get up.

The white light of magic had died out of Gerald's eyes, but he stepped towards the summoning circles and away from Jamie.

"You're right," Gerald said. "Power is worth everything. It's certainly worth your life."

He glanced at Nick, obviously all but used up, then laughed. He reached into the circle where Anzu stood.

"And I'm about to have everything."

Both of Anzu's hands shot out across the circle, like a vulture swooping down on his prey at last. Hands growing talons at the ends bit into Gerald's flesh, shadowy wingtips curved down savagely to envelop him.

Gerald's eyes went past blue into white, fierce shining white, like looking into the sun, like more power than anyone could bear. He laughed.

Then it was like a light burning out.

The light drained from white to blue to grey, until even the ashes of light were gone and darkness filled Gerald's eyes, as if someone had spilled shadows inside him, staining him forever.

There was nothing left of the balefire but smoke and darkness.

Nick stood, a looming black shape in the smoke. Jamie stepped up to his side, his eyes icy white fire in the gloom.

Sin and Mae both came forward and motioned to the Market to join them.

"A demon's mark on a magician means just the same thing

as a demon's mark on anyone else," Jamie said. He spoke softly but clearly, his voice ringing around the room. "It means you can be killed, controlled or possessed. Nick gave me power because he chose to. He did what I said because he wanted to. And he obeyed Gerald's orders because it was part of Mae's plan."

The magicians had already begun to recede from Gerald like the tide, as if realising how far from human company and comfort he had suddenly gone.

Whatever love or grief he had felt, it did not matter now. He had reached out for power above all, and got his reward.

Laura the grey-haired magician, Gerald's right hand, was crying, covering her face, her shoulders shaking uncontrollably. Sin had seen mothers cry like that for dead children.

Anzu turned Gerald's body slowly to look at her, face blank as a stone, and then he looked where Gerald had been looking in the last moment of his life, back at Jamie.

The mouth that had been Gerald's mouth twisted at the corners. Anzu moved, pulling a carved ring off his finger and threw it at Jamie.

Jamie caught the ring and Mae took it from him, slid it on to the finger of his remaining hand. The ring shone there, like the tears running down Jamie's face, falling from his magic-bright eyes.

"Which of you will surrender to me?" Jamie asked the surrounding magicians quietly. "Which of you will join the Market?"

Laura lunged at him.

"Never, you little monster," she shouted, palm lifted.

Nick caught her hand above her head and forced it down. Laura shook with horror, looking into his black eyes.

The magicians had never seen one of their own possessed before. It must have happened once, long years ago, and they must have learned to be careful enough that horror faded out of memory, and they were even able to believe Jamie's story that he could control a demon through his mark.

Sin had believed it herself.

She couldn't blame Gerald for believing it, too.

Laura tore her hand out of Nick's grip and ran headlong out of the room. No one stopped her.

Jamie looked around the room. "Will anyone surrender to me?" he asked, still quiet.

Helen of the Aventurine Circle, sword wielder, his mother's murderer, stepped forward with her fair head bowed.

"I will," she said. "If you will have me."

With a painful effort, Jamie smiled at her. "I will."

Helen came striding across the room, over the broken glass and the remains of two summoning circles, and knelt at Jamie's feet. He laid his hand on her silvery hair.

"Circle of my Circle," he said. "You are mine."

Helen rose and ranged herself behind her leader. Jamie's eyes travelled over the faces of everyone in the room and stopped at Seb, a faint question in his eyes.

Colour rising in his face, Seb said, "I was yours already."

Some other magicians came forward. Some retreated, slipping away and out of the door. Nobody stopped them, either.

"You made the right decision," Jamie said, when the last magician left swore to him. "I am going to take the magician's mark Gerald gave all of us, so that we could all share power. We have two demons who will share power with us now. Nick will give it to me, and I will give it to all of you. There will be less power than before, but there will be enough. And there will be no more killing."

Sin memorised the faces of the magicians who did not look relieved by the thought of no more killing, who looked even briefly furious about the loss of power. It was always useful to know who thought they had got a bad bargain.

"And for those of you who left," Mae said.

"Or those of you who may change your minds," Sin chimed in sweetly, and let her eyes fall on every face she had memorised.

"You all carry the magician's mark Gerald gave you," Mae said. "The channel between every magician in the Circle. And now the channel between you and the demons. Nick made a bargain with Anzu in the magicians' circles. You all saw it. When Gerald's body decays and dies, Nick will give Anzu another magician to possess. And another. Every magician in the Circle who keeps feeding people to demons will be fed to our demon, in time. And every magician who has already left, who will go to another Circle with Gerald's new mark, will open a new channel for us. Every magician in England who kills will end up possessed."

A full circle of victimhood, using the mark Gerald had been so proud of inventing against them, bringing on the magicians the same fate they had been willing to let fall on innocent people.

Only it meant that now the Market fed people to demons. No matter how guilty those people were, it was a terrible thing.

Sin did not have more than a moment to think about the guilt she had to bear, because the next moment Anzu moved towards her.

She remembered the promise she had made.

★

Gerald's body was already changing, Anzu changing a human being to suit his own taste, terrible beauty sweeping his face like a forest fire, hair running with gold.

He stood in front of Sin, silent and patient as demons had to be. It was only when he reached out and touched her arm, jerking his head towards the door, that Sin knew he wanted to go now.

Sin stepped towards him, separating herself completely from the others. If his fury was going to be directed at anyone, she wanted it to be her alone.

"I'm not going with you," she told him gently. "I was never going to go with you. I was lying when I said I would. Humans do that."

Sin closed her eyes and bowed her head.

He could kill her now, if he wanted. She refused to show fear and held herself braced. She knew the risks she had taken, making herself a bargaining chip in the demons' game.

And she'd never meant to go. She wasn't for sale.

She waited for a long time, and then the touch came. Light, against her stomach.

The pain from her wound dissolved under his fingers.

Sin lifted her head. Anzu's face was almost completely changed now, golden and still, like a face painted on a glass window.

He didn't kill her.

He nodded slowly instead and turned away. His hand lingered above hers, not quite touching, in what might have been a demon's version of a goodbye.

She wondered if he was doing what he'd said he would, doing nice things for her so she would love him, or if he'd listened to anything she had said about love, or if he had learned something from Nick.

He could not speak. She would never know.

He looked at Nick before he went. Nick met his eyes with a level gaze, his friend from another life, his enemy in this one.

The demons would keep their bargain, Sin thought.

Anzu walked out of the door. The magicians and the Market people shuddered away from him as he went on his silent way, all humans together caught in a moment of horror.

They had won. They did not need to keep up any pretence of power, when they had used it all.

Nick lay down, in the smoky ruins of the Circle, like an exhausted child. He lay down beside the still body of his brother.

Jamie staggered and Mae dived to catch him, both of them sinking but managing to stay up, Mae's arm tight round Jamie's waist. He sagged against her arm as if it was his only support, and spat something out on to the floor.

He lifted his face after doing it, and Sin saw blood dark on his lips and dyeing his teeth. His face was very white. His eyes were Mae's eyes for the first time, dark brown and human, and Sin found herself distantly shocked by them.

Sin could hear quiet spreading in Anzu's wake, through the house and then outside it, the battle stilling, over and won. She went to the window and saw it was raining, not a demon's storm but just the light grey drizzle of London, rain falling in the silent street.

A small sound made Sin turn round.

In the mess of the summoning circle, through the lingering smoke, she saw the new grey shimmer of Alan's hair.

His shoulders were humped, his back an arch of pain, as he struggled on to his hands and knees. He was making a low, terrible moaning noise. Sin knew that he was moaning and not speaking because Alan the silver-tongued, her smooth, cunning liar, had given up his words to a demon, had not used words in so long that they were lost for now. Animal sounds were passing his lips, nothing human.

"Nick," Alan choked out at last. His voice was destroyed, as if someone had been slowly strangling him for days.

He dragged himself up into a sitting position, and his outstretched hand almost reached Nick's body, fingers hovering over his shoulder, as if Alan was too scared to touch him.

Alan's hand finally fell on Nick's shoulder, very lightly, very gently, the same way Sin pulled the blankets over Toby when he was asleep and she did not want to wake him.

Nick lurched upward, shuddering, black eyes staring and terrible, like a dead thing come to unnatural life.

Alan did not flinch.

"Don't you ever," Nick snarled. "Don't you *ever* do anything like this to me again."

"Okay, Nick," Alan soothed him. "I won't. I promise."

"You're just lying," Nick said. "You said you'd never leave. You always lie."

"I know," Alan murmured. "I know. I'm sorry."

"I *missed* you," Nick raged, his voice cracking, and he put his head down, forehead pressed against Alan's knee.

Alan laughed a little, trembling and amazed, and Sin felt a rush of triumph, like the victorious adrenaline that always ran through her exhausted body after a successful performance, but multiplied by a thousand.

Mae laughed, her laugh a victory song even as she held her brother up, and Sin looked at her, knowing that their smiles mirrored each other, joyful and fierce.

Then Sin looked at Alan, and he looked back at her. He

looked so much older, or as if he had been through an illness everyone had thought would prove fatal. There were crow's-feet scored deep in the corners of his eyes, and his hair was thick with silver. His eyes had not changed at all, still dark steadfast blue and dear.

"Alan," she whispered.

He whispered back, "Cynthia, I'm here."

She had him back. The Market was safe. They had lied and murdered and now they had trapped the magicians, become almost as bad as the magicians, ready to see people as food for demons.

There was already one man possessed, walking through London in the rain. There would be more. The Market had to accept that. Sin had to accept that, what they had become in order to win.

It had been worth the cost. But it was such a cost.

Alan stroked Nick's hair with hands that could not stop shaking.

"Shh, it's all right," he said, lying again already, making the lie a lullaby. "Everything's all right now."

Sin turned back to the window, watching through the glass as that dark shape walked away through the rain, the human lost, the demon alone.

She had been in enough battles before to know victory was always bitter, and the bigger the fight, the worse the cost. But she hoped she would never again taste victory as bitter as this.

22

The Leader of the Goblin Market

THE LIGHTS OF THE GOBLIN MARKET WERE SHINING ON THE arching branches of the trees round Kensington Gardens. They were floating on the silvery surface of the lake, like lilypads with light instead of a lily.

Sin was dancing.

She was covered in tiny beacon lights like the one she had used in Black Arthur's house, shining like pearls with tiny candles set inside, and strung together across her skin with gossamer-thin threads of silver. It was a costume to brighten the old audience's eyes and dazzle all those for whom this was their very first Market.

The Goblin Market was spread around the lake on all sides, larger than it had ever been before, like a tiny city.

Sin knew there was nothing more important than opening a show with a bang.

She was dancing in silence by the lake, an illuminated apparition, her reflection a white shadow on the waters, her feet moving through the dark grass. People had started to gather, murmuring to one another, a hushed spoken start to applause.

Two tall torches were burning on either side of the lake.

The torches carved a warm, orange cave in the evening. There was a cold wind blowing, making the flames of the torches form strange shapes, as if they were dancers themselves.

The music started, lifting the scene to a whole new level. The drums of the Market started first, setting everyone's hearts to a new rhythm, and then Matthias led the twisting, turning and enchanting music of the pipes. Sin spun with them, brightness flowing round her as if the music had become a shimmering ghost and was turning her in its arms.

Low and sweet and simple came the sound of Alan singing, his voice changed but still beautiful, a song about love and trust in darkness.

Sin twisted her body as if moving like this was easy, as if she was made of water and light. Her hair lifted in the wind, streaming curls with more light trapped in them, and she moved as if caught by the current of the night wind, arms swaying above her head and then moving gently down, palms resting against her body.

She danced from the lake surrounded by trees gone sunset orange in autumn and night, through the Market, cutting a path to where the pagoda stood.

She held her face just so, looking at nobody directly and so looking at everyone, welcoming her audience.

Then she pulled the long knife from her bodice and threw it straight and true, and at the cue Chiara flung up the curtain hanging in front of the pagoda. The knife thudded into a wooden pillar, and the curtain was caught.

Behind the curtain, in the centre of the pagoda, stood

Merris Cromwell and Mae. Over their heads, among distant trees, a golden spire shone like a crown, the memorial of a queen's beloved.

Merris was all in black, her hair streaming black, too. It was dark enough that nobody could see the traces of red.

Mae was wearing tiny beacon lamps as well. Sin had designed both their costumes, as Mae did not really have the eye for showmanship yet; she tended to go overboard. Mae's dress was longer and lower, though, a softly glowing evening gown that cooled the brightness of her hair. Her eyes were shining.

"Mae of the Market," Merris said, her voice echoing in the night. "Will you take my people as your own, guard them and care for them, protect them with all your mind and all your body and all your strength?"

"I will," said Mae. "If they will have me. And if I do badly, they will be able to make a change. In seven years, I will call a meeting like this one, and I will call on Cynthia Davies. I will listen to the Goblin Market if they wish to take her as leader or keep me: I will lead the best way I know how, and in seven years if the Market wishes, I will follow her with all my heart."

Merris turned her black eyes to the Market. She had not wanted to come back, but Sin had contacted her through the necromancer now running Mezentius House. She had not pleaded or begged, but she had argued that it was the only way to transfer the Market, safe and entire. She had been sure that some part of Merris would still care.

And here she was.

"What do you say, Market people?" Merris asked. "Will you have her?"

Sin stepped forward before anyone else could, and said into the anticipatory hush, "We will!"

They got applause for the moment, applause for the dance and the whole show, applause that went ringing on and on as Merris put her hands to Mae's throat and fastened Celeste Drake's pearl there for all to see.

"I've done my part, I think," said Merris, standing in the shadows with Sin and watching her with Liannan's eyes.

Nick was hovering at Sin's back. Sin was not entirely sure if he was there as a silent threat, if he thought she needed protection from Liannan, or if he simply wanted to say goodbye.

"Yes," Sin said. "Thank you." She thought of Liannan and of Anzu, who had said he was betrayed. "And I'm sorry if you feel we took anything from you."

"Anything from me?" Liannan asked, a subtle change in intonation the only way to differentiate between Merris and the demon now. Her eyes slid to Nick. "Oh," she said. "Oh, my dear. He's just strayed a little. You humans don't live very long at all. A human lifetime to us, it's only the duration of a game. You forget every game, after a while."

"Not this one," Nick said.

Liannan smiled at him, sweet and cruel. "All right, my darling," she told him indulgently. "We'll see. I'm off to play my own game now."

She went over to Nick, her feet hardly seeming to touch the ground, and leaned up to kiss him. Nick jerked slightly away, and she only caught the corner of his mouth.

Liannan laughed as if she found him infinitely amusing. "See you later," she murmured, and moved away, easy and boneless in the night, swimming through shadows.

"Merris," called Sin.

She turned, the haughty face Sin knew so well smooth and young, but still the face she knew, half the woman she had cared for and half a demon.

But Sin was getting used to that.

"I loved you very much," she called out. "I wanted you to know."

"Yes, child," said Merris, in her old, impatient way. "I knew."

Then she was gone. Nick and Sin exchanged glances, understanding each other well enough, and turned back to search through the lights of the Market for Alan.

Liannan's open disbelief that Nick had changed, that the long, painful process of transformation could ever work at all, made Sin take especial note of all the magicians moving, some more obviously uneasy than others, through the Goblin Market.

She saw the fearless leader of the Aventurine Circle walking through the Market, using his usual method of diplomacy, which was talking at people blithely and persistently and moving on, leaving them stunned in his wake.

"He says after learning to talk to me, everyone else was easy," Nick said behind her. "Which is funny, as I never recall him having trouble talking to anyone at all."

Jamie's voice, addressing Seb and Mae and floating over to them, bore him out. Seb was walking beside Jamie as usual, but something about the way they were walking caught Sin's attention: Jamie's body angled back to mirror Seb's, perhaps. She thought this might be a date.

"I was thinking that what I need is a nickname," said Jamie. "A fearsome nickname. Like James Hook."

"I think that one's already taken," Seb told him, sounding utterly bemused but affectionate, and almost not embarrassed about it.

"Oh," Jamie said, downcast. "Really?"

"Captain Hook in *Peter Pan*," Mae informed him readily. "His first name was James."

Jamie frowned in thought. "Captain Hook was cool. I could go with that. What would you say to James Hook the Second? I don't really think I look like a captain."

"I think you're an idiot," said Nick. "Not that that's relevant. Except that it is always relevant."

"Oh, hush up or I'll be Evil Jamie again, and pull your hair," Jamie said lightly, while Seb and Mae both glared at Nick. Sin stepped forward to intercept the glares.

"Thanks so much for all your help with the lights, Seb," she told him. "You really have an eye for this."

Now Seb did look completely embarrassed. Apparently he could accept being gay, but coming out as artistic was a step too far.

Jamie looked impressed, though. "Oh, hey," he said. "They're great."

"Right," Seb said. "They're not that good. But. Um. I'm glad that you – that you like them."

Jamie looked confused, then surprised and dawningly pleased. He still did not seem terribly used to being liked.

He smiled, crooked and a little shy. "Yeah, they have a certain appeal I'm starting to appreciate," he said, and when Seb stayed there looking helplessly down at him, Jamie was obviously seized by an impulse, pulled him down and gave him a light kiss.

So definitely a date, then.

"Not a word, Nicholas," Mae said, with terrible warning in her voice. "I think it's nice."

"You're both deranged, and you always were," Nick

377

drawled. "I'm never going to be done getting you tiny lunatics out of trouble."

He did not sound deeply upset about it. Mae dimpled up at him. "We get you out of trouble right back."

She had changed out of her beautiful dress, which meant that Sin had been able to force her into it for all of twenty minutes. She was wearing a black business skirt and heels, which was not exactly Mae's style but which suited her somehow, and a pink T-shirt that read AND THEN THEY ALL LIVED HAPPILY EVER AFTER (BARRING DEATH, DIVORCE, ARREST FOR TAX FRAUD, THAT INCIDENT WITH THE POOL BOY . . .) The letters on her shirt got too small to read at that point.

Against her pink shirt was the dull gleam of the black pearl, the talisman safeguarding her from demons, the jewel that cancelled out a demon's mark. For at least seven years, and then they would see.

Nick looked away from Mae and at a random patch of grass.

"We could . . ." he said, and hesitated. "We could grab a cup of coffee. Sometime. You and me."

"Are you asking me out?" Mae inquired.

She waited for Nick's tiny nod, and then she was beaming, even brighter than before. Sin would not have thought that was possible.

"I don't know about coffee. I might hold out for dinner."

"We can do whatever boring thing you want," Nick told her.

Mae laughed. Sin thought she was trying for mocking and sophisticated, but Mae just sounded happy. "Ah, *l'amour*."

"I'll entertain myself looking at your face," Nick said. "You know I like that."

"Yeah," Mae said, beaming and beaming. "Sounds like a plan."

They couldn't stand around here talking all night. They had to be seen around the Market, shaking hands and walking through the stalls, and it was almost time to dance.

When Sin set off, Mae followed her at once. She caught on fast, that girl.

They had never dared hold the Market in such a public place, but now with the magicians' spells for privacy here they were, in a park surrounded by the purr of cars, a palace not so far away. The stall of lights was located on a statue of Queen Victoria, beacon lights dripping round her neck, a single love light hanging from her stone sceptre.

Helen the magician was standing at Carl's weapons stall, having an animated conversation about morning stars.

Phyllis's stand of chimes was gone and would never be set up again, but Ivy had put up chimes round the scrolls and tablets and old books in her stall. The chimes sang out softly as she moved around them, their song calling passers-by to her stall.

Sin stopped and spoke to Matthias, who was walking along with two older women behind him, making complicated hand gestures as they went. Neither of them, unlike Matthias, was Asian.

"These are my parents," Matthias said, and gestured to the women, his thin piper's hands moving with easy, fluid grace. He had his pipe tucked away.

"A pleasure," said Sin, and shook both their hands.

One of the women gestured at Sin after she was done shaking hands.

"She says she's heard a lot about you," said Matthias. "She's probably thinking about someone else. If you'll excuse me, there are a lot of gullible tourists to rook once I'm done showing my parents around. . ."

He laughed, dark eyes sparkling in his thin face. The other woman took his arm, her face much amused: she clearly thought her horrible little boy was hilarious.

Sin blamed it on the parents, really.

She just felt lucky she'd had good ones. Her father was walking through the Market for the first time in years, with Lydie and Toby in tow. He'd promised they would all come and watch her dance.

Later they would all go home together. There would be food on the table, the children would be looked after and Mae would be in charge of the Market for now, making reckless, brave decisions, even though she would obviously need a little help.

There was time now to rest, to do the right thing by Lydie and Toby, to work out exactly what kind of leader Sin wanted to be, and if she wanted to be a leader at all.

And there would always be the Market. There would always be magic, and the dance.

Jonas and Chiara stopped her next, asking where Merris had gone, and Sin had to tell them she'd left already.

"I've been thinking," Jonas said. "Do you think that necromancer at Mezentius House was Merris's boyfriend? At her age! That's nasty."

"I don't know," said Sin. "I'm planning on having a boyfriend at her age myself."

"Alan Ryves for life?" Chiara asked, making a slight face.

"That's the plan," Sin told her, and as if all he needed was to be called, she finally caught sight of Alan. He was talking to one of the magicians, an older man, but when he saw her looking, he excused himself and limped over the grass to join them.

"Doesn't matter if you disapprove," she told Chiara. "Everyone at school thinks he's a catch. An older man, you know. With a car."

She came a few steps to meet him and lifted her face to his, kissed him with her eyes half-closed under the Goblin Market lights. It didn't matter whether the Market thought she outshone him a thousand times or her school wondered how on earth she'd snagged him: they knew each of them had a hundred masks, and every one was true.

"Hey, Bambi," said Alan.

Sin smiled up at him. "Hey, Clive."

"Who disapproves of me?" Alan inquired. "If it's your dad, I can talk him round. Where is he?"

"My dad has seen Nick and is in a state of deep and profound thanksgiving at present," Sin informed him. "My grandma doesn't much like the idea of me and a white boy. But she's not here."

"So I'll come round for tea," Alan said. "Give me ten minutes."

"Don't disappoint me like this," Sin murmured. "Make it five."

She heard their new leader and her retinue calling out for them, so before the others reached them, Sin caught his face between her hands and kissed him one more time for luck.

"Now," she said, and looked round inquiringly. "Who is going to dance with me? Since I haven't convinced Alan to put our dancing lessons into practice – yet."

She looked at Nick and at Mae, both good choices, and then she got another surprise.

"If you don't mind," Jamie said, "I think I'd like to try."

Sin blinked. "Are you a good dancer?"

"I am."

"You're a man of many mysteries, James Crawford," Sin told him, and Jamie looked extremely gratified.

It would look good, the darling of the Goblin Market and the leader of the magicians, dancing together. It would be a symbol of the fact that all this could really work.

"If she's teaching you to dance," Nick said in a low voice to his brother, "I want to teach you how to use a sword."

"Well, if you would really like to," Alan responded, lazy and affectionate, as if he was promising Nick a treat.

Nick raised his eyebrows at Alan, and Alan grinned.

"More than anything in two worlds," Nick murmured. Alan leaned his shoulder towards Nick's, not quite touching.

"Learn to duel after you sing for me and Jamie," Sin commanded.

She wanted more people to hear him sing, wanted his voice to help bring the Market together, the voice she loved, the one that had called a demon in and made him understand.

It made Sin think for a moment of another demon, who had spared her for no reason at all, except that he might be beginning to understand, too.

Liannan might be right. This might all pass, so fast, time and hope slipping through their fingers.

There were other magicians besides the Circle that was now part of the Market, and demons still watching outside this world, hungry and cold. This gathering under the Market lights might not work.

But here they were, for this night at least.

And it might work.

This was the Goblin Market, where you could find anything, even a new side of your true self.

Sin reached out and took Jamie's hand, interlacing his fingers with hers, and stepped with him a little apart from everyone else: the demon and his brother, Seb the magician and her leader. She made them her audience and gave them her best smile.

"Come on, then," she said. "Let's dance."

Jamie smiled and followed her lead into the dancing circles. The lights strung along the boughs traced bright arches over them all, united for now at least. There was music starting, a fresh and beautiful tune, their new leader in her bright pink shirt presiding over them all. Alan's head was bowed over his guitar. Nick was sitting in the grass at his feet, like a child waiting for a bedtime story, ready to listen to a song. There was a silver, scythe-shaped gleam in her partner's dark eye.

For this one night, magic was everywhere.

It might last.

ACKNOWLEDGEMENTS

Trilogy accomplished! Which means more thanks than I can adequately express go to:

Karen Wojtyla, who was absolutely right about the book needing one last go-round, as she is about so much; Emily Fabre; and Valerie Shea. Also to Nicole Russo and everyone at Simon & Schuster for tireless marketing efforts on behalf of "Oh God, those demon books."

Kristin Nelson and everyone at NLA, for everything.

Venetia Gosling, Kathryn McKenna and everyone at Simon & Schuster UK, plus Scott Westerfeld and Justine Larbalestier, for so much, including an awesome UK tour.

All my foreign publishers, who without exception dazzle me.

Holly Black, who stayed up all night in London to read the first draft of this book, made it so half the edits my editor suggested were already done and is basically a Heroine of the Revolution. If you ever want a liver, Holly, I'll . . . get one somehow. Also, thank you for the most fun tour ever.

Cassandra Clare, who organised the secret writing location where half this book was written.

My amazing first readers: Saundra Mitchell, Justine Larbalestier and Karen Healey.

My family and friends, who for some reason have not yet put me on an iceberg and pushed me out to sea, as I understand the Eskimos do to annoying writers.

And if you're reading this? Thank you.